DARK EMPRESS

Tales of the Empire, book 3

by S.J.A.Turney

3rd Edition

For Lilian, who passed in 2015, is sadly missed, and without whose support the book would not have happened.

Also, to my father-in-law and mother-in-law, who not only gave me the love of my life, but who also keep me grounded and realistic.

I would like to thank everyone who made this book possible, and those who helped to bring this second edition into the world. Jenny, Lilian, Tracey and Sue for their work on the original, Robin, Liviu and Prue for their help and support on its release, and Dave for his help with this edition.

All internal maps are copyright the author of this work.

Published in this format 2016 by Victrix Books

Copyright - S.J.A.Turney

Third Edition

The author asserts the moral right under the Copyright, Designs and Patents Act 1988 to be identified as the author of this work.

All Rights reserved. No part of this publication may be reproduced, stored in a retrieval system or transmitted, in any form or by any means without the prior consent of the author, nor be otherwise circulated in any form of binding or cover other than that which it is published and without a similar condition being imposed on the subsequent purchaser.

Also by S. J. A. Turney:

Continuing the Tales of the Empire
Interregnum (2009)
Ironroot (2010)
Insurgency (2016)

The Marius' Mules Series
Marius' Mules I: The Invasion of Gaul (2009)
Marius' Mules II: The Belgae (2010)
Marius' Mules III: Gallia Invicta (2011)
Marius' Mules IV: Conspiracy of Eagles (2012)
Marius' Mules V: Hades Gate (2013)
Marius' Mules VI: Caesar's Vow (2014)
Marius' Mules VII: The Great Revolt (2014)
Marius' Mules VIII: Sons of Taranis (2015)
Marius' Mules IX: Pax Gallica (2016)

The Ottoman Cycle
The Thief's Tale (2013)
The Priest's Tale (2013)
The Assassin's Tale (2014)
The Pasha's Tale (2015)

The Praetorian Series
Praetorian – The Great Game (2015)
Praetorian – The Price of Treason (2015)

The Legion Series (Childrens' books)
Crocodile Legion (2016)

Short story compilations & contributions:
Tales of Ancient Rome vol. 1 - S.J.A. Turney (2011)
Tortured Hearts Vol 2 - Various (2012)
Tortured Hearts Vol 3 - Various (2012)
Temporal Tales - Various (2013)
Historical Tales - Various (2013)
A Year of Ravens (2015)
A Song of War (2016)

For more information visit http://www.sjaturney.co.uk/
or http://www.facebook.com/SJATurney
or follow Simon on Twitter @SJATurney

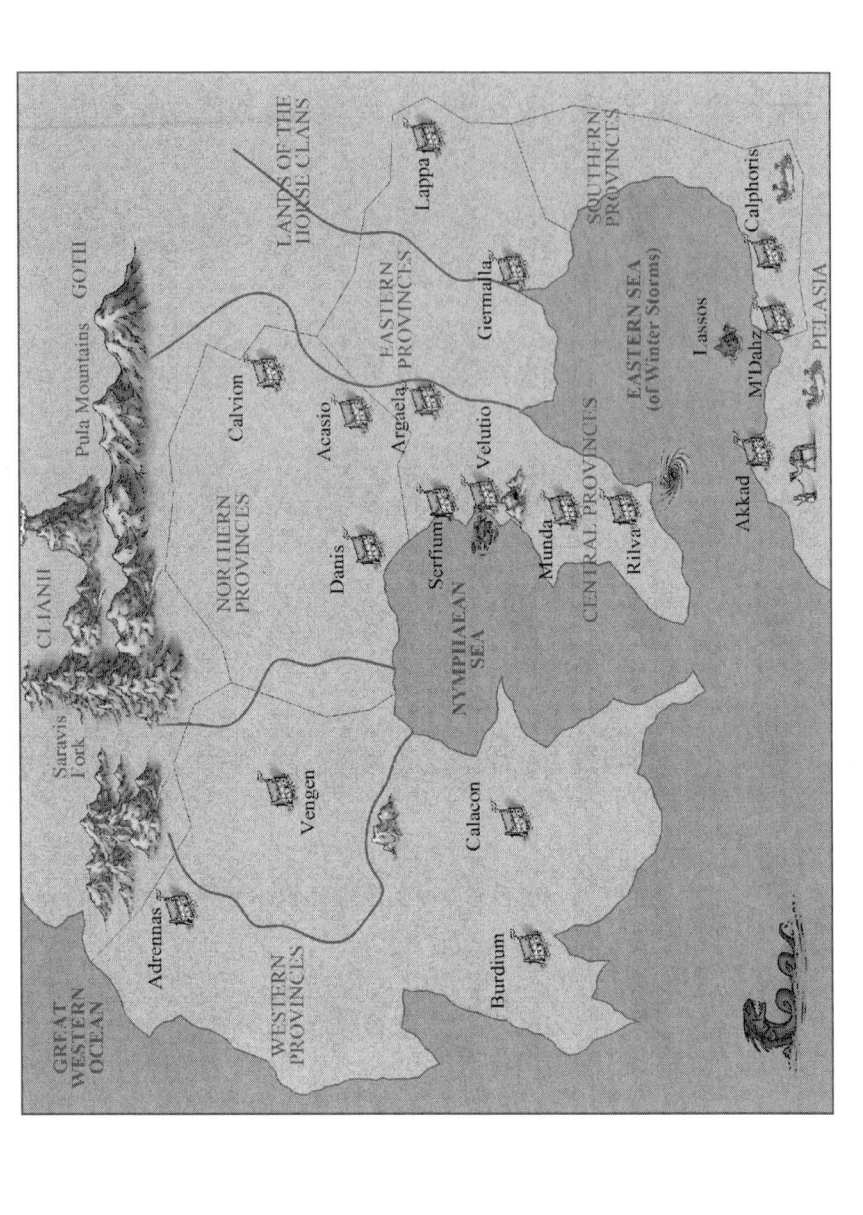

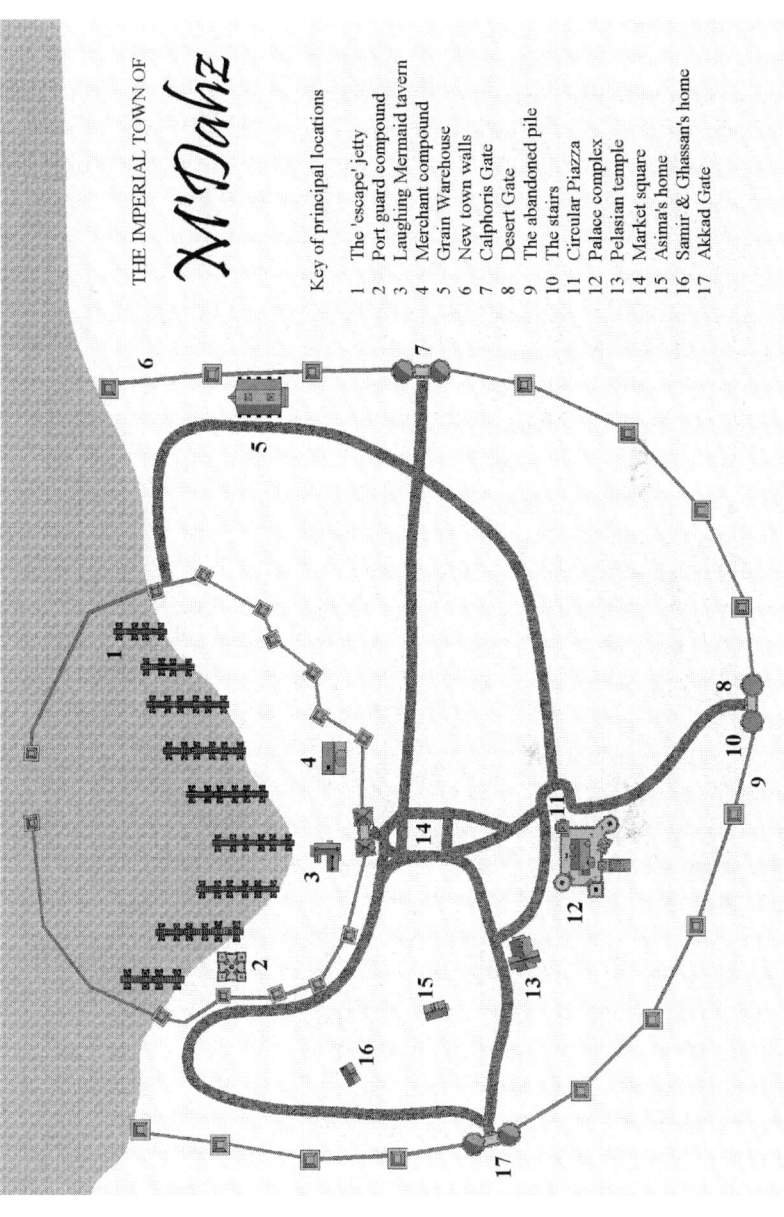

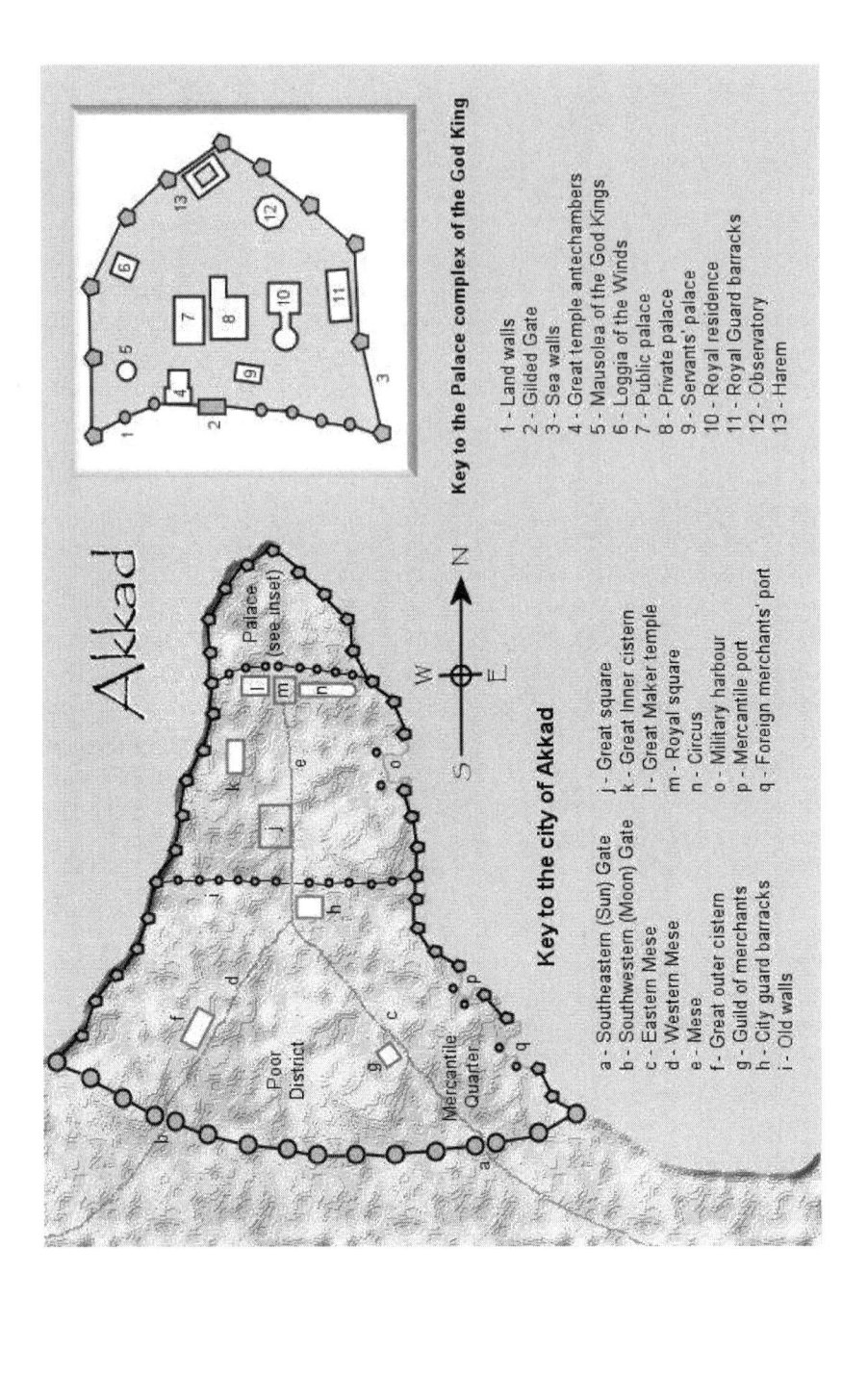

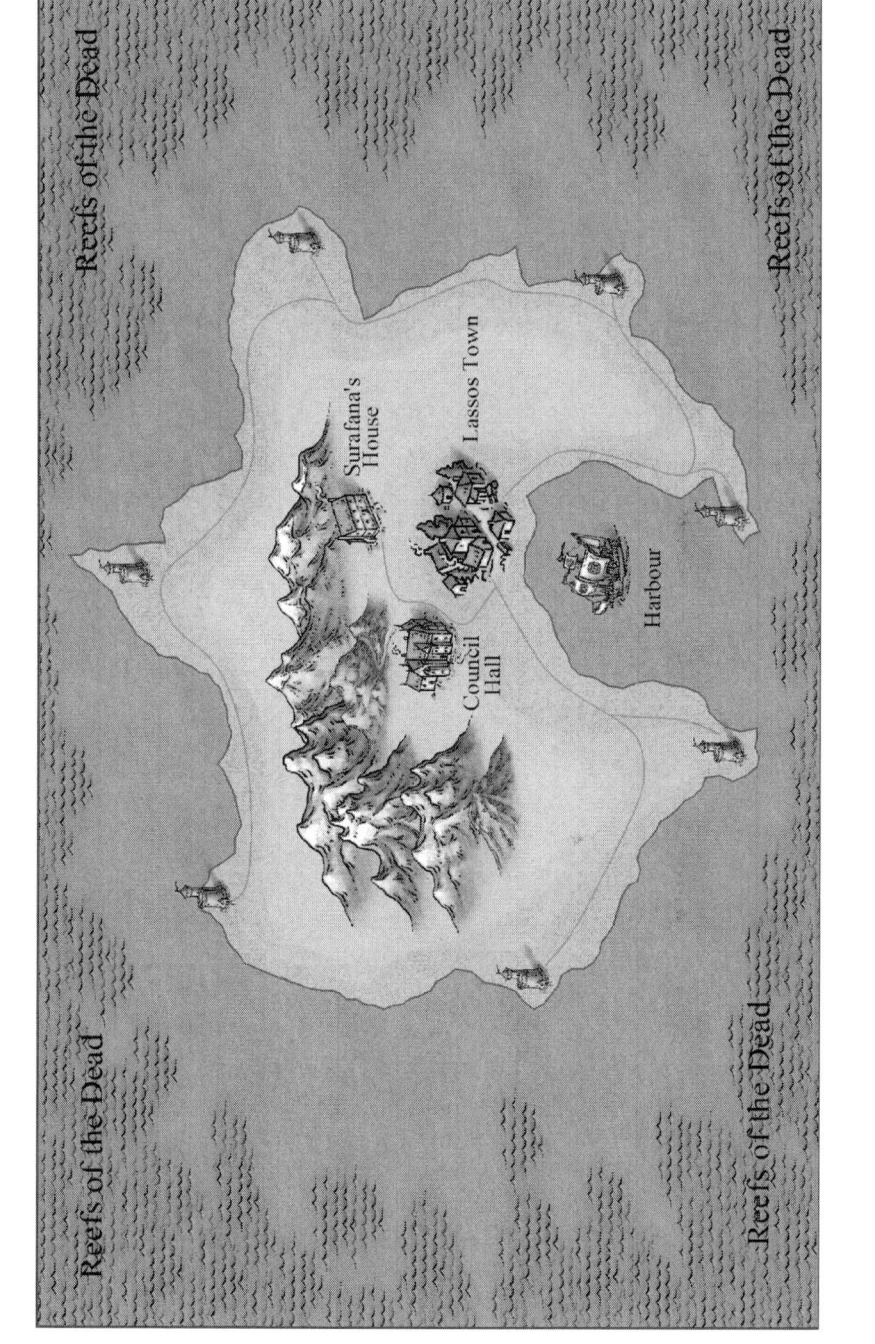

Prologue

If, in her later years, Asima described to someone the town where she grew up, which of course she wouldn't, she would have been spoiled for adjectives. M'Dahz was the last Imperial town before the Pelasian border and, as such, shared more of the characteristics of their swarthy mysterious people than of the great culture of the Empire. It was a border garrison, a mercantile port, trading post, and caravanserai.

It smelled of spice and of sweat; of work animals and of sweetmeats; of the sea and of the desert. It was a meeting of every world and a clash of mouth and eye-watering noises, sights and aromas. It was a maze of narrow streets and alleys, the ramshackle adobe houses often kept from toppling outwards by the heavy wooden struts that were jammed from side to side above head height throughout most of the town. To ward off the worst heat of the day and the periodic cloying sandstorms from the south, the people hung rugs over the beams, turning the alleyways into stygian tunnels and creating a labyrinth.

With the exception of the main thoroughfare that ran from the port to the Bab Ashra, the Desert Gate, the only part of M'Dahz that felt open and fresh was the palace compound, forbidden to all bar nobles, dignitaries and the military. A small and well-tended garden surrounded by elegant balconied residences, the compound presented a solid wall, free of windows, to the outside, shunning the dirty, smelly, noisy town that teemed with life.

The whole town sloped downwards from the desert to the sea, and it was said that a man could walk the streets of M'Dahz for a week without finding a road free of steps. It wasn't true, of course, but such streets were indeed rare, and every town has to have its little foibles after all. The town was self-styled as the 'Southern Bastion of the Empire' though in truth as much Pelasian or desert nomad blood pumped in the veins of its people as that of the Empire. And as for 'bastion'? Well the town had its walls, along with three grand gates, but the walls had long been abandoned as a defensive perimeter and more often served as the rear wall of a house than a barrier to potential attackers. In fact, for almost a third of their length the walls were now buried deep inside the town itself, invisible without requesting entrance to peoples' houses.

Space was at a premium in M'Dahz. Everything clustered together as close to the centre as possible, like a pile of broken pots, as the people tried to distance themselves from the outskirts where the dust piled up at the foot of walls and the sand had to be swept daily from the streets. There was certainly no park or garden; no green space; no fields or orchards. But then everything the people needed came from trade: dates and fruit and meat brought by caravan from the oases inland, or grains and meats by ship from Pelasia and the great Imperial cities.

People who visited asked merchants how anyone could live in the conditions they encountered at M'Dahz. But then the merchants would arch their eyebrow and ask in a concerned voice how anyone could consider living anywhere else. M'Dahz was dirty, noisy, smelly, at constant risk of sandstorm, barren and dry. But M'Dahz was life in its rawest form.

Asima would never speak of these things, or how she began as the daughter of a humble seller of animal feed before her rise to courtesan, concubine, and finally Empress.

Part One:

Childhood's End

In which journeys are started

They were seven years old when Asima first began to notice a change in the way the boys looked at her. It was not the lust, desire or hunger she would so often encounter later in life, but rather an indefinable need to be near her and to seek out her attention and approval. She would find in the coming days that she enjoyed their attention, but on that first day it surprised her, particularly given the strange timing that exhibited a subtle shift in the attitude of both boys, apparently independently.

It was a summer afternoon in M'Dahz, though only a local would have noticed much difference between the seasons in this arid, searing land. The heat was already unbearable to most folk, and only children, slaves and the duty-bound were in evidence beneath the fiery orb of the sun. The noise of the town was muffled as it rose from the stifled and shady alleyways beneath their coverings of rugs and blankets. A distant gong announced the call to temple for the faithful of the Pelasian divinity, but the subsequent clangs were lost among the noise of a town where life continued apace beneath the shady covers.

Asima turned to Samir, shading her eyes from the worst of the glare. The smaller of the two boys, Samir held the attention of girls older than he. There was something about that face, the way his mouth turned up slightly at the corners as though he wore a permanent knowing smile. There was a delightful, if wicked, twinkle in his eye at all times, and his bronzed skin and short, straight black hair were smooth, neat and perfectly complemented his fine oval face. His clothes, for some reason, looked stylish and carefully chosen, despite the fact that Asima knew that they were little more than rags; hand-me-downs from distant friends of his mother, washed so many times they had lost all shape and colour. And yet something about the way he wore them made them look princely.

Samir smiled and winked as he dropped into a crouched position, his muscles bunched and his tendons twanging. Asima nodded and turned to her other side. Ghassan was already in position as he turned to smile at her. Samir's brother, while officially a twin, was nothing like his smaller sibling. This was good, according to the traditions of the desert people from whom the boys' paternal line had sprung. Twins who were too similar were bad luck; bad magic. It was not unknown for the nomads to leave children to die in the sands because of their tragic similarity; but Ghassan was different, for sure.

Already a head taller, Ghassan had a slight curl to his hair and some parts of it jutted out in random directions. No matter how much their mother flattened, brushed, waxed or washed it, parts of Ghassan's hair were untameable. His skin was marked from an illness as a baby and yet the marks did not make him ugly or ruin his appearance; somehow, the imperfections added to the rugged power of his appearance and lent him a gravity he would otherwise have lacked. Where Samir's mouth turned up to a smile, Ghassan's was straight and flat, his expression serious. He was handsome in a way that appealed to some of the girls of M'Dahz, and mothers nodded sagely as they foresaw an eminently marriageable boy there. And yet, somehow, while Ghassan's clothes were almost identical to Samir's, on the taller boy they hung like badly sewn bags. Asima almost laughed as she nodded and faced forward, dropping to a crouch herself.

The girl was already pretty and was coming to realise it even at this young age. She had perfect skin, with a creamy texture that required surprisingly little upkeep, though her father chided her anyway for the amount of time she spent primping. Her almond eyes were beautiful, dark and warm, her lips a perfect bow. Her hair was long and carefully combed and pinned back, never cut more than a shaping trim as was the tradition of the Pelasians, for Asima had Pelasian blood on her mother's side. The only fault that marred her appearance in any way was her fingernails. Her mother, before she had passed last winter, had disciplined her repeatedly for the damage she was doing biting her nails down to the quick, though it had never stopped her. She was dressed, in a manner that would cause her father's heart to skip a beat, in just a white cotton vest and knee length trousers of the same thin material, her feet bare and her sparse jewellery removed and lying on the pile of more acceptable clothing by her feet.

She had jested time and again with the boys that her father would marry their mother one day and so she could never kiss them since they would end up being her brothers. But it was friendly banter and they all knew it. While the boys' mother was a handsome woman still in the bloom of late youth, she was poor almost to the point of slavery, eking out a living as a washerwoman for the mercantile classes. Indeed, it was at their mother's work where Asima had met the boys, her father being a factor for a Pelasian trader of fruit and having paid their mother a little extra to keep his daughter busy while he sorted problems with deliveries. Her father was far from a rich man, but his business kept him well enough that Asima really should not have been socialising with the likes of Samir and Ghassan.

But in that timeless fashion, the universe over, such boundaries of class meant nothing to the children, and forbidding them to play together merely drove them closer and closer. For the last year the three had become inseparable and even their parents had thrown their hands in the air in defeat and allowed the friends to continue their association, albeit restricted to times that neither adult was in sight.

And so here they were. The boys' mother worked her fingers raw in the cleaning vats beneath the blanket roof of the cloth market, despite the heat of the day, while Asima's father, busy as always, met with the captain of a ship newly arrived from Germalla across the sea to the north.

And the three unsupervised children?

'Go!'

As Asima shouted, the three figures, crouched and tense on the flat roof of the copperware shop in the street of a hundred martyrs, raced off across the dusty and hot surface, their bare feet hardened to the extreme heat radiating from the roof. Each week the route of the race changed, chosen by a different competitor, the three making sure that each of them had a fair say, though it was becoming clear that Samir was playing with them in designing his routes. The last two occasions that Samir had laid out the plan, both his companions had drawn a worried and surprised breath at some of his decisions.

The first jump was simple: across the three roofs to the next street, the street of the northern dunes. Northern dunes was a narrow alley and the carpet covering was only four feet below the rooftops here as a safety net. Ghassan was first over, his long and powerful legs giving him the thrust needed to easily clear the gap, coming down with a light thud and hardly breaking his pace before he sped up and was off again toward the tower of the Pelasian temple. Asima was next across, her small frame light and lithe. She landed awkwardly and stumbled for a moment, but was quickly up and off again. Behind her she heard the tell-tale thud and rumble of Samir landing and smoothly rolling to his feet once more without a halt in pace.

Across the rooftops they ran, gradually increasing in altitude as per Samir's route. The temple tower passed by on their right as they leapt across the nine sisters stairway, one of the few jumps with no carpet safety net and one of very few places on their run that could conceivably cause serious injury. By now Samir was at her heel like a terrier, while Ghassan maintained a short but convincing lead. Asima was trying to picture the path ahead, to identify any place where she could use her intimate knowledge of the town to gain the lead. Where would…

She was so surprised when Ghassan lost his footing and tumbled to a heap on the flat roof that she almost fell over him, leaping into the air at the last moment and performing a graceful manoeuvre as she skipped twice and then used her new momentum to clear the next street. She laughed as she landed on the other side and turned to see her lead over Samir had widened and that Ghassan, having pulled himself to his feet was now clearly at the rear of the group.

Turning her attention back to the terrain ahead, she drew a deep breath. She was in the lead now and had to maintain her advantage. She had only won two races this year and they had both been on routes she herself had set. To maintain face, she had to win one of Samir's routes. Asima could hear the laboured breathing of the smaller brother close behind her; so close.

Biting the inside of her cheek, she ducked sharply to the right, around the upper storey of the temple-hospital of Belapraxis, with its roof herb garden full of plants with bitter-sweet smells and healing properties. It was oh so tempting to stop for a moment in the blessed shade cast by the extra level of plaster wall, but there was too much at stake today.

Asima slowed as she neared the edge of the roof. Between this wall of the hospital and the grocer's at the other side of the street, a single beam ran across carrying the water pipe that fed the hospital from a cistern at the highest point of the town. With the increased altitude of the buildings here, the carpet ceiling was a good fifteen feet below and the fall would hurt even if she landed well; a bad landing on one of the supporting struts would be crippling if not deadly. Really, Samir's routes were getting crazy. Taking a deep breath and offering up her prayers to the four Gods whose names leapt easily to mind, she stepped out onto the beam and began to slowly inch across, placing her bare feet close in front of each other.

Almost half way across, she paused and dipped her feet in the open section of water channel to clean and cool them. Samir was close enough behind her she could hear him breathing tightly as he traversed the beam. There was no sound from further back than that. Biting her cheek once more, she risked turning her head to gauge her pursuit. Samir was perhaps twelve feet behind her. His short legs went against him in a straight run, but his cat-like grace and reflexes allowed him to pick up the pace in places like this.

Of Ghassan there was no sign.

Where had he gone? Surely he had not been so slow that they had lost him? She swallowed nervously. The alternative was unpleasant. Had he fallen at one of the jumps? If so, then dear Gods please let it be a good fall at one of the places where the carpets were close. There was no time to worry now; Samir was closing.

Turning carefully, she set off once more, her cool feet refreshed. Her grip would have been weakened as the beam became wet and slippery, were it not for the interminable dust that settled on every surface of M'Dahz and gave her good purchase on the wood. She concentrated hard. Staying ahead of Samir was important, but so was making it across safely.

Finally, after what seemed like an age, she reached the hot white roof of Jamal's grocery store and stretched gratefully for only a second before setting off at a run on the last leg of the route.

Up over a low dividing wall, past another roof garden and a quick, though awkwardly-angled jump, across the alley of the coppersmiths. A quick 'S' shape between the locked stairway entrances of three buildings and then a sharp corner next to a long drop... curse Samir for his insane routes. One more flat roof brought the last jump, a wide but straight leap across the stairway of Sidi M'Dekh. She smiled. There was no way Samir could catch her now; she was home free. She began to laugh wildly as she rounded the last corner to see the pole with the red rag that marked the end of the race.

And her face fell. Ghassan grinned back at her where he stood casually, holding the rag and leaning against the wall in the cool shade.

How had he done that? She racked her brains to try and work out where he had gone. How had he taken a short cut? It was theoretically a cheat, but there could have been no quicker way to get back up to the roof if he had fallen than the route they had both taken.

'How?' she demanded.

Ghassan's smile, all the more genuine for its rarity, held her for a moment as he bowed and proffered the red rag to her.

'I would turn the world upside down to see your face from this angle, Asima.'

She blinked for a moment and then smiled as Ghassan burst out laughing.

'You should have seen your face when you turned the corner and found me!' he howled.

She shook her head as Samir arrived and patted her on the back.

'No, I don't know how he does it either. It's that brain of his.'

The three children collapsed to the floor in the shade and scanned the rooftops at this, one of the highest places in M'Dahz. The Pelasian bell tower was just visible around the edge of the building, as were various turrets and high rooftops, but the main obstruction on the skyline here was the palace compound, and it was the looming and intriguing walls of that forbidden complex that captured the gaze of the three runners.

'One day.'

Both Asima and Ghassan turned to look at their companion. Samir shrugged.

'We've been almost everywhere there is to go above the town, but we've never set foot in the compound. Before the summer's out, I want to walk on the governor's roof.'

Asima and Ghassan nodded sagely, each privately considering the almost negligible chances of that ever happening. But there was something in Samir's eye that afternoon in the high places of M'Dahz; something that made Asima certain that nothing in the world of human endeavour was beyond Samir's reach if he put his mind to it.

Nothing.

In which changes occur

A year had passed. The rooftop chases had tailed off in the late wintertime, though not due to the conditions. After all, in M'Dahz the deepest winter was almost indistinguishable from high summer to all but the natives. No, somehow the thrill had gone, without them ever having set foot on the governor's roof as Samir had vowed. Oh, they still ran occasionally; perhaps once a month now, and it was always Samir who set the routes these days, but when the joy of the rooftops had palled a little, the three had sought out new thrills. Games had come and gone as the seasons turned, and had culminated in this, their latest test of nerves.

The port district of M'Dahz was a maze of warehouses, offices, palisaded yards, harbours, dry docks, houses and taverns. Every open space seemed to be filled with people, busily striding around with papers, boxes and sacks. Local merchants on business errands, factors visiting ship captains, dockers loading and unloading vessels and filling and emptying warehouses. And, of course, there were the fascinating visitors. Few of the foreigners that landed at the port made it into the depths of the city, staying close to their ships and cargoes and to the drinking pits that entertained them.

Among the busy and narrow thoroughfares, where ropes coiled around bollards and crates lay in abandoned unruly piles, Asima, Samir and Ghassan picked their way carefully, repeatedly ducking back and dodging the unheeding feet of sailors and slaves. The boys, dressed in the clothing of peasants, would be entirely unnoticed in the streets under normal circumstances, but Asima wore a shabby cloak over her good cotton clothes and had removed her jewellery once again so as not to stand out.

Ahead lay the warehouse complex of master Trevistus, owner of four merchant galleys, native of the Imperial capital and probably the richest man to currently walk the streets of M'Dahz. Asima swallowed nervously as the three of them ducked once more into the shadowy recesses of an unknown building out of the press of sweaty workers.

'This may be stupid, Samir.'

The lithe young man turned and grinned at her.

'Your definition of stupid is a little looser than mine. Getting caught would be stupid.'

Ghassan smiled enigmatically.

'She might be right, brother... this is a powerful man. One slip and we could be watching our hands as they're separated from our arms.'

Samir shook his head.

'Firstly, we're too good to be caught. Secondly, no one can hold on to me for long; I'm part eel... you know that. Thirdly: we're children. This man is a family man from the northern cities and they're all soft and sentimental. A sob or two from Asima and he'll send us on our way with a smile.'

Ghassan looked distinctly unconvinced but shrugged and then nodded. Asima rolled her eyes and finally gave her consent.

The three took a deep breath and slipped back into the busy street. A few more minutes and the high walls of Trevistus' compound loomed. Samir had thoroughly checked out the location yesterday. Within the enclosure stood four structures, one at each corner, leaving an open space in the centre that cluttered and emptied with goods and equipment like the tide.

Closest to the single gate, wide and strong, stood the two storey building with an external staircase that held the offices of the merchant, his factor, and the various clerks in his employ. On the other side of the gate stood the bunk house that catered for the crew of the merchant's ships when in port, a building busy at all times barring mid-evening when the men caroused in the local taverns. In the opposite corner stood the wealthy and elegant house of Trevistus himself, lived in for only a few weeks each year, and maintained the rest of the time by a permanent staff of servants and slaves. The final corner, the object of Samir's main investigation, was dominated by an enormous warehouse.

Ducking into a narrow side alley, the three crossed to the next street, from where the gateway of the compound was visible, guarded by mercenaries of foreign extraction; powerful and blond. Samir waved his companions back into the shadow of a porch projecting from the front of a smelly building called the Laughing Mermaid.

'Any time now.'

The others nodded and watched with growing nervousness and excitement in roughly equal quantities. Tense moments passed as workers and slaves traipsed past along the road, carrying goods or going about their various tasks, none interested enough to accord the three peasant children more than a passing glance.

Somewhere a horn sounded, announcing the arrival of another vessel at this meeting place of worlds. Samir tapped his foot impatiently and looked up at the sky, trying to gauge the time by the angle of the sunlight hitting the building opposite.

'We're here on time. They must be late.'

Ghassan, beginning to twitch slightly, pursed his lips and frowned.

'I cannot help but wonder how you came across detailed transport schedules for foreign merchants.'

Asima shrugged.

'Be sure there's some clerk somewhere wondering where his important papers are, Ghassan.' She turned and smiled knowingly at the smaller brother. 'You are a menace, Samir. And possibly a genius.'

Samir grinned and put a finger to his lips, gesturing over his shoulder with a thumb. In the street, four wagons, loaded to a point where the wood groaned uncomfortably, trundled past with interminable slowness, each drawn by an ox with a stoically resigned expression.

'Remember. Quiet until we're left alone. Take only one thing and nothing that will be missed. This is a game; a test... not a theft.'

Ghassan nodded and pointed.

'The third wagon. No guards; just a driver.'

Samir smiled and stepped backwards into the street, hidden from view of the general populace by the wagon itself. Gripping the side boards, he hauled himself with ease from the murk of the road and tipped over the edge into the mass of grain sacks. Ghassan shared a look for a fleeting moment with Asima.

'He's going to get us all killed one day', she said with mock seriousness.

Ghassan glanced past her at the cart and, quick as a flash and with no warning, tipped his head forward and kissed her; a brief peck in the manner of a nervous child, and then he was past her, hauling himself up into the cart.

Asima stood in the shadow for a moment, her eyes wide as she reached up in surprise and touched her lips. The world slowed as her mind reeled.

'Sssss!'

Snapping her head round in the mist of confusion, Asima saw the brothers peeking over the side of the wagon and beckoning as the vehicle had almost rolled on past the tavern. Shaking her head to clear it, she ducked out of the shadows and leapt onto the side of the cart. A hand appeared to help haul her up. She gazed upward into Ghassan's eyes and, taking a deep breath, clasped her hand in his. Suddenly, Samir was there also, helping haul her in among the sacks of grain, just as the cart passed from the building's shadow and into the clear view of the public once more.

Asima lay in the sacks, mulling over what had just happened. Above her, apparently unaware of what this meant, both boys peered between the boards to see ahead. Asima touched her lips again. She found herself smiling without the intention of doing so. Somehow, she had been waiting for a year for this to happen and yet had been completely unaware of her yearning until it had occurred. She looked up at Ghassan, unkempt and powerful, his noble brow and serious face intent on the task ahead.

And then Samir turned and unleashed a smile upon her and her surety exploded in splinters and vanished. She frowned as the boy turned back to his contemplation of the compound that rolled toward them with its looming danger. Shaking her head, she gritted her teeth. No time for this now, she chided herself, and clambered across the sacks to a position beside the boys.

The front cart was being led inside, while a clerk went through some papers with the driver of the second vehicle. At a gesture from Samir, the three children nestled down among the comfortable bags, covering themselves as best they could.

Minutes passed as they lay there, staring up into the endless blue while the noises of the port went on around them. And slowly, finally, the cart trundled forward. The three held their breath as the clerk approached, stopping only a few feet from them as he checked the manifest and clearances with the teamster. Such a short time passed and yet to the three of them it seemed an age of man had gone by.

Finally an agreement was made and the cart trundled slowly into the compound. As Samir had explained, drawing on information from his unknown source, the four carts would be drawn into the central space, not far from the warehouse, where there was sufficient space for unloading with the minimal distance to the place of storage. The teamsters, their job done for now, were given a chitty and escorted from the compound, where they would visit the nearest tavern while they waited for their carts to be emptied.

With a quick glance, Samir checked the compound over the top board. Someone, presumably an overseer, had gathered the workmen near the lead cart and was speaking to them in quiet tones. The teamsters were departing while the labourers' instructions were given, and the half dozen guards at the gate, bored beyond tears, watched the few women pass by in the street outside with half-interest at best.

With a grin, Samir beckoned to the others and clambered over the side of the cart, dropping lightly to the ground and running toward the warehouse, its great wide open doors welcoming him. Ghassan and Asima followed suit, their hearts racing as they slipped from the cart, across the open space unobserved, and into the shadow of the warehouse.

The three ducked around the inside of the doorway and stood with their back to the wooden walls, drawing a deep and relieved breath as they scanned the interior.

'What now?' Ghassan whispered. 'They'll be here in minutes to unload.'

Samir shook his head. 'We have at least ten minutes. They unload the carts onto small trailers and then wheel them in here. It's a complex business, but we've plenty of time to find something and slip out. Besides,' he added with a smile, 'it looks like they've got some sort of trouble. That man outside is keeping the workers busy.'

'You've still not explained how we leave here,' Ghassan sighed.

Samir grinned and pointed to the ladders that reached into the darkened upper corners of the warehouse, where they hooked onto the walkways.

'From the top level, we can slip onto the roof. From there we're the right height to cross the outer wall and drop into the alley.'

'That's a long drop.'

Samir winked.

'Not where I put the crates ready to drop onto, it isn't.'

Asima smiled. Samir always claimed to be the quick one, while Ghassan had the family's brains. To her acute eye, however, it was clear that the brothers shared every talent in equal amounts. For all their differences, they were every bit the match for one another.

Samir wandered along the wall among the crates, peering into occasional ones while trying to decide what trophy was most fitting with which to make off. With a shrug, Ghassan followed suit while Asima remained standing by the doors. There was more to think about today than mere trophies. With a sigh she picked up a small amphora of olive oil. That would do.

Her heart skipped a beat as a man strode into the warehouse mere feet away from where she lurked. She had been so absorbed in their task she'd not heard him approach. Besides, there should be no one coming here yet. Silently, holding her breath, she dropped down behind the crates, cradling her amphora like a newborn. As she vanished from sight, she noted with relief that the boys had already disappeared behind obstructions. They must have sharper hearing than her.

The man was tall; taller even that the nomads of the south, though he was clearly a man from across the sea to the north. Unusually large and imposing, he was dressed in dark leathers and a black shirt, with a finely-crafted chain mail shirt over the top. A curved sword hung at his belt, high and angled across him in the manner of a Pelasian. He had unremarkable brown hair, short and straight, and a neat beard covering a suntanned jaw. He walked as though he owned the world upon which he trod, though he was clearly no merchant.

With bated breath, she watched as a second man entered. This person was more than a head shorter and with blond hair, dressed in fine clothes and unarmed, gripped at his elbows by two unsavoury-looking men with Pelasian features and drawn blades. Asima bit her lip as the warehouse doors were closed ominously behind them by an unseen hand. The party of four men stopped in an open area of the warehouse and the rich man was dropped unceremoniously to the floor.

'Trevistus,' the tall man said, shaking his head with mock sadness. 'What am I to do with you?'

The smaller man coughed and Asima was shocked to see blood trickle from his mouth, flowing through a gap afforded by two missing teeth.

'I can pay you handsomely, Kaja,' the man replied, his gapped teeth whistling unpleasantly. 'There's no need for this antagonism. I'm a man with connections.'

The tall man – Kaja, as he had been called – shook his head.

'You used your connections to set a bounty on me; a large and very ostentatious bounty. Things like that can ruin a man's day. You have piles of money, but then money doesn't buy me peace of mind or heal my reputation, now does it, Trevistus?'

The merchant, his panicked eyes darting back and forth, stammered. Asima shrank down, fearing that somehow the desperate man would see her through the crates.

'But... wh... what can I do? I've sent a message cancelling the bounty. I am a man of means.'

'You were a man of means, Trevistus.'

The merchant's eyes widened and he assumed the bravado of the cornered man.

'You can't do this, Kaja! I have friends on Isera; in the government itself. My factor lives in the palace. He knows Minister Sarios... even the Emperor!'

The tall man smiled a horrible, feral smile.

'Emperor Quintus has enough on his plate at the moment. I hear his generals are now in open rebellion. The Empire's collapsing in on itself, my dear Trevistus, and the time has come for men like us. Men of independent means and supreme self-interest. Well... for men like me at least. Goodbye, my unfortunate friend.'

Asima closed her eyes as a brief whimper gave way to a gasp and was silenced with a slicing noise. There was the dull thud of a padded weight falling to the floor. She couldn't believe what she had just heard and offered thanks to every God that might be listening that she at least had not seen what just happened.

She almost shrieked as something touched her elbow. Snapping her head round in panic, her eyes met those of Samir, who was gesturing urgently for her to follow him. Beyond him, Ghassan nodded sharply.

The light-stepping journey around the periphery of the warehouse, hidden by crated goods, was tense and slow, and the three heaved a sigh of relief that, by the time they reached the nearest ladder and prepared to climb, the warehouse doors had opened and the occupants had left with their grisly burden.

A gloomy silence accompanied the children on their unnoticed escape.

In which relationships are forged

The next winter would turn the boys' world upside down. Asima had spent less time with the brothers since the incident at the warehouse and when they had seen her she wore a haunted look. Her eyes had darkened as though she slept little, and she had become taciturn. On the few occasions she had visited, she looked uncharacteristically frail and frightened and had taken to sitting wrapped in Ghassan's arms. Samir had pondered on this for a while, but had finally nodded and accepted that perhaps Asima currently needed Ghassan's sober strength more than his own optimistic humour.

Then late one evening, as their mother was preparing the main meal and the boys sat alone in the communal room, there was a knock at the door. Knowing that their mother would be too busy to answer and that she would become angry if she had to ask them, Ghassan and Samir rushed to the front of the house where the ill-fitting wooden portal kept the worst of the weather out. A visitor was an exciting prospect. Asima rarely came to the house, and would certainly never knock at the front door where her arrival would be noted by their mother.

As the door swung open, the brothers looked up into the weathered face of a tall man. Dark hued and imposing, he wore the travelling garb of a desert nomad. A bag slung over his shoulder, he was otherwise unburdened. Before either boy could speak, the man smiled, his teeth surprisingly straight, white and neat. The effect, against his dark face, was unsettling to say the least, but the smile seemed genuine.

'You boys have grown beyond measure and expectation.' His voice was rich and deep, with a touch of humour and warmth.

The boys stared and there was a crash from the kitchen as their dinner hit the floor in its earthenware pot, shards scattered across the tiles. Samir and Ghassan were still looking up in silent confusion a moment later when their mother came running across the common room and jerked to a halt, breathing heavily behind them.

'Faraj?'

The man's grin merely widened as he now stepped back to take in the three of them at the same time. Ghassan tugged at his mother's belt.

'Who is Faraj?'

He was rewarded with a brusque cuff around his ear as their mother stared at the man, various expressions pulling at her face. The visitor opened his arms and spread them wide in an almost placatory gesture.

'Whereas you, my dear Nadia, remain unchanged by the... oh, seven years since we last met?'

While Ghassan irritably rubbed his stinging ear and glared furtively at his mother, Samir was paying closer attention to the visitor. His sharp eyes had already picked out three details that had led him to form his own conclusions.

'Uncle Faraj?' he hazarded.

Ghassan's head snapped round and he stared at his smaller brother. Samir smiled as the visitor raised an eyebrow in surprise.

'You look a little like father did,' he explained. 'And you're a nomad with a barely-concealed sword on your back. And you've not seen mother for seven years, yet she dropped dinner at the mere sound of your voice.'

Faraj laughed and turned back to their mother.

'He's sharp, this one.'

Samir risked a glance at his mother, but she was too busy staring at her brother-in-law to care about disciplining the boys now. Shaking her head, she gestured to invite their guest inside. As she rushed to make the cushioned seating area as comfortable as possible, the big man shuffled inside, ducking his head at the threshold, dropping his bag to one side and unslinging the sword from his back. He winked at Samir and patted Ghassan on the head as he stretched. The boys looked at one another, shrugged, and closed the door before rushing over to join the adults.

As they reached the communal seating area, their mother pointed to the kitchen.

'Dinner is made, but the rice will have to be washed thoroughly, if it can be saved. Go to it, and serve on four plates and then you may join us.'

The boys nodded unhappily and, as they hurried off toward the kitchen, their mother called after them.

'There is a bottle of date wine I have been saving. Fetch it and two mugs.'

Ghassan rushed about collecting the bottle and mugs while Samir gathered the fallen rice bowl. The container had smashed into three sizeable pieces, but much of the rice with its rich herbs and spices had been contained within the surviving arcs and, along with the spare that was being saved for the next day, there would be enough for four dinners. The boys went about their tasks in desperate silence as they listened in on the conversation from the other room.

'You once said I was always welcome?'

Their mother drew a deep breath.

'And I meant that, Faraj. But you should have come before… when your brother passed. You should have come some time to see the boys. They were babes the last time you were here. You have been gone so long and with no word. I didn't even know you were alive.'

There was a brief uncomfortable silence.

'You are right, Nadia: my absence and lack of communication has been inexcusable. I have been fighting along the Pelasian borders in the southern desert, near the Shan'a Oasis. The Pelasian Satrap of the area has been encroaching on Imperial lands and we have defended as best we could.'

He sighed.

'But that has now changed.'

Again there was a silence.

'Changed how? Why are you here, Faraj?'

The desert soldier shook his head sadly, seen from behind by the boys as they toiled in the kitchen to finish the dinner preparations.

'The limitani are to be disbanded. The governor will not continue our contract. We have been told that payment for all limitani from the capital has stopped; payment for almost everything from the capital has stopped! They say Velutio and Isera are in chaos; that the Emperor is at odds with his court and his generals, and that we are a stone's throw away from collapse.'

There was a brief nervous laugh from their mother.

'People say such things. We have heard tales before, many times.'

'This is different,' Faraj objected. 'The Empire has abandoned us to our fate on the border. Even now, the more ambitious satraps are crossing the border and claiming parcels of Imperial land and we are not there to stop them. And so I have turned to the city. I must find employment.'

The boys, fascinated, began to ferry the dishes of food into the other room, trying to be unobtrusive while taking in everything they could.

'You will not return to the nomadic life?' their mother asked.

Faraj shook his head.

'It is too dangerous now. The satraps are looking for cheap conquests in their own bids for power. Only in the deepest desert would we be safe... or here, where Imperial power still holds sway. I will hire myself out in M'Dahz in whatever manner I can.'

He smiled sadly.

'I do not wish to burden you unnecessarily, however. I would ask to stay here until I am employed and have a little money. Then I can either find my own accommodation, or pay upkeep towards yours and stay.'

As the boys brought in the final dish and sat cross-legged on cushions opposite the two adults, their mother shook her head.

'I will not hear of it, Faraj. You will stay here like the family you are. It will be good to have your company, and the boys will prosper with a man's influence.'

She flicked a look at the two boys that made them turn their attention studiously to the food bowls in their lap. The brothers were well aware of the freedoms their mother's busy schedule afforded them and of the chance that the arrival of their unknown uncle would curb the more excessive of their activities.

'I thank you, my sister,' Faraj beamed. 'You are generous as ever.'

He reached forward to pour the wine and, as he did so, caught and held the eyes of the twins while continuing to address their mother.

'The boys must miss their father terribly. I will do my best to fill that gap.'

Ghassan's heart almost burst as he saw the wicked little secret smile their uncle flashed at them as he winked before straightening his face and turning away with the wine.

Samir and Ghassan listened half-heartedly to the rest of the conversation while sharing looks and unspoken thoughts. The meal progressed in quiet and polite tranquillity while their mother and uncle passed on every snippet of news they could think of and relived tales and events that pre-dated the boys. They waited patiently once they had finished until their mother noticed them and waved them casually away without interrupting her flow.

Samir and Ghassan rushed up the narrow staircase and into the small room that they shared, with its single rickety cupboard and two sleeping pallets covered with blankets. As soon as they closed the door, Samir turned to his brother and spoke excitedly under his breath.

'He's a swordsman, Ghassan; a soldier. He can teach us to use a blade!'

He grinned at his brother, but realised that Ghassan had hardly heard him and was staring over his shoulder. Turning, he saw Asima sitting in the darkness of their room, wrapped in a blanket against the night chill that blew in through the window from the wide desert. Samir rolled his eyes as his brother walked over to the bed, sat against the wall and wrapped his arms around their guest.

Samir, his own mind racing through the days to come, imagining lessons in swordplay and uncle Faraj taking them to exciting places and buying them treats, sat across from the pair and pulled up his own blanket against the breeze.

He must have nodded off, for he woke with a start, shivering as he tightened his blanket. Outside, the town had gone quiet, just the distant ring of a bell or shout of a drunken reveller breaking the silence. The only other noise was the sound of quiet conversation floating up the stairs from the room below. Squinting into the darkness, he glanced across at the other bed. Ghassan was fast asleep, still slumped against the wall and with his arms protectively around Asima who hunched beneath a blanket, gripping his wrist lightly.

But her eyes were open.

And they were fixed on Samir.

He blinked in surprise. The smaller brother always lauded his twin's intelligence, but he knew with unashamed certainty deep in his soul that, while Ghassan had a logical and retentive brain and would learn fast and easily, Samir was brighter. He would never remember a poem parrot-fashion like Ghassan, but his mind bridged gaps, solved puzzles and connected dots with lightning speed.

And he suddenly knew, just from one quick glance at Asima, that the girl may be seeking comfort from the strong brother, but her heart was already racing toward him.

A problem to be solved another day.

He closed his eyes and within moments he was dreaming once more of swinging a curved sword and standing on the ramparts of M'Dahz, defying the Pelasian warlords as they swarmed below him.

Some say that dreams can hold portents; glimpses of the world to come. Samir dreamed of many things that night; the last night the three would sit easily together.

In which things are learned, for better or for worse

The spring morning was glorious. It held that perfect blend. The sun shone bright in a deep blue sky, though that was far from unusual in M'Dahz, and the wind had turned northeasterly and was carrying a slightly salty but fresh and cooling breeze across the town and into the heartland of the desert. The meeting of scorching sun and cooling breeze was a welcome relief to the people and a note of positivity hung over the population as they went about their daily tasks.

The breeze was particularly strong up here on the tower of iron eagles, one of the more intact of the derelict turrets on the disused defensive walls of the town. The timber roof of the tower groaned under the load, but Faraj had assured the boys it was strong enough to take their combined weight several times over.

Samir squinted into the sun as he glanced along the line of the defences. He had dreamed more than once now of standing on these walls and fighting a heroic defence of M'Dahz. Fanciful, of course. From where he stood, the walls disappeared among the buildings of the city after the next two towers, where they had been used as the supporting walls of shops and houses. In the other direction the defences had entirely vanished after this point, leaving a long stretch of open land.

The clearing of a throat brought him back from his reveries. He turned to see uncle Faraj watching him with a raised eyebrow while Ghassan swept his wooden sword back and forth in practice swings.

Over the late winter and early spring, Faraj had quickly become an integral part of family life. The boys had almost forgotten what it had been like to have a father around, but everything had come flooding back with a welcome familiarity. The brothers had been as well behaved as possible for their uncle, reining in their more excessive habits. In return, Faraj had been thoughtful and kind and had begun taking the boys with him to interesting places and, when the occasion presented itself, buying them sherbet treats and fresh dates. But this was new and heart-stoppingly exciting. It was what

Samir had been hoping for since that winter night when their uncle had first arrived.

It had taken only a few days after his arrival for Faraj to secure a position as a mercantile bodyguard, with reasonable pay and good working hours and, as the boys had watched him over the months, they had realised why Faraj had experienced no difficulty in finding worthy employment. One evening, as they had been returning from the late market, a slightly inebriated cutpurse had dashed out from an alley and attempted to rob them at knife point. By the time the boys had realised what was happening it was already over. Faraj had the man pinned to the wall by the neck with the flat of his sword, still in its sheath and attached to his belt. He had been that quick. Samir believed that it was this incident, when the boys would have been in grave danger without their uncle present, that had led eventually to the ex-soldier's decision to teach them the rudiments of sword fighting.

Samir threw out his arm and shook it, freeing his muscles as much as possible. The wooden sword felt exceedingly heavy to him, but was excellently made. Had Faraj had a carpenter produce them or had he carved them himself?

Noting the glint of excitement in Ghassan's otherwise sombre face, he stepped forward and hefted the sword.

'This is so heavy, if I swing it, I shall fall over, uncle.'

Faraj laughed.

'Then you will have to learn balance quickly. The sword is heavy, yes. Heavier than a real blade that size. What you have there is a replica Imperial short sword at one-and-one-third weight. Bear in mind that the curved desert sword on my back weighs more than twice that. But you're right: you will find that the real Imperial blade is much lighter and easier to handle.'

Ghassan frowned.

'Then why practise with these?'

Their uncle smiled.

'Because you are lithe but not strong, either of you. Quick and supple, but without bulk. To hold your own in a real fight, you will also need power, and using this heavy sword will build your muscles. More than that; when I finally deem you ready for a real blade, you will find them so easy to use after the training sword that you will already have an extra edge.

Samir nodded. It made sense. He stepped forward once more and now the brothers faced one another across a short space. Faraj nodded.

'Very well. You are not armoured and these swords will hurt. If swung with enough force they will break a limb, so we are going to start light and slow. There will be no contact until I say that you are ready.'

He stepped between them and held out a long and sturdy stick.

'Swing your blades down and hit that.'

With some difficulty, Samir lifted the heavy sword, having to employ both hands as it neared head height. With some relief, he let it drop. Ghassan managed with one hand, his larger frame lending him extra strength, but the sweat on his brow told of the strain he was hiding. Neither blade connected with the stick as they fell.

'This may take some time,' Faraj laughed.

The sun rose slowly to its zenith and was already beginning its descent when the boys' uncle allowed them to rest for more than a minute's breather. Samir sat on the low wall at the tower's edge. His arm ached more than he had believed possible and, though Faraj had made sure they had regular draughts of water, he found himself salivating at the thought of the watermelon that he knew waited at home.

Ghassan was beginning to sag. Initially, his large build had lent him an advantage, but their uncle was no fool and had pressed the bulkier brother to reach higher and swing faster, thus placing a roughly equal exertion on both boys.

The man smiled as he watched the two boys' faces while they ate their bread and now-warm cheese and drank their tepid water like men who had just crawled out of the deep, parched desert. He stood, leaning on his long stick as he watched them. In such a short time, he had grown very close to his brother's family and had occasionally needed to remind himself that these were not his own sons, not that it made a jot of difference to how he treated them. He was firm when necessary, but generous and kind when the opportunity presented itself. Sword training, though, was a time for firmness, not kindness.

Once the boys had finished and were leaning back on the stonework, breathing heavily, he cleared his throat.

'Now, my boys. Time to start the real work.'

Both brothers made an exasperated face and shared a look that they hoped Faraj would not see.

'Come on… I have here padded leathers. Now, I only have jackets and gloves; no helmets or leg guards, and it will be extremely warm work under all that extra clothing. But you'll need it.'

As the boys staggered wearily to their feet and hefted their wooden blades as well as their screaming muscles could manage, Faraj dropped a heavy, padded leather jacket in front of them both.

'You need to be careful here. Your mother does not know that I am doing this and she would most certainly disapprove. If I have to take either of you home with a staved skull or a broken leg, we shall never get to do this again.'

The boys blinked and their uncle laughed.

'I do not mean to worry you, boys. The jackets are strong and the swords are blunt. So long as you keep your aim between neck and waist we shall all be fine.'

He smiled as Samir and Ghassan wearily hauled the heavy padded leathers onto their backs and fed their arms through the stiff sleeves before tying the thongs and donning the gloves.

'Very well,' their uncle nodded, 'we shall begin this by proving it doesn't hurt. I want each of you to take a swing at the other's arm. Only the arm, mind… no leg or head blows.'

Gingerly, Samir pulled back his blade and swung, landing a light blow with a thud that shook Ghassan a little. Ghassan grinned and returned the swing.

As they smiled, the brothers turned to look at their uncle. Faraj had one eyebrow raised and looked distinctly unimpressed.

'Hardly a real fight, is it? Now swing again, but this time put a little effort into it.'

Samir nodded and smiled at Ghassan.

'Ready?'

Ghassan laughed.

'Hit me, brother.'

Samir pulled back and swung again. This time, the blow hit with a heavy thud that knocked his brother to one side. Ghassan laughed and swung back before he had even righted himself. The return blow threw the smaller boy aside. The two burst out laughing and allowed their swords to tip downwards.

Faraj sighed.

'I recognise that this is exciting for you, but I must remind you that it is not a game. You are holding back because you are brothers and, while I understand that, you need to throw yourself into this if you are serious about learning.'

Samir shrugged.

'We are doing our best, uncle.'

Faraj tapped a finger to his lips.

'I do not think that this is true. I want you both to try. Keep your blows in the torso region, but swing as though your brother is trying to kill you. Imagine that is not Ghassan before you, but some Pelasian soldier intent on rape, pillage and murder.'

There was a brief silence as the boys glared at each other and then Ghassan pulled a face and both burst into hysterical laughter. Faraj sighed.

'I am sorry about this, boys, but if you are going to learn anything more than fancy posturing, you need to be willing to strike at each other as though it was your deepest heart's desire to kill him on the spot. And to do that, we're going to have to stop you kidding around.'

The boys slowly recovered from their laughing fits and straightened, trying to hold a serious expression on their faces. Faraj shook his head.

'I need you to concentrate on something that irritates you about each other. There must be something you argue over? A toy? A piece of clothing?'

The boys shook their heads but, as their faces came up again, Ghassan saw something in Samir's eyes; something dark; something worrying.

'There is nothing we argue over, is there Samir?'

The smaller brother shook his head.

'No, brother. Nothing.'

But Ghassan could not tear his gaze from those eyes. Something had cast a shadow over Samir's soul moments ago and Ghassan, for the first time in his life, began to fear his brother. There was something in Samir's gaze that he couldn't quite define, and he would shun any attempt to name it.

The two continued to lock eyes for a minute and Ghassan was forced to turn away from that look.

Uncle Faraj, unaware of quite what had transpired between them, nodded thoughtfully.

'Good. Now that you have finished giggling like a pair of school girls, we will try once again.' He turned to Ghassan. 'You first. Swing at Samir as though your life depended on it.'

Ghassan hefted the sword as Samir stepped slightly closer. He daren't meet his brother's gaze. Swinging the sword back, he let it go with as powerful a swing as he could really justify, looking up and meeting Samir's gaze only as the heavy blade closed on its target. The result was a loud thud that knocked the smaller boy from his feet.

Taking a deep breath, he reached out and proffered his hand to help Samir up. The smaller brother shook his head and looked up at Ghassan, whose face was a mask of concern, close to panic. Samir sighed and looked back down at the sandy timber beneath him. Ghassan was his brother. They were family, and Asima could do as she pleased, but Samir would never again consider what he had just now contemplated in the darkest recess of his mind.

He smiled at Ghassan; the warmest smile he could manage, and almost laughed out loud at the relief that flooded his brother's face.

'Is that all you can manage? I'd have knocked you to the next tower! In fact, I believe I will do just that in a moment.'

He grasped Ghassan's hand and hauled himself to his feet.

'My turn, lumbering brother.'

He grinned at Ghassan, and the taller boy smiled back uncertainly. Despite the jovial face and voice, there was still something lurking beneath the surface in Samir that unnerved his brother.

'Uncle Faraj?' Ghassan propped his wooden sword against the low wall. 'I'm not feeling very well. Do you think we could call an end to today?'

The weathered warrior raised an eyebrow.

'Perhaps it would be better to begin again on a morning when it is cooler. The afternoon heat is rather intense. Let us return to the house and see what your mother plans for supper.'

The boys helped Faraj gather the equipment and their uncle forced most of it into a huge bag that he slung across his back. With a last check that they had forgotten nothing, he set off toward the stair well at the corner of the tower. Samir hurried along behind, carrying the wooden swords. Neither of them was aware of the appraising look Ghassan cast at his brother's back while he hauled the food bags onto his shoulders and set off behind them.

Something had passed between them on the tower top that day and, although he knew beyond doubt what had been at the root of it, he could not bring himself to ponder too deeply on the matter. Suffice it to say that, while he loved his brother beyond almost all else, eight years of trust had wafted away in the light breeze this afternoon.

In which the world is seen to turn

The past three months had wrought huge changes, both physical and emotional, in the brothers, and no one had noticed the differences more than Asima. She had begun to spend more time with them again these days and passed many hours sitting in the shelter of their small room while her father, intent on some business errand or other, merrily presumed her to be in her room, reading and playing.

She lay on the floor on a thick blanket, her head cradled on Samir's crossed ankles. The smaller brother had changed the most. The physical training and exercise that their uncle was putting them through had bulked Samir out. Where he had been small and reed-like, now his muscles rippled beneath his shirt sleeves. He could lift Asima from the floor by one hand without breaking a sweat. He was toned and at the peak of his physical fitness. If rooftop chases had still held any interest for the three of them, Asima was sure that Samir would be unreachable.

But the greater change was in the boy himself. Something had changed in Samir's soul. It was as though a candle in his heart had been snuffed.

Oh, he was still a loving and charming person, and many candles still burned within him, but occasionally, when caught off guard, she could see the effect of that one light that had vanished. There was a shadow that haunted him sometimes. To begin with, she had feared this change in Samir and recoiled deeper than ever into Ghassan's arms. But then one evening, when she had seen Samir alone, she had seen that darkness cloud his eyes and, on an impulse, she had clutched him and held him so tight that she felt him gasp. As she looked up, she saw those shadows melt away and a light, stronger than ever, shine from within those sparkling eyes.

And that was it. She knew now that only she could heal whatever had broken inside Samir. They never spoke of it but, when he needed her, she made sure she was always there.

She looked across at Ghassan, who sat smiling at them, and she was sure his smile was false. The larger brother had become powerful indeed. They were approaching ten years of age now, but Ghassan was already a physical match for most of the men of M'Dahz. Indeed, he was already taller than some of the foreign merchants from the north, and yet his impressive physique was tempered now with a gentleness and humility. He often deferred to Samir when choices were made and seemed, at times, almost to be in awe of his brother.

Strange changes, indeed. But there had been changes in Asima too. Ghassan had held everything she needed; still did. There was nothing she could look for in a boy that she would not find in Ghassan. And yet the darkness within Samir fascinated and pulled at her and she found herself more often in Samir's arms that those of the taller brother these days.

And Ghassan must recognise that. It must sadden him. And yet he said nothing and merely watched them both with a fraternal smile.

It was a warm evening, and the breeze had died down just before dusk, leaving a cloying stillness that hung in the air as though the world held its breath. The faintest streaks of pink and azure hung in the west as the sun journeyed to the underworld for the night, where it would be renewed by the hammer and forge of the fire God. Soon, the boys would be called down for their evening meal, once Faraj had returned from his duties, and Asima really should go, although recently the boys' mother had become aware of her evening visits and, while raising the occasional meaningful eyebrow at her, had kept remarkably silent on the subject.

So she would probably wait here while dinner was prepared and, as was now often the case, Nadia would set out the meals and then call to the girl she knew was lurking upstairs. She would have automatically set a spare place for Asima. With the extra income Faraj brought into the household, they now ate well and could afford a little generosity. And her own father was so busy trying to keep his business afloat in what he kept referring to as 'the turbulent climate' that he often forgot to feed them, and they had to rely on a late supper of salad and cold meat.

Faraj would be weary but pleasant. He always finished late, as there was ever much to do in the port district. He…

She blinked as she heard the door open. Faraj was early?

'Nadia? Children?'

Their uncle's voice held an ominous tone that made Asima sit up. She had been around the family often enough to know that 'children' meant the three of them, and that Faraj presumed she was there. Had he meant the brothers, he would have said 'boys'. Ghassan and Samir began to move; clearly they also had recognised something in the man's tone. The three children hurried down the stairs, Asima keeping to the rear, to find Faraj, having hung his sword and bag by the door, seated with crossed legs by the low table. Bowls and plates had been laid out in preparation, but the food was far from ready by this time. The boys' mother had appeared from the kitchen and padded quietly over to sit at the table, gesturing the children to join them.

'What is it, Faraj?'

Their mother raised the question. It would have been impolite for one of the children to do so. Their uncle's brow was low and troubled, and his eyes were dark. He reached for the date wine in the centre of the table and poured himself a long draught, from which he took a pull before speaking.

'I am not sure where to begin...'

'Faraj?'

'Many rumours are flying around M'Dahz, and you will hear all of them within the next day, but I have the grains of truth at the centre of the rumours. I have confirmed this from several solid sources and the news is not good.'

There was a silence around the table as everyone waited impatiently.

'And you will like my decision even less than my news.'

Samir and Ghassan shuffled in their seat. Something leaden had settled in the pit of their stomachs. They waited what seemed an eternity for their uncle to take another swig and then continue.

'The Empire we serve and that shelters us has broken. Word arrived today at the port directly from the capital: the Emperor is dead. General Caerdin has revolted and burned the palace to the ground, General Avitus has named him traitor and declared martial law in the capitol; the army is in chaos.'

The family and their visitor stared in astonishment at Faraj as they listened to his tidings.

'Of course,' he went on 'this was all days ago; probably more than a week. It takes that long to sail from Velutio to M'Dahz. And for those of us on the Empire's periphery things become bleaker still.'

He took another swig.

'The Imperial navy has been recalled to the capitol. Without them, ships are prey to both pirates and Pelasian raiders, and so, on the dawn tide when the last Imperial warship in M'Dahz sails north, all the Imperial merchants sail with her. They will not risk staying this close to the border without protection. The garrison of

M'Dahz had been recalled to Calphoris by the Southern Marshal. The town is now defenceless and there is no protection for merchants by land or by sea. You know what that means…'

All of them nodded sombrely. With no protection and so close to both Pelasian lands and pirate waters, merchants would stop using M'Dahz as their marketplace. The desert caravans would dry up and the port would languish emptily. All trade would stop and the town would die. Samir shrugged uncomfortably.

'There are two possibilities then? A good and a bad?'

Faraj nodded.

'In the best future, the crisis in the capital will be resolved. A new Emperor will be crowned, the navy will be redeployed and everything will return to normal. That is possible, but it relies on many things beyond our reach and our control.'

He took a deep breath.

'Alternatively, Pelasia will take advantage of the situation and annexe as much land as possible. M'Dahz will then be the first to go, but at least it will survive as a Pelasian town, rather than vanishing under the sands.'

Again silence reigned and his audience dropped their eyes to the floor. Ghassan looked up worriedly at his uncle, his lip quivering slightly as he spoke.

'And what is your decision, uncle?'

Faraj shook his head sadly.

'The wealthy will flee M'Dahz, probably to Calphoris. Many of the poor will go too, but where they have homes and jobs here, they will become beggars there. We cannot flee, or we will lose the little we have. And so we must fight to preserve what we can. As soon as the sun rises, I go to the port to join the militia.'

Their mother shook her head.

'The militia are like thugs! They are barely paid and poorly trained and mannered. They are little more than a dog running alongside the Imperial garrison!'

Faraj shook his own head in return and slapped the flat of his palm on the table.

'No more. From the morning, the militia are the only army and navy M'Dahz has! All of those bodyguards, ex-limitani and pensioned soldiers in the town are joining tomorrow. We have to change the militia. We have to make it a force capable of holding off both Pelasia and the pirates until the Empire can heal its wounds and breathe life back into the port and markets of the town. There is nothing else. It is decided. Tomorrow I leave with the militia. We will be active by both land and sea and likely always busy, but I shall return as often as the Gods grant me the opportunity to see my family.'

The boys were both crying now and, despite her familial distance and the likelihood that her father could easily shift his business interests to Calphoris, Asima found that she was weeping openly for what would happen to Faraj and the brothers.

Their uncle straightened.

'I must do this. Though I will be torn from this household, I must go in order to protect it, so that there is still a house to return to when everything recovers.'

Brushing back the tears, Ghassan was the first to straighten and nod, bravely.

'We are too young to join you, uncle. I realise that. But you have trained us well and we will continue to learn and practice in your absence. And if the trouble persists until we are a little older and the militia will accept us, then we will come to stand by you.'

Faraj glanced at their mother's horrified face and her open mouth and quickly cut her off before she could speak.

'This will be over long before then, so make no unnecessary promises. I am pleased that you are both strong, quick, and bright, and can take care of yourselves and your mother, and even young Asima here if she requires it. Survive and stay out of danger so that we can be together again when the next Emperor sends his forces to save us.'

Samir nodded.

'We will, uncle.'

Silence fell over the room once again and was finally broken when their mother addressed the children in a small and cracked voice.

'Will you go to your room and leave me with Faraj for a time? I will call you when I have prepared the dinner.'

Nodding unhappily, Asima and the two boys untangled themselves and plodded slowly up the stairs to their room. Once inside, they could hear the inevitable explosion of tears and wailing from below before the door shut. Samir turned and looked at the others.

'You know what this means?'

Asima nodded.

'My father will move out in a matter of days and we will head to Calphoris. If we ever see each other again, it will be when this is all over and my father returns, if he even does that. I fear that we only ever stayed in M'Dahz because the place reminds him of my mother.'

She dropped to her knees on one of the blankets.

'I can't leave M'Dahz. I don't want to live anywhere else. I don't want to move, and I don't want to leave you.'

She wasn't entirely sure at whom that last was aimed, but the brothers both nodded sagely. Samir was the first to break the silence that followed, as he sat next to her and took her hand.

'Whatever happens is uncertain. Only the Gods know what lays ahead, not us. But the three of us are bound by bonds stronger than any Empire, and I tell you now that we will be together for many years to come.'

Suddenly Ghassan was sat at the far side, holding her other hand.

'Samir is right. We have braved injury and even death many times together, and we are here now, stronger than ever. If you go to Calphoris, then we will just have to come and find you when the time is right.'

Asima snuffled gently. She had begun to cry and was trying desperately to hold back the tears. And despite everything that had just happened, a world shattered into chaos, a future cast to the winds and a loved one to be ripped away from them, something deep inside her, that she was not sure she liked, felt a solid satisfaction that both boys were clinging to her as though their lives depended on her.

In which the field is levelled

The past two days had been chaos in M'Dahz. The military garrison had pulled out with no ceremony, merely collecting everything of value from their barracks in the palace compound, hauling it onto their backs, and setting off along the dusty road east to Calphoris. That was the day after the news broke like a wildfire across the town. That same day, the Imperial navy abandoned anything that did not belong on board their ships, hauled anchor and sailed north, accompanied by every merchant who had managed to liquidise his assets in time.

The town was already beginning to collapse. The militia had been called to the palace, where the local governor was on the verge of panic. The man had been sent by the Imperial government many years ago and, though subordinate to the provincial governor at Calphoris, had sole control and responsibility for M'Dahz, its port, military, all local settlements, trading stations and border patrol units. When he had arrived as an eager young politician, it had been a dream appointment for a pasty northern youth. Now, as a middle-aged and slightly portly gentleman, the position had suddenly become a disaster with vast responsibility for the lives of many innocents and no power or hope.

The governor had given the militia their orders with a note of sadness. He had spent hours during the night trying to allocate the meagre resources he was left with to control the trade routes, the town and the Pelasian border and had been left with an inescapable truth: he barely had enough men to control M'Dahz itself. The militia were to abandon the border, the desert roads and any outlying settlements. Split into two groups, one unit would begin to restore the city defences, tearing down houses to clear the walls of obstructions and building makeshift barricades where the lines of defence had long gone. The other unit would commandeer the six vessels in the port that belonged to absent foreign merchants and form a navy to protect those few who still had mercantile interests here. M'Dahz lived on trade and, if they could secure safe sea routes to the port, they could perhaps entice some of the other traders to return. Then, and only then, could they turn to protecting and building the desert trade links once more.

It was an ambitious plan, and almost certainly doomed to failure.

Faraj had been assigned to the navy and had embarked on a ship named the Pride of Serfium, heading out to his new career with a sad wave at the children standing at the port with their mother, jostled by the crowds of desperate folk seeking a safe way out of M'Dahz.

Already the markets were empty and many doors and windows hung open, the buildings abandoned as the inhabitants fled the perilous border region for the relative safety of the provincial capital of Calphoris. In just two days the life had left M'Dahz.

Asima hammered on the door of her father's study. There had been a great deal of crashing and thumping half an hour ago and then the house had slid into an ominous silence.

'Father?'

It had taken some time for Asima to pluck up the courage to knock. Her father was a serious man, disapproving of his child when she spoke out of place, but now she was worried.

'Father, are you alright?'

Her heart beating fast, the young girl leaned close to the door and placed her ear by the lock. The key was in the door at the other side. She could perhaps push the key out, but there was no gap at the bottom of the door, so that would hardly achieve anything.

She could hear no noise from within; just the background sounds of the town coming in through the room's only window, sounds of despair and desperation. But gradually, as she listened, she could pick out other sounds; faint sounds from within.

'Father?'

Snuffles and wheezes. Her father was crying; crying and scribbling desperately on paper at his table.

'Father, please let me in. I'm frightened.'

There was a long pause; true silence now. And finally the sound of a chair scraping back. Quiet, slow footsteps and then the turning of the key. Asima stood back expectantly, but the footsteps retreated once more and there was a further scraping of chair legs on the flagged floor. The girl stood for a moment at the top of the stairs, uncertain of what to do, and then finally took a deep breath, chewed on the inside of her cheek and reached out for the door, turning the handle slowly and swinging the door open as quietly as she could.

The scene within was a chaos that echoed the state of the town outside the window. Had they not been on the third floor in a locked room, Asima would have assumed that a brawl had broken out in her father's study. He sat at the table opposite, with his back to her, shaking slightly and occupying the only surviving chair; the other two were among the splintered and fragmented furniture scattered across the floor amid the general mess. Her father had clearly spent some time destroying his study.

'Father?'

Gingerly, she approached, stepping carefully between the debris. A bulky man, her father sat hunched over something on the table. He made no effort to acknowledge her presence and once more Asima's heart skipped a beat. Slowly, but with a determined gait, she stepped to one side and, reaching the end of the table, stood quietly.

The man looked up sharply and Asima's heart threatened to break. Her father had never been a man given to open displays of emotion, and even less so since her mother had died, but the last time she had seen grief like this assail the quiet man was on that day when her mother had been bound in linen, placed in a casket and buried, feet-downwards in the Pelasian manner in the cemetery of M'Dahz.

'Father, what is it? Please talk to me?'

When the man spoke, he voice was hoarse and cracked, his shaky hands gripping the edge of the table hard enough to whiten the knuckles.

'Asima... my dearest, darling girl. The light of my life and the song in my soul. You are your mother in all things and it breaks my heart to see it.'

'Father?'

'Asima, I just don't know how to tell you this; how to explain.'

The young girl bit her lip nervously.

'Whatever it is father, we can get by. You know that. We are strong.'

'You are strong, my love.'

He sighed and leaned back in his chair, his fingers detaching themselves from the table and sliding away the pen and the ledger over which he had been hunched.

'Asima, I have nothing. We have nothing.'

'I do not understand, father.'

'My business, Asima. My business is as a factor for a Pelasian trader. But I have received word that, with the withdrawal of Imperial support, the market in M'Dahz has collapsed and my esteemed colleague will no longer trade across the border. He has no further use for me. I had other interests with Imperial traders, but they have now fled across the sea to the north, taking their business with them.'

Asima shook her head.

'But father, you have stores of goods still in M'Dahz. Your wares will keep us until you can find new sources.'

The tired-looking man shook his head sadly.

'I believed so, but the boat I have a part interest in has been commandeered by the militia with no recompense, the traders at the oasis that owe me small monies will not venture close enough to the town to see me, and my store of fruit and perishables that is still worth a small fortune has been looted and devoured by the mob of waifs and strays at the port. There are no guards there to protect such interests now. I have been through all of my logs for import and export. I have nothing, my dear; only what is in this house. We have no more than those people who stole my food. We cannot leave M'Dahz. I cannot pay passage anywhere and we have nowhere to go.'

Asima stood stoically, her jaw set firm, and folded her arms.

'You are seeing only disaster, father, but remember this: we are both alive and healthy. We have a good house and clothes. You have possessions that are beyond the means of many that we may be able to sell, given enough time and investigation. You still have a solid reputation, and the future is not set in stone. Who, apart from the Gods, knows what lies around the corner? In a few days, a new Emperor could appear and bring peace and prosperity once more to M'Dahz.'

Her father stared at her. Such insolent words went against everything he had taught her. And yet it was sense; it was also precisely what her mother would have said to him had she still lived. Without a word, he reached across and wrapped Asima in a bear hug that almost crushed the wind from her.

'You are brave, my little jewel.'

Asima laughed.

'I was not looking forward to Calphoris anyway, father. The boys there are said to be pigs.'

He pulled his head back for a moment and stared at her in surprise. Then, suddenly, in a burst of unexpected and rare emotion, he burst into raucous laughter. As he laughed, he rocked back and forth, still gripping her tightly. Slowly the mirth subsided and he released her and sat back in his chair.

'Very well, my dear. I can see that in recent months while I have been chasing gold coronas with open hands, my little girl has grown wise and strong. Where I have failed alone, we shall now succeed together. If we are to make a go and survive in M'Dahz, we will have to work hard and I shall need you.'

Asima nodded thoughtfully.

'Do you trust me, father?'

For a moment the man's brow furrowed as though he failed to understand the question. Finally, he nodded and smiled.

'I have always trusted you, Asima. Enough to allow you to make your own entertainment around the town without my supervision. But now? For certain, I trust you more than ever, my girl. What have you in mind?'

Asima gave an enigmatic smile.

'It is time to work out what we have; an inventory of everything.'

Her father nodded.

'I shall do so…' he raised an eyebrow at his daughter.

'I, too, have my sources,' she replied.

Still with that enigmatic smile, she turned and left her father in his study while she ran down the stairs and out into the street.

Padding through empty alleyways and down numerous flights of steps, she made her way to the house of Nadia and her boys.

As was her custom, she approached the house from a rear street, climbed a ramp to a second tier of buildings and sidled along a ledge formed by ill-planned housing until she finally reached the window of Samir and Ghassan's room. The boys were sitting on one of the beds, throwing small darts carved from cedar wood into a cork board. They looked up at the noise from the window and smiled.

'Asima? We thought you would be packing. We were going to come and see you after dark.'

The girl grinned.

'You were worried that I would sneak away to Calphoris without saying goodbye to the boys I love?'

She ignore both the looks the boys gave her at those words and the small wicked feeling of satisfaction they elicited from deep within her. Smiling, she took a deep breath.

'I shall not be leaving M'Dahz. Father and I are to stay here.'

Ghassan blinked.

'But your father's business...'

Samir grasped his wrist.

'... has failed, hasn't it Asima?'

She nodded. Of course clever Samir would be a step ahead as always.

The smaller brother nodded thoughtfully.

'Looters or the military?'

She shrugged.

'A mix of them both, unfortunately, along with some bad luck.'

She straightened and folded her arms.

'However, I look at this as not so much an end as a beginning. Where there is chaos and desperation, there is always an opportunity. Father still has some resources and inventory. What we need to do is build on that; to find a market for the things we have left. But father only knows of finance and trade, whereas you and I know M'Dahz; the real M'Dahz, not the one that rich traders know. I know that between the three of us we can turn a small store into a large profit.'

Ghassan smiled.

'So you need our help? You'll have it, of course.'

Samir nodded emphatically, but Asima shook her head, smiling.

'My father will not understand such a thing, but employees he understands. I am here on his behalf to offer you a job. The three of us will work for father.'

She sighed.

'Of course, at the moment, he cannot afford to pay you. You would have to wait until we are successful for a wage, but I truly believe we can do this.'

Samir shook his head.

'I have no need of your father's money. You both need it more than us.'

Their friend gave a short, light laugh.

'That's not exactly true, is it Samir? Since your uncle left, most of the money has gone once again from this house. Come now, accept the deal.'

Ghassan nodded and proffered his hand, Samir following suit.

'You speak a lot of sense, Asima. What is the first step then?'

'We need to go and visit father. He is drawing up a full inventory of what we have. Once that is complete, we will go out into M'Dahz and find buyers for everything.'

Samir grinned.

'We shall crack M'Dahz like an oyster and collect the pearl from inside.'

In which tidings are brought

The town of M'Dahz languished hopelessly for the next few months, eking out an existence from the few desert traders desperate enough to sell their wares that they would brave coming this close to the troubled border, and from the occasional Calphorian merchant willing to face the possibility of pirates and Pelasian patrols for the high prices they could charge in the region.

It was far from a comfortable life, but it was a life, when all was said and done. After an initially hopeful start, when the seaborne section of the militia impounded two vessels and brought the navy's strength up to eight ships, they soon encountered violent resistance from both pirates and a few Pelasian vessels that felt confident there would be no reprisals. Now, after four months of campaigning, the militia had achieved a few small victories, but were back down to a strength of four vessels and were beginning to lose heart.

The defences of the town had been bolstered by the land militia. The new walls were poor and badly-constructed when compared to the heavy fortifications from the height of Imperial power, but they enclosed the nervous population and were well-patrolled by armed militia. M'Dahz endures, the people said. It was the only positive thing anyone could really find to say, these days, and so the people said it often.

Asima and her two partners stood on the jetty waiting for the fleet of small two-man fishing boats to return. The flotilla speckled the water near the horizon and would reach the dock in ten or fifteen minutes, at which point the three children would fill the baskets in their cart with fish and take them back to the secure warehouse.

The past four months had seen an almost spectacular revival of her father's trading interests. After a slow start, business had picked up rapidly for them and Asima had even talked of employing others, though had finally decided that the business should be kept between them. The girl was shrewd and, with the addition of Samir and Ghassan's quick minds, her father was astounded at how rapidly his stores replenished and his coffers refilled.

Samir and Ghassan, as the months went by, were repeatedly taken aback by just how vicious and cutthroat Asima was capable of being in business deals. She showed no sign of sympathy or compromise in her dealings, despite the fact that the people they were trading with were often old acquaintances of her father and most were in a similar financial state to themselves, desperately trying to survive in the impoverished town.

Still, it was Samir and Ghassan's knowledge of the city and their intuitive ideas, combined with Asima's strength and wily approach to business, that had turned her father's meagre surviving assets into a going concern once more. They may not like having to be hard on people with whom they sympathised, but it was doing so that was pushing them into a more comfortable position themselves.

And tonight their fish stock would go into storage so that tomorrow it could be distributed among the market traders and fill the ever-hungry bellies of M'Dahz.

Samir frowned and held his hand to his brow, shading his eyes from the late afternoon sun. Something was wrong.

'Ghassan?'

'Hmm?'

His brother turned from the warehouse wall at which he had been idly staring, counting the bricks.

'Ghassan,' his brother repeated, 'look at the flotilla. What do you see?'

Ghassan, they had discovered, had the sharpest eyes of the three of them and was probably the most observant. He had spotted the bad dates they had been about to purchase last week, and a month ago had spotted a pirate vessel on the horizon in plenty of time to get word to the Calphorian captain with whom they had been dealing to bring his boat back in to dock.

Ghassan peered out into the bright light, trying to make out the many small shapes amid the glittering, sparkling waves, muttering under his breath. Finally, he removed his hand from his brow and shrugged.

'Twenty eight small fishing boats, all very heavily laden. Bodes well for us, brother.'

Samir shook his head tensely.

'I'm not so sure, Ghassan. Twenty eight, you say? And you're sure?'

'I could count them again, but there are twenty eight. Why? Are some missing?'

Samir's jaw hardened.

'Quite the opposite. There are only twenty three fishing boats in M'Dahz.'

Ghassan blinked.

'I know these things,' Samir shrugged. 'I pay attention.'

He turned to find Asima, who was standing a few feet away from them by their cart, involved in yet more dealings with one of the dock workers.

'I think we may have trouble,' he called to her.

Asima waved away the worker and joined Samir, who explained the discrepancy as Ghassan once more shaded his eyes and stared out across the water. Definitely twenty eight. And heavily laden. There must be so much fish…'

He bit his lip as he scanned across the boats once more.

They were far too heavily laden.

The flotilla was getting closer now and more detail was visible. Twenty eight boats, but not twenty eight fishing boats. Samir had been right. Twenty three fishing boats, for sure. And five lifeboats. Ghassan suddenly found that his heart was racing. He knew what was weighing the boats down now, even before he could confirm it with his eyes. He turned to the smaller brother, his mouth dry.

'Samir… they're lifeboats.'

Samir stood still and silent as his eyes drifted from Ghassan and back to the bay, where they slid across the open water to the collection of small vessels rowing their way to land; rowing their way to safety?

Ghassan turned his own gaze back to the flotilla and nodded wordlessly as he confirmed with horror what he already knew to be true. The boats were devoid of fish. The men of M'Dahz rowed for land, but their cargo lay in bloody, soaked heaps among the ribs of the vessels. Not all were corpses, though most were clearly beyond hope. A few of the men rowing were bloodied and wet, but alive and making for home.

Militia. All men of the militia of M'Dahz. And, as they came closer and closer to the docks, every face was bleak and hopeless. Samir's own mouth was now dry as he stared out among them. Asima was between the boys now, her hands on their shoulders in a gesture of strength and support.

'It could have been any of the militia ships,' she said hopefully.

Samir shook his head, unable to speak in more than a low croak. Ghassan reached across and squeezed his brother's wrist before turning to Asima and shaking his own head.

'Each of the militia ships carries only two lifeboats. That was all that could be drummed up.'

He turned back to the fleet that were now jostling and manoeuvring into position by the jetties.

'Five lifeboats means at least three of the four ships.'

Asima fell silent once again, not trusting herself to speak any further.

Quietly and unhappily, the men from the boats climbed onto the jetties and went about the sad and grisly business of finding carts to transfer their bloody cargo from the boats. The brothers watched with bated breath, their eyes playing across the crowd of sailors, looking for the man they somehow already knew would not be there.

As the last figure shuffled up the wooden walkway, Samir collapsed backwards onto a sack of grain awaiting removal. Silently he sat there, staring at the chaos, as Ghassan hurried down the jetty and began to examine all the bodies piled in the boats.

Asima gripped Samir's hand. She didn't know what to say, but the chances were not good. She watched and realised she was biting her cheek once again, a habit she had been trying to kick recently. She had realised that many of her little habits were signs of weakness or insecurity and, as the main negotiator for her father's business, she could no longer afford such girlish tendencies.

She continued to watch, clutching the silent Samir, while Ghassan ran from boat to boat, stopping the men as they carried their ghastly cargo from the dock to the carts, and checking each body. Finally, he stopped and shuffled slowly back towards them.

'He's not there, brother.'

Samir sagged a little more, but Asima straightened purposefully.

'Well that's good, then. Faraj may be alive. His ship may be intact.'

Ghassan shook his head sadly.

'The insignia they're wearing are from all four ships. No one escaped. If uncle Faraj is not there...' his voice cracked and tailed off.

He sat with a heavy thump next to his brother.

'If he's not there, then he either drowned or he's been captured.' He took a deep breath. 'And given what the pirates are said to do to their prisoners, best to hope that he drowned.'

Asima stared at the taller of the two brothers, but realised that Samir was nodding sadly.

'Pirates?'

The three of them turned at the sudden rude interruption. A militiaman, bleeding profusely from a cut above the eye and with a damaged arm tucked limply into his belt, stopped on his way to a cart.

'Pirates, you say?'

Ghassan nodded, uncertainly, and the man shook his head.

'No pirates, lad. This was Pelasia.'

Asima blinked.

'But they wouldn't dare? Even with the army gone, Calphoris is only a day distant, with the governor's forces.'

The man laughed a hollow and unhappy laugh.

'Calphoris will be looking to its own defence now. They'll not sally forth to protect a third-rate little crossroads like M'Dahz.'

The man sighed.

'Pelasia comes, my dear. Pelasia comes now, and there is no one to stop them. The satraps have made their opening move and destroyed our ships. Best get indoors and stay as quiet as possible and hope the invasion is quick and painless.'

With a last, sad look at the three children, the militiaman shambled off among his peers. While their small exchange had occurred, one of the men must have announced the news, as roars of distress and groans of despair went up among the civilians among the docks and as the three of them sat on the grain sacks, the world exploded around them. People ran in panic this way and that, rushing to find their loved ones and either hide within the houses of the town or flee and hope they would make Calphoris before the satraps of Pelasia could catch them.

Ghassan nodded sadly as he watched the people rush in a mindless panic and turned to Samir.

'Will the rest of the militia fight, do you think, brother?'

Samir nodded.

'They are men like our uncle. Can you imagine Faraj rolling over and showing his belly to the Pelasians?'

He sighed.

'No. They will fight.' He swallowed sadly. 'And they will die.'

Ghassan shrugged.

'And we will fight and die with them.'

As Samir nodded, Asima turned to them, a shocked expression on her face.

'What?'

The two boys merely shook their heads sadly.

'But you're ten years old!' she barked. 'The militia will send you home.'

Samir sighed.

'Asima, when the Pelasians come it will make no difference. We can fight as well as any man in the militia now. Faraj trained us well. And we have to try; for you and your father… for mother.'

'But you'll die!'

Ghassan nodded sadly once again, but Samir turned to look at her.

'I have been dreaming of this for a long time. I had always assumed it would be glorious and we would be the victors, but that seems unlikely now. And yet, many times in my mind I have stood on the walls and watched the Pelasians come. It no longer frightens me.'

He grasped Ghassan's wrist.

'Let the Pelasians come.'

In which M'Dahz changes

The last twenty four hours had been frantic for most folk. At Samir's estimate, a third of the town's population had left through the east gate for Calphoris. The road between the two places must be thronging with refugees. A few of the hardier folk had found weapons and joined the remains of the militia where they gathered at the great market to plan the next step.

The commander of the M'Dahz militia was a man named Cronus, a mercenary from the northern lands who had settled in the town over a decade ago. He had proved to be a strong and intelligent commander and had, as soon as the militia had mustered, gone to see the town's governor, only to find that the palace compound's gate had been shut and barred. No amount of cajoling had drawn a response from within. The governor had withdrawn in solitude; the militia were on their own.

And so Cronus had found himself and his men in sole charge of the defence of M'Dahz. No questions had been asked of anyone who joined them and no one, regardless of age or ability, had been turned away.

By the time the sun had set, every man the militia could muster had been given a position on a wall or tower or in one of the makeshift redoubts in the port. No one returned home now. Should it be days of waiting, the men of M'Dahz would remain in place on the walls, huddled in blankets against the cold desert night and sweating through the heat of the day.

But the wait would not be long. Outlying scouts had returned around dawn to report a Pelasian army on the move and already in Imperial lands. The desperate and wild-eyed rider had reported a veritable sea of black-swathed bodies on the move and, when the commander had asked how many the army numbered, the scout had merely replied 'all of them' and gathered his own gear to flee the town.

There had been a few desertions during the night. In fact, from their current position, the boys could see gaps that had opened in the line of defence. Even now, some of the men on the defensive circuit glanced wistfully over their shoulder at the dubious safety of the narrow streets.

It seemed curiously fitting that the brothers found themselves stationed with five other men on the very tower where uncle Faraj had begun their sword training those months ago. Now, though, as they glanced left and right, the wall was clear of obstructions and, where there had been open land before, there was now a new gate and a hastily-constructed wall, all with their own guards.

'Do you think their navy will attack the port at the same time?'

Samir shrugged at his brother's question.

'Who knows? They'd be stupid not to, but that's if they have a navy. I heard Cronus talking about them. There are three satraps around the border area, but only one of them rules coastal land, so what we're facing depends on who it is that's coming. It might be one satrap, or two, or possibly all three.'

He sighed.

'The one thing the commander said is that this must have been started without the consent of the Pelasian crown. Apparently their God-King is an ally of the Emperor.'

'Was an ally,' the taller brother corrected. 'There is no Emperor now. As they say in the gambling pits at the port, "all bets are off".'

The boys fell silent. Indeed, no man on the walls spoke in the eerie and oppressive morning light. The only sound that accompanied their tense anticipation was the gentle rumble of the wind blowing over the sand dunes and through the empty ways of the city. Samir shuddered.

'The dunes are noisy.'

Ghassan frowned.

'Too noisy. That's not just the wind.'

As Samir fell silent and held his breath, the taller brother shaded his eyes and gazed into the distance. In their current position, they were on the highest part of the defensive circuit of M'Dahz, with the road into the deep desert heading out in a diminishing line before them, marching off to the oases and their date farms. The dunes came very close to the city here, where the desert met the sea. More than a century ago, an enterprising civic leader had created a levee of stone to keep the drifting sands away from the town. The levee had been buried beneath the endless dunes for many years now, so high were their crests and so deep their troughs. Sailors from the north who bothered to venture to this side of M'Dahz were often amazed by the desert. It was said that the sands south of M'Dahz formed waves higher than were ever seen on the seas.

And it was from one of the deep troughs that Ghassan watched the first Pelasians emerge. Tales of the Pelasian armies abounded in the folklore of the south. They were said to go to war with more pomp and splendour than the retinue of most Kings. In the old stories, the column of black-clad warriors was preceded by chariots bearing banners and effigies, musicians and acrobats. High-stepping, painstakingly-trained horses would convey the army's leaders to the conflict.

The old tales were wrong.

There was nothing splendid about the flood of black that washed like a sick tide from the deep sands. Like a million locusts swarming across the sea of gold, so thick that hardly a grain was visible between them, descending on M'Dahz to strip it bare.

No musicians; no banners and acrobats. Just company after company of black-clad death-bringers. Spearmen, then archers, then heavily-armoured infantry; three varieties of predator in waves, over and over again. And alongside, escorting them in long-filed companies, came the cataphracti: cavalry so thoroughly armoured that every inch of both man and horse was covered with shining steel plate. Untouchable. And along the periphery, the light skirmishing cavalry in small parties.

The sight was breathtaking; terrifying and marvellous at the same time. And despite the certain dread of death that grasped Samir's heart and pulled it down deep into his gut, all he could find to think was how hot those cataphracti must be under the desert sun.

Ghassan was breathing heavily close to his ear. Groans could be heard along the wall from the less disciplined militiamen. In his head, Samir performed a couple of swift calculations based on the size of each infantry and cavalry unit he could see. He whistled through his teeth. Even counting only the enemy he could see, and there were clearly more yet to arrive, the Pelasians must number more than ten thousand men. He had performed a head-count at the market meeting and estimated the militia to number a little less than three hundred. The odds were around thirty five to one. While he had been under no illusion that the militia could hold the forces of Pelasia away from the town, the truth of their predicament suddenly struck home. It was like a rat trying to hold back the sea. If this satrap simply wished it, he could dismantle the entire town in less than a day with no appreciable loss of men.

'Are we foolish, Ghassan?'

His brother blinked in surprise.

'What?'

'Are we making a brave last stand to prove our worth as men,' he asked, 'or are we simply throwing ourselves onto the pyre of our pride?'

Ghassan opened and closed his mouth a few times, but no sound was forthcoming. He stepped next to his brother and watched as the last of the enemy came into view.

At the rear of the great army came a small mounted party, with one man clearly at the centre. As the army drew itself to a halt beyond the missile range of the wall, the man on his single, gleaming black steed rode forth from his group, accompanied by half a dozen riders with large oval shields. They trotted through the deep sands past the many units and out into the open land before the walls.

As the man came closer, the brothers peered down at him, assessing this man who posed such a great threat. He was tall, dressed in fine, though understated, clothes and armoured only with a shirt of interconnected steel leaves. A black scarf wound around his head and neck and covered the lower half of his face against the abrasive sands. A long, curved sword hung at his side.

Though he had several men with him armed with great shields, he rode alone into arrow range, apparently unconcerned, and finally stopped ten yards from the gate, his horse snorting and prancing impatiently. The impressive satrap looked up at the defences. For a long time there was a tense and uncomfortable silence and then, finally, he unwound the black scarf and leaned back in his saddle, rubbing his smooth, clean shaven chin.

'Boys!' he called out in a strong, surprisingly light and almost musical voice.

'Boys, old men and merchants!'

There was another uncomfortable silence.

'I have claimed M'Dahz and its surrounding lands as part of my demesne in the name of Pelasia and the God-King. I care not what you think or call yourself, but you and your land and possessions are now Pelasian.'

There was a low rumble of dissent among the defenders, but with no identifiable source or audible words. The satrap nodded as though answering some internal question.

'I give you a very clear choice. You many fight to defend your precious hive, though if you choose to do so, you will all die; I will take no prisoners. Then your women and children… those few of you old enough to have children…' a condescending smile crossed his face. 'Will have to face a life without you, poor and alone until they die unremembered.'

He drew a dagger from his robe and threw it point first into the sand before him.

'Or you can surrender the walls of your town, open your gate, accept your satrap willingly, and you may return to your life.'

He allowed his horse to prance dramatically for a moment as his words sank in, and then settled to stillness once again and lifted his face.

'I know that your town is dying a slow death since the Empire left you. Pelasia offers rebirth. We bring trade, peace and prosperity once again.'

He grasped the loose end of the scarf and began to wind it once more around his neck.

'Or we bring death, fire and oblivion; the choice is yours. You have five minutes.'

Without waiting for an answer and apparently unconcerned for his safety, the satrap turned his horse and walked slowly away from the walls. Ghassan and Samir watched as the man approached a low pavilion that was in the advanced stages of construction at the near periphery of the Pelasian army. Food and drink was being unloaded and delivered into the heavy-framed tent and the satrap dismounted and entered, brushing aside the hanging door and disappearing from view.

Ghassan continued to stare at the enemy, conflicting emotions and thoughts battling in his mind. He hardly noticed as Samir dashed over to the rear edge of the tower.

'Ghassan!'

He turned at Samir's hissed whisper and joined his brother at the parapet. Down in the shadows behind the gate, commander Cronus was standing at attention, with three of his senior men alongside him. Along the street from the centre of the town a small party was approaching. The boys had rarely ever seen the governor's guard; a hand-picked mercenary unit from the northeast, they were resplendent in silver and white, with plumed conical helmets and banners flying from their pikes. And in their midst came the governor. None of them were mounted; it was simply impractical in the streets of M'Dahz.

'What will he do, d'you think?' Samir asked quietly. His brother shrugged.

'What can he do? He must surrender or join us on the walls.'

The Imperial party stopped below the gate and, while the white guards stood stiff and proud, the governor strode out forward to meet the militia commander. For some reason he looked ludicrous to the boys; an overweight man of more than middle years, used to good living and peaceful bureaucracy, in a white uniform, armed and armoured and with a plumed helmet beneath his arm.

The two commanders entered into a brief, muttered conversation and finally Cronus stepped back and saluted. Ghassan squinted into the shadows and was almost relieved to see the strained look of deep melancholy on the commander's face.

'He's going to surrender, Samir. I don't think Cronus likes it, but he's acquiesced.'

Ghassan clearly hadn't realised how loud his voice was, for men nearby turned sharply to face him, accompanied by an audible sigh of pent-up dread being released. The tall boy lurched back from the wall as the governor and his militia commander threw their heads back and gazed up toward the source of the comment.

The brothers held their breath for an eternal moment, and the strain slowly passed. Below, the governor's voice demanded that the gate be opened.

Ghassan and Samir rushed to the far side of the tower and gazed down into the bright sunlight as the governor, along with Cronus and the white-clad guards, strode out onto the sand, the gate remaining wide open behind them.

There was a brief flurry of activity around the pavilion and, casually and without fuss, the satrap emerged unarmoured. Stretching, he gestured to the guards nearby. As the brothers watched, their breath held, the Pelasian guards turned a number of crossbows on the approaching nobleman. Secure and safe, the satrap stepped to the edge of the carpet, keeping his unbooted feet out of the rough sand.

'Governor Talus. How good of you to come.'

His expression was hidden as he bowed deeply with an almost snake-like fluidity. The governor and his party came to a halt a respectful distance away. As the white guardsmen came to attention, the governor stepped forward, drawing his sword. For just a fleeting moment, Ghassan pictured the defiant governor skewering the black-clad satrap. But no.

In an age-old gesture, the governor stepped a little closer, reversed his sword, dropped to one knee, and proffered the hilt to his enemy.

'In the name of the Imperial governorship and the people of M'Dahz, I hereby offer you my sword as your vassal. M'Dahz is yours, my lord Satrap. I offer you not only my loyalty, but that of my people, in the hope that you will accept us as vassals and not prisoners, to join your lands and bring glory and prosperity both to our town and to its new master.'

Samir whistled through his teeth again. It was a bold stroke; to not just surrender, but try to maintain M'Dahz as his own command under Pelasian rule. Samir found he was holding his breath once again. Audacity like that could just as easily be punished as rewarded.

For a long moment, the satrap glared at the governor before finally pursing his lips and nodding.

'I will accept your offer, Talus, with conditions. If you wish to continue to govern M'Dahz for me, I will hold you responsible for everything that happens here. I keep things tightly-reined and peaceful in my demesne and I expect you to do the same. For every incident of unrest or dissent of which I hear, I will carve a piece from you to remind you of your situation. Do you understand?'

He stepped back and, as his face came into view, Samir found he was biting his tongue. The satrap that had been so smooth and calmly-spoken was more than he had initially appeared. There was something about his expression that sent a shudder down the boy's spine, something snake-like and cold. This was not a man to cross; nor, he mused, was this a man he was inclined to trust.

They watched as the governor nodded and swore an oath. Wordlessly, the satrap reached down and accepted the hilt of the Imperial sword, holding it between thumb and forefinger as though it were something dirty and unpleasant, and tossed it carelessly into the pile of debris resulting from the pavilion's construction.

Ghassan turned to Samir.

'When I look into those dead eyes, I suddenly find I envy those who fled M'Dahz.'

Samir nodded thoughtfully, watching their new ruler.

'We need to find Asima and tell her the news.'

In which Pelasian might is encountered

Asima looked up at the white-clad guard as she grasped the handles of her bag.

'Where are we going?'

The guardsman turned his strange, pale blue eyes on her and shrugged beneath his cuirass of iron plates.

'Fast.'

His accent was strange and thick, like date wine that had been left too long in the open air. In the aftermath of the Pelasian arrival, Samir and Ghassan had dropped in, breathless, to deliver the tidings before running off to find their mother, and the guard had arrived ten minutes later with orders to collect Asima and her father. They had been allowed a brief pause to collect one bag of possessions to take with them; no more. The guard had been silent and singularly unhelpful in reply to their questions; likely the man spoke their language badly. For a few minutes her father had argued with him, but he soon gave up. These were the governor's own guard and there was no one safer in M'Dahz in whom to place one's trust.

She hefted the weighty bag on her shoulder. Despite her acquisitive nature, Asima had been totally unaware of just how many possessions, even treasured possessions, she had. Selecting few enough to fit in the bag had been a tough and heartbreaking task, made all the more painful by the irritated glares and impatient shuffling of the guard.

Her father appeared in the doorway, his own considerably smaller bag over his arm.

'Come on Asima. We must go.'

'But where?' A note of petulance had entered her voice.

'Where else, girl. To the palace… this is the governor's guard. Now stop arguing and hurry.'

Asima fell silent, her lips flattening in an angry line, and strode past the two adults into the stairwell. Behind her, her father and the guard shared a look and then followed on.

Outside, in the street, the guardsman drew his blade; a northern sword, longer than a standard Imperial one. Hefting it meaningfully, he pointed up the street and the three of them set off through the winding maze of alleys and passageways toward the high walls of the palace compound.

Along the thoroughfare they turned left and climbed the stairway toward the next highest level of M'Dahz. The guard's face when Asima occasionally saw it was set in a grimace as though he were expecting trouble at any moment; indeed, the way he held his sword suggested he was prepared for constant attack.

Strangely, there was no sign of movement in the streets. Clearly over a half of the town's population had abandoned their lives and fled to Calphoris, but there were noises among the streets and buildings of M'Dahz; noises that didn't bear too much listening to. A scream cut through the general hubbub and, now that Asima concentrated, she realised that most of the sounds were those of wanton destruction and sobbing.

A sudden shout attracted her attention as they passed an open door. Risking a quick glance at the interior, she caught a brief sight of a black-clad figure raising something metallic. There was a gurgle and Asima turned her head away and closed her eyes, fervently wishing she had not looked in the first place.

As they strode on, she found herself and her father drawing closer and closer to the white-clad guardsman. What was going on? This appeared to be the looting and pillaging of a victorious army; she had heard stories of what the soldiers of a conquering force were capable. But from what the boys had said, this had been a peaceful surrender and takeover of power; the governor was nominally still in charge of M'Dahz. There was a dull thud from an alleyway on her right. She noticed the guardsman's head snap round towards it and kept her own gaze locked on the way ahead, biting her cheek once again.

What was going on?

Slowly and nervously the three of them climbed the streets to the palace compound. The gates, always shut against the possibility of theft or wilful damage, were wide open. Where previously no guards had been visible from outside, now black-clad Pelasians in shirts of splinted mail stood by the gateposts watching the street carefully. Within the walls, the only figures visible were Pelasians. Asima looked across sharply at the guardsman walking with her, but the man kept his expression neutral and his eyes straight ahead.

As they approached the gate, the Pelasian soldiers shifted quickly as if to bar their way, but relaxed as they recognised the white and silver uniform of the governor's guard. The guardsmen gave a professional salute to the two men who merely glanced at him and then waved disinterestedly toward the internal buildings.

Inside, Asima sized up the situation in short order. There were several buildings in the compound, and she was aware of the purpose of most. Black figures strode in and out of them, often carrying goods one way or the other, even in the guards' barracks. The only building that seemed to be escaping the worker ants of the Pelasian force was the governor's residence, tall and elegant and with four white-clad guardsmen standing to attention around the entrance, watching the activity in the courtyard with distaste.

As the guard led them across the courtyard toward the governor's building, Asima glanced around her and noted with interest the small party of four people just arriving at the gate, well dressed and carrying bags, escorted by another white-clad guardsman.

As they reached the entrance to the house and the guardsmen stepped aside, the next group caught up with them. A nod of recognition passed between her father and the portly gentleman in the other party.

'What do you suppose this is all about?' her father enquired quietly.

'Not sure, but I'm damn glad I'm here and not one of the poor folk being beaten to death that we passed on the way!'

Asima's heart skipped a beat. Ghassan and Samir and their mother were out there somewhere.

'Why are they doing this?' the man asked.

'I've no idea,' her father replied, shaking his head, 'but I suspect we're about to find out.'

The guards escorted them up the ornate steps and into the house. The first storey consisted mainly of a large hall, with several doors leading off. A floor of decorative multi-hued marble lay beneath them, while wide, beautifully curved staircases rose to both sides, meeting at the far end to create a wide balcony that overlooked the hall. Guards stood on the platform, while the hall below thronged with people, all well dressed and from the lower nobility or wealthy mercantile class. In this one room stood most of the wealth of M'Dahz.

Asima and her father, along with the new arrivals, tried to find enough space to stand comfortably. Minutes passed, accompanied by a low murmur of troubled conversation, and heads turned occasionally as further groups of blessed citizens arrived and were ushered into the room.

Finally there was a brief conversation in some strange guttural language between the guards outside and one of them stepped forward and closed the door.

Asima cursed her imagination. Was it her own thoughts or the influence of Samir and Ghassan's quick minds that made the situation suddenly worrying and uncomfortable? It occurred to her momentarily that everyone in M'Dahz who was of worth to a conqueror was gathered in one room. The old adage of eggs and baskets leapt to mind and she found herself looking carefully around the stairs and at the guards, searching for something that might signal a doom for those present.

Her imaginings of a gruesome end flittered away as the door above the stairs opened and the governor, with two of his aides, stepped up to the balcony rail and waited for silence to fall across the hall. Once the assembled crowd had noticed the new arrival and every face was tilted up toward governor Talus, the man cleared his throat.

'I expect everyone here would like an explanation.'

There was another unhappy murmur that came and went quickly.

'Satrap Ma'ahd has set his men loose in the city. I have lodged the strongest complaint with his second, but the satrap is unwilling to grant me an audience.'

Asima noticed for the first time the tired and defeated expression on the governor's face.

'It seems,' the man continued, 'that the satrap had promised his men a sacking of M'Dahz, and he intends to keep his word despite my attempts to end this without incident.'

He took a deep breath and Asima noted the way, though his face maintained a strained composure, he repeatedly slapped his palm on the balustrade in irritation.

'I am quite simply unable to protect the people against this wanton destruction, but I have done what I can: I have taken in those we deem the most valuable of our citizens to protect you from the worst of these troubles.' He glanced sidelong at the guard commander next to him. 'I can only hope that my doing this without seeking the satrap's approval is not enough to anger him, as that may well place us all back in direct danger.'

He straightened.

'I have had rooms prepared for you all in this building. There is little space and things will be cramped. You are, sadly, required to share living space. I can only apologise for the conditions, but I had to try and save as many people as I could. Once I leave here, my staff will help you all settle in and see to the provision of food and bedding. I, regrettably, must visit our new overlord and attempt to smooth things over and secure your safety. If all goes well, the satrap is mollified, and the army run out of places to loot and rape, then it is my fervent hope that you will all be able to return to your houses in a matter of days. Thank you for your patience and I hope that we will ride this through safely.'

With a bow and a sombre look, the governor turned and left the balcony. There was a long, uncomfortable silence, and then suddenly the noise burst like a dam and angry and despairing voices flooded the room. Asima looked up at her father, who had remained silent and gaunt.

She had her own worries.

Samir and Ghassan burst through the door to find their mother sitting cross-legged by the wall, rocking slowly back and forth.

'Ma?'

The woman raised her face sharply and the boys saw with heartbreaking sadness the tears running down her cheeks.

Samir sighed. What more could the Gods have thrown at their poor mother? Her husband had died long before his time and left her all but penniless to bring up two headstrong boys. There had been a brief interval when Faraj had returned and things had once more become easier and hopeful. And then the Empire had left and Faraj had gone off to fight and die.

And then her boys began to follow in his footsteps. They had prepared themselves for death this morning; it had seemed inevitable. She had ordered and then cajoled and finally begged Samir and Ghassan not to go with the militia, but they had been defiant and proud. Strong. Like their father and their uncle. And then they would be dead like their father and their uncle. Likely their mother had spent the morning preparing to be utterly alone.

But miraculously, they had survived. Nadia wiped the tears from her face and blinked.

'Samir? Ghassan?'

As the boys ran across the room and threw themselves at her, their mother opened her arms and turned to them.

'Then there is no invasion? But I can hear fighting…'

Samir hugged his mother with rib-breaking force. Ghassan sat back a little. His face was not the mask of joy she had expected.

'Not entirely, mother. The governor has surrendered M'Dahz to Pelasia, but their army is laying waste to the town anyway. It is the Pelasian way when victorious to sack the conquered town. They will harm us and destroy our property throughout today and tonight. Tomorrow they will stop.'

Samir nodded.

'It is horrible, but it is true, so we must leave here. We are a way down the slope of the town from where the army entered, but they will reach here long before nightfall and when they do…'

His voice tailed off, but all of them knew what would happen when hungry Pelasian soldiers spotted the still-handsome Nadia. According to some stories that were told about the Pelasian men, it was possible even that Samir and Ghassan would also be in danger.

'We've been thinking as we came back,' Ghassan said, grasping his mother's wrist. 'Nowhere in M'Dahz will be safe until at least dawn, so we must leave the town.'

Nadia shook her head. 'You think fast, my boys, but their army surrounds the town. There is nowhere to go.'

Samir grinned.

'Yes there is, mother. There is only one place that is safe tonight.'

He shared a glance with Ghassan and they both nodded.

'The satrap led his entire force across the desert. This means he has no navy. We take two or three of the small fishing boats, some heavy blankets and food to last a day or more and we row out from the port and along the coast until we find somewhere safe to moor.'

Ghassan smiled at the relief on his mother's face.

'We can return once the town has settled.

Nadia had to smile at her sons. They were often a source or worry or grief but then, when troubles seemed insurmountable, they were also a source of wonder and pride.

In which Asima denies the Gods

Asima crouched by the window, hugging her knees and gazing out between the filigree shutters. The past eight months had plodded by in a blur of misery; not only for her, but for every captive soul in this benighted place.

Governor Talus had visited the satrap in the wake of that disastrous first day and made his case for the safety of the people in his care. His presumption had cost him his left eye, burned out with a heated blade on the floor of the council chamber of M'Dahz, and yet the sacrifice of that eye had bought the safety of those in his house. The satrap had granted sanctuary to anyone in the governor's mansion but had made it perfectly clear that this rule applied solely to the building itself.

The looting, burning and abuse had slowed through that first night and had stopped the next morning, leaving M'Dahz damaged, burned, and in a state of shock. One or two of the more daring refugees in the house had taken this as a sign of safety and had collected their belongings, despite the warnings of the guards, and left the complex, returning to the town. Severed heads both old and young decorated the main gate for weeks thereafter as a reminder that sanctuary stopped at the governor's doorstep.

As the weeks rolled past and the captives mooched around their packed quarters, despair became the theme. Every morning was greeted with sobbing from somewhere in the building and every night ended with a tense and oppressive silence broken only by the Pelasian temple bells.

The first two months saw a thinning of the crowds in the house. A few brave adults had left at night, climbing down the outer wall and running through the maze of alleys in an effort to flee the cursed town and reach Calphoris. Perhaps they made it; certainly their heads never returned to the spears above the gate. Others, enterprising as they were, had brought great wealth with them to the palace and had visited the Pelasian overlord and bought their freedom with breathtaking sums.

Sadly, others had succumbed altogether to despair and had taken their own lives quietly in the night. The months had not been kind.

Asima sighed. She had no idea what was happening out there. Were her friends still alive, she wondered? What of her house? This whole situation set her teeth grinding. Her mother was Pelasian and had been a beautiful and kind woman. Merchants from across the border had traded at M'Dahz for centuries. The Pelasians she had known had always been a kind and exotic people, so why had the Gods seen fit to send the most heartless and twisted son of a whore in the whole world to crush the people of M'Dahz? Three satraps held lands at this border, so why him and not one of the others?

She knew why not, of course: because Gods did not exist and misery and cruelty were the baseline of the world. She had toyed with the idea that Gods were a fiction when her mother was taken from her years ago, and nothing she had seen since had given her cause to change her conclusion. As she sat staring across the roofs, something fell into place in Asima's mind. She had always been fast and smart; perhaps not quite as fast or smart as Samir, but she would always come out on top, because Samir was soft. Asima was, and she recognised this in herself, quite capable of hardening her heart and combining an iron will with her other talents to achieve her goals.

And that was why she would survive all of this. Maybe the boys would, or maybe not. She could no longer afford to gaze longingly out of the window and hope for them. Whether they were alive and well or not, they were lost to Asima now and, unless she wanted to sit here and wither away in the shadows, she was going to have to do something to save her father and herself.

She turned to look at him, sitting dejected in the shade by the wall. She had not seen a hint of a smile in eight long months and the light had all but gone out in his eyes. A quick glance around told her that they were practically alone, the only other occupants of their living space currently standing out on the roof and breathing clear air.

'Father?'

'Mmm?' The man looked so much older now and had lost a great deal of weight.

'Father, I want you to listen to me.'

He turned to frown at her. A year ago he would have disciplined Asima for speaking to an adult in such a fashion. Now, even the thought seemed absurd. He merely frowned and shrugged.

'Father, I am going to do something and I want you to be prepared, as I am not sure how this will work out. You won't like it, but we have no choice.'

A raised eyebrow only; she squared her shoulders and went on.

'There is no magical solution coming, father. No Gods or heroes are going to strike down the satrap and save us; he is not going to have a sudden change of heart. If we do not do something we will slowly wither away in this building until we crumble and die.'

For a moment it looked as though he might argue, but slowly, unhappily, and silently, he nodded.

'So, father, I intend to seek an audience with the satrap. I am the daughter of a Pelasian. I have Pelasian blood in my veins and I need to make him see that.'

'Asima…'

'No, father. I know what you are about to say, but this is the way. There is no luck and no fate, father. We make our own futures and I, for one, do not intend for mine to be as a prisoner.'

'Asima, you cannot…'

His voice tailed off as the girl stood, proud and defiant. She was eleven years old; still a girl. In two or three years' time he would normally have been looking for a husband for her but now, while there was no longer any hope of that, she had blossomed in captivity; grown adult too early. There was something about her that reminded him so much of her mother; and the thing that he knew clearest, without a shadow of a doubt, was that he could no more stop her now than he could stop the sun setting. Biting his lip, worried, he nodded.

Tenderly, she reached down to where he sat on the floor and placed her hand on his shoulder, leaving it there for a moment before she straightened, held her head high, and strode from the room. In a mix of pride and fear, he watched her go.

Asima strode from the room and round the corner into the corridor before she stopped and allowed the violent shaking to take hold. She could force herself to appear confident in front of her father; had to, in fact, or he would stop her. But now that she was alone, she could allow the fear she felt rooted in her belly to manifest, just for a minute.

She leaned against the wall and rubbed her temples before folding her arms around her chest and fighting the rising gorge of fear. She couldn't allow herself this kind of weakness.

Straightening, she shuffled along the wall to the large mirror, where she examined herself carefully. Despite her complexion, she looked decidedly pale, she thought. Pinching her cheeks, she carefully re-pinned her hair and, re-appraising herself, nodded in satisfaction.

Bracing herself and clenching her teeth, she strode to the stairway and began to descend. On the ground floor half a dozen white-clad soldiers eyed her with surprise as she approached. The one nearest the door, bearing a black and white striped crest on his helmet, stepped in front of the doors.

'You need to stay in house. Dangerous out.'

Asima found herself blinking in surprise. In her time here, she'd not heard any of the northern guardsmen speaking her language though, now she thought about it, some of them must do in order to communicate orders. She smiled at the guard officer.

'Thank you for your warning, kind sir, but I must insist on being allowed out.'

The guard shook his head and smiled a condescending smile in return to her own.

'Run along, girl. Go to father.'

Bridling, Asima felt the heat rise in her cheeks. How dare this man talk to her like that? She made to step forward, but the guard reached down and gently held her back. She stopped struggling and stepped back. This was both ridiculous and undignified. The guard would clearly not accede to the demands of an eleven year old. She could hardly face her father and ask him to speak to the guards. Biting her cheek and then chiding herself irritably for it, she glared at the guard officer and then turned and stalked away, back up the stairs.

Months of being trapped in this luxurious prison had given her endless time to explore. With the exception of the governor's own rooms on the top floor and the temporary guard quarters on the ground, she had examined every nook and cranny of the building and, with her customary cunning, had long since discovered three private routes out of the building.

Frowning as she reached the top of the stairs, Asima glanced this way and that. The easiest exit, from the first floor balcony onto the roof of the stables, was blocked as a couple of other prisoners occupied the terrace looking out across the compound. Clicking her tongue in irritation, she made her way up the next flight of stairs. The third route would be dangerous and should be avoided if at all possible.

Hurrying now, she turned along one of the corridors on the second floor and rushed along to the end. From here, she could edge along the roof of the balcony below where the couple stood and reach the exterior wall. From there she could walk safely around the perimeter, high above the stable block, and descend next to the council buildings where the satrap now held court.

Asima was so busy planning her route from the window that, as she rounded the corner, she walked straight into the elderly nobleman and his wife.

'I am dreadfully sorry, master… ma'am.'

The man barely glanced at her, passing her by and hurrying along the corridor toward the stairs. The woman, however, grasped her by the shoulders.

'Whatever are you doing alone, child?'

Asima floundered.

'I... ah...'

'Come with me. We must find your father.'

Shaking her head, Asima tried to find words, an excuse to deny this lady.

'I have something to do, ma'am. My father knows...'

The lady turned her forcefully and began to propel her along the corridor in the direction from which she had come. Asima blinked in surprise and made protesting sounds. The lady stopped, turning her by the shoulders and glaring at her.

'This is not the time to throw a tantrum, young lady.'

Asima was so surprised at the force in the older lady's voice, that she stopped struggling as she was turned once more and directed along the corridor behind the old man.

'You are the daughter of the merchant that resides in the room of glittering peacocks, yes?'

Again, Asima was taken aback. Had she been that noticeable?

'Yes, ma'am.'

The woman nodded and gestured to her husband.

'Pass the word on. I will return this wayward stray and then join you.'

The man nodded and made his way toward the higher level and the governor's rooms, while Asima and her escort made for the descending staircase.

'Ma'am...' Asima began in a questioning voice. Something about the lady's manner was beginning to alarm her. The noblewoman cut her off with a waved finger.

'It is not becoming of young ladies to question their elders. Come along.'

Asima hurried on with the lady as they turned corners and marched along corridors until once more she entered the room where her father sat staring into nothing. As the two approached, the man looked up in surprise.

'Lady Shere'en?'

He struggled respectfully to his feet and bowed his head. Even in their current circumstances there were matters of etiquette when dealing with someone of the lady's stature.

'I have come to return your precocious little jewel. She is, I fear, up to no good, given the desperate attempts she made to lie about her reasons for sneaking around the corridors.'

Asima's father nodded meekly.

'I apologise for her, lady.'

The woman shook her head.

'That is not necessary, master merchant. She is headstrong and clever, this one, and in our dire circumstances, she can be forgiven many things.'

She sighed.

'Now, however, is a bad time to be wandering alone. Something is happening in the great square. We have seen from the roof. There is fire and the noise of combat. Pelasian soldiers are mobilising in the courtyard. We may all be in danger.'

Asima blinked again and craned her head to stare at the lady behind her. Now that she concentrated, she could hear many things. Distantly, across the roofs of M'Dahz, there were sounds of fighting and screams. Closer by, on the balconies above, she could hear worried conversation and groans. Warning bells chimed around the Pelasian barracks of the city and soldiers gathered in the complex outside, shouting orders. Something was happening and, from the sound, it was something dreadful.

In which unrest occurs

Samir and Ghassan crouched in the shadow of the vine-covered pergola on the roof of a low building fronting on to the great square of M'Dahz. From their earliest days out and about in the town, they remembered the square as a place of life, colour, noise and commerce. The grand bazaar was located here on an almost permanent basis, only closing up when the public space was required for festivals or parades.

In these oppressed times, however, the bazaar was strictly controlled and only licensed on two weekdays. Flags of Pelasia and the Satrap Ma'ahd festooned the walls and poles; a constant reminder to the people of their new master.

But not today.

It had begun only a few minutes ago, although the boys had been aware of the plan for some time. The resistance, which had begun on the night of the invasion under the mercenary Captain Cronus, had been slow and careful in developing. As Pelasian soldiers had burned, raped and murdered their way through the town that night, Cronus, already disenchanted with the manner in which the government had yielded and capitulated to the invaders, had gathered the militia near the docks. A decision had been made and the resistance movement that resulted had steadily grown in strength and number over the succeeding months.

After just two days hiding out in a secluded cover two miles from the walls, the boys and their mother had, slowly and cautiously, taken their boat and returned to the town under cover of darkness. As soon as Ghassan discovered what the militia were doing, he and Samir had approached Cronus and volunteered. The grizzled mercenary had accepted them as scouts and since that day the boys had quietly gone about their business in M'Dahz, attracting no unwanted attention and yet gathering information through watchful eyes and attentive ears.

The resistance was now twice the size of the militia who had initially stood on the walls and watched Ma'ahd and his men arrive, whereas three quarters of the satrap's force had returned to the family holdings in Pelasia. The odds, while still steep, were considerably better now than they had previously been.

Many of the members of the resistance, spurred on by Pelasian atrocities, were twitching with the need to make a move, but Cronus had expressly forbidden any such activity. It was all about subtlety and timing. The force had picked up more and more members over the months and had received illicit caches of arms from both seaborne and desert sources and had kept them in hidden locations around M'Dahz, preparing for one great event.

And this morning had been a flurry of hidden activity as resistance cells across the town gathered their arms and moved silently through the streets. The plan was simple. Some had complained about it, of course, but Cronus had been adamant. It had to be simple, well-timed and above all, it would require sacrifice.

Volunteers had been called for for the demonstration. In all likelihood, many would not survive this, but the demonstration was necessary; a diversion for the main event.

Grinning at Samir, Ghassan opened his shuttered lantern, the light from the candle burning within hardly visible in the brilliant sunshine. Samir tipped a small amount of his precious oil flask onto the Pelasian flag that hung from the spar that jutted out just below the roof line. Glancing across the square to other rooftops, he smiled.

'Now.'

Ghassan nodded and withdrew the candle, touching the burning wick to the flag. The great, heavy banner leapt into flames, fire rippling across the surface and roaring in the silence. With perfect timing, all around the square Pelasian flags burst into flame as scout groups of men too young for Cronus to accept as soldiers carried out their own acts of defiance.

With a roar, the main group of protesters rushed into the square from three side streets, converging among the burning banners, and made for the Pelasian guard barracks that occupied the once proud civic hall. The two black-clad guards on duty beside the door took one look at the advancing mob and disappeared inside, closing and bolting the door. Samir could not see their faces, but smiled grimly as he imagined their panicked expressions.

The force of over a hundred protesters rushed up to the building and began to hammer at the doors and windows, others rushing to the buildings on either side to gain access to upper floors.

Ghassan nodded with a deep sense of satisfaction. Finally they would get to do something. They just had to hope now that Cronus had been right and that the Pelasians would react in the predicted manner.

Ghassan and Samir dropped below the low parapet and watched, tensely, as events unfolded. The barrack was a three storey building, standing proud into the square, but abutted on either side by houses and shops of two storeys. The Pelasians had taken some pains to bolster the defensive capabilities of the building, reinforcing the doors, placing bars on the windows and heavy wooden shutters. It would take an hour for the rebels to gain entrance, but the Pelasians would now begin to panic. There was no rear exit from the building, as they had walled it up as part of their defensive adjustments and they were outnumbered two to one by their attackers, so issuing forth from the building would be extremely unwise. They may be able to hold it for a long time, but the building had no well and would burn easily.

The mob could quite simply torch the building. Samir and Ghassan knew that wouldn't happen. It could turn into a blaze that destroyed half the city, but the Pelasians didn't know that. They would have to do something and Cronus had predicted what that something would be.

Samir, counting under his breath, grinned as he saw the door on roof of the building fly open. He turned to his brother.

'The captain underestimated them. They panicked quicker than he said they would.'

Ghassan laughed and focused his exceptional gaze on the three figures that issued from that door. Just as Cronus had said they would, two of them hauled up to the parapet one of the great horns that were once used to warn ships away from port during sandstorms. Shaped like a narrow cone six feet long and supported at the flared end on a hinged iron pivot, the great horn took a great deal of effort to get a powerful sound from. Indeed, as the boys watched with quiet mirth, the three men took turns breathing deeply and blowing into the horn. There were a number of low honking noises; loud, certainly, but not loud enough to reach the reinforcements they needed at the palace complex.

Finally, after a little discussion, one of them seemed to arrive at a conclusion and positioned himself.

The blare that issued was still quieter than the port hornsman would have managed, but would carry a warning to the complex, and that was all they needed. Satisfied, the three men blew a half dozen more blasts, gradually increasing in volume, and then returned to the open doorway. Ghassan slapped Samir on the back.

'That's it. It's all in Cronus' hands now.'

Samir nodded and was about to reply when where was a cry of alarm from the square. Turning, he gazed down once again, just in time to see an arrow pass through the neck of one of the resistance.

'Oh no…'

Ghassan lunged to the edge and joined him, staring down in dismay. The Pelasians didn't carry bows in the town. They were of little use in the narrow streets, so the guards relied on their spears and swords and slings if needed, so why did they have bows now? As he watched, he realised with cold dread that he already knew the answer. Groups of a dozen black-clad and heavily armed Pelasian soldiers had appeared in all the side streets, blocking the exits from the square. As the boys watched, more arrows whispered their deadly song as they emerged from windows all around the square and thudded into the crowd of protesters outside the barracks.

'It's a trap!'

Already the numbers below were thinning out but Samir stared in horror as he saw more guards emerge from the doorway on top of the building. Most ran to the edge and began to drop stones onto the crowd, but two were carrying a huge copper pot slung between two poles and which, judging by the way it swayed, was very heavy.

Samir averted his eyes. This was one of the oldest of defensive manoeuvres, but Samir had no wish to watch its grisly effects. Ghassan grasped his smaller brother.

'We have to go!'

Samir was shaking gently.

'They'll burn. They'll all burn…'

Ghassan hauled the other boy to his feet and glared at him. Drawing his hand back, he gave Samir a stinging slap across the face.

'Wake up, brother. They have seen the flags. They know we're up here. We have to go now, or we will burn with them!'

Samir stared at him, shocked, for a moment, and then nodded. As they ran across the roof, heading for one of their old routes that would take them unnoticed far from this place of danger and high above the ground, Samir shook his head sadly. How could they have dared to hope? Now the resistance was finished. M'Dahz was lost.

For the first time in many years, Samir found himself crying as he ran.

Across the town and far up the slope of M'Dahz, Captain Cronus and the commanders of the resistance crouched behind doors and walls and listened to the stifling silence punctuated only by occasional mutterings of the guards at the palace complex nearby.

A distant boom from the horn in the main square rang across the town and Cronus clenched his teeth and made several hand signals to the nearby commanders. The signal at last. Now the civic barrack block in the square was under siege and the Pelasian soldiers, outnumbered almost two to one, would be trapped within the barracks.

Cronus found himself thinking sadly on those hundred volunteers in the square. They would have to keep pounding at the doors until the first sign that reinforcements were on the way. As soon as the Pelasian soldiers appeared in the square, they would have to run for their lives and few would escape.

He ground his teeth.

But their sacrifice would draw the soldiers from the palace, leaving the satrap and his upper echelons badly protected and at the mercy of the honest citizens of M'Dahz. Once they had the commanders, they could call an end to this and drive the invaders out and, when that was done, no other satrap would consider attempting a repeat of this horrible mess.

As he watched tensely, there was a blast on a horn within the complex and the gates opened. A swathe of heavily armed black-clad soldiers marched out of the encircling wall in columns, turning and splitting into three groups that took separate roads toward the square to speed their arrival and deployment. Cronus watched them go from his position behind the low wall, making a rough count of the men. As the last men filed out of the gate and left the small plaza outside the complex, he made a quick mental calculation. Almost a thousand men. That would be most of the Pelasian complement in M'Dahz now. There would be a thousand or so more stationed in various places around the walls and at the port and sundry other locations, but there couldn't be more than a couple of dozen left in the complex to stop the almost four hundred conspirators.

This was it. They finally had a chance.

Cronus watched and listened carefully. Taking a deep breath, he cautiously crept from his hiding place along the wall and to the low gate. A quick glimpse and he could see that the gate guards were standing at attention. The sounds of the soldiers marching away seemed to have faded. Now was the time.

The captain took a deep breath and then bellowed 'now!'

The resistance poured from gates and doors in the surrounding buildings and ran out into the street, converging in the small, circular public space and running for the complex gate. It was a strange sight, Cronus thought as they ran; hundreds of heavily armed men charging into battle, but doing so in relative quiet. The Pelasian soldiers may be out of the way and marching to the diversion in the square, but there was no reason to test their hearing and risk tempting them back.

The two guards at the gate disappeared within as soon as the mob entered the open spare. The gates began to close very slowly. Cronus had been counting on that. The portals were heavy, constructed of solid wood reinforced with bronze plates. There was no chance of them being closed in time.

Triumphantly, the mass of elated citizens ran through the gate, brandishing their weapons, ready to deal with whatever defence remained for the satrap. Cronus was, due to his positioning in the square, among the rearmost of the converging units and what happened next unfolded with the dreadful efficiency of a carefully-laid plan.

The charge came to a sudden stop in the courtyard of the complex as the ground burst into flame. A huge horseshoe of oil that arced out from the side wall was now a deadly blaze; a wall of fire blocking any hope of access to the interior buildings of the compound. Already the momentum of the charge had driven dozens of the attackers into the flames and their screams were echoing from the walls of M'Dahz.

Cronus came to a halt, his world shifting to slow motion and he turned with a cold weight in the pit of his belly, somehow knowing what he was going to see. Every street that led from the small piazza was filled with black figures, silently marching back toward them.

How could they have known? Someone had betrayed them. Someone had sold out any hope of the freedom of M'Dahz. With a sickening finality, he turned to face the nearest Pelasian unit and straightened his back.

'If we're going to die, lads, let's make them remember us, eh?'

Amongst cries of rage and hatred and screams of the dying, the last defenders of free M'Dahz charged to their doom.

In which endings become beginnings

Samir and Ghassan trudged through the street with heavy hearts, their heads bowed and watching only the feet of those in front of them. There had been no escaping this time and no hope of being saved by the resistance. Every last man involved in either of the attacks had been butchered mercilessly and their bodies carted several miles into the desert where they had been left to rot.

There had been a pregnant pause for a few hours after the incident during which the brothers had dared to hope that repercussions would be limited to the resistance themselves.

Such was not the case. The gates and harbour had been sealed off and patrols increased around the edge of M'Dahz during that quiet time; that deep indrawn breath before the real evil began.

Then, during the height of the afternoon heat, the Pelasian military had begun to sweep through the town. This was no victory looting or search for culprits, but a simple rounding up of every living being in M'Dahz.

So thorough had the satrap's men been that even the infirm had been rounded up, their relatives or neighbours forced to carry them. Newborn babes cried in their mothers' arms. Even the homeless beggars were collected. Every last soul in M'Dahz was gathering by the southern Desert Gate, as Samir and Ghassan knew. They had the best hiding places of anyone in the town and the best knowledge of the hidden ways and yet even they and their mother had been found behind the garden wall on the roof of the neglected Imperial cult temple.

And now, here at the gate, finally were gathered all of M'Dahz. Samir shook his head slightly. Not true, he corrected himself. Those who lived now in virtual seclusion in the governor's palace complex were not here. What had happened to them would remain a mystery.

He looked up at Ghassan, who was examining the ranks of the Pelasian guards who surrounded the sadly depleted population of M'Dahz. He had once heard someone estimate the population of the town at something like twenty thousand people. At a rough estimate, he would guess there were less than three thousand people here, and that was everyone.

Orders were being given by the gate, but that was on the other side of the crowd and the boys could not hear the details from where they stood. Something was happening, though.

As they watched, the first few of the population were led up the staircase on the inner side of the south gate. Slowly and dejectedly, they trudged up the steps to the top of the wall, where they were then directed out along the parapet. Ghassan ground his teeth.

'Whatever they're going to do, it will not be pretty.'
Samir nodded grimly.
'I know what they're going to do. So do you.'
Ghassan closed his eyes and shook his head.

'How did it get this bad, brother? Every time I think M'Dahz has reached the bottom of the well of the damned, we get kicked down a little further.'

Samir nodded.

'It continues to grow more and more hopeless, Ghassan, but when things are truly hopeless… that is when you need hope more than ever before. We will do whatever it takes for as long as it takes; endure whatever the Gods and the satrap can throw at us and we will survive. Because all things change and one day things will be better.'

Ghassan stared down at his smaller brother in surprise. There was a strange certainty about him, something that actually gave the taller boy just a flicker of hope; a tiny light in his heart, wrapped in pride.

'Things will be better, Samir.'

Though, as they nodded and returned their attention to the activity ahead, the very idea of things improving seemed impossibly far away. Samir continued to watch as the scene unfolded, while Ghassan averted his eyes sadly.

As the folk of M'Dahz were led along the wall there was a scream. Samir nodded sadly to himself as he watched the first person in the line plummet from the wall to land on the rocky ground below, his head smashing like a watermelon. The fall was perhaps forty feet. Few would survive the drop and many of those that did would be smashed beyond repair. Surely the satrap did not intend to execute them all? Who would he have to be merciless to?

As he watched, the line of prisoners was marched along the wall and the next few were directed to the steps to descend to ground level once again. Samir clenched his teeth and counted as he watched.

'One… two… three… four…'

As the smaller brother peered between the figures before him, he saw the fifth prisoner jabbed with a staff and pushed across the parapet by one of the guards. The man made no sound as he fell, though Samir would never forget the sound as he landed. Was he brave to have held his silence, or perhaps stricken by such shock that he was unable to speak?

'One… two… three… four…'

Another scream; this time a woman's voice. He was unable to see as a large, bald man obscured his view at the last moment.

'Every fifth person, Ghassan. One in five.'

The taller brother shook his head in disbelief.

'Then we have to leave; to escape…'

Samir pursed his lips.

'Not possible. I've looked at every angle I can think of, but the satrap's got us covered. The only way out of here is along the wall or through a thousand heavily armed guards.'

'Someone has to do something.'

Samir shook his head.

'He's broken us. Have you not seen? Months ago the guards would have had to physically push the people up the stairs. Not now, though. They're acting like cattle. The satrap points and the people walk. M'Dahz is done for. When we get through this, we need to make some rather important decisions, my friend.'

'When we get through this?'

'One in five. The odds aren't too bad.'

Ghassan stared at his brother.

Suddenly the crowd nearby was beginning to move. The pace along the wall was picking up. One, two, three, four… scream. One, two, three, four… scream. There was something sickeningly comforting about the one, two, three and four.

Ghassan continued to stare at his brother as Samir turned to face the now moving crowd and walked forward. The taller brother stared for a moment and then turned to look up at their mother, who had been silent throughout the whole exchange. She hardly appeared to notice him. Her expression, dead and glassy, was unchanged by the horror around her and the only hint Ghassan could detect that she was even aware of her surroundings was a slight twitch at the corner of her eye with each fresh scream from the wall.

With a deep breath, he turned to face the horror and took a step forward.

Slowly, with solemn and dreadful certainty, the entire crowd shuffled forward, gradually filtering into a line as their neared the gate and its stairs. Samir turned as the ascent grew ever closer and locked his gaze on his brother.

'Things will be better, remember? Hope.'

Ghassan nodded and clasped his brother's hand tight. As Samir shook and then let go, they both turned to look up at their mother. As the satrap had broken M'Dahz, the whole experience had broken Nadia; such was clear. Her eyes stared ahead in their glassy oblivion, not even flickering down toward her children.

'Mother?'

Ghassan reached out and grasped her hand.

'Mother? I don't want to do this without hearing your voice again.'

There was no reaction. Her eye twitched once again at the shriek from close by.

'Mother? Please speak to me.'

A tear welled up in Ghassan's eye and he started as Samir grasped his shoulder and turned him forward once more.

'Leave her alone, Ghassan.'

'I can't.'

'You must.'

Samir grasped his shoulders, the whole line coming momentarily to a halt.

'Mother is gone, Ghassan. She's not here any more, and she's better off wherever she is. Don't bring her back and make her face this. It's not kind.'

Ghassan stared at his brother.

'But we can't let her go on like this…'

'Yes we can, Ghassan. When we get through this we can take care of her; get her some help. But right now the best thing you can do for her is leave her alone.'

The taller brother continued to stare as Samir turned his back once more and picked up the pace to catch up under the watchful dark eyes of the guards by the gatehouse tower. Taking a pace forward, his toes touched the first step. Slowly, with his heart pounding, Samir began to climb the staircase. Behind him, he could hear Ghassan's breath, fast and close to panic, by the sound.

Moments passed and finally he was high enough to see along the wall. A woman was thrust out into open space as his eyes settled on the queue. Without even realising he was doing it, he counted the intervening prisoners.

Eighteen.

His mind raced.

Ghassan… It would be Ghassan.

Ghassan wouldn't let him change that. His brother was too noble in his heart to let Samir do it. So it would have to be quick…

Fifteen.

Very quick!

There were five guards at the point where people were being thrown off. They were busy in solemn conversation but looked up regularly to examine the queue. Samir was pleased to note that they did not look happy with their lot. Perhaps there was hope for these people after all?

Gritting his teeth, he waited for a moment until they looked away and suddenly ducked to the side and came back up behind his brother. Ghassan looked round in shock.

'What? Why…'

The taller boy suddenly realised what his brother had done.

Eleven.

'No, Samir…'

Ghassan tried to push past his brother, but one of the guards rushed across, his attention once more on the queue, and separated them.

'No one changes,' the Pelasian said flatly.

Nine.

A man Ghassan thought he recognised as a shopkeeper on the street of wild winds disappeared with a bellow from the parapet.

'Samir!'

The smaller boy shook his head.

'Hope, Ghassan. Look after mother for me.'

'Samir!'

Seven.

The taller boy's eyes were wide as he stared at his brother. He couldn't let this happen. He'd always assumed that if it came down to that, he would be the one to sacrifice himself for Samir and not the other way around.

Four.

There was a shriek from ahead. Horribly close ahead.

Three.

'I'll see you on the other side, Ghassan.'

Two.

Ghassan stared at Samir as the smaller brother was suddenly pulled away from him. Nadia pushed the boy behind her and looked down at her son for the last time. The guard made to change the order back, but another black-clad Pelasian stopped him and shook his head sadly.

'Survive, my boys. Survive and prosper.'

Ghassan reached out, tears streaming suddenly down his face, but his fingertips failed to reach her, as one of the guards hauled him back and pushed him on toward the stairs. As she stopped and, with deliberate slowness, the soldier pulled back his staff, Nadia turned her back on the weeping boy being taken further away to safety, and looked down at Samir. The smaller boy, always, she thought, the stronger one, had a single tear in the corner of his eye. He gave her a sad smile.

'Goodbye, mother.'

She gave him a sad smile and, without waiting for the guard, took a step from the wall into the open air.

Samir turned away and blocked out the next moments as best he could before walking on toward his brother who shuddered his way toward the stairs.

Hope. There had to be hope.

In which Asima's life takes an unexpected turn

The attempted coup by the M'Dahz resistance changed everything in the town. The satrap, having spent so many months as a barely-disguised tyrant ruling through the powerless governor, finally abandoned all pretence of care. The morning after the executions, posters went up across the town reminding the population that M'Dahz was a Pelasian city now, in the province of the Satrap Ma'ahd, and warning that the last quarter he would ever consider giving had now been given. Any further individual infraction of the strict rules to be imposed would be rewarded with a very painful and public death, and any larger-scale civil disobedience would result in the systematic extermination of every last occupant of the city and their replacement with Pelasian settlers.

The dead from the southern wall were left where they fell for seven days by order of the satrap and no one was allowed near them. To the horror of those who lived nearby, not all of the victims had died when they fell, but lay among the stinking, grisly remains of those who did, limited by shattered limbs as they wailed and begged for days until the heat, starvation and wild creatures of the desert who dared come so close to the walls finally killed them off.

Asima had heard the tales of what had happened and how it had been dealt with and found herself curiously unmoved; a trait she was seeing more often in herself and that she felt should worry her more than it did. While she recognised what a horrifying thing the satrap's judgment had been, she could not help but blame the stupidity of the plotters. Why had they tried? If they had just tried to reason with the satrap, none of this would have happened anyway.

Besides, she had heard Pelasian soldiers in the compound close by the governor's house talking about the incident and many of them had, privately and out of earshot of their superiors, spoken of their own dismay over the events of that day.

Not all Pelasians were cruel and, if people had only given Ma'ahd no cause for alarm, he would likely have soon returned to his hometown and left the governor to run M'Dahz. Then everything would have been more or less back to normal.

But no.

Because of the idiotic activities of the so-called 'resistance' the satrap had, instead, rooted himself ever deeper in M'Dahz and had brought the rule down harder than ever on its inhabitants.

But while these fools could bang their drums and shout their slogans and continue to bring down the wrath of the conqueror upon their heads, Asima was resolved to make her life and that of her father easier however she could. The problem was, the actions of those idiots in the militia had placed the satrap in a particularly angry and unresponsive mood and the problem of how to approach him now was a thorny one.

She sat on the decorative chair, staring at her reflection in the mirror. She had always known she was pretty, and the way Samir and Ghassan used to look at her had confirmed that this was not merely narcissism, but an accurate appraisal of her appearance. And yet, even being conservative with her opinion, she could see that she had begun to change over this past year and was filling out, becoming voluptuous and more truly beautiful than girlishly pretty. The timing was unfortunate, when she thought about it objectively. Another year or two and she could probably have had the satrap eating from her hand.

She smiled.

'I will have him eating from it, regardless.'

Her attention was drawn to a sudden intrusion in the corner of the mirror. For a moment, in a fashion that threatened to worry her, she was irritated at her father for having interrupted this introspective viewing of her face. She turned and smiled her most devastating smile.

'Asima...'

'Father?'

'My dear, you have been sent for, and I do not know whether you should go.'

She laughed lightly.

'What are you saying, father?'

'Satrap Ma'ahd has ordered that you present yourself. I know that that is what you have been intending to do anyway, but, for all your wits and precociousness, my dear, you are still a girl and still my daughter. I fear that perhaps you should flee instead.'

Asima laughed again.

'Flee where, father, and how?'

Her father's brow furrowed.

'I know that you have your ways; secret ways in and out of the building. Use them, Asima. Get away before Ma'ahd gets his claws into you.'

'Father, you worry too much.'

Straightening, she walked across the room and patted him on the shoulder.

'Things will be fine, father. I am of Pelasian blood, remember.'

With a last glance back, she checked her reflection in the mirror and nodded with satisfaction. She needed to look her best for this.

Along the corridor and out into the main hall, she was busy planning how she would sweep into the satrap's presence like a graceful swan. It was all about impression. It was about making herself important and worthwhile. It was…

She stopped for a moment at the balcony above the stairs. There were black-clad soldiers marching around the ground floor of the governor's residence. Surely they did not mean to break their promise and invade the governor's own house because of the acts of a desperate group of lunatics?

And yet, as she watched, she realised that there was not a single white-clad Imperial guardsman to be seen. The Pelasian army was in the mansion.

Frowning and scanning the soldiers, she spotted a particular figure in the centre of the ground floor hall, directing the men this way and that. She recognised the bald head and aquiline features of Jhraman, the satrap's chief vizier. Jhraman had been the man who, over the past months, had delivered the conqueror's words to the captives here and who had listened to their questions and requests and delivered them back to his master.

Always a shrewd judge of character, Asima had early formed a favourable opinion of this small, hawk-like man. While he was utterly loyal to Pelasia and his satrap, he was a man of reason, with a remarkably light sense of humour and a kindness of spirit that his master lacked. Her eyes locked on him, she quickly and quietly descended the staircase.

Instinctively, as she reached the bottom of the sweeping stairs, her gait dropped into a sweeping, ladylike manner and she flicked her hair back just as Jhraman turned to see her.

'Asima,' he smiled. 'You are looking as glorious and radiant as the daughter of the sun just as you always do.'

'Master Jhraman,' she replied lowering her eyes while flicking her lashes dangerously. 'Thank you for your kind words. I believe the satrap has requested my presence? You require so many men to escort me?'

The vizier gave a tight laugh. Something in his manner warned her not to play too many games with him today.

'Hardly, Asima. The news will be circulating soon enough, I am sure but, sadly, I must inform you that governor Talus hanged himself last night.'

In a testament to her iron composure, Asima barely blinked, though her mind raced through many avenues before arriving at a conclusion she daren't voice. Instead, she feigned shock.

'But why?'

Jhraman shook his head.

'The reason is immaterial. Regardless, he is being cut down and will be taken to a place of burial today with appropriate honours. Sadly, this means that his guard are no longer appropriate here and are being deported back to Imperial territory.'

Asima nodded sagely. Whatever the satrap would secretly have liked to do with the white-clad Imperial guardsmen, he would not dare risk it. Even with the Empire in chaos as it was said to be, Ma'ahd would not push his luck any further. The Emperor had abandoned M'Dahz, but these soldiers were citizens from the north.

Likely their presence in M'Dahz was an ongoing impediment to the satrap. Perhaps that was even the reason Ma'ahd had had the governor take his own life? She blinked as she realised the implications of all of this. No governor meant no guards, but it also meant no sanctuary; no protection. The satrap's men were here because they were commandeering the mansion. They would then eject the occupants at the very best. At the worst…

That just did not bear thinking about.

She frowned at the vizier.

'May I enquire as to why the satrap has sent for me?'

Jhraman shook his head and sighed.

'I believe your father mistook the request I made. You are not to present yourself to him, child, but to me.'

An alarm went off deep inside Asima, but she maintained her composure, her frown still aimed at the small man before her.

'Master Jhraman?'

The vizier cast his eyes back and forth furtively. They were practically alone, with the few soldiers nearby busy and at the edge of earshot.

'His Majestic and Imperial Highness, the God-King himself is, I fear, displeased with the manner in which the satrap has conducted this affair. I have advised my master that a gift, or donation, to an appropriate value will buy the satrap his majesty's support for the coming year.'

'I am to be a gift?'

Asima mentally chided herself. Such an outburst was hardly productive, and she had almost shrieked like a fishwife. Several of the guards glanced in their direction and she blanched at the look of displeasure in the vizier's face.

'Be quiet and calm, child, or I shall have to discipline you.'

His shoulders relaxed a little as the guards went about their business once more.

'His majesty is a good man with a strong appetite for... healthy young women,' he concluded, colour rising in his swarthy cheeks.

Asima blinked.

'You mean...'

'Yes,' the man replied with an embarrassed smile. 'You and three other young ladies of my choosing will be sent to Akkad, to the harem of the God-King. By Pelasian law no girl of less than thirteen years of age may be taken to a man's bed, but rest assured that it will take at least two years for you to learn the ways of the court.'

Asima found she was shaking her head.

'You have no choice in the matter, Asima. Accept it and be pleased. Whatever you may think of this now, be assured it is a good thing. You will be taken from this barren cesspool and to a place of unimaginable wonders and delights.'

He smiled a very genuine and warm smile.

'And your father, being the father of someone so potentially important, will be well looked after. I will see to it myself.'

Asima stared at the man before her.

'When do I leave?' she asked in a small voice.

Jhraman pursed his lips.

'Tonight. Take a few hours to say your farewells and gather anything of personal value. Travel light though, as many of your things will be inappropriate and, upon your arrival, you may be made to discard them. An hour before sunset a caravan will leave, accompanied by cataphracti and soldiers. The journey will take many days but, with the consignment being so delicate and valuable, you will travel only in the late afternoon and evening time and early in the morning, when the sun is still cool. Pelasian way stations will shelter you for the nights.'

Asima found she was shaking her head again, though not in denial. Already, her lightning mind was racing ahead, planning the coming days. She would not be alone. Three others, who would very likely all be beauties and probably wealthier and higher-born than her. But they would not be as bright or as cunning. By the time the caravan reached Akkad, they would be to her as crows are to eagles. She must be, as her father used to say, 'the best thing on the menu'.

Akkad had best prepare itself. The Pelasian capital held many of the great wonders, but it had never tried to contain someone like Asima.

In which childhood ends

Samir sat by the low table in the common room of what he used to think of as their family home.

'I couldn't find her, Ghassan.'

The taller of the two boys shrugged.

'That's probably a good thing, brother. I want to remember her as she used to be, not as how the jackals and buzzards have left her.'

'She needs to be buried.'

Ghassan's brow furrowed and his eyes took on a hard edge.

'She needs to be avenged, Samir, not buried.'

Samir sighed.

'Vengeance is hollow, brother. Survival is important. That is the lesson she taught us; the last lesson.'

The two lapsed into silence for a moment. Something here felt wrong. It had been days since the horrors that had ended their mother's life and any hope for a free M'Dahz. The dynamic between the brothers felt strained and odd. Their whole life there had been a third person. Oh there had been occasions when the two brothers had been alone, for certain, but not for a length of time, and never with important decisions to be made. Their father had been there, and then their mother, and uncle Faraj, and even Asima. But now they were utterly alone.

'Do you think Asima will return?'

Samir blinked at his brother's question.

'Would you?' He sighed. 'No, Asima will not return to M'Dahz. The important question, and the one that we seem to continually dance around, is what we should do now.'

Another uncomfortable silence followed as the brothers met each other's gaze.

Since the deaths, the boys had grieved in their own way, and subtle changes were now evident in Ghassan, who had become quieter and more serious than Samir had even known him and his eyes held an iron resolve that worried his brother. Samir swallowed nervously. This had to play out exactly right.

'Whatever we do, we will need to do it soon, Samir. The supply of food is dwindling and we will not be able to afford to eat in a few days. I have no intention of surviving the invasion and the horrors of Ma'ahd's reign just to die of starvation in a back alley.'

Samir nodded.

'Agreed, but the question is: what? There's nothing in M'Dahz we can do, short of crime, and those folk who fled to Calphoris are probably as poor and hungry as we are. If Faraj was still alive…'

Ghassan nodded in silence.

'We have to leave M'Dahz though, Samir.' His eyes darkened. 'We need to avenge mother, whatever you say.'

'Survival, not vengeance, Ghassan.'

'Both.' The taller brother straightened. 'I'll bet the Imperial army is still functioning in Calphoris. We can sign up with them and protect the rest of the Empire against Pelasia; possibly even drive Ma'ahd back out of M'Dahz in time.'

Samir shook his head.

'Even if the army is still in Calphoris, if we signed up, they'd send us to the other side of the world where the men are all pale with fair hair and it get so cold the water becomes solid. But Calphoris will have lost Imperial support by now, brother. The Empire is so far away and crumbling. Calphoris will be on its way to becoming what M'Dahz is now.'

Ghassan shrugged.

'Perhaps that would be better still. They will still have a militia and will be watching the satrap carefully. And their militia will be far larger and stronger than ours, as Calphoris is a big city. And if it's the militia we can probably lie about our age easier.'

Samir was still shaking his head.

'That's not the way, Ghassan. To sell ourselves into military service? It's a waste of our talents. There will be other paths that will open to us.'

The taller brother shrugged.

'We have to leave M'Dahz. That is clear, Samir. South into the deep desert is unthinkable. Neither of us has the slightest idea how to survive there. West is Pelasia and, given our current situation, I do not think that would be an advisable choice. No ships that dock here travel across the sea to the north and, anyway, the north is cold and their water turns solid and chills the bones. That just leaves east to Calphoris. Whether you think the army or the militia are a bad idea or not, there is now simply nowhere else to go, my brother.'

Samir sighed and nodded.

'That much is true, yes, though I would rather try to make my fortune there than become a soldier and die in a border war for someone else's good. We are clever and enterprising, Ghassan. We saved Asima's father from poverty.'

They lapsed once more into an uncomfortable silence. The subject of Asima's father was a touchy one that neither brother felt comfortable dealing with at this point. They had become aware of Asima's fate when those who had been under the governor's protection found themselves suddenly without support. A few had disappeared without trace, presumably having fallen foul of the satrap for some reason, but the rest had been forcibly ejected from the complex into the town, their more valuable belongings impounded beforehand, to make their way as ordinary citizens.

The boys had spoken to a group of survivors, eager for news of the friend of whom they had seen nothing in so many months. The fact that Asima and the other girls had been sent to Akkad for the God-King's pleasure was something that neither brother had so far allowed themselves to ponder on. Still, this meant that she was safe, at least. Her father, however, had been found by the satrap's vizier and had last been seen disappearing into Ma'ahd's palace.

'Very well.' Ghassan stretched. 'We can agree that whatever we do next, we need to do it in Calphoris?'

Samir frowned and bit his lip. The idea of abandoning everything and committing to the provincial capital for the future felt like a betrayal and, though Ghassan's logic was unassailable, Samir had his plan. Finally he nodded.

'We head east. Have you given any thought to how and when?'

Ghassan shrugged.

'As soon as possible. And on foot, I suppose. It's not as though we can afford camels or horses.'

Samir smiled and reached behind him, rummaging in his pack. A moment later, he withdrew a small hessian bag that was clearly heavy and which clinked when he dropped it to the table. Ghassan stared.

'That's money?'

Samir nodded.

'From where?'

'It belonged to Asima's father. I doubt it will do him any good right now wherever he is.'

'You stole from Asima's father?'

Outrage pushed Ghassan's voice up a notch and the question ended in almost a squeak.

'After a fashion. They had already gone to the palace when I found this. Their house had been turned upside down by Pelasian soldiers, and I can assure you that they took everything he had that was of any real value.'

'So how did you find that?'

Samir gave a cheeky grin.

'I've known where he kept his emergency fund for a long time, Ghassan.' He straightened. 'And this is an emergency.'

Removing two pouches from a nearby cupboard, he neatly divided what looked to Ghassan like a small fortune, dropping half into each container. With a nod, he slid one pouch across the table to his brother and tied the thongs of the other to his belt, tucking the pouch down into his pocket for added security.

Ghassan frowned.

'Why are you splitting it now?'

For a moment, Samir flinched slightly. Then he smiled. 'Just in case. One man carrying too much money is asking for an unfortunate accident.'

He straightened once more.

'We will need to leave tonight, while it is dark. In fact, if we wait until the early morning, we can leave when the moon passes to the underworld. That should give us almost two hours at this time of year to get past the walls and out along the coast before sunrise.'

'That seems sensible,' Ghassan agreed. 'We should leave as far from a gate as we can. The port is out of the question, though, as I've heard Ma'ahd is having shipping watched and searched now.'

Samir nodded.

'There's a place not too far from the eastern end of the port where the walls are very close to a number of warehouses. We can get into the warehouses before the moon rises fully and wait out the night there. We'll need some rope to get down the other side of the walls, but then we can be half a dozen miles away from M'Dahz before the sun comes up.'

'About ten miles along the coast is a village with an animal market. Asima's father used to trade with them. I've never been there, clearly, but I suspect his name will carry some weight there.' He picked up the pouch in front of him and tied it to his belt. 'And now we can afford a horse.'

Samir answered with a grin, his heart racing now. This was the time.

'There is one more thing, though.'

Ghassan shrugged.

'Yes?'

'I have something else to do before we go and it could be dangerous…'

The taller boy frowned.

'What?'

Samir winked and touched the side of his nose.

'I'm afraid I can't tell you yet, Ghassan, but I will reveal all later.'

'How am I supposed to help if you won't tell me what you're doing?'

'You're not supposed to help,' Samir countered. 'Sorry, Ghassan, but I'm doing this alone. Go to the warehouses in the Street of Running Dogs as soon as the sun sets. There are three buildings in a row. The central one was a grain warehouse and has the best access to the wall. There's only a jump of about four feet. We can do that in our sleep, and there should be a lot of rope in there for us to use.'

Ghassan held up his hands to object, but Samir pushed them out of the way.

'This is not a negotiation, Ghassan. I will meet you at the warehouse before the moon sets and we will run for Calphoris. But… and this is important… if anything happens and I cannot get there, you cannot afford to wait. If the moon sinks and I am not there, you must go. If I can, I will find you in Calphoris later.'

The taller boy was still shaking his head and objecting vehemently.

'Ghassan,' Samir said quietly, 'you must do this, as must I. Do not panic. I will in all likelihood be there.'

Ghassan continued his refusal.

'How in the name of the seven faces of Ha'Rish would you find me in Calphoris? There are more people there than anywhere else on this continent!'

'You know me, brother. I could find a single rock in all of the deep desert if I set my mind to it. Now promise me: wait for me, but only as long as you can. When there is full darkness, whether I am there or not, you will run for Calphoris.'

Ghassan remained silent, his eyes locked on his brother.

'Ghassan!'

'Alright. But you had better be there, or I shall curse your name to the Gods.'

Samir grinned.

'Tonight we end the curse, Ghassan. From tonight, we will be blessed. Changes. Things will be better, remember?'

Ghassan took a deep breath and nodded.

'Then I will run to my errand and I will see you by moonlight in the grain warehouse on "Running Dogs" yes?'

Ghassan nodded once again and the pair clasped hands.

With a smile, Samir hoisted his pack over his shoulder, cast one last look at his brother, and then walked slowly to the front door and left the house.

In which we look to the future

Samir strode down the empty, dark street a hundred yards from the house without looking back. At the corner, where the Street of Dancing Fools ran back up the hill toward the gate that faced Akkad and Pelasia, he crouched and withdrew a bag, a cloak, and a sheathed sword from behind a stack of boxes.

He took one last, sad look back up the street.

It was sad, for certain, but Ghassan would never understand or approve. Life in M'Dahz would change sooner or later, and Samir knew with certainty that he was one of very few souls who could survive this and prosper. He would find a way to live in the town and eventually to turn things around.

But the way ahead of him was, for the foreseeable future, a life of running and hiding, of consorting with thieves and murderers and living on the very edge of the law until the laws were once more worth abiding by.

Ghassan was too noble in thought for that. He was too straight and would never even think of what Samir was proposing to do. His brother would be safer in Calphoris with his precious militia, wearing a uniform and living to a code of duty.

One day, when everything was put right and the wounds that had been opened in their home had healed, he would find Ghassan and they would return to the house of their mother. After all, they were family.

With a sigh, he hefted the sword and tore his eyes from the house where his brother waited before making his way down the street toward the port.

The last rays of the sun had left the streets of M'Dahz almost an hour ago.

Ghassan crouched in the rafters of the grain warehouse, peering out through the hole in the roof at the city's defences and leaning on his pack for support. The Pelasian soldiers patrolling the wall passed every ten minutes or so and there would be plenty of time for him to sling over a rope and drop to safety. If he placed it right, the rope would remain unnoticed at least until sunrise.

It saddened him a little that the walls of his hometown were patrolled like a prison, the watchful guards directing their gaze inward more often than out, preventing their captive populace from fleeing the clutches of the twisted Satrap Ma'ahd.

He sighed and fought back the panic once more.

He knew with cold certainty that Samir would not come. Whatever his brother was planning it was clear to Ghassan that he had no intention of meeting at the warehouse. The dividing of the purses; the enforced promises; most of all, the look on the smaller boy's face as they had clasped hands that last time. Samir would not come.

But Ghassan knew with equal sureness that he had to go. He had to do this, even if he never saw Samir again. Someone had to find a way to bring the hand of Imperial justice at Calphoris against this Pelasian butcher who had destroyed everything and murdered everyone that they had loved.

Ma'ahd would pay for his crimes.

The desert nomads have a saying.

'When something is broken it should never be discarded. So long as the pieces remain, the whole can be remade.'

The moon set slowly over M'Dahz and a new day dawned.

Part Two:

Making Ends Meet

In which Samir's plans are changed

Samir shook his head to free it of the fuzziness and regular pounding. Stupid really. He should be more careful. He'd end up in trouble one of these days.

Six months had passed since he and Ghassan had gone their separate ways and Samir would have to admit eventually that he had squandered and wasted most of the time. The first few nights he had frequented some of the less reputable areas of the port district, hoping to make contacts or even friends among the criminal classes.

At the age of twelve, Samir was still small for his age, though the events of the preceding years had given him a slightly drawn and haunted look that advanced his years somewhat. In addition, dark facial hair had begun to manifest recently, surprising Samir somewhat. It had taken some work, regardless of these developments, to gain and maintain access to the drinking and gambling pits of the port. Even with the Pelasian control and a seriously diminished population, these establishments managed to survive. In fact, given the level of misery in M'Dahz, their patronage had actually increased rather than falling off.

At first, Samir had been content to sit and take in the general atmosphere, trying to work out the associations and connections between the various unsavoury patrons he had selected as likely contacts and listening intently to any snippets of conversation he could catch.

Soon, however, he came to realise that someone such as he stood out in these establishments, and not because he was small or young; given the state of M'Dahz these days there were many waifs and strays that made their way here looking for work or a handout. No, what made him stand out was the way he always sat on his own, never drank and was seen to be paying too close attention to things that did not concern him.

The issue had become clear to him after he was dragged from one bar and beaten repeatedly in an alleyway. He had not returned to that establishment, turning his attention to alternative locations.

And in what he thought of as 'phase two', several weeks after Ghassan had left, he began to throw himself into the part, learning some of the games that went on in the gaming pits and trying several of the drinks on offer until he discovered what was palatable and what was not. And, as he had gradually become accustomed to the drink and the games, and experienced a little success in the gambling dens, he had finally begun to fit in. Two months into his new life, he had at last reached the point where people paid no attention when he entered or left a bar.

Soon he found he was being offered work by some of the other occupants; just small things to begin with; the running of an errand; delivery of parcels or messages. He began to carry his sword with him where he could and a sharp knife everywhere else. Gradually, he became indistinguishable from those other young men who performed small tasks for the underworld of the district.

But what had begun as an attempt to ingratiate himself into the habitat of the criminal classes had quickly grown beyond his control. As the weeks passed, Samir found that he was so busy running dubious errands, making money and maintaining his persona as a small time crook that he had no time to apply what he was learning to any of his grand plans for the future of the town. There was simply not enough time to try nudging these people toward his goal: guerrilla activity against the Pelasian masters.

And yet, with this new life came a certain respect, albeit from the lowest orders of the town. And money and influence, of course. Only two months down the line, Samir had already reached such a stage in his career where he now had three boys running errands for him; he had unquestioned access to most places in the port district and the ear of some of the most dangerous men in the town.

What came along with this as baggage was the carousing. The late nights, gambling and drinking were changing his habits and he had become more or less nocturnal, having to allow at least two hours of an afternoon to clean himself up and let the thumping hangover fade before looking to his daily tasks. He had sought to infiltrate the criminal classes in M'Dahz. Half a year later, however, he had become the criminal class of the town. Ghassan would never have recognised his brother now.

And yet, with all his late night forays and sessions, last evening was unquestionably the worst he had yet suffered. He couldn't even remember leaving the last place. There had been a fight over a purse of coins. He remembered that and felt his upper lip, wincing as he found the bloody cut and the missing tooth. That explained some of the throbbing. Even wincing made his head hurt. His entire body ached as though he had been attacked with branches, which was distinctly possible given the events of the night that he *could* remember and the length of time as yet unaccounted for. He tried to smile to himself, but the pain this brought in his gums, lip and head made a smile beyond hope.

He was obviously still somewhere close to the port, from the briny smell. At least the gulls were being silent, which was a blessing. The usual morning squawking of a thousand gulls might just have killed him this morning.

Samir shuddered and, very slowly and with great care, pried open his eyes, trying to ignore the fresh waves of pain and nausea that light and colour brought with them.

'He's awake.'

Samir blinked. A face several feet away from him grinned a malicious grin, showing several missing teeth. The pain in his mouth, face, head and screaming muscles forgotten in an instant, Samir's reactions took over. Scrambling from his side onto all fours, he backed away and felt himself bump into a wooden structure. What in the name of the great mother was going on?

His eyes became accustomed to the low light, and he focused on the face before him as the other figure came up from floor level into a crouch. The lad was younger than him, though probably bigger regardless. He had clearly seen the losing side of several fights by the marks and old wounds evident on his face and arms. He wore a cloth wrapped around his forehead and a leather waistcoat that allowed him to display the several gold chains hanging round his neck and the bronze armlets and bracers he wore.

'Who are you?'

The boy ignored him and grinned again.

'Awake and conscious.'

'Good,' replied a voice from the shadows behind the boy. Samir squinted and tried to make out the shapes in the shadows. There were more than one. Perhaps a dozen people.

'Who are you and where am I?'

There was a chorus of laughter.

'This is not as funny as you think,' Samir barked. 'I'm an important man. There are some very dangerous people who will miss me and be extremely unhappy with you.'

The laugher moved up a notch and for the first time in many months Samir's confidence foundered. He licked his lips nervously and winced as his tongue touched the fresh cut.

Slowly, the other figures moved forward out of the shadows. In other circumstances, Samir might have laughed, they were such an assorted bunch. He had once seen a carnival, a great religious festival that had been organised to celebrate the millennium of the Empire's foundation. His father had called it the 'freak show' and the scene in front of Samir reminded him so closely of it that he found it impossible to avoid smiling. Tall, fat, short, thin; some missing limbs, some with one eye, some with misshapen body parts. Not a one of them older than fifteen at a guess.

Samir sighed.

'I am tired and hung over. I have a lot to do and no time to play. If you intend to rob me, do so now. I have nothing on me of value, barring a few coins left over from the evening. If you're just wanting to pick on me, then let's get this over with so I can get to my work.

The laughter from the second boy who had spoken was deep and rich and disturbed Samir further. There was something about this he didn't like at all. He had dealt with bullies many times. This was somehow different. This other speaker was clearly the leader. Older than most and taller than all, he was bulky and lighter skinned than the rest, almost like the foreign merchants from the north. One side of his face had been tattooed with intricate designs and whorls. Something about the boy suggested he was not one to be taken lightly.

'Show him, Afad,' the leader said without taking his eyes from Samir.

Samir kept this tall boy in his sight while trying to follow the movements of the one who had watched him wake. This 'Afad' made his way across to a wall in the shadows. There was a bang and a creak and suddenly a square hatchway opened in the wooden wall. Light poured in, illuminating the face of the smiling boy and picking out sharply the shape of the others.

Samir shrugged.

'So? You're all very pretty, I'm sure.'

The leader laughed.

'You misunderstand. Go and look.'

Trying hard to keep his eyes on the rest of them, Samir, backed away along the ribbed wooden structure behind him, toward that small square of white light and the grinning boy next to it. As he approached, he made motions for the other to move away and, with a shrug, Afad shuffled back toward his companions.

Samir closed on the light, feeling around his belt as he did so. No surprise there. His knife had gone, as had his purse.

And then he reached the hole and, quickly, so as not to grant too much opportunity to the potential attackers, he peered through the hole.

As his world shattered and the shards fled from him, the gathered children in the dark almost entirely forgotten, Samir blinked at the foamy water and the wake flowing past the wooden hull.

'Shit!'

Once again a chorus of uproarious laughter burst out in the shadows.

'Shit!'

'You may have been important in M'Dahz, little one, but here you're just fresh meat.'

Samir's heart raced. He was good under pressure and he knew it, but this was so far beyond his territory he really had no idea how to react. He swallowed. The important thing was to stay in control of himself. That way he had a hope of gaining control of the situation as time progressed.

Setting his jaw stubbornly, he turned to the assembled crowd, fighting down the panic and compacting it in his gut into a hard resolve.

'Very well. We're obviously some distance from M'Dahz now. You're clearly not a Pelasian vessel and the Empire won't be sending ships here these days. The militia have gone and merchants are not in the habit of pressing unconscious drunks into service.'

He smiled a smile that he hoped was as irritating and condescending as it felt.

'I assume therefore that this is a pirate vessel and I am now, whether I like it or not, in fact, a pirate.'

Though no one replied, there was a chorus of vaguely affirmative noises from the other occupants of this dark space. Irritating, because now Samir was going to have to build up the respect of his peers from scratch once again and learn the ropes of this place. Clearly, short of a suicidal escape attempt to swim dozens of miles of open sea, he was stuck here for now and would have to make the most of it.

He smiled to himself. Perhaps this was actually a blessing in disguise. While he had entered his new life at M'Dahz with great plans of using the criminal classes of the town to foment rebellion against the Pelasians, he had to admit how easily he'd let himself slide into the simplicity of a life of few morals and lost sight of his original purpose.

Pirates! Pirates could be a great deal more use than a few smugglers and thieves.

His smile widened. All the more reason to push this as far as it would go. If you needed respect, the first thing to do was to test your limits. Once you knew how far you were allowed to go, you knew what you had to continually exceed to gain respect, or at least fear.

'I've met pirates several times. Saw a captain behead a merchant in M'Dahz once. And since pirates are, in my experience, grown men with brains and cunning, I can only assume that you are either captives or that perhaps you clean the shitters, yes?'

Several growls greeted this comment. Samir began to relax. Some crowds were so predictable it was almost a shame to play them.

'Well? Any of you young ladies got enough of a voice to tell me what ship this is.'

The leader at the back folded his arms and sat back on a crate.

'You are either exceptionally brave or monumentally stupid, boy. My lads will tear you to pieces for that.'

Samir shrugged.

'Bring it to me. I have gutted Pelasian captains, learned to fight well from a desert warrior and dirtily from the docks of M'Dahz. And I am not remotely afraid of any of your catamites, my friend.'

The figures, barring the leader who remained seated on his crate, began to step slowly and purposefully forward from the shadows. Samir nodded to himself. This was going to hurt, but it was the first step to gaining a level of control.

With a smile, he scanned around and found a rib-shaped piece of timber perhaps two feet long and slightly curved; part of a broken barrel, probably. He hefted it for a moment and turned to face the advancing crowd.

'Alright. Who's first?'

The white horses of possibility rushed along the side of the ship as they danced from crest to crest, keeping pace with the beatings just audible from within the hull of the great dark vessel.

On the raised rear section of the deck, beneath the large building-like canopy, Captain Khmun shifted his gaze from the wide horizon ahead to the two sails which billowed.

'We're losing the wind, Sharimi. Break out the oars.'

He cupped his hand round his ear and grinned.

'And you'd best go break up the fight. The boys need to take their seats.'

The first officer returned the sly grin and bowed. As he ran off shouting commands, Khmun rubbed his bristly chin and stared off ahead into the distance, trying to focus on the island that would not be visible for days yet.

The 'Dark Empress' was heading home.

In which a journey is completed and one begun

Ghassan stared up in wonder. Although his whole life he had heard the merchants in M'Dahz talk of the glorious city of Calphoris as though it made his home town look like a desert hovel, he'd not been truly prepared for what he saw now.

It had been so long since he had set off in the dark moonless night from the walls of M'Dahz with visions of a quick run and then a five day ride along the coast to the capital of the province that he had lost count of the sunrises and sunsets he had seen.

What had begun easily had soon become complicated beyond belief. He had run through the night and had hoped to come early the next morning to the trade station where he would buy a horse or possibly a camel for his ongoing journey.

The light had gradually grown with that first dawn and he had approached the trade post with some caution. Even though the chances were that, even if the rope had been found, the Pelasian military would hardly expend men on a manhunt unless someone important was found to be missing, there was no reason to tempt the lady of fate.

The station had been quiet and, as he'd approached, he had realised just how quiet. No trading post was that silent, let alone one that specialised in animals. Obviously the place was still used, since the smell of dung had been fresh and pungent enough to assail him as he reached even a hundred yards' distance. Perhaps, now that there were so few traders on the roads, this place was only maintained by nomads who would need to stay there occasionally.

Biting his lip, he had approached slowly and in a crouched, tense manner. Somehow he hadn't believed his rationalisations. Something had been wrong with the place and, as he'd reached the boundary wall that formed part of the horse corral, he had spotted the first signs of trouble. A broken blade lay partially covered by the sand. Once again he had found himself thanking the Gods for the gift of sharp eyes.

Ten minutes he had waited, obscured by that wall, listening for any sign of movement, before he had ventured within the post.

Formed of three buildings and two tents with four separate corrals and an enclosing wall, the trade station had clearly been occupied continuously by a number of men and a great many animals of different sorts, up to a matter of days or even hours before. Equally clearly, the peaceful occupation of this mercantile centre had ended quickly and violently.

Not a single animal was to be found at the site and no bodies had been in evidence, though Ghassan had found a number of ripped fragments of garments and shards of metal belonging to weapons and armour.

Most disturbing had been the gobbets of fresh blood on the floor of the main building, clearly where the fighting or, more likely, the executions had taken place.

Despite the lack of corroborating evidence, he had become convinced almost immediately that this was the work of the Pelasian invaders, probably in some form of revenge for the attempted coup in the town.

Whatever the reason, he had now been faced with several weeks' walk to the city of Calphoris, a walk along the coast, down near the shore and away from the road where patrols might find him.

Sighing, Ghassan had set off and headed east once again.

Later that afternoon, he had almost walked to his own demise.

A whole day of repetitive terrain and the quiet lapping of waves on the sand had become like a mantra, driving the young man into a stupor as he plodded ever on. It was almost soporific and he had his head lowered and his thumbs tucked into his belt as he'd rounded that headland. As he thought back on it now, he became certain that he'd even been whistling a childhood ditty as he went.

And there, on the beach beyond the headland, had been a patrol of black-clad Pelasian light cavalry, cooking freshly-caught fish for their lunch. He had been so surprised, shocked out of his mental haze, that he'd stood there like some sort of practice target, silhouetted against the sapphire sky, as the first rider had spotted him.

Ghassan was far from a stupid young man and years of having to keep up with the mercurial thought processes of his clever brother had honed his instincts. Shaking his head slightly, he had turned and run up the slope toward the road inland, making sure he moved far enough back west as he went so that he'd disappeared from their view.

As soon as he'd done so, he had then ducked back the way he came and dropped to the ground to peer over the headland. Sure enough, the riders had clambered onto their horses and ridden towards the road. With a smile, Ghassan had then run down onto the gravelly shore. Briefly he'd considered stealing the fragrant baked fish, but quickly rid himself of such dangerous ideas. Keeping his eyes darting around the periphery for warnings of the scouts coming back this way, he had carefully run across the beach to the opposite headland, making sure to keep to the hard, stony part of the shoreline and stay off the sand that would betray signs of his passing.

After that incident, he had travelled much more slowly and very carefully. It would take the best part of a month at that rate for him to reach the city, but he would be more likely to arrive unharmed. Besides, he could catch and cook fish as he went, which would prevent him from starving, and fresh water could be supplied using an arrangement of three pots to boil sea water and then collect the dripping steam, a trick any desert-coast dweller quickly learned.

Many times over the next three weeks of travel, he had considered alternative routes. The road would have been so much quicker but, several times, he had spotted Pelasian scouts or patrols, so the idea had been quickly shelved. The only other possibility had been deeper into the southern desert but, while he was almost guaranteed to see no Pelasians there, the desert held its own perils.

He knew where the oases were supposed to be and, in principle at least, knew how to extract water from succulents he might find. But it was very easy to lose your way in the desert and the chances were that he'd be walking to his death. Besides, if you were not a native of the dunes, there was every chance the sand devils would catch you, and Ghassan had no intention, at this pivotal point in his life, of being eaten and left a stripped carcass in the deep sands.

And so the days had dragged on and on. He had begun by keeping a rough track of the time but, towards the end of the first week, he had given up such meaningless ideas and merely settled for whether it was morning, afternoon or night. By the end of the second week he'd given up trying to remember what day it was and had vowed that, when he finally reached his destination, whether he became a soldier or a mercenary, whether he was rich or poor or somewhere in between, he would make sure that he never ate another chunk of baked bream or boiled seaweed again as long as he lived.

And now here he was. With a sigh of relief, Ghassan let his pack fall to the floor beside his leg. His legs ached a little, but the constant daily exercise had built up his muscles enough that he hardly noticed it any more.

He was finally safe from Pelasian patrols, standing before the great white marble gates of Calphoris. The massive arch rose up above him, to a height of perhaps a hundred feet. The sides of the gatehouse had once been great cylindrical white towers, though in more troubled times some governor had given them a great dark, square, buttressed stone casing that covered the lower half.

The top of the gate, resplendent in its white marble battlements, was surmounted by five great golden figures. As he examined them, it occurred to Ghassan's jaded mind that the chances of them being anything but highly-burnished bronze was tiny. No amount of guards in the world would stop a good thief from taking pieces off the statues if they were really gold.

The walls of Calphoris made M'Dahz look like a poorly-protected village. Inside, the tips of a multitude of white and bronze towers rose toward the azure heavens. The great gates themselves were clearly bronze-plated, and heavy enough to stop the hardiest of battering rams. Calphoris had money; glory; a past. He smiled. A future.

Approaching, he took careful note of the two men in uniform standing in a bored fashion to either side of the gate, They were not members of the Imperial army, certainly. Ghassan had seen enough of the Empire's soldiers in his youth in M'Dahz that he knew not only the insignia for the southern Marshal's army, but also of half a dozen of the specific units based in the south, their rank insignias and their armour standards.

While these two were clearly professional soldiers, their tunics and cloaks clean and pressed, their armour polished and correct, the insignia and some of the equipment was different. Ghassan was immediately impressed. These were obviously the militia as it existed in Calphoris. Certainly a step up on that of M'Dahz. Clearly, then, Imperial support had pulled out of the provincial capital too.

Taking a deep breath, Ghassan straightened and tried to look as adult and serious as possible. The guard to the left of the gateway watched as he approached, his expression carefully neutral. Ghassan swallowed as he came to a halt, his pack over his back and the sheathed sword hanging conspicuously from the bundle.

'Excuse me. I need to know where I would go to sign up?'

The guard blinked, clearly surprised at the question, though his composure never faltered.

'How old are you, lad?'

For a moment, Ghassan wondered about lying. Would it stand him in any better stead? But the only real way forward if he was going to commit to this properly would be honestly.

'I am almost thirteen, sir.' A slight exaggeration, but basically true.

The guard nodded. Ghassan had truly expected the man to laugh and was further impressed by these men as the soldier looked him up and down with a professional eye.

'You might be better coming back in a few years, to be honest, lad. If you sign on now, you'll have seniority when you hit sixteen and we get the new recruits, but it means you'll have three years of getting the shitty end of the stick; all the nasty jobs.'

Ghassan shrugged as professionally as he could manage and almost lost control of the heavy pack on his shoulder.

'I'm willing to do whatever comes my way. I just want to sign up.'

The guard nodded again.

'Fair enough, lad. Go through the gate and head up the street until you pass through the arch of the old walls. You can't miss it.

The next street on the right after that leads to the military compound.'

He laughed.

'And the spice market, but I'm guessing you'll be able to work out which is which.'

Ghassan smiled.

'Thank you, sir.'

'Why so determined?' asked the soldier as Ghassan shouldered his pack once more, preparing to set off.

'I'm from M'Dahz. I've watched the place collapse under the Pelasians and I want to protect the Empire and make sure M'Dahz is as far as they get.'

'I heard things in M'Dahz were pretty dire. If you're hoping for revenge, though, this isn't the way.'

Ghassan frowned and the guard shrugged.

'This isn't the Imperial army any more, lad. We don't go conquering enemies now. This is the army of Calphoris and we fight to protect our city, our lord and our territory, whether it be from Pelasians, desert nomads, pirates or even other Imperial cities. You might as well know that before you sign your life away as a scout in the cavalry or a skivvy in the navy.'

Ghassan smiled. There was no humour about his feral look and for a moment it even shook the guard at the gate.

'Sir, I will do whatever is required of me for now, but I can assure you that some day I will march back into M'Dahz and I will kill any Pelasian who gets in my way.'

He gave a small bow, his teeth still clenched in that non-smile.

'Thank you for your assistance.'

Taking a deep breath, Ghassan straightened once more and strode purposefully through the gates of Calphoris toward his future, whatever it may hold.

In which Pelasia opens her arms

Asima was tired of travel by the time the armed caravan arrived at Akkad, but not half as tired as she was of her companions. The journey had taken three weeks, most of which had involved travelling with interminable slowness through a constant, monotonous sea of sandy waves, punctuated by the Pelasian way stations.

Though comfortable, these establishments, mostly built around oases or crossroads, were home to cackling old men who made their living from the government supplying shelter for the military and those who could pay their way. They made a healthy living, so she felt safe, knowing they would do nothing to jeopardise that, but this did not stop them leering and making vaguely suggestive comments.

The seemingly endless tracts of sand began to show signs of tailing off after two weeks and each morning for the last few days she had noted a more fascinating world passing them by. They approached a low mountain range, passing through it across a saddle and from that point on, the landscape changed. Beyond the mountain range were low hills and, as they made their way toward the capital, reaching out on its promontory into the sea, she began to see farms and fields of wheat. She had been told by her father that Pelasia was the world's greatest supplier of grain, but had always assumed this to be an exaggeration, given the fact that it lay at the edge of the Great Southern Desert.

She might have enjoyed that last week, as they passed inhabited towns and actual rivers with fishermen. She might have marvelled at the almost miraculous changes in the landscape. Unfortunately, after two weeks trundling across the desert in the company of the vapid witches she had been saddled with, she had almost lost the will to live, let alone any interest in her surroundings.

Asima's fears that she would have to work to become the shining jewel among the gift sent to the God-King were soon assuaged.

Sharra, clearly the eldest of her companions, was the only one that seemed to have been gifted with the ability to outthink a dormouse. She would be the only real competition, and Asima was hardly worried about her. Sharra was tall and elegant and had skin the tone of dark honey with long lustrous hair. She was well-spoken, educated and from a wealthy family of M'Dahz. However, she was also clearly mad. She had spent the entire journey separating herself more and more from the others and complaining and moaning to the escort. She had no intention of 'abasing' herself in Akkad. Prideful and rebellious, she had tried to escape no less than five times during the journey. Despite her looks and her intelligence, Asima smirked at the thought that Sharra would be lucky to last five minutes in the sort of situation they were heading for.

Kala, the youngest, was… there was simply no way to put it kindly. She was a moron. Pretty, certainly, though not the prettiest of the four, she had been confused from the beginning. Unaware that Pelasia was not part of the Empire, she had smiled as they left and asked sweetly if she would get to meet the Emperor. Asima had sighed in despair. Kala was woefully unaware of her own gender and the role they were to play in Akkad. Indeed, Asima had, in a fit of sympathy, begun to try and explain why they were being taken to the God-King but, after having to explain in intimate detail some of the terms she was forced to use, she soon gave up and told Kala that she would find out soon enough.

Nima completed the tragic group. Nima was the closest to Asima in age, appearance and social class. She could have been a real problem, had she not been prey to no less than three problems. Her speech impediment was subtle and no true issue until one was forced into, say, three weeks close confinement with her. And so long as she tried to avoid words with an 'r' in them, she would be fine there. Her memory, on the other hand, would cause more issues. She had continually forgotten her companions' names throughout the journey and often couldn't think of the correct words for the simplest things. The great tragedy of Nima, though, was that she was friendly in the way an excitable puppy was friendly, and this led to her talking fast. Nima loved to talk, and when her companions finally became tired of the endless stream of prattle, she would look out of the wagon's window and talk to herself. At these times, Asima would try her hardest to shut out the noise.

The three of them had driven her mad throughout the trip. One sulking and complaining and trying to run away, slowing down the journey on several occasions; the other two chattering away like some sort of trained birds in a market and making about as much sense. At times she had found herself wondering whether the vizier Jhraman had selected the three prettiest and best-bred girls to send with her without actually speaking to any of them, or whether he had been exceptionally kind in sending her off with women that would be no competition to her.

Asima sighed. When they arrived she would find out more of what she was up against. The women in the harem of the God-King would be a different proposition entirely to these three mindless drones. It occurred to her briefly that if she really wanted to cause trouble for Ma'ahd, she should be equally disagreeable and make the satrap's gift into a joke, angering the God-King. But M'Dahz was not her concern. Asima's chief concern had to be her own future now.

They arrived at the great gates of the Pelasian capital in the late afternoon as the sun sank behind the great white city. People said that Akkad was built of marble. It was called the 'white city' or the 'city of cloud' but as they passed through the bulb-arched gate, Asima realised much of that was a façade. The city walls were of stone and mud-brick, whitewashed, while the gates were faced with marble. The various government, military, or wealthy buildings they passed were certainly white, either marble or faced with it, but the majority of the ordinary buildings of the working folk of Akkad were of brick.

Yet Asima could see how the name had come about. From a first impression, the city dazzled the visitor's eyes, with the walls, the high palaces and towers all gleaming in the sunset and the brick walls down at street level and hidden from view. The gate led to a wide boulevard, lined with cypress trees at regular intervals. The road was paved with perfectly flat, interlocking stones in a manner that Asima had never seen before. The pedestrian walkways to either side, where the trees marched ahead up a gentle slope, were of a white stone that looked a little like marble, but was a powdery white and failed to gleam. At regular points along the street, rings were driven into large blocks for the tethering of horses and the evidence of an advanced drainage system pointed clearly to the fact that Akkad, at least occasionally, experienced rainfall.

The 'Mese' as she would later learn its name, passed through the city from the south-eastern gate, criss-crossed by many other thoroughfares, major and minor, and met with another great road coming in from the south-west. The resulting street, also called the Mese, marched up a continual rise until it reached the great promontory that jutted out into the sea and held the palace of the God-King, along with the architecture of government and many gardens and terraces.

The ride through the town was, she would have to admit, one of the high points of Asima's life. Not only was Akkad magnificent in every way, visually and architecturally, with wide, clean streets, beautiful white towers, surmounted by bulb-shaped domes, temples and columns, statues and arches, but there was more than just the sight of glory.

After dusty and dry M'Dahz, with its mix of animal and spice smells, Asima simply could not believe that a city that was home to more than a million people, a centre of trade and the home of one of the world's greatest militaries, could smell so fresh. The gentle sea air was infused with a flowery aroma. Lotus and jasmine filled the streets in carefully-positioned gardens and the smell was heavenly. There was a slight tang from the spice market, but the heady mix merely added to the fresh and scented air, rather than ruining the experience.

Asima was astounded to find that she was relaxing, despite the constant prattle of her companions. Ignoring them, she leaned out of one of the carriage windows and cast her gaze over the people they passed.

The Pelasians seemed to be quiet, gentle and happy; a far cry from the Satrap Ma'ahd and his wicked machinations. It was more than possible that life here could even drive the memories of the past few years from her.

The road finally reached the top of its incline, passing out onto the plateau of the headland. The centre of the promontory was given over to a great plaza of gleaming white, surrounded by fruit trees, laden with oranges, lemons and limes. Ahead, the most ornate gateway Asima could ever have imagined stood amid walls of white marble and bronze decoration. Above the gate, with its statues and friezes, its peacock-feather columns and golden latticework, rose a great gilded cage with its own bulb-dome. Songbirds twittered and flapped within, gracing the square with their musical dialogue. Off to the left, to this side of the great walled enclosure, stood the temple district, with the great temple of The Maker in all its pink marble glory and many, many slender belfries. The right hand side was occupied by the arcade that marked the near end of the great circus of Akkad, used for horse racing and public displays.

She had little time to marvel, however. The carriage was escorted to the ornate gateway where the God-King's personal guards stood. Here, the cataphracti on their armoured horses bowed and took the rest of the escort with them, riding off to the rear to some unseen barracks. As Asima watched with interest, a unit of the God-King's guard appeared through the arch of the gate after a short pause, and took up position around the carriage and the wagon behind them. There had been a full minute in between guards when any passer-by could have approached the travellers and it was a testament to either the reputation of the God-King's guard, or the law-abiding nature of the citizens that the carriage remained unvisited throughout the handover process.

An officer gave the order and the guards began to march forward, the carriage trundling between them, beneath the great decorative arch of the royal Gate with its aviary. Within, the palace was a maze of beautifully-tended and carefully organised gardens and lawns, punctuated by scattered trees that smelled of fresh citrus fruit. Between these gardens stood various ornate and beautiful white and pink buildings, with apses and arches and rows of windows. A grand theatre rose from behind a row of poplars, the seating visible between the trees.

The carriage rolled forward along a wide pathway between two great structures with ornate windows. Inside, the wittering of the two girls was becoming hard to ignore, overriding the sounds from outside. Asima sighed and pushed open the grill on the window, drawing aside the net that kept the sand out during desert travel.

One of the God-King's guards walked alongside only a few feet away. She smiled at him, though he kept his eyes firmly forward.

'Am I allowed to ask anything?'

The guard remained stony silent and Asima sank back into her seat. The place was beautiful and exciting, and she was genuinely interested in the buildings they passed. Still, there would be time for her to learn more later.

The column continued on through the gardens and between buildings for a full five minutes before coming to a stop in front of a huge building. Square and unexciting, this structure stood at one edge of the peninsula, a steep incline running from its foundations down to the sea and the rocks below. Regardless of the inaccessibility of the slope, the defensive walls had been continued precariously around above the waterline on a ledge.

After the wondrous buildings of the palace complex, Asima was a little disappointed by the great, grey, square edifice, which showed little evidence of decoration or exterior windows, they being few and far between.

She made to enquire of the guard as the carriage door was opened but then changed her mind. He would not answer anyway, and she had no intention of showing an enquiring mind in front of the vacant passengers that accompanied her.

She had made sure she was ready and was therefore the first to exit the carriage. Stepping lightly down to the fold-out stair, she alighted with the soft crunch of gravel beneath her sandal. She raised an eyebrow questioningly at the guard but, before she could ask anything, a sharp feminine voice snapped from nearby.

'Do not dawdle. Your belongings will be brought on. Now follow me and be quick about it!'

Asima, keeping her face carefully neutral, stepped around the carriage to see that the doors of the great square building had opened. Guards stood by the entrance, but the figure addressing them from the doorway with its jarring hawk-like voice was not exactly what she had imagined. Instead of the gaunt, thin woman with a stern topknot that she had seen in her mind's eye, the figure in the doorway was a middle-aged man, quite rotund and dressed in elegant silks and satins. As she hurried toward him, the other three hot on her heels, she studied the man. He was wearing makeup and, she had to admit grudgingly, it was beautifully chosen and applied.

As she came to a halt before his upraised hand, she glanced through the door behind him and was relieved to see that the interior of her future home was, in fact, beautiful. Gardens and lawns could be seen within, surrounded by porticoes and balconies. Of course. This was not designed to be dull for the occupants, but to hide the glories that lay within.

She smiled.

'Wipe that inane grin off your face, girl!'

The portly man sighed in a feminine fashion and placed his fists on his hips.

'I am Mishad, your overseer and tutor. I can see we have a lot of work to do, so we'd best get started. You have a long afternoon ahead of you, ladies, but first we had best peel you out of these "things"' he eyed their attire with distaste, 'and have you bathed, oiled and perfumed. Then perhaps my nose will unblock itself.'

As he turned, the guards approached to close the doors behind them.

'You will note that the guards do not follow us,' he said as he walked through the arched hallway toward the garden. 'There are no guards within the building. No men are permitted within the harem.'

Kala blinked and turned to tap Asima on the arm surreptitiously.

'Why is he allowed in then?'

Asima sighed and rolled her eyes.

'Once we've had a little rest, Kala, and we're alone, I'll explain it to you.'

In which advancement is earned

The Dark Empress rode through choppy waters. Samir stood near the prow. He had been aboard for several weeks now and things were not improving. That first morning he had taken the beating of a lifetime, though he still remembered with satisfaction how, when they had been pulled off him by the first officer, he had inflicted enough damage on his attackers that four of them were unable to take their place rowing for a few days.

Now, as he prepared to haul on the rope when the shout came, he was still a little bruised and numb. That first day had been a lesson to his 'equals' on board. They had attacked him a number of times since then, but these days they did so in small groups with someone on lookout and they only attacked when they were sure of catching him off guard. On the bright side, they stuck to body blows these days in an attempt to keep their bullying hidden from the elders.

Such behaviour was both a gift and a burden for Samir. He had to be watchful, and had avoided several attacks through his quick wits, though he periodically suffered a flurry of clandestine blows. But despite this, he still considered there to be upsides. That he was worthy of such effort suggested that they felt threatened by him, which was a powerful thing to know. It also cleared his conscience. There was nothing that would stop him using them when the opportunity presented itself. And thirdly, he was pretty sure that one of the crew, a man called Marcus with one eye and a scarred scalp, was aware of the troubles. He had caught an occasional look from the man and was at fairly sure he had a potential ally there.

So now it had become a waiting game. He just needed the opportunity to present itself and give him the 'leg-up' he was looking for. In the meantime, the enmity of these boys was useful in ways they were unaware of.

He peered into the spray and the mist, which hung low over the sea here and meant they were nearing Lassos. Samir was eager for a glimpse of this almost mythical place. The ship had docked there four days after his arrival but at the time he'd been suffering rather badly, with three broken ribs, a puffed-up and closed eye, an immobile arm and numerous cuts and bruises. The ship's doctor had refused to let him leave the room put aside for him until he could pass three very simple tests of strength and agility. He'd almost passed one at the time and been put back down by the doctor until he was better healed.

Since then, the Dark Empress had been back out on another, unfortunately unproductive, patrol for weeks, before returning to its home port.

As a child in M'Dahz, he and Ghassan had heard of Lassos, of course. The pirate isle was infamous in legend of the southern continent. Somehow, though within only a few days' striking distance of numerous ports, the mysterious island had remained hidden from the navies of two empires and numerous inquisitive explorers. Some said that the island moved; that it drifted on the mist. Samir had his doubts.

He'd always had his doubts about the 'reefs of the dead' also, though weeks onboard had now shaken that from him. Subtle and careful questions around some of the older sailors made it perfectly clear that, whatever he might think, they themselves were in no doubt. And so, as they now approached this most mysterious island, Samir realised he was holding his breath in anticipation of what he might see.

'You: get aloft!'

Samir turned in surprise, but it seemed the pirate's command had been addressed to one of the other young mates nearby. Samir returned his attention to the prow and tightened his grip on the rope.

'All hands prepare!'

There was a long moment of ominous silence, made all the more uncanny by the mist that was now beginning to envelop the prow of the ship. Samir listened desperately and kept his eyes peeled. He could now see only twenty yards in front of him and, as he quickly turned his head, at most a third of the length of the deck stretching out behind him before it became lost in the wispy grey.

He whispered a quick prayer to the luck Goddess and peered ahead once more.

'Bring to!' the cry went up from the stern. Commands were relayed in short order around the ship, but Samir was already hauling on the rope and beginning to furl the sail before he was told.

As the rope tightened, he found himself drawing close to one of the men he didn't know, who was busy doing something arcane with a rope on the other side of the mast. Samir smiled at the man, but was ignored as he continued about whatever the task was.

He continued to haul on his rope and turned briefly to look out over the prow. The ship was slowing to a halt now as the sails, already deprived of wind in this still environment, were furled. The twenty or so rowers who had been sent to their seats ten minutes ago were rowing gently against the direction of travel, bringing the whole ship to a halt.

Samir dropped the rope in an instant, the cord burning his hand as it ran through his palm until he caught it again.

'Back!' he bellowed as loud as he could.

The man nearby looked up in surprise and then followed Samir's gaze and dropped his own rope, cupping his hands round his mouth.

'Abaft! Take her abaft!'

The man rushed over to Samir, who stood, gripping the rope, mesmerised with fear at the jagged, black, glistening rock that drifted toward them with slow and deliberate momentum. Behind them, desperate orders were bellowed out.

'Shit, shit, shit, shit, shit…'

He looked around at the voice and realised the man next to him was making signs to ward off evil.

'Gods won't help now', Samir said quietly and grasped the tip of one of the half dozen spare oars that were sheathed beneath the rail down the side of the ship near the front. Hauling on it, he heaved it over the rail, surprising himself with the strength he appeared to find from nowhere.

Gritting his teeth, he jammed the oar in a dip between the rails and aimed for the rock that was now almost upon them. Throwing all his weight behind the oar. With a worrying cracking and crunching noise, the oar struck home on the rock. For a horrifying second Samir was convinced it had broken at the end of the blade and they would run afoul of the hazard. Then the full, solid wood of the oar shaft hit the rock and Samir was physically lifted from the deck by the blow and hurled several yards back against the mast.

As he picked himself up, he realised the other man had gripped the oar and was desperately fending off the rock. The now desperate rowing and careful manoeuvring, combined with the push of the oar, turned the ship slightly and the rock came alongside, drifting along the side of the hull like a menacing sea beast. The man let go of the oar and the item dropped into the water and bobbed away. Slowly, once again, the ship came to a halt.

The man was saying something to Samir, but his attention was otherwise engaged. The young man stared out from his position at the rail into the mist.

This was no solitary rock. The reefs were here and as dangerous as imaginable. Glistening obsidian points rose from the turbulent waters, white froth dancing around them and fading, only to be replaced by more as the next wave hit. The rocks were everywhere. Ahead of them and beside them, behind them somehow and, he turned to confirm this… yes, at the other side too. How in the name of the seven faces of Ha'Rish had they got here, right amid the rocks?

His mind reeled. It was, he supposed, theoretically possible for a ship to fit in some of these narrow gaps between the pointed hazards, but the Empress was not a small ship and it would be difficult under even the best circumstances. In the mist? Never.

But the reefs, regardless of their danger, were only rocks.

Samir's gaze only took them in in passing.

Figures stood on the shards. All around them. Figures in dark, wet, drab clothes. Many appeared to be wearing grey robes like those of a priest, but duller and darker. And wetter. And infinitely more frightening. The silent figures watched the Dark Empress as she sat, motionless, among the rocks and the mist.

Toward the rear of the ship someone was shouting orders. Sounded like the first officer. The commands were very precise;

how many degrees the wheel needed turning; how many rowers should begin and in which seats; how many strokes a minute the man at the drum should beat out.

None of the commands would affect Samir in his role here, not that he would be listening even if they did. His attention was riveted on the figures staring at the ship; staring, he felt, directly at him, or into his soul. He shivered.

The nearest figure he hadn't noticed at first and let him to question his eyes. A girl of perhaps seven years of age sat in her ragged clothing on the very rock that had almost fouled them. Her arms reached up, outstretched; beseeching? Inviting? He shuddered once again as he realised he could just make out the reflection of his silhouette at the boat rail in the girl's glassy, black eyes, sunk deep in her grey face.

This was clearly impossible. Not only could he not imagine the ship managing to get into this strangely cramped position, but the girl had not been there when he'd pushed the oar at the rock. Somehow this whole thing must be some kind of illusion.

Frowning, he picked up a spare belaying pin and cast it at the rock, smiling as he realised how simply he had seen through this trickery.

The wooden pin bounced from the glistening rock with a noisy 'crack' and disappeared into the water with a plop. Samir sagged slightly. Impossible, yet definitely real.

The man nearby thumped him lightly on the shoulder.

'Don't throw things at them. You hit one and you'll have some bloody bad luck…' he looked around nervously. 'Maybe we'll all have some bloody bad luck!'

Samir blinked.

He'd been looking forward to seeing this mythical place and suddenly now, while he was this close, something was making the hair stand up on the back of his neck and he would just as rather be almost anywhere else. It felt like he would never be warm or see the sun again, such was the damp cold of the mist that stuck his shirt to his chest and the dismal grey all about them.

'Fucking captain!'

Samir blinked and turned to look at the man that had just smacked him on the shoulder.

'What?'

'Captain Khmun! Came in too fast. Should know better.'

Samir bridled, though he wasn't sure why.

'Someone with an ounce of sense ought to knock him down and take over. Someone who actually knows how to sail!'

Opportunity knocks so rarely that sometimes you miss it. Samir had seen opportunities slip past him several times in his life, unaware at the time that they were important. The events of the last year, however, had taught him the value of luck and opportunity, and he had been actively waiting for a moment like this for weeks of agonising beatings. Luck presents opportunities, but you still have to grasp them.

'Shut up!' he said, vehemently, and louder than he'd intended.

Without waiting for a reply from the surprised man, he turned, the other belaying pin he'd been grasping on the rail now gripped tightly in his hand. He span with no warning, his arm swinging out with its heavy timber weapon. His aim was true; his aim was always true.

The narrow end of the foot-long, heavy wooden pin smashed with force into the man's face. There were two instantaneous cracks. Samir was agonisingly aware that one of them was his finger, caught between the man's cheekbones and the timber. The other, judging from the explosion of blood that showered his own face, was the man's nose shattering beyond repair.

Samir straightened and watched as his victim, unconscious instantly from the blow, toppled backwards onto the deck, landing like a sack of grain.

Without turning, he closed his eyes, biting his lip against the pain in his hand. The captain was so close behind him he could feel Khmun's eyes boring into his neck; almost feel his breath. Opportunity knocks.

'Why?'

'Borderline mutiny, sir. With respect, you need to watch him.'

The captain fell silent, though Samir could almost see him nodding thoughtfully.

'When we've docked, clean yourself up and tell the watch that I want to see you.'

Samir turned slowly and carefully, keeping his eyes deferentially low and nodded.

'Of course, captain.'

Khmun laughed.

'The bowed head is a nice touch. You, I can use.'

Samir smiled to himself.

All you have to do is answer…

In which pecking orders are established

Asima stood by the golden latticework window and peered down. There were precious few external windows in the royal harem, and most of those were inaccessible to the girls. It had taken her a long time to find a window that looked out toward the rest of the palace complex rather than over the sea. Such a window was to be found in the antechambers of the mistress of the gates.

The woman, whom the girls had privately nicknamed the 'Witch of Akkad' was in charge of the security of the harem and the keeping of order and, initially, Asima had run afoul of her several times. She had been trying hard to fit in and to become a model occupant and yet the rules were so strict, or at least, those enforced by the witch were, that Asima's natural curiosity had led her into conflict until she began to learn how to play the game. Fortunately, over those first few weeks a greater problem arose for the mistress of the gates, in the form of the continually rebellious Sharra who seemed to have little regard for personal safety and no fear of punishment. The girl had made four bungled attempts to leave the harem in the first week, including a laughably traditional 'blanket rope' down the walls to the precipitous sea cliffs.

And so Asima's curiosity had begun to go overlooked. She had explored every place she could get to within the harem, though there were a number of doors that were securely locked and barred that sealed off whole areas.

In this time of adjustment, her opinions of the whole situation here and of the nature of the Pelasian royal household had been changed rapidly, as her eyes had opened to what Pelasia had to offer other than the wicked Satrap Ma'ahd. She had taken the natural leap in assuming that the harem was little more than a decorative prison for those women the God-King took to his bed.

How wrong she had been; the harem was so much more. Truly, it was home to those women who were wives and concubines of the God-King, or lovers who had the potential to become one of the official companions. But the harem was more than this. It was also the home to the female members of the God-King's family, including his mother, four aunts, two sisters and six girl children. More than a prison, the harem was a place of protection and seclusion for the royal women, and a place where girls were taught the ways of the court and Pelasian society in order to make them fitting brides for the God-King, or for other nobles or Princes if the God-King decided not to take them.

So Asima had learned over those first few weeks that most of her waking time was already allotted to lessons in etiquette, history, deportment, the application of makeup, massage and the use of oils, the geography of Pelasia, literature and so much more. She had never dreamed there could be so much to learn.

It had been at least two weeks before she had settled in enough to plan her time efficiently. There were twelve hours of lessons each day. Given that the daily routine for bathing, dressing and making up took a little over two hours, that meals took up at least an hour of the day, and that the girls were expected to sleep for eight hours to prevent unsightly shadowing of the eyes, that left Asima with less than an hour of freedom each day.

Careful planning had led to a streamlining of the preparation process, which granted her an extra hour in the morning and to the discovery that there were three hours in the late evening, once the girls were assumed to be settled in bed, when the witch and her cronies would play games of dice, drink sweet wines and smoke the water pipe, and the corridors were free to roam.

And so it was the late evening when Asima did her exploring.

Three weeks or so after her arrival, Asima had been sneaking around the upper galleries above the gate area; the night indeed when she had discovered the very window she now stood at, when she had bumped into Yasmin for the first time. She had nearly died of fright as she slowly and silently crept around a corner, walking on the sides of her feet to keep the pressure she applied to the floorboards as narrow as possible, and collided with a smaller girl coming the other way.

They had both made an involuntary squeak; the sort that someone who is where they know they should not be makes when they manage not to shriek.

As the two had picked themselves up, they had looked one another up and down, appraisingly. Yasmin was beautiful, and obviously lithe. She had to be a little older than Asima, but was clearly still a student here, as Asima had seen her in classes. In a mere glance, the girls had instantly summarized one another, both clearly aware of what the other was up to. A smile had broken the moment and a wary alliance had quickly formed between the two girls.

As the older girl, Yasmin would be presented to the God-King a year before Asima. She would therefore have seniority and a full year to ingratiate herself before Asima became a threat. Thus Yasmin was comfortable with the newcomer for at least a couple of years. Similarly, Asima knew there was nothing she could do about her new ally at this point, short of physical violence, and that Yasmin would know many things about the harem and could be of use. For the moment, the two girls recognised that they were the 'cream of the crop' among the young ladies waiting for their time.

After that, things had become easier and much more interesting. Yasmin had warned Asima who to watch for and who could be trusted. Over the following weeks, a campaign of advancement had begun. As far as the other occupants of the harem were concerned, Asima and Yasmin barely knew one another even by sight, and such anonymity granted surprising power. Messages were passed secretly and evidence planted to lower the status of those who currently stood out above the two girls.

Ladies who were so straight and noble Asima wondered how they managed to bend in the middle found themselves disciplined for possession of stolen sweetmeats and smoking pipes. Gradually and slowly, and with infinite subtlety, Asima and Yasmin moved up the ranks of the almost four dozen girls in training.

Each year, on the feast of The Maker, the girls of age would be presented to the God-King in the temple and he would choose three, in sacred memory of the three aspects of the creator. Three girls would become wives or concubines, out of perhaps twenty or more. The rest would wait until the next state occasion, when they would all be presented at the palace to the hungry eyes of princes, satraps and senior commanders of the Pelasian military as potential brides or concubines.

Asima and Yasmin had been determined to be among those chosen, and since they would be selected a year apart, they were no threat to one another until they were both in the royal court.

Almost two months after she arrived at Akkad, Asima had caught sight for the first time of the God-King of Pelasia. He was nothing like she had expected. For no real reason, the picture she had formed in her mind was of an overweight, overbearing and over-dressed fop who would have carpets rolled out before him as he walked and rose petals cast beneath his feet. The ancient tales in the Empire spoke of the Pelasian God-Kings as such.

This man was so far from that, Asima had found she had trouble adjusting her thinking.

She had been standing and recovering with three of her classmates after a gruelling athletics lesson, at the edge of the gardens and close to the gate passage, when the gate had been opened and the light from beyond flooded into the dark aperture, picking out the decoration on the walls and ceiling.

The God-King had come for one of his wives. Asima had learned that no King of Pelasia retained his name; to call him by name was disrespectful. He was simply the God-King. But even he, as a man, was forbidden entry to the harem; not that he would have tried, it seemed.

Pelasia's absolute ruler was a man in his early sixties, at a guess. He could be older and very well preserved, but he was certainly no younger. Tall and lean, he dressed in simple black, almost like one of his soldiers, the only thing that marked him being the symbols of the royal line stitched into his cloak in gold and the very simple gold circlet on his brow. He was clean-shaven, with short grey hair and piercing bright green eyes that reminded Asima of a cat caught in the light. Almost the precise opposite of Asima's imagined ruler, the God-King was a simple and noble man, handsome in an almost indefinable way, who carried such weight and gravitas that even standing in a room full of kings, emperors and princes, he would still stand out.

Asima instantly recognised that this was a rare figure indeed, and could understand now why the wives and concubines she had occasionally encountered spoke with such love and reverence of the man. Asima had smiled at that moment and had settled into her role, determined that her future would be at the side of this unsettlingly attractive older man.

Asima and Yasmin, after the second month, began to divide their time better. Now that the order of precedence in the harem had changed enough to move them both close to the top, their campaign of character assassination slowed. Now they need only keep themselves among the top runners, while allotting more time to learning those things that would make them stand out among their contemporaries.

Since that day she had seen the God-King before the harem gates several more times. It transpired that one of his most favoured pastimes was hunting and, once he had returned from a morning out with his court, he would often call at the harem and take one of his wives or concubines with him to the palace until the morning.

Discreet enquiries had further strengthened her resolve and bolstered her favourable impression of the God-King. It would appear that, despite his reputation for his – 'appetite' seemed the most appropriate word – the God-King was charming and respectful and often took one of his favourites merely to spend the evening playing games of towers or listening to poetry or taking night time walks among the gardens.

By the start of Asima's fourth month at Akkad, she had been a little disturbed to realise that she was happier now than at any time in her life. Moreover, she had more direction, determination and resolve that ever before and the potential for a fabulous future, living beyond the imaginable means of even the wealthiest merchant.

Toward the end of the fifth month, however, the pace in the harem changed. In seven more weeks the festival of The Maker would begin in Akkad and across the country. There would be a series of events in the capital over several days, culminating in the events at the great temple, where the God-King would choose three new ladies. Preparations in the harem became manic and lessons would be cancelled for the younger students for a whole month in order to concentrate on preparing those older girls for the upcoming event.

Asima had suddenly found she had unexpected time on her hands and saw considerably less of Yasmin. It was good to become accustomed to that, though, for in the very near future she would likely see nothing of her for a while. Those girls who were being groomed for the festival began to be taken out of the harem on escorted occasions and shown other areas of the palace; introduced to those people they would need to know. They were permanently occupied with preparations and the younger girls virtually ignored.

And that was why it had been such a surprise when Yasmin had found Asima daydreaming in one of the solar rooms and dragged her hurriedly to the stairs and back up to the very corridor where they had first collided. Along a little further and they had reached the witch's antechambers and this very window.

And now Asima stood at the window, frowning at the palace grounds as Yasmin tapped her fingers on her folded arms tensely.

'What are we waiting for?'

'Just be patient', the other girl replied.

They could hear, muffled by the distance and corridors, the ringing of bells. Asima shook her head.

'That's your call, Yasmin. You have classes.'

'I don't care.'

Asima blinked.

'If you miss your classes you'll be punished. And it will be noted among the people that really matter here.'

Yasmin smiled broadly.

'Yes, I know.'

'What?' Asima said incredulously. 'Are you trying to ruin everything we've been working towards?'

'As a matter of fact, I am.'

Asima turned her head and stared in the shadowed hall at the nearest thing she had in Akkad to a friend.

'What?'

Gently, but firmly, Yasmin grasped Asima's shoulder and turned her back to the window.

'Look.'

Asima, baffled and shocked, did as she was told. A small group of riders had come in from somewhere out of view to the left. There were eight... no, nine. Their horses were steaming and had obviously been ridden hard. All of them wore the plain black of soldiers, though one wore a cloak with gold designs similar to that of the God-King and, as he dismounted and slowly removed the black scarf wound around his head, also wore a circlet.

Asima stared and the strangest thing happened: the man with the circlet turned and cast his gaze across the wall of the harem almost as though he knew he was being observed. Asima caught her breath. The man was like a younger version of the God-King himself. Handsome and tall, he was clearly one of the royal line. Not one of the God-King's sons, though, since they both had yet to reach manhood, while this specimen had clearly done so a while ago.

'Who is he?'

Yasmin grinned.

'He is the reason I miss my lesson. He is the reason I shall be punished several times in the coming weeks and he...' she sighed and Asima recognised the hopeless adoration in the sound, '... he is the reason I shall not be selected by the God-King.'

'Yasmin, I will grant you that he's handsome, but the God-King is both God and King. There is no one in all the world higher than he. Why settle for the moon when the sun is within reach?'

Yasmin stared at her as though she were insane.

'Look at him, Asima! Just look at him. He will be mine. You can have the God-King. I will have Prince Ashar Parishid for my own.'

'You know him?'

Yasmin nodded, grinning like a fool.

'We have spoken. He has been in the palace for a while during our escorted visits. He apparently used to spend much of his time at Velutio but, since the Empire has collapsed, he's come home. I stumbled on a walk through the main palace's garden. The witch went to whack me, but Prince Ashar stepped in and stopped her. He helped me up, Asima! A prince helped me up!'

Asima smiled a calculating smile as she examined the man below.

'Then I hope things go well for you, Yasmin. I really do.'

And she really did. She knew the ropes in the harem well enough now and had no use for Yasmin, and the idiot girl had just taken herself out of the running. There was nobody left that Asima considered a threat. She would be a queen soon enough.

In which Calphoris encounters Pelasia

The ship lunged forward through the waves like a hungry animal in sight of food. The call had gone up a few minutes ago that a Pelasian sail could be seen around the headland, and the 'Wind of God', a former Imperial navy vessel now crewed by the Calphorian militia, furled the sails and began to hammer out a rhythm for the three banks of oarsmen.

Ghassan, too young still to serve in an official capacity with the militia, stood ready in the stern of the ship. Resigned to his lot after months of bailing out water by hand during heavy storms, scrubbing the deck in the searing sunshine, and helping clean the wooden bowls after the serving of meals, he was really rather grateful to have such an exalted position as rudder monitor.

While there were officers, marines, pilots, oarsmen and so many other important positions on board, Ghassan's most important duty to date appeared to have been sitting quietly out of the way and making sure that no lines or random flotsam became entangled with the rudder. A month ago, one of the militia's ships had encountered just such a problem during an engagement with pirates and had been unable to manoeuvre. They had been lucky to escape with their lives, and now it was standard practice for one of the juniors to be set on permanent duty during any engagement watching for exactly that problem.

Ghassan clicked his tongue irritably as he glared malevolently at the rudder. The Wind of God, and he still had no satisfactory answer as to which God that was anyway, had so far, in his five months of service, tracked two pirate vessels and lost them in the open sea, apprehended a smuggler in a small trading ship, and driven off several unlicensed fishing vessels. And now that they finally were facing a Pelasian, he was at the back, in the dark, watching a plank of wood. Still, back here he was close enough to listen in on the conversation of the officers on the deck above.

'It's a Pelasian, alright, and a military vessel to boot. We're on a line for attack, captain, but you need to give the word.'

Ghassan, sitting in the shadows beneath, separated from the oarsmen further forward by wooden bulkheads, nodded vigorously to himself and willed the captain on.

'It's a thorny problem, Sater,' the captain replied.

In the silent darkness, Ghassan shook his head.

'These are contested waters. What we do here, Sater, will set a fairly important precedent. If we attack and the satrap of M'Dahz has his vessels in these waters with the full backing of his government, we could find that we've inadvertently started a war between Calphoris and Pelasia.'

Ghassan could almost hear the first officer nodding thoughtfully.

'But if he's just testing the waters, captain, and we let him be, we're more or less granting the Pelasians control of these waters. Can we afford not to act, sir?'

The captain made a grumbling sound and then shouted along the deck.

'What's she doing?'

'Still coming on slowly, sir. She's not picked up speed. I don't think she's in an attack position.'

'But she's definitely a military vessel?' the captain replied.

'Yes sir. New, too. Didn't think this satrap had such big, new ships.'

Ghassan frowned and listened on.

'Sater, I need your honest opinion', the captain said flatly. 'Our lives and careers might all ride on the next few minutes.'

There was an uncomfortable silence. Ghassan glared angrily at the rudder as though it were trying to ruin his life. How could they not see? Did they not know the Pelasians?

Before he even realised what he was doing, Ghassan was on his feet, the perils of clogged and tangled rudders entirely forgotten. As he passed the doorway between the bulkheads, he entered the main rowing section of the ship.

Powered by both sail and oars depending on requirements, these 'daram' vessels as they were known in the south, were the standard military ship of the old Empire. Equipped with a ram, three banks of oars, three sails, a housing at the rear for all senior command functions and a tower amidships armed with ranged weapons, they were the perfect military vessel. The problem was that, over the centuries since their innovative appearance, the style had been copied and converted for their own use by the Pelasians and private fleets. Indeed, many pirates used daram they had captured.

The oarsmen turned to stare as this young man strode insolently past them, though they never once faltered from their professional rhythm. Along the length of the hull, below decks, the first two ranks of oarsmen sat, the inner row several feet higher than the outer and interspaced so that the oars had plenty of room.

Without acknowledging any of their looks, Ghassan stormed past them and to the stairs that led up on deck.

As he climbed towards the daylight, Ghassan swallowed nervously. He wasn't absolutely sure what he was doing, but someone had to do something and nobody else seemed to want to act. Still, it was a dangerous choice. To leave his post was to invite a flogging alone for, though still underage for active service, he was nevertheless paid by the militia and had taken the oath. To approach the captain and speak out of turn? Well, if he was unlucky, in an hour or so he might find himself bobbing around in the middle of the wide sea with nothing but a plank to call a friend.

As he reached the deck, he turned for a moment and glanced over his shoulder. The Pelasian ship was heading straight for them and he knew; couldn't say why or how, but he knew with absolute certainty that if they didn't act fast, the Pelasians would be on them.

'Captain!'

He now began to run along the deck. The top row of oarsmen in the open air stared at him in surprise. The upper deck rank would only join the beat and dip oar to water when full speed was called for.

Now, some of the junior officers were stepping to intercept him. He could see the marines standing in position. They were formed up but clearly not ready for action, their weapons sheathed. The captain and first officer turned to look at him as he ran toward them. He managed to get within almost ten feet before the crew grabbed him and pulled his arms round behind his back.

'What the hell do you think you're doing, boy?'

The speaker was a marine officer, the commander of a boarding party by the emblem on his upper arm; Ghassan had a good memory for insignia.

'With respect, sir, I must speak to the captain.'

The man grinned condescendingly.

'Oh you must, must you?'

'What is the meaning of this?' bellowed Sater, the first officer, as he approached the fracas.

'Urchin from below says he must speak to the captain, sir.'

Sater looked Ghassan up and down. The first officer had a good reputation among the men and Ghassan bowed his head respectfully.

'Talk to me, boy.'

Ghassan nodded. This was more than he could hope for.

'Sir, I don't know how to explain this, but you've got to attack.'

The various men holding him laughed though, Ghassan noted with a small amount of relief, Sater did not.

'And why does a rudder monitor sitting in the dark, barely old enough to shave, believe he has reason and right to dictate command policy?'

The comment sounded condescending, and yet there was something about the way the first officer looked at him that suggested it was a truer question than the others knew. Moreover, Ghassan had presumed a boy like him was basically invisible to the senior crew, and yet Sater had known his job.

'Respectfully, sir, I'm from M'Dahz. I've met the Satrap Ma'ahd, stood with our militia against him. I know how he thinks and what he's capable of.'

'Go on…'

Imperceptibly, the officers' grip on his arms loosened enough to prevent the discomfort he had been feeling.

'Sir, Ma'ahd didn't have ships before the invasion and the only coastline he controls is M'Dahz. It's common knowledge that M'Dahz has been abandoned; nobody raised an eyebrow when he invaded us, and there's virtually no trade traffic at the port these days, so he has no real need to defend his territory. Besides, sir, these waters don't even belong to M'Dahz.'

He swallowed.

'Also, Ma'ahd is not popular with the Pelasian God-King. He had to send offerings to mollify him after invading M'Dahz, so it's very unlikely this incursion is supported by the Pelasian government. Then there's the fact that this is a brand new ship. That means, since Ma'ahd has no other coastline, that he's set up a military shipyard in M'Dahz. If he just wanted to protect the port itself, he'd have bought second hand ships off one of the other satraps.'

Sater was nodding to himself as he listened. Ghassan rattled on.

'Sir, Ma'ahd is almost unstoppably greedy, conniving and treacherous. He is by now aware that M'Dahz is hardly the prize he expected and is probably already deciding which tower of Calphoris would look best with his banner hanging from it.'

Sater frowned. 'I understand what you're saying, lad, but why then send just one vessel into our waters? It's not a tactically sound move.'

Ghassan fell silent. He honestly didn't have an answer to that, but he knew beyond a shadow of a doubt that the closing black sail meant grave danger. The quiet was broken by the captain; Ghassan hadn't even been aware that the man had joined them.

'It's quite simple when you think about it. If the boy's right and Ma'ahd is building a fleet with the intent of conquest, then he can't make a play for somewhere as important as Calphoris without his God-King's backing. If he's unpopular, then he needs an excuse; a reason for invasion to take to his God-King.'

Sater shook his head in amazement.

'He's expecting us to attack them. They'll fight us off and then run away. Then we'll have initiated combat and he'll have his excuse. Then we must sail on by. We can't attack them, sir.'

The captain's face was a mask of doubt and Ghassan realised he had reached a crucial moment.

'With respect, sir, all that may well be true, but I know how Ma'ahd works. If you don't attack him, they'll have the advantage on you and we'll never leave here to tell the tale. He won't want word of their presence leaking out, or his plan falls through.'

Both Sater and the captain were nodding now. The marine officer narrowed his eyes.

'Permission to have my lads stand to and load the artillery, captain?'

The captain frowned for a moment and then nodded.

'Very well. We can't stand down or they may just sink us without a fight. And we certainly can't let them get away if we do fight. So, quite simply we have to win, and we have to sink them.'

He turned to the others around him.

'Have the men stand to and everything made ready, but do it carefully, subtly and quietly. Don't let them know we're preparing.'

Ghassan felt the grip on his arms disappear.

'You,' the captain said, pointing at him. 'You have an uncanny insight into this. Get aloft in the rigging and keep your eyes open.'

Ghassan saluted and, as he ran off, he heard the captain ordering someone else to the rudder. Things were looking up.

As he ran past the midship fortification, he saw the artillery master loading the giant crossbows and the catapult and, most impressive of all, rolling the massive inflammable ball of wadding onto the firing mechanism while a man stood to with a lit taper.

He scrambled with a recently-practiced expertise up the rigging to the spar at the top where the current lookout, an older boy nearing active service age, nodded a greeting.

'What's up?'

Ghassan pointed at the ever-nearing ship.

'Seen anything odd yet?'

'Not really,' the other boy shrugged.

'Where are the marines then?' Ghassan asked with a grin. 'That's a military vessel about to meet a potential enemy in open sea. The marines should be on deck.'

As the lookout blinked in surprise and nodded, Ghassan's smile widened.

'We've got them by the balls!'

Without offering any further explanation and leaving the lookout with a blank expression, Ghassan jumped down from the spar and slid down the ropes as fast as he could go. Dropping the last ten feet to the deck, he went into a roll and came up running until he reached the artillery master with his crew among the wooden battlements amidships.

'Sir?'

The officer turned and frowned at the grinning boy.

'What?'

'We can end this in minutes, sir.'

He noted the doubt on the man's face and pointed back at the Pelasian ship.

'No sign of their marines, sir, but a ship like that should be ready with them on the deck. That means they're hiding ready to board, sir, and they can't be below deck, 'cause they wouldn't have time. That means they have to be crouched down among the upper deck oar seats along the edge.'

The artilleryman frowned.

'You sure about this? If you're wrong, we could be in real trouble.'

Ghassan grinned.

'I'm not wrong. Aim the catapults and the fire thrower along the gunwales and we'll take out most of their marines in two shots. After that she should be easy, sir.'

The officer frowned for a moment and then nodded.

'You'd better be bloody right, lad.'

Ghassan, his grin still wide, saluted and, tuning, ran to climb the rigging once more. He was right. He knew, beyond certainty, that he was right. He also knew that the captain was watching him with interest, and that any minute now, and because of him, they would sink the first ship Satrap Ma'ahd had sent to the east.

First blood, Ma'ahd. This one was for his mother and all of those who died on the walls of M'Dahz that terrible day.

In which five years have passed

Asima sat back against the red velvet cushion and examined her nails critically. No matter how much time she spent on them they never quite seemed to look right. Tetchily, she reached around for the goblet of rich, sweet palm wine and took a less than ladylike gulp.

She also noted with a strange mix of irritation and nostalgia the slightly crooked angle of the index finger on her left hand as she buffed. A smile crept across her face as she remembered that time three years ago when she had been among the girls taken to the great temple for the choosing. She had, and this had really surprised her, been entirely unaware of the conspiracy of hatred that had grown among the other girls during those two years of preparation. She hadn't realised just how petty, angry, and even subtle, the others had been.

The morning of the ceremony, while the festival was in full swing outside, the girls had been allocated five hours to prepare themselves and Asima had discovered with growing impatience that everything she needed to help her get ready had been vandalised or disposed of.

The fight that had ensued had ended satisfactorily for Asima in most respects. She had managed to acquire everything she would need from the four girls she knew to be behind the worst of the activities. She had fought hard but had been clever, keeping her blows to areas that would not show and would be hard to prove. The only permanent mark she had received had been her own fault: a broken and now slightly-misaligned finger from a badly-aimed blow that she would need to keep hidden for a time. The others, however, had fought like wildcats, randomly and angrily. Their blows had been aimed for maximum discomfort instead and Asima had smiled through her painful split lip as she returned to her room.

She knew exactly what she was doing.

At the mirror, she had examined the mess the girls had made of her. Reaching down with the brush, she had been about to apply the concealing makeup over the already blackening eye, but had smiled, wiped the blood from her lip, and tended instead to her hair.

Once they were ready, the twenty six girls had been taken to the gate of the harem where the witch had examined the ranks critically. She had moved down the two lines nodding with satisfaction until she reached Asima. Her eyes had bulged so dangerously that Asima had been afraid she was going to have some sort of attack but, instead, she had merely shaken her head in despair as she noted the bruises and the red weal on Asima's forehead. The mistress had long since given up any hope of impressing her will on this one.

And then the guards had escorted the girls across the paths and between the lawns to the private gate that led from the palace grounds directly into the precinct of the great temple without having to enter the public square. Asima had smiled to herself once again as they mounted the steps and entered the narthex, keeping to one side and out of sight of the closed doors into the temple proper.

There they had rested for several minutes, awaiting their cue. Asima had been aware of the girls glaring at her and had given them a surreptitious wave and a sweet smile that had reopened the lip and send a slow trickle of blood across her teeth.

A huge gong had announced that the ceremonies had reached the appropriate point and two of the lesser priests had opened the gate as the royal guard lined the narthex along either side. They couldn't enter the church under arms at any time and were here merely as an escort. But the girls hardly needed them. Two years of training had prepared them thoroughly for this moment.

As the doors swung wide, the two lines of girls, side by side, had entered the great domed temple, walking slowly and solemnly down the open walkway between the rows of seated nobility, priests and wealthy citizens.

The God-King, still in plain robes, yet oozing a commanding presence, stood on the dais to one side of the altar, attended by three priests and his nephew, the Prince Ashar. Asima sighed as she looked around the rows of so many people as subtly as possible. Yasmin's hopes of becoming Ashar's princess had been dashed last year. She had carefully worked everything out and deliberately failed to appeal to the God-King.

When she, along with the other girls, had been presented to the nobles the month after she missed the God-King's selection, she had positioned herself and pouted just enough to attract the prince's attention and Ashar had chosen her for the first dance. Asima, watching from the gallery where the younger girls were to observe the events of a state occasion, had initially been pleased for her friend, but Yasmin's hopes had been shattered a moment later. She had smiled up at the prince and slowly, as passionately as she could, she had pursed her lips and leaned in to kiss the prince.

Ashar had pulled back ever so gently. He had not made it obvious, for fear of embarrassing her, but had clearly rejected her. Even from the gallery, Asima had seen the look of confusion and dismay in Yasmin's eyes. The prince had leaned forward and whispered something to her.

Six days later, Yasmin had entered the harem to collect her things and follow her new husband-to-be, the Satrap Khelid, and Asima had stopped her.

'I'm sorry about Ashar,' she had confided, 'but, you know, many of the noblemen's preferences lie in… another direction.'

Yasmin had smiled sadly.

'Not Ashar, Asima, but he put me straight. He doesn't like the court or these occasions. He'd only been there because the God-King asked him, and he said quite clearly that he was not looking for a wife for many years yet. I had the distinct feeling he was already pining for someone else.'

The witch had appeared then and hurried Yasmin along to the satrap who waited patiently outside the harem for her.

And after all that time, here was Yasmin once again in the great temple watching events unfold for Asima and standing at the side of Khelid, not far from the dais. Asima had been pleased to see what appeared to be a genuine smile on her friend's face. Khelid was a handsome enough man and, as he had turned and looked down at Yasmin, there was adoration in his gaze. Asima had smiled as the lines approached the dais.

Slowly, in time with the quiet beat of the drums, the girls had stepped into position and then turned, bowing from the waist to the assembled crowds, before returning to face the God-King, the prince and the priests.

The high priest had rattled on with an incantation and then a speech that Asima only half heard. She wasn't a follower of any God, let alone the Pelasian maker. Patiently she had waited, aware at all times of the warm, gentle trickle of blood into her mouth.

The speech had finished and finally the God-King had stepped forward.

'Here goes,' Asima had said to herself and held her breath, only to discover that the God-King had begun to make a speech now too. She'd sagged slightly and then, remembering where she was, had straightened. Slowly, finally, the speeches had come to an end and a fanfare blared. Asima had found her patience ebbing and hoped this would be it, finally.

The God-King had taken one more step and reached the end of the front line of girls. Slowly, he had moved along the row, casting his gaze over them. The rear line, in which Asima had been disgruntled to find herself, had been spaced so that they were fully visible between the front girls. Asima, determined, had smiled, but with an air of insolence. Given her condition, a meek, wet grin would hardly give the right effect.

The God-King had nodded and whispered things in his nephew's ear. Ashar had shrugged a couple of times and whispered back; clearly the God-King valued Ashar's opinion highly. With a nod, they had come on ponderously. This was no mere ceremony for the God-King; the decisions he made here would affect his personal life for at least the next year. More nods and consultation and then…

The God-King had stopped directly in front of Asima. It was the first time he had come to a complete stop during the ceremony. Asima had smiled in satisfaction as the God-King had reached across to Ashar, who was busy studying the girl they had last discussed, and tapped him on the upper arm, pointing at Asima.

The music in the background would make it exceedingly difficult for anyone close by to hear, let alone the general public in their seats, but Asima was close enough and sharp enough to catch the whole exchange spoken beneath their breath.

'Look at this one!'

Ashar had peered at her and, despite her resolve and her surety, Asima found herself suddenly experiencing doubt. There was something about the black-clad prince that unnerved her. It was as though he was staring directly into her soul and dissecting her motives. The Prince frowned at her and shook his head. He knew. He couldn't possibly have known how Asima had schemed and worked everything since her arrival here, how she had ruined the chances for her main competitors and played every opportunity to her own advantage, even that morning's beatings. But somehow Prince Ashar Parishid distrusted her.

'This one is more trouble than she's worth, uncle.'

'Sometimes a little trouble is good for the soul, Ashar.'

The prince had nodded unhappily.

'That is very insightful and certainly true, my King, but mark my words. This one will do you no good. Her smile is bright and her mood is mischievous, but her soul is black. Take her if you must, but remember what I say.'

The God-King had straightened and, in a breach of etiquette that had never been seen in generations of this ritual, he had spoken to one of the girls. He had smiled at Asima and addressed her directly.

'My nephew warns me off you, young lady. What have you to say for your unique appearance this morning?'

Asima had lowered her head slightly in respect and taken a deep breath.

'Majesty, I am considered a threat by many of my peers and they act according to their fears. I do not fear and shall not hide what I am. If your majesty deigned to choose me, you will know from the very beginning what I am.'

The God-King had laughed.

'Outspoken and honest? That will truly be a change among my companions.'

He had given her a nod of respect and moved on along the line. Ashar, however, had let his glance stay on her for some time, boring into her very being. Finally he had shaken his head sadly.

'Honest, indeed.' It had not been meant to be heard, but Asima's hearing was sharp.

As the ceremony had concluded, one of the priests had come along the lines and selected the three girls that would be taken in by the God-King and his household. Asima had been so sure that she had already been stepping forward when the priest came to her.

She had noticed, that day in the great temple, that one of the other two chosen girls was Sharra, her companion now for years and the most rebellious and insolent girl that the witch had ever dealt with. Clearly the absolute ruler of Pelasia had a soft spot for insolence.

A bird flew past the ornate window, casting its shadow briefly over Asima and pulling her back in from her reverie.

She sighed and left her nails alone at last, turning her attention ostensibly to the book before her, but in truth looking over the top at the three girls at the other end of the solar. The game had been far from over when she had been selected. No, indeed. The game had then begun in earnest. In the three years she had occupied the concubines' section of the harem, she had continued her campaign of discrediting the competition, though any activity she undertook outside the harem remained above board, due to the watchful eyes of the ever-present Prince Ashar.

She smiled behind the book as she examined Lady Dierra, her next target. She had been itching to cause a fall in the standing of the God-King's favourite concubine for months, though Dierra kept Asima at arm's length and was guarded about her actions.

News had arrived this morning that Prince Ashar was to leave Akkad for a time on a mission to Velutio, the capital of the Empire, and with no Ashar to watch over the God-King's women Asima would move swiftly up the ranks.

She was no longer a girl, but a woman of sixteen years and some weeks, and she was already a concubine to the most powerful man in the world. Given enough time to manoeuvre, within a month or two she would be in a position to be taken as wife instead of concubine. Then would be the greatest challenge of all…

To disband the harem and become sole queen.

In which we see that the years have been kind to Samir

The Dark Empress lunged violently through the water, rounding the sandy spur that jutted from the island. Ten minutes ago they had been plodding along, using only two sails and no oars, the crew resting and relaxed, trying to decide whether to drop anchor and go ashore to collect fresh water. And then the boy aloft above the main sail had called out.

A merchantman had appeared around the far side of the island, visible over the humped sandbank only from the lookout's position.

Within moments Captain Khmun had called the orders, the sails had been unfurled and altered, three rows of oars extended and dropped into the water and the Empress sallied forth to confront the target.

Not many years ago, Samir thought as he watched the boys with the rigging, he would have been there, hauling on ropes and climbing the sails. Strange how things worked out, but then he'd been planning his advance on board since the day he arrived.

And here he was now at sixteen years old. Still short for his age, but lithe and wiry, with his straight hair brushing the base of his neck and shoulders, Samir's face had filled out, giving him a heavy jaw and dark bristles that defied his attempts to stay clean shaven, attempts that had ceased a year ago now.

With a sigh, he squared his shoulders, allowing the chain mail shirt to settle into a more comfortable position over his heavy tunic. Blinking away a sudden spray of salty water, he grasped the hilt of the heavy blade at his side and cast his glance over the men on the deck before him.

'Alright, lads. Let's not have any cock-ups like last time. A sailor's precious little use with one arm. Felix and his men will take the wheel and rudder and then move to the sails and the hatch. Our job is to neutralise whatever marines they have on board so that Felix can do his job. Got it?'

There was a rumble of assent from the men of Samir's boarding party.

'They'll probably not have any marines anyway, Samir.'

He narrowed his eyes.

'It's possible, but not likely. In the last couple of years we've earned a bit of a reputation, Jaral. I've heard the merchants have started to eat into their own profits to hire mercenaries and guards. Chances are there'll be warriors on any vessel in these waters.'

Again there were nods of agreement.

Samir sighed. It was definitely getting harder. Khmun and Sharimi had consulted with the senior sailors and suggested the possibility of heading east or north; moving to more traditional Imperial waters, where the Dark Empress was as yet unknown. They could still be just about within reach of Lassos and yet raid waters towards Germalla. Samir had panicked for a moment at the thought of moving so far away from M'Dahz. His intention had always been to reach a position among the pirates of Lassos in which he could begin to use them to move against Ma'ahd and reclaim his home.

He had already allowed himself to lapse once into a wasteful life in the docks of M'Dahz and forgotten his overall purpose. He would not allow himself to do that again. Marshalling every argument at his disposal, Samir had turned his considerable talents at persuasion to keeping the captain and crew of the Empress close to the southern coast.

Soon, though, he would have to find a way to gather the various captains together and move on M'Dahz. The idea of promoting it to them as a second Lassos, a potential pirate haven in the border zone, had played around in his mind a few times, but the position was so dangerous, and the fight to claim it would be so tough, that he would need to offer a great deal more incentive to make it an attractive proposal.

He shook his head. In the meantime, he had a job to do.

'Everyone ready?'

There was a murmur of assent from his men once again. They would not shout; no reason to risk giving too much warning to the oblivious merchant merrily wandering along at the other side of the sandbank.

Slowly, almost ponderously, the merchant came into view around the slope at the end of the sand bar. There was, as always, a pregnant pause while the quiet predator raced in at an angle toward them. Then, suddenly, someone on board must have spotted the Dark Empress, for cries went up aboard and there was a sudden burst of panicked activity. The merchant began to lean away from them and turn on an escape path.

Samir laughed quietly. This was a slow mercantile vessel; little more than a barge with a sail. They'd not get very far before the swift ex-military Empress was on them. Obviously their military complement was not overly large, given their desperate attempt at flight.

The boarding party were clearly as eager as he and, as he listened, he could hear someone in Felix's party abaft urging the Empress on toward her prey.

He smiled as he stood, tensely, watching the impressive speed with which the powerful pirate vessel gained on the cumbersome merchant. As the minutes passed, the details became visible on the target ship. The crew were running around as though their panicky desperation could prevent the inevitable. Samir gripped the rigging next to him as the Empress lurched slightly in the wake of the merchant. The trader captain had done very well to turn such a slow beast away from them in this time and in such a tight curve. He must really be very good.

He nodded to himself as he watched. He was about to ruin a man's livelihood, but such were the perils of the sea and better they met the Empress than some of the other ships that worked out of Lassos.

Khmun had once been part of the Imperial navy, long ago, and held certain principles that were sadly lacking among most of the pirate captains. The captain of the Dark Empress, while now infamous for the sheer number and value of his achievements, had also managed to maintain a reputation that, unchecked, would turn him into some sort of folk hero.

Samir's captain always gave the opposition the opportunity to surrender their cargo without further incident. If this was not acceptable, then he would take the vessel and its cargo by force, but always with as little injury and loss of life as possible. Most of the captains would simply kill most of the captives, ransoming the more important ones. Khmun held to the principle of mercy and always allowed the crew to leave on board their own lifeboats. If the enemy had been particularly courageous and deserving, he may even take their cargo and leave them with their ship intact.

This set of very military principles had spread to one or two of the other captains, who could see logic as well as mercy in the method. Dead merchants were no danger, but neither could they buy new ships, re-equip and then bring fresh cargoes your way. There was a small group of what Samir considered gentlemen captains among the more vicious cutthroats of Lassos.

Another lurch and they were almost on the enemy vessel. With a few crisp commands from Captain Khmun, the Empress swung out sharply to starboard and then back on line. Within a few moments they would start to come alongside the merchant, at which point Samir and his boarding party would swing over and put paid to the marines on board, clearing the way for Felix.

As the two ships closed, something occurred to Samir. They would have to manage the boarding action very carefully, as the side of the merchant vessel was considerably higher than that of the Empress. He frowned. How could that be? This was a laden and slow merchant. It should be floundering around several feet below their own deck level. And the Empress was light and riding tall.

'Shit!'

The men of his party turned to him in surprise.

'Sir?'

'Something's wrong, Rin. I think we're in trouble.'

Without waiting for questions, Samir ran across the deck and glanced up at the lookout.

'Can you see anything unusual?'

The lookout looked down in surprise and then quickly spun around and cast his gaze across the horizon. Samir heard the string of expletives very clearly.

'You blind ass!' he bellowed up. 'How many and of what?'

By now other members of the crew had caught on to the sudden flurry of activity amidships. The lookout shook his head.

'One ship, but she's a daram, the same as us.'

'Flag?'

The lookout squinted and shaded his eyes with his free hand.

'Can't quite see, sir, but I think it's pale green or pale blue.'

Samir was already running toward the captain at the stern before the boy had finished.

'Sir. Daram closing in behind us and the idiot boy lookout can't tell who it is, but it's clearly not Pelasian. Could be Calphorian or some private force. Also, the merchant's got far too much freeboard, whereas she should be wallowing low in the water. Sir, she's not carrying any cargo. We're in the jaws of a trap.'

Khmun rubbed his chin for a moment.

'Any marines on board the trader?'

'Not that I've seen sir. I think it was just bait.'

The captain nodded.

'Then Felix can board her. We'll set her crew adrift and fire the vessel. If we can get her ablaze we might be able to use her against the other daram. In the meantime, though, we'll have to fight them off and make sure they don't board us. Think you can do it, Samir?'

Samir laughed.

'Soldiers don't know how to fight dirty, captain. We'll keep them quite busy until you're ready for whatever you want to do.'

The captain clasped hands with him for a moment, and then turned his attention to shouting commands among the crew. On the way back to his men, he passed the second boarding party and Felix grasped his elbow as he passed.

'I'm over manned for the job, Samir. If there's no marines on there, I only need a dozen men. You take the rest with you; you'll need 'em.'

Samir considered arguing for a moment, but Felix was right. He beckoned to half the men in the group and they followed him back along the ship to where Samir's party stood waiting.

The heavy military daram was bearing down on them with speed and purpose. Any minute now they would be in trouble unless Samir and his men could keep them occupied and the captain came up with one of the clever manoeuvres for which he was famed. Samir turned to his men.

'We're going to have to board them to give the captain time to do what he needs to. If we just try to stop them getting aboard us, we'll end up fighting among our own oarsmen. So as soon as the damn ship gets close enough I want everyone over there. Once we're across gather into groups and we can start doing some damage. Three groups. One by the main sail amidships, one making their way toward the rear where the officers are and the third in between. Alright?'

There were shouts of agreement and Samir turned back to examine the ship bearing down on them. Certainly Calphorian. What the hell were they doing so far to the west?

In which a rift forms

Ghassan leaned against the rail and watched the pirate ship intently. The captain was good. The moment the lookout had spotted the Wind of God, the men on board the ship had reformed very quickly. Rather than panic and try to run, which would have been disastrous for them, since the militia vessel was running at maximum pace, while the pirates had slowed to deal with the merchant as they pulled alongside, the captain of the Dark Empress had continued what he was doing but reorganised his men.

'Captain? He's only sending a few men on board the decoy. He's formed the rest up to stop us.'

The captain nodded sagely. He had come to rely quite heavily on the sharp mind and eyes of Ghassan and within a year of reaching full service age, the young recruit had already been promoted to a junior officer position.

'Suggestions?'

Ghassan shrugged.

'We still outnumber them, sir, and this Khmun seems to be a clever and honourable man. I don't think he'll make it a fight to the death. We just need to prove to him that we are not willing to back down and he'll do so to save his crew.'

The captain continued to nod.

The militia warship closed with impressive speed on the pirates. Ghassan twitched as he gripped the hilt of the blade he carried ready. He would lead the second boarding party, having considerably less experience than lieutenant Shufi. The Empress came ever closer and, with a nod, Ghassan had one of his men ready the grapples.

As the gap between the two vessels rapidly narrowed, Ghassan realised flames could be seen beyond, on board the merchant ship.

'The bastards have fired her. I hope Khmun let the crew go first or I'll skewer him myself.'

There were nods of agreement among his men.

He counted down under his breath the seconds until the pirate ship, with its complement of mismatched criminals lining the rail, reached the point where grapples could be thrown.

'Four... three... two...'

He blinked in surprise as the first rope from the pirate ship crossed the gap and the heavy iron grapple fell among his men.

'What?' he bellowed in disbelief as he and his men were forced to drop their own grapples and duck out of the way of the iron missiles that shot over from the pirate ship, scraping across the deck and anchoring themselves among the rowing seats and on the rail.

'They're boarding us? Are they insane?'

There were cries from the men on board the Dark Empress and the militia vessel lurched as twenty strong, bulky pirates hauled on the ropes and dragged the two ships together. Several of Ghassan's unit lost their footing as the two vessels met with an almighty crash. This Khmun was supposed to be unpredictable and clever, but this was plain crazy.

And with no further pause, the world exploded into a chaos of noise, movement and violence. Without an order being given, the pirates hurled themselves across to the militia ship, taking advantage of the surprise and the fact that the soldiers were temporarily off balance.

Behind the boarding party, the top deck oarsmen on the pirate vessel, currently superfluous, unshipped their oars and stood ready to repel any militia boarders that made it past the initial attack. Given the fact that they'd taken the pirates by surprise with little over a minute to react, Ghassan couldn't help but be impressed by the precision and coordination the men of the Dark Empress exhibited.

He had no time to appreciate the matter as he suddenly found himself under the direct attack of a crazed and excessively ugly Pelasian-looking man with a jagged, saw-edged sword. Desperately, he jumped back out of the way of the first swing of that horrible weapon. Righting himself, he felt the mast behind him. Taking a deep breath, he let a blank mask fall across his face and waited as though in terror. The pirate grinned and swung the terrible blade again. In a sharp movement, Ghassan ducked to one side and the blade bit into the heavy timber mast.

The pirate started in surprise and Ghassan righted himself and lunged with his own blade. The ugly fellow was surprisingly quick, though, and, as this officer went for him, the pirate grasped one of the soldiers by the shoulder and hauled him between them as a shield, forcing Ghassan to arrest his blow sharply or face impaling one of his own men. With a laugh the saw-blade pirate flicked a mock salute at him and then disappeared in amongst the flurry of men.

Ghassan took advantage of the brief pause to take stock of the situation. The pirates had used the confusion to form into three distinct groups. The first was engaged here amidships with Ghassan's men. The mess was well-planned, preventing the other militia boarding party from getting involved. Instead, the second militia unit were trapped behind his own, trying in vain to cross between the two ships, but held at bay by several rowers flailing dangerously over the gap with their heavy oars.

He turned to look back along the rear of the ship and saw that the other two groups of pirates were also well placed. The furthest group were now engaging the officers at the rear and keeping the helm busy. The Wind of God would be unable to manoeuvre until the area was freed of attackers, but the third group had positioned themselves between the two areas of fighting like a wall of ugly and were severing the ropes and rigging that controlled the sails.

Ghassan shook his head in amazement. Despite being outnumbered and in a poor position, the pirate captain had managed to turn things to his advantage. The militia troops were trapped and mostly useless, while the pirates were rapidly gaining control of the helm. But this was all temporary. As soon as the first group here broke under the weight of militia numbers, the soldiers would begin to sweep along the deck and would soon deal with them all. What did they hope to gain by preventing the militia from manoeuvring? What?...

With a sinking feeling, Ghassan grasped the rigging by the main mast and hauled himself a couple of feet higher so that he could see over the fighting.

'Oh, shit!'

Nearby, one of his men looked around in surprise, only to be dispatched by a pirate.

The merchant hulk, now fully ablaze, was being led around the stern of the pirate ship with ropes and kept at a safe distance with oars. Slowly, but with infinite menace, the roaring timber inferno was rounding a corner and bearing down on the bow of the militia ship.

The pirates weren't trying to take the ship; they were stopping the Wind of God escaping the oncoming flames!

Ghassan dropped back down and brushed his dark curls from his eyes. He saw one of his lieutenants pull back from the action and grabbed him by the shoulder.

'Simos? We need to break through to the captain and get that rudder turned. They're bringing a fireship down on us.'

A frightened look passed across the man's face.

'Don't panic,' Ghassan yelled at him. 'Just get the men formed up and have them begin trying to turn the tide back so that we can push through until they break.'

The man looked at him in momentary confusion and then saluted and started bellowing orders. Ghassan nodded. All they needed to do was break through. They didn't have to kill all the pirate boarders, just get through them and help recover the helm and the senior officers. The next problem was to buy them some time to pull it all off.

Taking a deep breath, he climbed the rigging and began to pull himself along it above the heads of the fighters. He'd momentarily considered using this route to get to the rear, but the middle group of pirates who were not engaged in combat had now fully severed the rigging, preventing just such a possibility.

Irritably, he clambered toward the bow, where the other militia unit were disorganised, some of them fighting off the swinging oars of the pirates across the narrow watery channel, others trying to get involved in the main melee, and yet more merely standing and staring in horror at the blazing inferno bearing down on them.

Shaking his head, he caught sight of his opposite number.

'Shufi! Get your men organised. You need to get the oars out and use them to try and hold that thing off! We're trying to free the helm.'

The officer stared up and him and then nodded and began issuing the appropriate orders. Satisfied that there was little else he could do to improve the situation, Ghassan once more cast his glance around the ship, trying to take stock of how things were progressing.

He was lucky indeed to have chosen that moment to look around, as he saw the knife hurtling toward him through the air in time to avoid it. The blade sailed between the ropes where the young man had been moments earlier and clattered down to the deck harmlessly as Ghassan dropped to the ground and drew his sword to deal with the new assailant.

'Brother?'

Ghassan's eyes opened wide at the voice. As his head came up to see the source of the thrown blade, his mouth fell open. Samir had changed, for certain, with the passage of so many years, but there could be absolutely no doubt as to who this was, his knife-throwing hand still frozen in the air, the other gripping the blade at his side.

'Samir?'

The smaller brother laughed.

'You went to join the army! What are you doing at sea?'

Ghassan shook his head angrily.

'I went to join the militia and that is what I did.'

'To fight pirates?'

Ghassan growled and changed hands with his sword.

'We fight whoever needs fighting. We've already taken blood against Ma'ahd several times, but you?'

Samir was disappointed to hear a mixture of astonishment and disgust in that last word that was almost spat at him.

'You?' Ghassan repeated. 'You became a pirate? You abandoned me to the desert to live a life of crime? Mother would disown you!'

Samir's face hardened.

'That's not true. And I never intended this. Things just happen sometimes, Ghassan, but my goal is ever the same as it was; the same as yours, even: to take the fight to Ma'ahd and free M'Dahz.'

Ghassan spat on the floor.

'Crap! You're a killer and a thief now. When we retake M'Dahz its people like you we'll be keeping out!'

Samir shook his head sadly.

'These soldiers have you thinking too simply, Ghassan. You fight your war, and I'll fight mine. In a few minutes we'll be free of you and we'll leave. And because we're thinking and reasoning people, we'll leave you be and go our own way. We don't need to fight.'

'That's a coward talking,' Ghassan growled. 'You're supposed to be a pirate, Samir; a killer.'

Samir shook his head.

'I am what I am, brother, but I'll not fight you.'

With a sad look, Samir turned his back and sheathed his sword, striding toward the gap between the boats. As he went, he called out to his men.

'They've got enough to deal with now, lads. Get back aboard and cut the ropes. We'll be a long way from here before they can get going.'

He clambered up to the rail and stopped in surprise at the sudden pain in his neck. He turned, astonished, to see Ghassan behind him, sword raised and blood running down the razor edge, dripping to the timbers of the deck.

'Ghassan?'

Samir put his hand to his neck. It was just a small flesh wound that would heal quickly, but it was a wound nonetheless. He glared at Ghassan and spoke through clenched teeth.

'You will have to sort out your rigging before you can make sail again, you'll have to be careful around the burning merchant, and our men have put your artillery out of commission and jammed your rudder. You won't be able to follow us or fire on us.'

He growled.

'We're leaving now, Ghassan. For the life of every one of your men, do not try and follow us across or we will be forced to take a more violent approach.'

He wiped the blood from his neck and flicked it at Ghassan, spattering red droplets across the uniform.

'And there is blood between us, Ghassan. For the sake of mother at her rest, I will not kill you now, but rest assured that the next time we meet I will give you no quarter.'

'Nor I you,' barked Ghassan.

Samir, turning to make sure the last of his men were disengaging and crossing back to the Empress, threw a last vicious glare at his brother and jumped across.

Some days were designed to test a person to his very soul.

In which the wheel has turned many times

Samir prodded the fresh wound above his right eye. The last engagement had been one of the most precarious yet. He smiled weakly as he looked down into the foamy water racing past below the rail. Yesterday had been his twenty-second naming day, and the event had passed him by, almost entirely unnoticed. Indeed, he'd still not have thought about it now, had the crew not made something of it.

When they'd scuttled the Pelasian merchant the previous afternoon, they had cast the survivors adrift in the lifeboats and then spent the next hour stacking and storing the booty that would have to be transported back to Lassos where the affectionately-named 'Eyeball' could add them to the Empress' takings roster and move them through his 'channels' to various ports of dubious ethics on the eastern coast.

A few hours later, Samir had been examining the cargo when he had been accosted and dragged, kicking and arguing, back up the stairs to the deck. It had been a natural assumption that his time had come. He'd risen through the ranks on board the Empress so damn quick that he'd put a lot of peoples' noses out of joint in the process. Indeed, when Sharimi had been laid to rest two years ago, the victim of a heavy artillery bolt during a boarding action, Khmun had barely glanced at any of those who probably had much better claim to the position, and had promoted Samir to first officer without a moment's pause.

Of course it turned out, as he was dragged, blinking, into the sunlight, that they had a few naming day 'surprises' for him: several uncomfortable and even painful practical jokes and games at his expense and then enough date wine and powerful spirits that he felt lucky to be alive this morning. That being said, there was a reason he'd spent the last hour leaning over the rail and 'alive' might prove to be a relative term.

He spat away the unpleasant taste in his mouth as he drifted off once more into musings on past events.

It was no surprise to Samir, really, that Khmun had chosen him on Sharimi's death. He had proved himself time and time again over the years. His uncanny knack for tactics, combined with Khmun's genius for innovative thinking in combat, had resulted in the Empress racking up almost twice as many captures as any other vessel that worked out of Lassos.

The name 'Scourge of the Seas' had been heard applied variously to the Empress herself, to Captain Khmun and recently to his infamous first officer, Samir. And yet, despite their fearsome reputation, the officers and men of the Dark Empress were proud of the fact that they could sometimes take a merchant down without inflicting any permanent harm on the crew. Often the mere threat of violence, combined with the name of the dreaded vessel was enough to bring about a peaceful surrender. Certainly their kills were among the lowest in the ledgers of Lassos. It all went to bolster Samir's growing reputation.

Those who had beaten Samir repeatedly in those first weeks on board had changed as much as he. The weak, greedy or stupid ones had died early on through bad luck or their own actions, while the clever and loyal ones had been finally forced to accept the fact that Samir appeared to have been born for this life. Indeed, several of them professed a grudging admiration for this man that they had tormented as a boy. Afad, the first face he'd seen on board, was now a boarding party chief and a trusted lieutenant of Samir's.

He turned his rubbery, sweaty, pale grey face to the water once more and groaned as a fresh wave of sickness overtook him and all thoughts but the regret of the morning after were forced aside.

A full minute of such horrendous activity and he finally settled back in ragged breaths to feeling weak and draping himself over the rail. Occasionally he would hear a gentle laugh somewhere. It wasn't that he couldn't hold his drink, so much as that *no one* could hold that amount of drink! He would occasionally look up when he heard a laugh and give the man a weak smile. He could have disciplined them for taunting a superior, but this wasn't the navy. Order relied as much on trust and respect as on discipline. Besides, his head might crack if he tried to shout at someone.

Now, where was he…

Ah yes. Every man on board could be considered a rich man by the standards of Samir's youth. Certainly any one of the officers could have afforded to buy Asima's father…

He blinked and focused on the water rushing past. Curious. While he had been forced to think about Ghassan quite a lot over the years, he'd not given a thought to their childhood friend for so long that it took a moment's dredging his memory to construct a reasonable image of her in his head.

He smiled as he remembered her; headstrong and controlling, almost always, he now realised, playing the emotions and affections of he and Ghassan against one another. His thoughts drifted to the sands of Pelasia for a moment and he wondered how she was doing now, even what she was doing now. Was she still in the harem of Akkad? Knowing her steadfast refusal to bow to the will of others, she may well have been executed by the vicious satraps or the royal family by now.

That thought brought with it an unexpected sadness, but he soon brushed that aside. No. She would be alive; probably alive and well. Asima was a survivor as much as Samir; probably more so. She would probably be running Pelasia before long.

She must be a stunning woman now.

Samir realised with a laugh that he was starting to drool and hoped beyond belief that this was a further effect of the hangover and not some childish infatuation coming back to haunt him. Besides, she'd been closer with Ghassan most of the time...

Ghassan.

Why the hell had he had to join the naval militia, of all the stupid, brainless things to do. Samir had been pressed without choice. Ghassan could have done anything, but no. And Calphoris liked to think of itself as a continuation of the collapsed Empire that continued to wallow, treating its militia as if they were still the Imperial army; all straight-laced and order and discipline. If only Ghassan could see that the driving principles of the militia allowed for no grey areas and had killed off his ability to reason beyond the blind acceptance of orders. Then he and Ghassan...

His jaw hardened.

No.

Samir was sick of feeling guilty and sorry for his brother. It had been Ghassan that had drawn blood when Samir refused. Ghassan had been the one to label him a murderer and bring their mother into it. Samir had been happy to let things go.

Over the last few years, with the increasing reputation of the Empress and her crew, interest in her capture had grown and it had become the life goal of many militia captains – and probably many Pelasians too – to capture the pirate ship and put an end to her activity.

The ridiculous thing was that, with such attention being paid to Samir's ship, those captains who had fewer morals were considerably freer to go about their bloodthirsty and murderous business. Samir had seen some of the nastiest captains at Lassos buy Khmun a drink for taking the heat off them.

The last half dozen years had brought a few near misses between the brothers. Samir had privately explained the situation to Khmun and the captain had agreed that, in addition to the desire to save the crew from unnecessary loss of life, the fact that someone on board the Wind of God may be able to predict their tactics meant that they should avoid contact with that particular vessel at all costs. On a personal level, Samir knew he must stay out of contact with Ghassan. What had been done could not be undone and they had both sworn to give no quarter when next they met. As far as Samir was concerned, that simply meant that they must, under no circumstances, meet.

There had been a number of engagements with ships of the Calphorian militia and black vessels bearing the flags of the satraps of Pelasia, but in all this time, Khmun and Samir had succeeded in pulling out of any engagement that involved Ghassan's ship. The closest Samir's brother had managed to boarding the Empress was last year when they lay in wait, hiding in a cove near the current arbitrary border of Satrap Ma'ahd's lands. They had just been getting underway when the Wind of God appeared around the headland at full speed and ready for action. The artillery master on board the militia's daram had managed to strike their foresail with a flaming mass and the resulting combustion and panic had almost cost them their lives.

Khmun and Samir, thinking quickly, had sacrificed a lifeboat to save the ship, filling it with combustible materials and quickly severing the ropes so that it dropped to the water behind the Dark Empress. As they did so, Afad and his men managed, with only a few minor wounds and burns, to cut the flaming sail free. As the drum began to beat out the rhythm and the oarsmen rowed as though the guardian of the underworld were slavering at their heels, the crew dumped the burning mass into the lifeboat and watched it explode into a fresh inferno.

The Wind of God had been forced to reverse their oars and arrest her speed as much as possible to gain the time and space to turn and avoid the burning obstacle, by which time the Dark Empress was already accelerating and racing across the waves to freedom.

By the time they'd gone half a league, the replacement sail was already up and the artillery armed and positioned. Twice in Samir's time on board they had come very close to disaster with Ghassan's ship and both times they had been saved by fire.

The time was coming when he would have to deal with matters, though. He would soon be forced to move on either Ghassan or the Satrap Ma'ahd. Samir had tried several times, both on board and back in port at Lassos, to persuade the captains that M'Dahz was a prime target and that Ma'ahd needed removing for their own safety.

That last was true, as well. Ma'ahd had constructed quite a navy over the years since he had taken M'Dahz and the black ships plied the coast dangerously close to Calphoris and even close to the island of Lassos, though should they ever find it, which was said to be impossible, they could never navigate the reefs of the dead.

There was another long pause in Samir's train of thought as he retched repeatedly, failing to bring up anything. He slumped once more, his mind spinning. What was he thinking about? Oh yes… the reefs.

No… Ma'ahd.

That would have to wait, he'd finally realised, until he was a captain in his own right, though such a time may not be far off.

Though Khmun had made no announcement, things were falling into place that suggested a certain sequence of events in the coming days.

Firstly, Khmun had, over the last year, increasingly involved Samir in his strategy and planning meetings. The captain had shared what wisdom he had with his first officer and seemed to Samir to be grooming him for the position.

Secondly, there was the wound. A few years before, a lucky shot from a defender on a Calphorian ship had sent a missile through Khmun's leg and the arrowhead had lodged in the man's knee. Though it had been removed and the captain had made what he deemed a 'full recovery', Samir had noted the wincing that went on whenever the ship lurched or shook. Moreover, Khmun had acquired that age-old mystical ability to predict cold and wet weather by the discomfort in his leg. Khmun was starting to tire of life aboard ship.

Finally, there was the matter of the council of twelve. The council was to the pirates of Lassos what a government was to a country, and the head of the council, a retired captain by the name of Surafana, was ailing fast. Word among the drinking pits of Lassos was that Khmun was the favourite to replace him.

Of course, the moment Samir could be sure would be when Khmun gave him the compass. In seven years of serving in various capacities on board the Empress, Samir had never found anyone that could tell him how the captain navigated the reefs of the dead, and it had only been with his ascension to the position of first officer that things had been made relatively clear to him.

On every ship based in Lassos, only two men knew the secret. For centuries the captains had used the so-called 'dead man's compass' to find their way through the reefs. There were said to be only two of them, and no more would ever be created. And, even as first officer, in two further years Samir had never seen the compass but, in a way, that was comforting. The day Samir knew that Khmun was ready to retire and Samir to take his place as captain of the Empress would be the day that Khmun showed him the compass and explained its use.

The time was coming for Samir to take on the ultimate challenge that life on board the Empress had to offer, and when that time came, he would use it to turn the wrath of the most dangerous men within a thousand leagues on the Satrap Ma'ahd. Whatever Ghassan thought he was doing, Samir had not lost focus on the goal ahead.

Soon, Ma'ahd... soon.

In which a fleet is found

The wind rushed through Ghassan's hair as he leaned over the prow and gazed ahead. Without taking his eyes off the black sail some distance in front, he sniffed. There was a barely-perceptible change in the wind and he bellowed commands over his shoulder back to the men under his command. Captain Jaral, way back at the stern with the other officers, would receive any appropriate information, passed from man to man along the deck, while relevant instructions would reach the correct people en-route.

Since Ghassan's promotion to second in command this summer, there had been a shift in the purpose of the Wind of God that only he and the captain seemed to have recognised. There had, over the last year or more, been fewer and fewer complaints among the merchants of Calphoris concerning pirate activity. Looking into the incidents that had been reported, along with information from other sources, it was clear to Ghassan and his captain that the pirates of the coastal waters had inexplicably turned their focus toward Pelasian shipping.

Inexplicable to most, but not to Ghassan. On first discovering the situation, he had recognised instantly the hand of Samir. Somehow, probably through gaining higher rank, Ghassan's brother had managed to steer the pirates to more Pelasian targets. Oh, it wasn't a black and white situation, by any means, since there were still incidents with Imperial merchants; even horrible ones. But the frequency had declined.

Moreover, Ghassan had noted with a sense of optimism, the Dark Empress had not been in a recorded incident with Imperial shipping in at least a year. Samir had turned his attention at last to the wicked Satrap Ma'ahd and that suited Ghassan just fine.

The end result of this shift in pirate activity was that Ghassan had managed to persuade the captain also to take more of an interest in the movements of Pelasian shipping, though, in truth, he hadn't taken much persuading. Over the years, they had located and chased down the Empress numerous times. They had almost caught her once, but the pirate crew seemed almost prescient. They were always either already running when the militia turned up, or prepared to get away at a moment's notice. Though Ghassan had tried to the best of his ability to take the pirate vessel, he found that somewhere, deep inside, he was profoundly grateful that they'd never managed to capture Samir.

Besides, the Pelasians were making a nuisance of themselves these days. Though years ago the militia had put paid to Ma'ahd's attempt to extend his territory east, sending missives after that first meeting to the God-King in Akkad, demanding that he keep his satraps under control, there was still a constant threat.

A line had been drawn, metaphorically speaking. Watch posts of both the Calphorian militia and the Pelasian Satrap had been constructed from the coast into the desert sands, glaring at one another warily over a half mile of unoccupied land. Less defined was the sea border and, while Ma'ahd had irritably agreed to keep his shipping in Pelasian waters when pressed by his God-King, his interpretation of what constituted 'Pelasian waters' was fluid at best.

So the Wind of God had taken it upon itself these past months to patrol the border region between the two powers, making her presence known and making sure she was to be found whenever a Pelasian ship crossed the line, chasing them back into their own territory.

Ghassan and the captain had considered what they would do if ever a Pelasian vessel decided not to run, or if they ever caught up with one while still in their waters. To leave it unmolested would be to invite further incursions, but to attack and sink the vessel might be considered an act of war by the God-King. It was a thorny problem and the compromise had been a decision that, in such circumstances, they would capture a vessel, strip it of anything useful and valuable and then escort them to their own waters before releasing them: a solution nobody could legitimately complain about.

And now it looked as though they would have their first opportunity to test the theory.

The Wind of God had come entirely by surprise upon the Pelasian scout half an hour ago, clearly a long way inside Calphorian waters; much further in than any vessel they had previously spotted. The arrival of the militia daram around a headland had shocked and panicked the Pelasians and the scout had turned as sharply as possible and begun to rig their sails to flee as fast as the wind would take them.

The daram was already at speed and bearing down on them, but the scout was light and fast. It would be a race.

And so, for just over a half hour they had been chasing down the small, single-sailed ship. There had been an appreciable closing of distance between them, but the result would be tight. In just over five minutes they would reach the contested waters and then the political ramifications of what they did would be less sure.

But the artillery master had reliably informed them that within a couple of minutes they would be in range to fire. At that point, the sails would be targeted, and then the hull. The scout would flounder and slow until they caught and dealt with it…

…as long as the artillerists were on form, anyway.

Ghassan, his teeth clenched and the spray lashing him repeatedly across the face, leaned further forward, urging the daram on desperately. The time had come to chastise these bastards for continually pushing acceptable boundaries. Besides, it was Ghassan's life goal to twist the knife in the side of the Satrap Ma'ahd until he could be properly dealt with. Minutes… it would all come down to a matter of minutes.

There, ahead, was the headland that marked the end of official Calphorian territory. Beyond that lay half a mile of free waters before they entered those belonging to Pelasia.

Minutes…

Ghassan frowned.

The headland was the point at which the border towers ended. This spur held an Imperial watch tower. The promontory at the far end of the next bay would hold the Pelasian one. The cove between was anyone's water, but safer for everyone to stay out of it. Such was not the cause of Ghassan's frown.

There was activity on the watch tower.

He frowned and shaded his brow from the bright sun, focusing his exceptional vision on that small wooden tower with its roof of thatch, its small palisaded compound that sheltered the complement of three men and its array of signalling devices.

He had realised that one of the men in the tower, almost half a mile away, was waving frantically. He was trying to discern the situation when he suddenly turned completely blind. Damn it!

The men in the tower had resorted to the signalling mirror, flashing the reflected sunlight at the ship and directly into Ghassan's eyes. Half a mile was too close for the heliograph to be used. That was for long-distance signalling, the morons! He turned away, blinking, and could see nothing but amorphous purple and green blobs. Continuing to blink, trying to restore his sight, he reached out for the rigging boy he knew to be nearby. Feeling the boy's shoulder, he grasped.

'See the signals coming from the tower?'

There was a silence and it took a moment for Ghassan to realise the boy was nodding. He grunted.

'Tell me what they say.'

Staring down into the shadowy area of deck and blinking was rapidly restoring his sight, but there was no way he was about to risk that again. The trick when at such a short distance from the source was to look in the right direction, but not directly at, the signal.

'It's warning us to turn round, sir...'

Ghassan frowned.

'Do they say why?'

There was a silence and Ghassan was trying to decide whether the boy was waiting for more message or had merely nodded or shaken his head. He looked up and the blurred shape resolved itself into the rigging boy staring off into the distance.

'Fleet ahead, sir!'

'Fleet?' Ghassan replied incredulously.

'Yessir!'

Ghassan, still blinking, looked toward the tower as the warning was repeated. The boy hadn't misinterpreted. That was clearly the signal. Ghassan shook his head. What to do? Could they afford to just let this go? He ground his teeth.

There was simply no choice. It was possible the message was false. What if the Pelasians had taken control of the tower? That was unlikely. If there was a fleet here, though, it had to be Pelasian and why in the name of the seven faces of Ha'Rish would they build up a fleet in sight of the Calphorian watchtower?

The questions were simply more numerous than any hope of answers.

'Take the word back to slow her down. Not to stop, but to slow the pace and be ready to come to a full stop or full speed at any moment. And hurry!'

Ghassan watched tensely as the headland neared, while the distance between the Wind of God and its quarry continued to close. His sight was improving all the time.

'Come on…' he found himself whispering under his breath, willing the ship to slow. He realised he was now actually nervous of what might be waiting around the headland.

As he watched, the ship showed signs of slowing, the gap between the Pelasian scout and themselves opening up finally. Hearing footsteps running up behind him, he turned, coming face to face with the captain.

'Sir.'

'What's going on, Ghassan? We almost had him. The artillery master's about to explode.'

Ghassan nodded sagely.

'I can understand that, sir. I was looking forward to this myself, but we were warned off by the watch tower.'

'Why?'

Ghassan opened his mouth to reply but, as he did, the answer appeared before them, stretching across the waters of the bay.

'Shit.' Both officers turned to look at one another.

As the Wind of God continued to slow, drifting forward, the headland passed by, ponderously, on their left. Ahead, the small black scout vessel sailed into unclaimed waters, out of their jurisdiction, and directly toward the mass of black sails that dotted the sea's surface like an ebony disease.

'That's one hell of a fleet,' the captain said, shaking his head in disbelief.

'Looks like three fleets massed together, sir.'

'How'd you work that out?'

'The flags, captain. Flags that I can see of three different satraps.'

The captain turned to the men gathering behind them and silently staring.

'Back to your places, men. Pass the word to turn as sharply as possible and get the hell out of here.'

He turned back to Ghassan.

'Do you think we'll have time to rescue the guards from the tower?'

Ghassan shrugged.

'I don't think there's any rush, sir.'

'What?'

'I don't think we're in any immediate danger.'

The captain boggled at him.

'Ghassan, what are you blathering about?'

'If that fleet was gathering to come against us, firstly they would have removed the watchtower guards so they couldn't warn anyone; secondly, they wouldn't have ships in our water just in case this very thing happened; thirdly, they would be gathering the fleet in Pelasian territory, out of sight of our scouts. By the time they got here, they'd be at full speed and it would be too late to warn anyone.'

He frowned and a slow but uncertain smile spread across his face.

'I think we're looking at a symptom of civil war, captain. There are no ships there flying the Pelasian flag or the God-King's banner. Just three satraps' flags, and I think they're all unpopular border lords. They're gathering in unclaimed water so that no Pelasian sees them in advance. Those bastards are being gathered to go against their own, captain. It's the only answer.'

The captain narrowed his eyes.

'I hope you're right, Ghassan.'

The young first officer nodded.

'They're not bothering with us. They've seen us, but they're not even sending a scout out toward us. They just don't care; it's simply not about us any more.'

The captain smiled.

'We may just have caught a break here, Ghassan. A civil war in Pelasia would keep them occupied and off our back for a while; give us a breather.'

'I'm not too sure about that, sir. The authority of the God-King is the only thing that's keeping the worst of the satraps under control right now. I dread to think what these three lords would be up to if they didn't have to answer to the throne.'

The captain blinked.

'You really think they'd have a chance against the crown?'

'Satrap Ma'ahd doesn't do things unless he is fairly sure of success, sir.'

'It may be, then, that the man we've been watching anxiously for the last decade is our main hope. Gods, I hate it when politics get too involved in the military.'

Ghassan shrugged. An image of Asima being dragged from a burning palace rose unbidden in his mind.

'It's in the hands of the Gods, sir, not us.'

In which Samir has to move fast

The Dark Empress rushed across the sea, bouncing from crest to wave crest and throwing spray up in a wall that burst over the prow and washed across the deck. Samir grinned a feral grin as he set his gaze on the black sail ahead.

It had taken a great deal of wheedling and arguing to persuade Captain Khmun to come this far into Pelasian waters. Khmun had now been confirmed as the successor to Surafana on the council of twelve and was uneasy straying too far from Lassos at this juncture. The captain had been dubious about Samir's unwavering desire to take the Empress against any black sail to be found at sea and the very idea of heading deep into Pelasian waters was just asking for trouble.

Still, Samir had persisted and had finally won the day. He had wanted to see M'Dahz, even if only from a distance; the port must now be churning out Pelasian ships and a hive of activity, given the number of relatively new vessels they had spotted bearing the insignia of the Satrap Ma'ahd. Finally, Samir had sold the idea to Khmun as a scouting mission, highlighting the need to know more about what the satrap was up to with these new ships he was building.

In truth, there was some validity to that mission goal, but what Samir really wanted to achieve was twofold: to see M'Dahz once again after a decade gone, and to insult the satrap as much as possible by sinking his ships, preferably within sight of the town.

And two leagues from shore they had spotted a Pelasian scout ship. At such a distance, Samir couldn't quite make out the pennant, and the vessel could belong to any satrap, but it was clearly Pelasian. At that point they had been a little to the west of M'Dahz, not far from the old Imperial border and their quarry had taken flight as fast as the small, nimble scout could manage, heading directly south toward land.

Samir, wary of getting too close to land so far west, had requested a decision of the captain, though Khmun had deliberated surprisingly little. The vessel had seen them and it was a matter of pride to chastise them for that. The Empress had a reputation to maintain, after all.

It was also a matter of pride to the officers and men of the Dark Empress that no vessel in the Sea of Storms could match her for speed. Khmun had set his considerable naval expertise to streamlining the hull, re-working the sails and masts and organising the placement of his oarsmen to maximise their strength. Every time the Empress chased down a fast ship or escaped one due to an extra turn of speed on the oars, those men were put down for an extra ration of liquor or share in the booty. The incentives had had impressive results.

So, despite the impressive pace of the lightweight Pelasian scout, the pirate vessel continued to gain on them, closing the distance as the miles rolled past. The ships had quickly come into full sight of the coast, previously visible only as a thin line of hazy brown on the horizon. In what appeared to be a pathetic attempt at evasion, the scout tacked to port and began to run along the coast, some distance from shore. At this point, the hills and dips of the coastline had become distinguishable and a dark smudge rising from the horizon some distance to the east had to be M'Dahz. Samir smiled. If they timed this right they could sink the scout within plain sight of the port watchtowers.

The dark smudge that...

Samir shook his head. His eyes must be playing tricks on him.

The smudge had moved.

If only he had Ghassan's sharp eyes.

No. The smudge was definitely moving. And that meant that it wasn't M'Dahz at all.

He frowned and his eyes widened.

They were ships. There were definite sail shapes that could be made out if you looked carefully enough.

'Shiiiiiit!'

Samir turned and ran along the deck, shouting to the captain, but Khmun was already busy. Samir realised with horror that the lookout aloft on the main mast was shouting warnings, but pointing astern.

'Oh no.'

His heart sinking, Samir ran to the rail, casting his eyes to the wake behind them and then, with growing dismay, in a wide arc out to sea on the port side of the Empress.

The shapes of black Pelasian vessels were dotted on the horizon in every direction. What had to be a sizeable fleet was moving up from the east, the smudge on the shore, while a wide cordon of Pelasian warships tightened a net around the pirate ship. They were coming from almost every angle.

He ran to the shelter at the rear where Khmun was slamming his fist on the balustrade in anger.

'Should have stayed away from the shore, Samir. What was I thinking?'

Samir shook his head.

'My fault sir. I dragged us into this. Question is: how do we get out?'

The captain shrugged

'There's no simple solution there, Samir. Whichever way we turn there's trouble. Best hope is to pick a target and try and break through where the cordon's weakest.'

'That's not going to work, captain, and you know it. By the time we meet them, even the thinnest area will mean three to one odds. There has to be another way. Come on sir, you can do this.'

Samir tried to keep the note of desperate hope from his voice, but had clearly failed by the look on his captain's face.

'You wanted to fight Pelasians, Samir. Now might be the time.'

The young first officer growled and shook his head.

'I didn't mean a suicide engagement, captain.'

Khmun shrugged again.

'Nothing else for it. At least we'll take one or two of them with us.'

Turning to the deck, the captain began bellowing orders. Samir ignored them, settling down to think as quickly yet clearly as he could. West and north there were 'haraq'-class warships; south was the coast, and east was the fleet he'd mistaken for M'Dahz...

Mistaken as a blur on the coast.

The coast.

He turned back to the captain, taking a deep breath.

'Pardon this, sir, but...' he turned to the crew and raised his voice. 'Belay those orders! Take us in toward the coast at full speed.'

There was a strangled silence. Khmun stared at Samir but, noting the grin spreading across his first officer's face, he nodded.

'Do as he says, lads!'

As the changes were made swiftly and efficiently and the Dark Empress gave up pursuit of the scout, angling directly toward the coast, still two miles away, the captain dropped down from the raised deck platform to where Samir stood, grasped his shoulder and pulled him over to the rail.

'What's your plan?'

'We can slip by them, sir,' he shrugged.

'Are you mad?' Khmun blinked at him. 'Slip by where?'

Samir grinned.

'Alright, sir. I've got good eyes, but it took me a while to realise that black smudge was ships and not the town. The heat haze on the land makes everything a little blurred and uncertain from out at sea. We need to get to shore as fast as possible. Then we'll turn sharp west and head out deeper into Pelasian waters. With any luck, they'll continue to close on where they think we'll be. I'm sure they won't expect us to head further west.'

Khmun slapped his forehead.

'You know why that is, Samir? Because there's more and more Pelasian warships that way. We've no idea what we'll be sailing into. Besides, you mistook the fleet because it was black against the brown land. Our sails are white. We'll be visible for miles!'

Samir laughed.

'I'd rather sail into the unknown than into what we do know. And if we furl the sails and rely on the oars, we'll be almost invisible against the shore. Trust me, captain. I know we can do this.'

Khmun stared at him for a moment and finally shook his head in amazement.

'You really are something, Samir. If you and that brother of yours were on the same side, no other ship on the ocean would be safe. Very well, let's do it your way. Better than being sunk by a Pelasian haraq while trying to break out.'

They returned to the raised command platform that gave a clear view in every direction not obscured by a mast. The coast raced toward them, brown and speckled with rocky coves and inlets and low headlands, growing every moment. Samir smiled to himself. For every foot the coastline seemed to grow to him, the Empress would shrink to the slower warships closing in behind. Any moment now, even the masts would become invisible against the backdrop of cliffs rather than sky.

Now was the time to pull his little manoeuvre.

'Furl the sails!'

The crew, taken by surprise, rushed to follow orders and, in a testament to their abilities, moments later, the three heavy sails crashed to the deck and were shuffled out from underfoot.

'Alright, men,' Samir shouted. 'Keep the sails ready. We'll need to raise them sharpish when we're out of danger, so that we can run. We're going to head toward land for another minute or two and then bank sharply west along the coast. During that minute I want anything white or colourful or brightly polished below deck level. We're going to blend in with the coast and slip past them, so we need to be as brown and unobtrusive as possible.'

There was a note of relief to the low comments and affirmative noises among the crew. Clearly they had been hoping for one of Khmun and Samir's miraculous ruses and it looked as though the first officer had a trick up his sleeve.

As Samir watched tensely, the men went about their tasks, stowing anything that might draw unwanted attention and preparing everything for a sudden turn of speed the moment it was needed.

Counting down under his breath, Samir watched the cove and the headland looming ever closer. This had to be done right. They had to be as close to land as it was possible to be, but not quite close enough to beach, or they'd really be in trouble.

In his head he tried to estimate the distance to shore and then calculate the depth of the water. A dromon had a shallow draft for such a large ship, but this was still very tight.

He took a deep breath and closed his eyes for a moment, expecting the crunch of gravel at any time.

'Starboard sharp!'

The oarsmen and the rudder master responded instantly and, without the wind in the sails to push them off course, the ship turned tightly and, mercifully, without the sound of wood grazing on gravel. Within a heart-stopping half minute the ship was turned and racing along the coast toward Akkad and the heart of Pelasia.

'Hold it steady now, lads.'

He and the captain shared a look for long moments and, as the ship battered on in silence, Khmun glanced up and called to the lookout.

'What are they doing?'

The lookout remained silent for a moment and then replied.

'I think they're continuing on, sir…'

There was a long, tense pause.

'Yes, sir. They've not turned. I think they've lost us.'

An explosive venting of air echoed round the ship as almost every member of the crew released the breath they had held for over a minute.

'Samir, there are times when you surprise even me.'

The young first officer grinned at his captain and turned to look along the deck. Things were back under his control, where he liked them. A quarter of an hour's journey along the coast and they'd be well away from any pursuers. Then they could set sail once again and head out into the open sea. His need to see his home town had almost cost them…

His train of thought was interrupted as an arrow came from nowhere and thudded into the railing a few inches from his head. He snapped his head round in shock to see a scout party of Pelasian riders on the headland, firing from horseback. There were only perhaps a dozen, but Pelasian horse archers were renowned the world over for their accuracy and rate of fire from the saddle. The Empire had employed them as mercenaries many times and, with the speed the Empress was currently achieving, the archers would have no trouble choosing targets.

'Get us out of arrow range of the coast, but no more!'

Scanning back along the deck, he spotted the artillerists loading the fire thrower and growled loudly.

'Stop that! If you fire that thing we'll be spotted five leagues away!'

The artillerists, taken aback by the ferocity of his tone, changed tasks and began loading the bolt throwers and taking pot shots at the horsemen. They would never hit them, a moving target from on board a moving vehicle, but it was making the Pelasians wary and causing them to pull back a little, which would give the Empress time to get out of range. Once that was done in half a minute, nothing would catch them.

He turned, sighing with relief, to ask the captain's opinion on keeping the bolt throwers loaded while they travelled the shoreline and realised in horror that Khmun was not where he had been.

His eyes dropped to the deck. The captain lay propped where he had fallen by the railing, an arrow protruding from his neck and blood running down his throat and back and soaking his tunic.

'Captain!'

Khmun issued a wheezing noise and grasped Samir's breeches, hauling him down to deck level. In a hollow voice, accompanied by an unpleasant bubbling noise, the captain addressed him face to face and very quietly.

'Get them home, Samir. Get them to Lassos. You know where the compass is and how to use it now. Time to practice the hard way.'

Samir nodded absently, as he started to pull away.

'I'll fetch the doctor…'

Khmun rasped what could have been a laugh.

'I'll be dead before he gets here, Samir.'

The young man suddenly found he had tears in his eyes; most unfitting for a pirate officer. And yet, it had happened again. Every father figure he found was taken from him. Every father figure he found was taken from him by Pelasia! He growled and the flow of tears stopped.

'I will get them back for this, captain. I will string up every last Pelasian east of Akkad for this.'

Khmun made that rasping, bubbling sound again. It was a laugh.

'Oh, Samir…'

Whatever had been the captain's last planned words, however, would never be heard. With a rattling sound, Khmun passed to the other world, supported by the rail and his trusted lieutenant. And now Samir had to do the worst thing imaginable: to tell the crew their captain had died.

Captain Samir of the Dark Empress, his face bleak and angry, bent and gathered up the body of the fallen captain.

'All free hands to the stern!'

Another death for which to repay Ma'ahd. The focus of the Dark Empress was about to narrow.

In which Asima progresses

The harem was a place of rules and discipline, but those rules changed depending on the position and rank of the occupant and, if one knew how to play the game well, they were surprisingly flexible.

Asima had learned early on in her days as an official concubine of the God-King that she had a great deal more freedom and authority than before, though the women who lived at this exalted rank took various differing viewpoints on their newfound power.

Tanita, one of the other two women who had been chosen alongside Asima, seemed to drift happily along, content with her role and enjoying what freedoms she had. Sharra, as always, continued to complain about her captivity and seemed to have taken this authority and used it to separate herself from the others.

Asima saw in the relaxing of control the opportunity to advance.

It had taken her a couple of years to get to know all of the wives and concubines, their foibles and traits, and to work out exactly where in the line of seniority they all stood. This was only somewhat important to her plans, of course, since some who were considerably more senior than Asima were now old or ugly or both, and therefore posed no great threat to her… barring one.

Keshia was now sixty three and, frankly, not looking her best. Asima had initially placed her under the 'people not to care about' heading, but had learned quickly that Keshia held a special place in the heart of the God-King. She had been his first wife and they had married before he had even ascended the high throne. He must have been so like Prince Ashar in those days.

Keshia, despite her age, was as much a threat as those eight years of chosen that followed Asima and the many that came before. And yet many of them were so mundane that they blended in with the wall decorations. There were, to Asima's surprise, more than a hundred women in the harem that the King had apparently never sent for and who lived lives of anonymity and great freedom. It had been this that had given Asima her greatest idea.

There were one hundred and seventy of the God-King's women in the harem. Of those, a little more than sixty ever actually saw him and those women were divided in Asima's mind into those above her, those level with her and those beneath her.

The more than thirty women beneath her, she kept her eye on, just in case they decided to make a play. Of the others, six women Asima believed were as favoured as her in the God-King's eyes, and only one of those was a wife rather than a concubine. The rest, eighteen women who outranked Asima, were all wives and, while a wife officially held higher rank than a concubine, such distinctions were quite blurred in the palace of Akkad.

Now, the only way to compete with the rest was to change her status completely, which meant either raising her own, or lowering that of those above her. Over the past six years, she had moved gradually up the ladder until it was often her that the God-King sent for when he needed companionship; moreover, flatteringly, it was as much her advice and conversation that he required as her beauty and her... other talents.

Now, however, she needed to become a wife. Once that happened, she would be perhaps tenth in line and would be in a position to jostle her way higher.

And so, here she was, strolling out of the great private palace at the centre of the complex, her hand resting lightly on the God-King's arm. Timing was everything and it had taken every tool in her arsenal to keep the ruler of Pelasia busy until the appointed time. Finally, she had smiled and told him sweetly that she was ready to return to the harem now.

'What route shall we take, my dear?' the handsome man had asked. 'The jasmine by the Loggia of the Winds is particularly fragrant at the moment.'

Asima had, as always, marshalled every argument and conceived of every possible problem before joining the God-King tonight. She shook her head quietly and, smiling, gestured out north.

'I would rather, if it suit your majesty, pass by the orchard. The smell of the lemon trees between the observatory and the harem is fresh and pleasing this time of year and, to visit the Loggia, we would have to pass the kitchens of the public palace at the time the slops are discarded.'

The God-King had laughed and squeezed her hand.

'Then the observatory and orchard it is. I might, if time allows, go inside and see what patterns the stars have formed for me tonight.'

She had smiled. That wouldn't happen. Not tonight.

And so now they walked down a paved white path between rich lawns and toward the northernmost point of Akkad. Ahead, the pentagonal towers of the palace walls rose up like the great horns of some silhouetted beast, the crown of its head formed by the dome of the observatory. Away to the left, beyond the citrus grove, stood the sombre bulk of the harem.

The moon was intermittently covered by scudding clouds that prevented too much silvery light from playing across the gardens, and Asima had to narrow her eyes discreetly to pick out any details on the observatory.

A relic from the days of the God-King's grandfather, the observatory was a three storey structure of white marble and porphyry. Octagonal, each face was smooth, punctuated between floors with purple decoration and surmounted by a domed, grey roof with portions formed of delicate glass.

The ruler who had originally had the curious building constructed had been convinced that the stars held some power over events in the real world and that, if man only learned how to read their patterns, he could predict the future. It was a belief that was commonly held to be erroneous, though nobody would say so in relation to the God-King's family.

Tonight, however, there was a certain ring of truth to this.

If everything was going according to plan, the observatory would herald certain future trends and foretell at least one specific event.

They strode down the gentle slope from the palace toward the structure and its adjacent orchard, the King humming a tune that the musicians had played through dinner, while Asima smiled and kept herself as calm and steady as possible. Periodically she looked up with her head lowered, casting surreptitious glances at the observatory. There was nothing to be seen there. Not a surprise. There would be in a minute, but not if the God-King kept up that irritating humming.

'Listen, majesty. Do you hear the gentle song of the nightingale?'

The God-King tilted his head slightly.

'You must have good hearing, Asima? I hear nothing.'

'It is faint, majesty, but beautiful.'

Her companion fell silent, listening intently for the birdsong that existed only in Asima's head. At least he was quiet. He may be handsome and kind, but the aging ruler of Pelasia had what

Asima considered to be some of the world's most irritating habits. She would cope with them in return for the power they brought, but really she would have to do something about changing him once she was in charge.

They approached the marble octagon, moving now into the shadow cast by the palace's high walls. The paved route would take them around the building to the door on the north side and, from there they could walk across the springy turf between the citrus trees back to the harem.

Well, she could. The God-King would be busy.

Almost there and Asima found she was holding her breath. Silently, she admonished herself and tried to relax. Appearance was all too important right now.

And it was with a happy smile and an easy pace that she and the God-King rounded the octagon and came face to face with the couple in the shadowed doorway. The God-King was so startled that he almost cried out for the guards, one of which would be patrolling the wall top nearby.

Asima allowed her face to slip into the practiced look of horrified disbelief at the sight of Sh'a'lah, the King's second wife, locked in the embrace of one of the black, white and gold-clad royal guard.

The God-King's face was everything that Asima had hoped. If she picked apart his expression, she could find horror, anger, betrayal, disbelief and sadness though, as she watched, the proportions of those emotions changed in a split second from heavy disbelief to extraordinary anger.

The couple, tightly held, took a second to notice the God-King. Sh'a'lah had been so involved in their kiss that she had been making strange squeaking noises. As the full knowledge of what had befallen them spread across her face, the second most powerful woman in the harem, five years older than Asima and a born princess in her own right, fell to her knees, her forehead touching the floor, abasing herself before her master.

It was impossible in that frantic moment to identify the soldier's expression, as most of his face was hidden in shadow and they only saw a flash of his eyes and a brief blur of his skin before he turned and ran, silently, into the shadows of the orchard.

The God-King, despite his fury, ignored the soldier as he ran and, instead, turned his gaze downward to glare angrily at the woman on the floor.

'Sh'a'lah?'

The woman made whimpering noises but no identifiable words came out. She would be terrified beyond her wits' end. The penalty for adultery among the God-King's women was to be crushed to death. There would be no trial, no alternative, and no hope of reprieve.

A small part of Asima that was still the girl that had played jump-rope and raced around the roofs of M'Dahz with the brothers felt sorry for Sh'a'lah and the fate she now faced...

... but the part of her that mattered mentally ticked a box on a chart and shuffled names on a list.

She held her silence, maintained her look of shock and horror, and stepped back, disassociating herself from events as the God-King grasped his second wife's wrist and hauled her to her feet, his face white with rage. Instead, she thought deeply about what she would need to do now, once the God-King had brought the guards and had the woman detained.

It had taken Asima three months to find a guard who was greedy and amoral enough to consider enticing the queen and playing the gigolo with her. It was a dangerous task and she had been paying the soldier a small fortune each week for his continued help and his silence. Of course, she had left nothing with him that could be proof of her complicity if he had spoken of her requests, but it was better that he hadn't, for otherwise plans would not have been brought to fruition and this would never have occurred tonight.

There would be two or three days of chaos in the harem and the palace as the King raged. Sh'a'lah would be repeatedly interrogated and tortured until her nails were gone, her fingers broken, her nose slit and all manner of horrible acts perpetrated. She would be able to say no more than that the guard had wooed her and she had accepted his attentions, for that was exactly what had happened.

The gentle manoeuvring and prodding that had come from Asima would be forgotten as mere generalities in harem life. She had been careful to be as subtle as a woman could be. No... no trace would lead back to her.

The only loose end left would be the young guard who had courted her, but that was hardly a worry for Asima. During their last meeting tonight to finalise the arrangements, she had taken the opportunity to slip him a cup of wine laced with a lethal but slow-acting poison. He would first notice the cramps in an hour or so and would then be dead within minutes. She had practiced dosage and timing on a variety of animals in the gardens over the past three weeks and was satisfied that the guard would never have the opportunity to tell anyone what had happened. Of course, he wouldn't anyway, for he would then be staring death in the face alongside Sh'a'lah, but this way was more sure.

As an additional touch, she had left the vial of poison in his room. When the body was found it would be assumed he had taken his own life after realising what he had done.

In the aftermath, a week or so from now, the order in the harem would change drastically. Far from everyone moving one place closer to the most favoured position, around a dozen of those wives above her, those who were known to be close to Sh'a'lah and would now be tarnished by her failure, would fall from favour. That would be enough, given Asima's recent good favour and the gifts and surprises she had in store, to push her into the top few of the God-King's chosen. Within a month she would now be taken to wife. Of that she was certain.

She allowed her thoughts to return to the present.

Guards were now rushing through the trees and across the grass to their master's calls. Sh'a'lah sagged in his grasp, broken and hopeless. Sad in a way, as she'd always been nice to Asima, and was so perky and full of life. Not for long, though.

The next challenge would be to deal with the sixty three year old favourite, Keshia.

Tonight Asima would move on to her new project.

In which Asima's world changes once more

Asima woke to commotion and instantly settled into an evil mood. She needed her rest. It had been five days since Sh'a'lah had been executed and things had only just begun to settle down in the harem after the tremendous shakeup that had followed. Asima needed her sleep, in the name of all that was sensible. Gritting her teeth, she pulled the satin pillow over her head and pressed its smooth, cold exterior over her head, squeezing her eyes tight and willing sleep to come back in what was clearly a futile gesture.

For almost two minutes she lay there, the noise (and what a noise it was) muffled by the pillow, but far from silenced. Finally, an expression of indignant anger on her face, she hauled herself out from beneath the lustrous, expensive covers and crossed the room to her robe, which she threw on furiously. Someone would pay for this, possibly even with skin and hair!

Growling like some predatory wildcat, Asima strode to the door of her room and was about to throw it open and demand silence of the chattering creatures obviously filling the corridor outside, when suddenly some sixth sense made her stop and take her hand from the latch.

That was not excited chatter or happy conversation. What was going on out in the corridor, though she could not make out the words, was evidently shocked and panicked babbling. In a moment of awareness of her vulnerability, she slipped the second additional lock shut and backed away from the door.

Why so many in the corridor outside her apartments? The answer was clear as it dropped into her thoughts. With her current high position, she had managed to acquire rooms away from most of the others, and with one of the few external windows. There was no reason for other girls to be anywhere near her apartment, but the corridor outside also held two more windows that faced north, over the cliff and the walls far below, and out to sea.

What had happened? Had one of the girls thrown herself from the window in despair? It had happened before and more than once from this very corridor. The fall was invariably fatal from here. Her heart in her throat, Asima rushed back through her ornate rooms, past the bed, so recently disturbed, and into her day room, where the window looked out over the sea in a breathtaking panorama. There were crimson drapes, heavily backed, to cut out the light when necessary, but Asima never bothered closing them. She slept in a different room and was not in the day room when she sought darkness.

Wondering what sight, grisly or exciting, awaited her, she crossed to the window and cast her glance immediately downwards. The moonlight was bright and illuminated everything below and before her.

The ground outside the harem wall continued level for only a few feet and then fell away precipitously, turning into rocks and jagged cliffs and ending twenty feet above the water in a ledge upon which the walls strode around the bluff. There was activity on the parapet; perhaps someone had thrown themselves off after all?

Asima, her interest piqued, glanced right along the wall to see the faces of several of the lesser concubines projecting from the windows. They were not looking down. With a strange, sinking feeling, Asima turned her head and followed the direction of their gaze.

She must have been blind not to notice it immediately.

The open sea beyond the walls was dotted with vessels, some ablaze, others gradually sinking to a watery grave. As she watched in shock, a ball of burning mass shot up from one of the haraq warships and gracefully arced out over the sea, its reflection in the black waves eerie even at this distance, before it came down, smashing through sails and rigging on board an identical ship.

What the hell was going on?

It registered in mere moments that all of the vessels involved in the huge and vicious naval engagement below were Pelasian, with the traditional black sails. From here she would have no hope of identifying the flags on board, but some of them must be the royal fleet based here at Akkad. It was unrealistic to believe such a fight would occur below the city without the royal fleet being involved.

And that meant Pelasians attacking Akkad.

Which meant only one thing: civil war.

What was it with the men ruling this world? All Asima wanted was a happy and rich life of peace and plenty, and every time she managed to find a niche and start decorating it the way she liked, some mindless ruler attacked and wiped everything out.

She growled. First Satrap Ma'ahd at M'Dahz, and now someone else here. The Empire was known to have well and truly collapsed nearly two decades ago, but why did Pelasia feel the need to follow suit.

'No!' Asima barked to herself. She was not having this. Not again. She was damned if she'd spent so much time and effort hauling herself up the ladder only to have the wall moved away as she neared the top. She had dishonoured, destroyed and downright murdered over a dozen people to get where she was now… She paused and frowned as she realised how bad this sounded when she said it flatly. There were extenuating circumstances.

'Besides,' she said to herself soothingly, 'that's how the game is played. I just play better than most.'

Setting her jaw, she examined herself in the mirror and, tutting irritably, lit the lamps to give herself a clearer view. Could be worse; her hair, long and straight and dark, stayed relatively neat no matter how disturbed her night was, and a few quick strokes with the brush along with two or three of her golden pins would soon make her look divine once more.

A servant eunuch had laid out her clothes for the morning and, since she had a lunchtime engagement with the God-King, they were among her best and most enticing. That would be fine, and as for the making up? Well, Asima had the practice down to such an art these days that she could accomplish a better look than most professionals in a mere couple of minutes.

She set to work with a vengeance and, within five minutes, was ready, giving herself a last critical look in the mirror. Yes, that would do. She had to be prepared for anything but, whatever happened tonight, she had to look divine enough to come out on top of the situation.

Smiling wickedly, she paused at the door and sprayed herself with a light burst of perfumed oil fragranced with musk, poppy and jasmine.

And then she was out. It gave her a small feeling of satisfaction to note the baffled and amazed expressions on the faces of her lessers as she swept regally past them in the corridor, perfectly attired and made up, and smelling of heady nights in the harem gardens. Perhaps the thing that astounded them the most would be that they panicked and wailed as they watched what could be the end of everything, while Asima maintained her usual calm composure. She knew some of the younger girls had spread a rumour that she wasn't entirely human and she had done nothing to discourage the talk. A little mystery and fear all added to her power.

Leaving the gaggle of hysterical women behind her, Asima strode along the corridor, down the two flights of stairs and out from the hall, through the decorative archway and into the central courtyard.

As she approached the main exit of the harem in its dark, recessed tunnel, one of the eunuch doormen, armed with a long, curved knife, stepped in front of the door. He looked distinctly unsure of his situation and had to glare at his companion guard and motion before the other eunuch joined him. Asima came to a halt a few feet from them and folded her arms defiantly.

'A thousand pardons, lady Asima, but you know the rules.'

Asima smiled, then laughed with absolutely no humour.

'Get out of my way, you pointless, poisonous half-man!'

The eunuch stayed where he was, a shocked expression spreading across his face. Asima sighed.

'In case you were unaware, we are being attacked by a force of traitors by sea and therefore almost certainly by land as well. If Akkad is about to fall I will stand by the side of my God-King and face it with him.'

The humourless smile returned.

'If you do not step aside, I will take your knives and use them to remove any parts of you that still protrude.'

The guards, likely awed by her reputation as much as her ferocity, shared a look and wisely turned the gate key before stepping aside.

Delaying for a moment, she took the time to give the guards a good hard stare before striding away into the night. The trick was in paying attention and devoting time to the details. That one last glance would stay with the guards for years and add to her reputation, so long as there was a future for her reputation to carry into.

The gardens were strangely quiet and yet busy. As Asima strode with purpose along the direct path to the royal residence, she saw small groups of servants and guards going quickly and resolutely about their business in a worried silence. And yet, despite the flurries of activity everywhere, the only noises she could hear came from outside the walls: crashes and bangs out to sea and what sounded like vicious fighting in the city beyond the palace gate.

Without paying to too much attention to what was happening close around her, Asima set her sights on the building ahead and made for the entrance. As she approached, the door opened and three servants rushed off toward the public palace, carrying bundles of something.

For a moment, Asima wondered whether she had been premature. Perhaps the God-King was in one of the palaces rather than his residence, tending to affairs. Perhaps, given his strength and abilities, he was armoured already and helping defend the palace.

No. The guards would not allow him to put himself in danger. He would be in the safest place in Akkad.

Striding purposefully, Asima pulled open the door to the residence of the God-King. The entrance hall was filled from side to side with heavily armed and armoured soldiers of the royal guard, archers positioned on the balconies above. The guard were clearly taking no chances of the enemy reaching their master.

As she walked toward the line of steel and bronze, she glanced into the side chambers and noted with satisfaction archers and soldiers positioned at all the windows. The building was well defended. Behind her she heard movement and, glancing back over her shoulder, she noted with approval the four guards lifting the heavy beams that would fall into grooves and bar the door in a moment.

Hardly premature. Just in time, in fact.

The captain in command of the guard gave a military half-bow as he recognised the royal concubine approaching and, with a curt command, the soldiers parted to allow her through. She glared at the captain and he was taken aback, blinking for a moment before recovering himself and straightening.

'Ma'am?'

'You just let me through without a single question?'

The captain cleared his throat, aware that somehow he was now treading a fine line.

'Ma'am? You are concubine and favoured of the God-King.'

Asima growled.

'We are being attacked by Pelasians, captain. No one should be trusted.'

The captain was crestfallen as Asima swept past, awash with annoyance, and made for the stairs. Behind her the guards closed ranks once more. Asima chided herself as she climbed. It had been petty, but it made her feel better. When events beyond one's control threatened, it was always satisfying to make someone feel less than oneself. In a strange way it passed a small amount of control back.

At the top of the stairs, she noted with satisfaction the second line of soldiers guarding the entrance to the main apartment complex. The men parted once more to allow her in and she wondered briefly whether to repeat her admonishment, but decided against it.

Opening the door, she stepped inside and Bashi, the God-King's chief manservant greeted her in the corridor.

'Lady Asima? I am surprised to see you here?'

Asima bowed her head. Bashi had a great deal of power and influence and, should tonight turn out well, she would need to remain on his good side.

'Master Bashi. As soon as I discovered what was happening I rushed to my Lord to be by his side and to offer him support and comfort, should he require it.'

Bashi nodded.

'This is good. The master is tense, my lady. Please attend just a moment.'

Asima stood in the entrance chamber and examined her nails as she heard Bashi enter the apartment and announce her. She also heard the strain and slight sound of relief in the God-King's voice when he asked the servant to admit her. By the time Bashi returned, she was already walking toward the main room. He smiled and passed her to go about his business.

The God-King, resplendent in his plain black, with the circlet on his brow and his jewelled sword slung at his side, smiled at her, though there was a sadness and a hollowness to that smile.

'Asima, I am grateful you came. Surprised, but grateful.'

He reached his hands out to her.

'Surprised, my lord?'

The God-King laughed sadly.

'You are ever the game-player, my dear. Ashar warned me about that from the start. But for all your wickedness, life here would have been duller without you.'

Asima frowned.

'Majesty, you speak as though the game were already lost.'

The God-King sighed and sat heavily on the couch.

'For your own good, you would do well to leave. I have already sent Ashar to collect the twins and ferry them to safety. I have seen the red stars from the observatory. My grandfather saw them the day before his death, you know.'

He sighed.

'Several of my satraps have risen against me with armies and fleets they have constructed in secret and I have not had enough warning to pull in allies. My fleet is lost on the sea floor to a surprise attack and most of the walls of Akkad are now under their control. The noose tightens around my neck, Asima, and if you are here when they come, you may well hang alongside me.'

Asima shook her head.

'You are a God, my love. They cannot kill you.'

A true laugh.

'I am well aware of my simple mortality, Asima, and I do not think that you believe in any God, regardless. No, I shall die tonight and I would have you away somewhere safe, but I am glad that I saw you once more. You would have won, you know? I just cannot resist you. You would have been Goddess and queen had I lived. How sad.'

Asima found that she had a genuine tear in the corner of her eye.

'I shall go nowhere, my lord. I shall be by your side when they come.'

The God-King Amashir IV, absolute ruler of Pelasia and divine power smiled sadly.

'Then let us sit and drink wine while we wait.'

In which the wheel turns again

Asima gripped the arm of the chair so tight that she felt her nails cutting their way through the delicate satin cover, her knuckles turning white. A few feet away, the God-King sat with a sad, stoic calmness, his legs crossed and his gaze firmly affixed on the door. The sounds of vicious combat at the entrance to the palace had died away only moments before and the echoes of steel on steel still rang around the corridors of the residence. There was a pregnant pause as Pelasia held its breath.

'The time is upon us, my dear. Time to go.'

Asima shook her head and dug her nails ever deeper into the chair arm.

'It is no use making such a noble gesture, my love. I appreciate the thought, but there is no need now; your death would be pointless. Find somewhere to hide.'

Again, Asima shook her head, her face pale. She was wracked by uncertainty. When she entered the building, this was exactly what she'd planned to do, though she had also considered several alternatives. It was a calculated risk, that if the attackers succeeded she would appear noble and loyal enough to stand out above all the other women who hadn't come here. It was all about raising her profile before anyone else had the chance. But now there were feelings of regret and real loyalty creeping in and she hadn't felt these emotions since the days of her youth in M'Dahz.

She sighed as the God-King turned to her.

'Consider it a last royal command if you must, Asima.'

It was almost worth arguing. Her profile was… something in Asima's subconscious flashed her images of a potential future. She could see how clearly impressive she would look once the usurper had felled her master and she strode calmly from behind the curtains, looking regal, stunning and entirely unfazed by the horrifying events around her. If anything it would be all the more impressive.

With a sad smile, she reached out and grasped his hand. As she did so, the fresh sounds of battle broke out on the stairway and landing outside the apartments. The God-King squeezed her hand lightly, smiled once, and then turned back to face the door.

Asima stood and made her way across to one of the drapes that hung as a divider, separating the more intimate lounging area from this formal reception room. Her choice was hardly random. She had selected it as a possibility when she'd first entered the room twenty minutes ago. There was sufficient dark, heavy material to hide a full person thoroughly, with enough light, wispy, netted areas for her to be able to watch events unfold whilst unobserved. Moreover, given the drapes' position between the two rooms, it was quite reasonable for one of the concubines to be in the intimate chamber rather than the reception room. With a quick glance at the door, she ducked behind the material and held her breath.

The wait was not long. The fighting at the head of the stairs was over almost before it began. Asima swallowed and kept herself still as she heard footsteps approaching the door.

There was a rattle and then a creak. From this position, she could just see the door's edge as it opened and was so surprised at the sight that unfolded before her that she almost laughed. The Satrap of Siszthad!

The satrap, one of the more powerful and yet certainly one of the least popular at court, had been absent from the seat of government for over two years, following an unfortunate incident involving a serving boy. He was, to Asima's mind, one of the most thoroughly unpleasant and repulsive creatures the Gods had ever let loose in the world.

The man who made his way into the room was more than a head shorter than the God-King, so rotund that no armour would go round his bulk. He waddled more than walked and his complexion was oily and sick, his eyes small, dark and beady. In essence, he was everything the God-King was not. Siszthad jerked his head to one side, his neck making an unpleasant cracking noise and his topknot swishing like a horse's tail over his bald, shiny head.

His strange waddle was accentuated almost humorously by the clicking of the silver and ebony cane in his hand, like a third leg preventing the spherical nobleman from rolling over. Asima shook her head in wonder. Siszthad was wealthy and powerful with a lot of land, certainly, but... this? This unpleasant, piggy little pox-hound had masterminded a coup that had felled a dynasty of four centuries' standing? It seemed ridiculous.

The satrap came to a halt, sweating, before the God-King, who stood, slowly and regally, to tower over his usurper.

'Siszthad? This was never your doing. You have neither the strength nor the intellect for something like this.'

Guards in black began to enter the room, fanning out on either side of the two men. Asima growled under her breath as her view was partially obscured by the two in front of her. The satrap laughed, a high-pitched, feminine noise.

'Amashir...'

To Asima's surprise, the God-King reached forward and gave the small man a backhanded slap hard across the cheek.

'You will refer to me by my title, you worthless piece of camel hide. I am God-King as long as I live, no matter what you do to me!'

'Easily solved,' said an unseen person.

Asima jerked at that voice. As the guards had finished filing into position, two other men had entered to stand at the rear. One was a satrap she vaguely recognised; handsome and dark, a man of nomad blood from the deep desert regions. The other had been mostly obscured by guards and the drapes. She knew the satrap ruler of M'Dahz's voice well, though.

'Ma'ahd!' the usurper squeaked. 'What do you mean?'

'Oh, for the sake of reason!'

Ma'ahd stepped forward, brushing the smaller man aside, and pointed to the nearest guards.

'This man was a King and a God, so make it quick, but do it now.'

There was a brief hesitation and then two guards stepped forward. One reached out for the God-King who made no attempt to defend himself. The guard grasped the God-King's wrists and pulled his arms around behind his back. The tall, elegant ruler smiled at his three enemies.

'You are committing treason, murder and ostensibly deicide. The stars have a way of coming back round and taking their revenge on such people. Remember that. The stars will burn red for all of you, in time, so enjoy your reign for now.'

Without another word, and without waiting to be forced, the God-King bent at the waist, extending his neck. The second guard drew a long, curved sword with a horrible rasping sound and lifted it high above his head. Pausing for a second, he looked to the Satrap of Siszthad for confirmation. Ma'ahd sighed.

'Just do it.'

Asima watched with a mix of hatred, awe and sadness as the living God that ruled Pelasia fell in two, his body crumpling and, as the guard let go of the wrists, slumping to the floor. The head rolled several yards and came to rest in front of the darker-skinned nomad satrap. Siszthad turned and addressed Ma'ahd in his squeaky voice.

'Burn the horrid thing. I want rid of anything that reminds anyone of that man!'

Ma'ahd shook his head.

'That is not enough, Siszthad. His head must go above the Moon Gate as a warning.'

The man who had plagued Asima for most of her life gestured to the guards and pointed at the head and the body. Without waiting for further commands, the men gathered the remains and began to carry them carefully from the room.

Behind the drapes, Asima's head spun. She had been prepared for a usurper, but not for a triumvirate, and certainly not for Ma'ahd. She could make her future secure with almost anyone, but this would complicate matters. How would they rule together?

She shook her head and concentrated on the three men who were now fully within the chamber. At a perfunctory gesture from Ma'ahd, the corpulent little man took the seat so recently occupied by the God-King. The dark satrap bent and, retrieving the simple gold circlet, passed it to the seated man.

Asima frowned. There was further activity at the door. As she watched, the high priest of the creator, along with half a dozen of the most important ministers in Akkad, was ushered inside at sword-point.

'Knees!' barked the darker satrap in a rasping, dry, desiccated voice that sent a shiver through Asima. The seven men dropped to the ground, those who were too slow aided in their descent with a blow to the back of the knees delivered by an unseen guard.

Ma'ahd smiled a smile that told Asima more than any words could.

'King Amashir is dead. I shy away from the title God-King, for clearly he was no such thing. There will be no more Gods ruling Pelasia; just men. You will now kiss the floor and accept the blessing of your new King, Paranes of Siszthad... Paranes I.'

There was a silent pause and Asima could imagine what was going through the minds of the seven men. The guards gave the witnesses a few random clouts with the hafts of their weapons; not enough to damage, but enough to goad them into action.

As the men gave their oaths of allegiance and collapsed, grovelling, to the floor, Asima shook her head. She would survive and probably even prosper. Ma'ahd and the other satraps were clearly intent on the power without the prestige; becoming the de facto power behind the throne. That meant they would be no immediate threat to Asima, as long as she extended the same courtesy to them. Siszthad would be the one to rule and he was no lover of women; he was known to have a thing for boys, and mostly for unwilling boys. If he ever sent for a woman from the harem it would probably be to produce an heir, but it was unlikely even that would make him do so.

He was a horrible creature, and physically repulsive, but he was also stupid, greedy and gullible. Asima would be able to claw her way to the pinnacle of Pelasian society just by playing the man. She…

A noise distracted her, and she swung her head to the private chamber behind her, tastefully decorated and furnished, and graced with three ornate windows and a balcony. Her heart in her throat, she realised the shouts of warning were coming from outside. What now?

Weighing her options, she sighed and moved as lightly as she could from behind the drapes, across the other room and to the balcony. Stepping outside, she glanced down into the grounds and took in the events below as shock made her grip the rail of the balcony.

Black-clad guards were running across the lawns, chasing a single figure on horseback. The horse was a magnificent white mare. She knew that, because she knew the rider. Prince Ashar raced for the stairs leading up to the walls near the gate and she found that she was urging him on; to escape. Strange that: Ashar had never trusted her; never been a friend to her, and yet she felt that on some unspoken level he understood and appreciated her. He was a conundrum, that one.

Other guards were closing the net. She realised with a hint of sadness that Ashar had been charged with saving the God-King's twin boys and yet his hands were empty as he rode desperately, looking for a hole in the tightening net. Ashar would now be the last direct member of the Parishid dynasty; four hundred years of rule in Pelasia in the form of one man, fleeing the palace in the night.

As she watched, Ashar wheeled his horse, shouted something she didn't quite hear, and raced toward the thinnest area of the cordon. Timing his move impeccably, the prince urged his horse to a jump and cleared the closing guards with ease. As confusion reigned and the black soldiers rushed around trying to change direction and follow their target, Ashar rode up the wide staircase to the top of the land walls.

Behind and below him, men ran across the lawns and began to climb the stairs, but Ashar had a strong lead on them. As other guards appeared from towers and ran out onto the walls, Ashar climbed dexterously onto the saddle of his horse, turned to face the palace, gave a last, elegant bow to the memory of his uncle, and dropped backwards out of sight, disappearing from the wall top into the street that separated the palace complex from the great circus.

The fall from there, forty feet down to hard paving, should be fatal, or critically-injuring at least. And yet, this was Ashar Parishid. In the years Asima had known the prince in Akkad, he had never once done anything foolish or without having planned it through first. The prince would be alive and well and leaving Akkad...

... for now.

She heaved a sigh of relief and turned to see the three lords standing in the room behind her, guards filing around the perimeter.

'Lady Asima, I believe,' the Satrap Ma'ahd smiled mirthlessly. 'I am given to understand that you were one of Amashir's favourites and that you were one of my girls from M'Dahz. It seems I chose well.'

Asima smiled meekly. No time to push things, now.

'My Lord Satrap.'

Ma'ahd nodded, deep in thought and then turned to a guard and gestured at her.

'Take her back to the harem; and while you're there, do a complete count of wives, courtesans and other women. I fear we may have to perform a cull. Amashir had a broad palate.'

The look of complete unconcern on Siszthad's face brought a mix of dry humour and disgust from Asima.

She could survive a cull. She had survived far worse.

Part Three:

Cargoes

In which a new page of history begins

Ghassan shuffled his feet nervously and glanced sidelong at Captain Jaral. In the past few years, their life had become surprisingly mundane.

The Pelasians seemed to have turned their attention west, toward their own people. The civil war there may have been short and brutal, but the resulting peace had been long and just as brutal. For three years now Pelasia had cut off most of its remaining ties with the Empire or, at least, with the former territories of the Empire. Black ships had rarely been seen anywhere near the border zone, concentrating instead on keeping the new reign imposed on an unhappy and restless population.

Consequently, the only target for the militia was the pirates and, with what was essentially the closure of Pelasian waters and therefore a massive increase in Calphorian military concentration on anti-piracy activities, the villains were generally staying well away from the coastal regions and picking on the occasional brave merchant who crossed the open sea.

It had been rumoured that the Lord of Calphoris was considering reducing the size of his navy and pushing any spare militia into the land forces. The idealistic side of Ghassan approved of the move and realised that a reassignment to dry land could be a step toward his goal of directing the strength of Calphoris against M'Dahz. The practical side of him also realised, however, that since Satrap Ma'ahd was now one of the top men in Pelasia, any move against them would likely result in Calphoris being squashed like an insect under the weight of the Pelasian army.

Also, frankly, he'd grown to love life at sea.

And so it was with some trepidation that he stood now with his captain outside the doors of the Lord's council chamber in the palace of Calphoris. The next few minutes could change his life entirely; he could even be pensioned out. He swallowed nervously.

'Enter!'

Ghassan straightened his hastily-washed uniform and watched as the huge cedar doors swung slowly inwards to reveal the great court chamber of the provincial capital. The Lord of Calphoris sat at the far end not, as Ghassan had expected, on a high throne surrounded by vassals and servants and plotting campaigns on grand maps. The Lord of Calphoris was, in fact, sitting at a plain wooden desk with two elderly men and scribbling furiously while discussing something in low voices.

Ghassan looked around at the room. Large and high and fancy enough in which to hold great state occasions, the hall was certainly the largest single room Ghassan had even seen. Poles jutted from the wall high on both sides, having once held banners of some kind. The room was of white and yellow marble, with an inlaid and patterned floor.

He looked at the captain, who shrugged and gestured forwards.

The two men fell easily into step and strode with a clacking sound across the hard floor. As they approached the far end, the Lord looked up and blinked. Sitting back as they came to a halt and saluted, he frowned and then nodded.

'Captain Jaral and Officer Ghassan of the "Wind of God" yes?'

'Sir.' They both replied in the affirmative. The Lord of Calphoris, ex-Imperial provincial governor and the most powerful man south of the sea was a surprisingly small and mousy nondescript man in an ordinary, plain tunic and breeches. He scratched his chin and fixed the two of them with the most piercing gaze Ghassan had ever seen. Those emerald eyes seemed to have weighed up Ghassan's worth in a glance. This, despite his ordinary appearance, was an exceptionally intelligent man.

'I have important news to impart to you, gentlemen. Please… stand at ease.'

As the two sailors relaxed a little, though not enough to appear insolent, the Lord leaned back and stretched.

'You have been in port for three days. I believe…' he fished around among his papers, found one and ran his gaze down it. 'Of sixty two militia craft in varying sizes, the "Wind of God" is the only one currently in port and the "Shadu's Arrow", which we are not expecting for several days, will be the next.'

He smiled as he leaned back.

'It is good to see the navy so active, though I might prefer a few vessels close enough to afford protection to the city.' He shrugged.

'Did either of you see an unusual vessel arrive this morning?'

The captain nodded.

'There was a fast northern courier bearing a flag I didn't recognise, sir. A raven, a dog and a cat or some such. Looked a lot like the old Imperial flag. A new lord in contact, sir?'

The Lord smiled.

'It was actually a raven, a wolf and a lion; silver on black. If you had looked carefully, you would have seen the crown between them also.'

Again, those piercing eyes weighed the two men up.

'News, as I said; brought on a courier ship from the north. Important news that directly affects myself, you and your crew, and indirectly everyone in Calphoris. But for now I want the flow of this news restricted. I need you to remain collected and deal with this professionally, yes?'

The two men frowned and nodded, uncertain of what was happening around them. The Lord breathed in and out several times and then straightened.

'There has been something of a development in the interminable power struggles of the central provinces, gentlemen. A week ago, give or take a day or two, Lord Avitus of Velutio met the infamous general Caerdin in battle somewhere near the capital. It would appear that, although the general himself did not survive the battle, his liege lord has been crowned Emperor; the first in two decades to dare claim the title.'

The surprise was evident on the sailors' faces and the Lord of Calphoris smiled quietly.

'According to my dispatches, this Darius, as he is called, has received overwhelming support from the northern and central provinces. The Imperial government is being reconstituted and commissioners sent to all Imperial territories to aid the transition of power as soon as things are settled at Velutio and on Isera.'

He sighed sadly.

'There are a number of lords both here in the south and along the eastern coast that will be unwilling to accept the mastery of a new Emperor and may well declare independence. I, on the other hand, am more than satisfied to return to my original role as governor of Calphoris if the commissioners will allow it, and I believe they will. By declaring for the new Emperor, it is entirely possible that I have made enemies for us of several of the more powerful lords in the southern provinces. Do you see why I bring this to your attention?'

Captain Jaral tapped his lip.

'With respect, my Lord…'

'Governor or "your Excellency" will do nicely, I think.'

'Excellency, what does this mean for the militia? Are we to be disbanded, maintained, or integrated into new forces?'

The governor shrugged.

'I have only the bare bones of the matter at the moment, captain. I cannot imagine that men of talent and experience will be wasted. I am sure there will at the very least be a place for you. But let me come to the heart of the matter; the reason I sent for you, then.'

'Sir?'

The governor sank back into his chair once more, glancing briefly at the two old men who continued to work at their ledgers without looking up.

'Until we have further instructions from the Imperial council, I must do what I feel is prudent for Calphoris. As you are aware, I have allowed the naval branch of the militia to operate very loosely, under the authority of each individual captain, reporting only to the militia commander at Calphoris. Commander Pharus has always steadfastly maintained that such was the only way to operate an effective militia navy.'

'Yessir.'

'For now, however, I need someone to coordinate naval activity, to plan strategies and to dispatch the various militia vessels appropriately to new assignments as they return to port. It may be weeks, or even more than a month before we receive any further instructions from the capital and we have cities to the east who may declare against the Emperor and a growing and turbulent situation to the west.'

Ghassan frowned.

'Excellency, Pelasia has been quiet for years.'

The governor sighed, his expression inscrutable.

'That brings me to the rest of the news in the dispatches, gentlemen. It would appear that the scion of the last true royal house of Pelasia, Prince Ashar Parishid, took the field alongside the new Emperor and General Caerdin and defeated the de facto ruler, the Satrap of Siszthad, in that same engagement.'

The young first officer blinked in surprise.

'Sir? Pelasians fighting in the central Imperial provinces?'

'Yes,' the governor shrugged. 'It does seem odd, doesn't it? In the days of the old Empire, Pelasian units were a standard auxiliary force in the military, but never whole armies of them becoming tied up in Imperial politics. Still, it is not difficult to see how, with the fractured Empire and the usurped throne of Pelasia, there could be sympathies among aligned factions.'

He stretched and tapped his chin thoughtfully.

'The problem we have now is that Siszthad was not alone in his coup in Pelasia. There are other noblemen who will be taking this news rather badly and, depending upon how Prince Ashar and the new Imperial government handle matters, we could see increased activity at the edge of our waters, or even assaults on our shipping or outposts.'

Ghassan shook his head in disbelief.

'Satrap Ma'ahd is basically in control of Pelasia right now and I would say he's too careful to launch a war on us when there's trouble coming back at him from overseas.'

The governor nodded.

'In fairness, young man, regardless of Siszthad's title, I think you will find it's been Ma'ahd that has controlled Pelasia for years and, while he may be concentrating on the potential return of Prince Ashar, M'Dahz is one of his power bases and his main shipyard these days, so he may feel the need to make his presence felt on our border, regardless.'

He shrugged.

'Until we receive further word from Velutio, I want you, Jaral, to coordinate the fleet. As soon as you leave here, go and see the commander Pharus and he will make arrangements for staff, banners and documents of authority to be delivered to you. I need you to make sure we still have an effective presence against pirates, and to put some ships to patrol in the east as you see fit, but make sure you have enough of a force to deal with any Pelasian threat.'

The governor smiled and tapped the side of his nose conspiratorially.

'And don't go spreading the word about the new Emperor beyond those who need to know yet. I've made no official announcement and don't intend to until I've slept upon it. As far as most folk are concerned until further notice, this is a mere reorganisation of the militia. Let's not start a panic or a riot with unconfirmed rumours, eh?'

'Also,' he added, pinching the bridge of his nose, 'let's give it a few days and make sure this Darius is still in power with his head on his shoulders once the dust settles.'

The captain saluted.

'Sir, I'm not the most senior captain in the fleet, you understand?'

'You are, however, two things,' the governor smiled. 'The most renowned and popular captain and first officer in my navy, with a fearsome reputation, and the only one currently in port. Now get to work, Jaral.'

'Of course, Excellency.'

The captain turned on his heel and strode from the room, Ghassan hurrying to catch up, still shaking his head in amazement.

'Captain, what does this mean for M'Dahz? Do you think the Prince Ashar will be leading an army or a fleet back from the north to retake Pelasia? If he does, what will happen to my town?'

'Calm yourself Ghassan. I realise that you've always wanted to go back to M'Dahz and personally behead that sack of shit satrap but, whatever may happen to the town, Ma'ahd has been living at Akkad for years now, controlling the throne. He may be beyond even your reach there.'

Ghassan nodded glumly and Jaral gave him a fatherly smile as they left the hall's foyer and the doors were closed behind them.

'We'll have to head back to the ship as soon as we're done here and inform them of the change in status and orders. Then I'll have to look for somewhere appropriate in the port to set up a headquarters; we can have staff and equipment sent to the ship in the meantime.'

'I presume, sir, that the crew will have a few days' shore leave until the other vessels have all arrived and you've set their orders and are free to come back out?'

Jaral laughed.

'Hardly, Ghassan. I'm going to be a little busy from now on and, from what the governor said, we'll need to get the ships out and patrolling as fast as possible. I'll need to be on top of the situation at all times, with reports from every ship that comes in, changing the groupings and position of the navy as required. Gods, I may even need to put in a request to construct or buy more vessels.'

'But...'

'Ghassan, you're more than capable of captaining the ship and you know it. Just make sure you follow the orders I give you and don't go off on one of your personal crusades to hunt down Ma'ahd or your brother. There are other things to be done right now.'

Ghassan shook his head.

'I'm not sure how the crew will take it, sir.'

Jaral smiled.

'I think you'll find they've been expecting it for some time.'

In which events take a surprising turn

Things had been unsettled for some time in the palace. Asima had made the most of the last three years, but had been continually beset by difficulties. The Satrap of Siszthad had taken no interest in the harem, finding his entertainment in less reputable directions. As a result, things had become static among the women. With no master or husband, the women were not required to leave their harem, were even forbidden to do so. In this stilted, lifeless situation, Asima had taken to playing games with her fellow inmates, turning them against one another and watching the resulting mayhem with interest.

Causing discomfort among her rivals was her only diversion, though, and even that had begun to pall after a few months. After all, she was at the pinnacle as it was, and playing the game repeatedly when you'd already won was no fun at all.

She had wondered whether, given Siszthad's notorious preferences, one of the other two important satraps would come to the harem to take a woman, but they had not done so. On one of the rare occasions, half a year ago, when a guard had come to the building on a chore and had shown a little humanity to the women, Asima had quizzed him about the three satraps.

She had been surprised initially to learn that Siszthad had led an army across the sea to track down Prince Ashar and strike a deal with the Lord of Velutio. It had seemed strange for the little piggy hedonist to embark solo on such an impressive military campaign, but then it would have been the other two pushing him into it, and Asima was sure they considered their figurehead King to be thoroughly expendable.

The dark-skinned nomadic satrap apparently already had a harem of wives he had brought with him from the desert as he 'despised' the softer, lighter women of the coastal regions.

And as for Ma'ahd? According to the guard, Ma'ahd simply had no time for them. He was busy effectively ruling the country and planning expansion, and that left few hours for frivolities.

Life had become dull, but still Asima kept herself alert; on the edge. When things were quiet, in her experience, it was almost always a prelude to busier times. And, indeed, it would appear that busier times were arriving. This morning, one of the younger girls who was so far below Asima on the ladder that she felt almost friendly toward her had come with news that the palace was a hive of activity.

Asima, of course, had been blissfully unaware of this. Her apartment looking out over the sea meant that the only activity she ever witnessed in the palace were the guards patrolling the walls far below. The younger girls, though, desperate for excitement, had taken to hanging around the window that Asima and Yasmin used to frequent and others that were more readily accessible these days.

She had listened half-heartedly for a moment, reasoning that what the girl thought of as a 'hive of activity' could be anything, but it had appeared she was correct. The stables had apparently been emptied, the horses, camels and carts of the palace loaded up.

Asima had frowned and gone to her window. Sure enough, the guard had been changed. The common arrangement, to which she was now very accustomed, called for two guards to each stretch of wall, passing one another as they patrolled, with one more in each tower and more on duty below and out of sight. Now, however, there was one guard alone patrolling the two stretches of wall and three towers visible from her window.

That was why she now found herself standing like a sneaky child at the narrow window of the kitchens close to the harem's main gate, watching as the guard were paraded back and forth, kitted out for a campaign. Whatever Ma'ahd and his crony were up to, it would appear that it would take them out of Akkad and that could be dangerous for him. Even in such seclusion as the women now suffered, the mood of the populace was common knowledge. The ruling triumvirate was not popular, it seemed. Hardly a surprise, particularly given the respect that had been accorded the God-King Amashir.

Asima frowned as her eyes strayed from the marching soldiers to the heavily laden carts being marshalled in the gravel area between the public palace and the mausoleum. What in the name of sanity were they taking that weighed down so many carts?

Her frown deepened as two servants left the public palace, carrying something large toward one of the carts, under a sackcloth covering. As she watched in interest, one of them got their feet tangled in the cloth and it slid off. The large, filigree gilded shutters that protected the God-King's reliquary flashed in the sunlight.

Asima growled. Ma'ahd wasn't going on campaign; he was simply leaving and taking whatever he wanted with him. She scoured the grounds for more signs of the satrap's greed and suddenly spotted the man himself with one of his officers striding toward the main harem door not ten feet from her window. Holding her breath, she ducked back out of sight. The two were deep in conversation as they approached, but their voices were low and quiet. Asima strained to hear as the two men stopped outside the closed door.

'Will they leave the building, sire?'

'They'll have to, Siva. See to it. Let's make this quick. The storm approaches.'

Asima frowned for a moment. Storm? It was a perfect day. There…

She adjusted her thinking to the likelihood of a metaphorical storm. Something so huge was about to happen that Ma'ahd and his men were leaving Akkad and raping it of anything valuable. She allowed herself a small crooked smile. Ashar… that had to mean Prince Ashar. He was coming back for his throne.

Her smile slid a little. Things might be bad right now with that unpleasant pig on the throne and the two most callous satraps in the kingdom running things, but at least they had no opinion of her either way. Ashar, on the other hand, had never made any secret of the fact that he distrusted and disliked her. It would appear that she was about to be delivered from an uncaring captor by one who actively disliked her. What sort of choice was that? Moreover, where were they being taken? Ma'ahd and his ally held no interest in the women of the harem.

As the great doors of the harem rattled and creaked open, Asima's heart lurched and the colour drained from her face as she became sure of their fate. Ma'ahd was raping the city but had no interest in the women, so they would not take the girls with them. But he would leave nothing for Ashar. In the brutal world in which these satraps lived, a retreating soldier left nothing for the enemy.

The women would be killed, probably along with the servants of the palace. Then, very likely, the whole complex would be put to the torch, and maybe even the city, so that when Ashar arrived there was nothing but soot and wreckage awaiting him.

She realised she was growling gently. Her hand closed on something and she looked down in surprise. She had grasped one of the cleavers hanging from the rack above the heavy wooden bench. Now why had she done that? If she'd believed in Gods or fate, or indeed anything but her own will, she might have put that down to some hidden influence.

Smiling coldly, she walked quietly along the wall of the kitchens, parallel with the entrance corridor of the harem; a foot-thick wall all that separated her from the two men. She approached the kitchen door with a little trepidation and paused, listening. This portal led back out into the central courtyard of the harem beside the entrance passage. She heard Ma'ahd and his man stop nearby; heard the satrap clear his throat and begin to address the harem in a clear voice.

'Women of the royal bedchamber! We no longer have any need of you and the time has come for you to escape this prison. You are to be set free.'

Behind the decorative door, Asima snarled. She knew exactly what sort of 'escape' and 'freedom' the man was talking about. Well, she was not going to curl up and accept her fate quietly.

Outside she could hear girls rushing out of the doorways around the building and into the garden, chattering with excitement. Could they really be so dense and short sighted that they believed the masters of Akkad after leaving them to rot for three years actually intended to free them? Just how stupid were some of these women?

She heard a hoarse chuckle from the officer.

Without a plan; without forethought or even taking a breath in preparation, Asima ripped open the kitchen door and stepped out, directly behind the captain of the satrap's guard. In that brief moment she took in the entire scene. The women were filing out into the open square from which Ma'ahd addressed them. The guard officer was armed, but the weapon was sheathed; Ma'ahd likewise.

With no grace or elegance, Asima swung the heavy cleaver to her left, her eyes fixed on Ma'ahd and not even breaking her step as she tugged the gleaming blade back out of the man's neck, hearing the unpleasant sounds as it snapped a tendon and left the spine almost severed.

Behind her, Captain Siva of the palace guard, his eyes bulging in shock, collapsed to his knees and then, one hand going to the huge chasm in his neck, toppled gently forward, making gurgling noises.

The whole assault had been so brief that she had already taken her next swing before Ma'ahd, his eyes wide with surprise, had begun turning to see what had happened.

Her blow took off Ma'ahd's left arm just above the elbow, the razor-sharp, heavy blade continuing on to dig into his ribs. He stared at her, his mouth opening and closing as he registered the gruesome damage she had just inflicted on him.

The whole world, having slowed to a crawl for Asima as she dived into her assault with no thought and delivered her initial blows, suddenly sped up and left her in a minor panic. What in hell's teeth had driven her to do this? Before her, Satrap Ma'ahd was recovering his composure. The wound was crippling but far from fatal. He roared and reached around with his right hand to draw his long, curved sword.

Asima swallowed and sighed. No going back now; she had to finish it.

As the wounded tyrant began to draw his sword, the blade rasping against the metal edge of the scabbard, Asima kicked him in the kneecap with as much force as she could muster. There was a satisfying crunch and, sword still half sheathed, Ma'ahd cried out in pain and fell heavily on to his back.

Now they were fighting on Asima's terms and not his. Like all of her plans, carefully constructed over many years of harem life, this one had to be played out in the appropriate steps, and carefully. First: the element of surprise. Well, she'd accomplished that easily. Second: leave nothing for your victim to use against you.

Taking a deep breath, she drew back the cleaver and let it fall with all the power she had behind it. The satrap, agonised and in shock, floundering on the floor with a missing arm and a shattered knee, could do nothing but watch in horror as his other arm, hacked off above the wrist, scraped across the gravel and came to a halt beneath a decorative rose bush.

'What?' he managed, blood bubbling around his lips as he managed to speak in a wheezy whisper. 'Why?'

Asima smiled and the effect made the satrap recoil as far as his position allowed.

'You invaded our town, burned our homes, killed our people, turned on your own country and usurped your King, among many other failings. There are countless reasons, I'm sure, why people want to see you dead, Ma'ahd. But not me. You see, I have changed since the days you sent me away from M'Dahz.'

As she spoke, she stooped and finished the job of drawing his curved sword from the sheath, flinging the cleaver, covered in viscera, into the bushes away from them. She became aware of the horrified silence that filled the garden and the increasing proximity of some of the other women, who were slowly closing in from behind her. They were hardly a worry.

'Quite simply, Ma'ahd, you took a happy young girl and turned her into me. For that I suppose I should really thank you. I am far stronger and more powerful than I could ever have hoped to be as Asima the merchant's daughter.'

She paused in her speech for a moment to bring the long curved blade down in a precise blow that severed his other leg below the knee. The satrap shrieked. Third step: make sure you have them exactly where you want them and there is no escape.

She turned and the women approaching her stopped in their tracks.

'I'd wait there, ladies. I'm rather enjoying myself and I don't know whether I'll be able to stop at two.' She licked her lips hungrily.

Without paying any further heed to them, Asima turned back to the maimed and bloody mess below her. He was flailing, but not a single limb remained intact to obey his brain's desperate commands to flee this mad woman.

'No.' Asima stated flatly. 'I've long ago got past hating you. I'm sorry if it bruises your ego, your lordship, but there are girls in this building that I consider more of a threat than you. No... I couldn't have cared less about you.'

She gave three light slashes with the blade, delivering random cuts across the man's torso, eliciting new cries of agony.

'No. This is quite simply self-preservation. I will not go to my death, Ma'ahd. Some of these women may be stupid enough to think you might free them, but the only thing I'm not sure of is whether you would have had us shot full of arrows or simply locked us in a shed and set fire to it.'

And the last step? Make sure the game goes on long enough to enjoy it. She delivered a few more painful cuts. He was bleeding quite profusely now and his face had become gaunt and grey, the hollows of his eyes taking on a purple tint.

'More even than that, you see. Prince Ashar never liked me much. I don't think I'll thrive under his reign, but I may be able to begin closing the gap between us when I present him with your neatly severed head on a bed of rose petals.'

Without taking her eyes from the groaning heap below her, Asima gestured over her shoulder with her free hand.

'You girls... get me a few hundred rose petals and a silver serving dish. Satrap Ma'ahd's reign is over.'

The last thing the mighty Satrap Ma'ahd, power behind the throne of Pelasia and conqueror of M'Dahz, ever saw was the happy grin on the face of a blood-spattered beauty as she went to work, sawing through his neck with his own sword and whistling a lullaby as she did it.

In which borders are redrawn.

Asima stood glowering at the new King of Pelasia. Ashar, calm and collected, leaned back in his seat and placed his feet upon the table in a relaxed fashion.

'I understand you have a problem, Lady Asima.'

She eyed him coldly and nodded.

'I am well aware of the fact that you do not like me, Majesty. I never expected to fulfil the same place with you as I did your uncle, but this is madness. It flies in the face of tradition!'

Ashar laughed lightly.

'Tradition, Asima? You would lecture me on Pelasian tradition? Unless I am mistaken you are only partially of our blood, born and bred in Imperial lands. Who are you, really, to take the high ground with me?'

Asima grumbled.

'I am the woman who dealt with Ma'ahd for you and prevented you returning to a ruined city. At least give me that.'

Ashar paused for a moment, a thoughtful look on his face.

'I will give you that, yes. I do not believe for a moment that it was motivated by selfless honour, rather than self-preservation and personal gain. It so happens that our goals coincided for a time.'

He sighed and sat forward once more, cradling his hands on the table.

'Asima, the world has changed. Pelasia has changed. For all their greed and wickedness, the three usurpers have changed the role of the Pelasian ruler forever. I shall not be a God-King; merely a King. I also have no need of a coven of women to fulfil my desires. There is only one woman I have ever wanted, and she and I will see out my reign together. I am disbanding the harem and that is all there is to it. You should be glad.'

'Glad?' Asima said, her voice rising with a dangerous edge. 'Majesty, I was plucked from a comfortable and innocent life, put through hell and managed through my own strength to claw my way to a good position. And now you, ostensibly the hero of this little play, wish to take that away from me again. What do you intend to do with all the noble and delicate women you cast aside and make homeless?'

Ashar smiled.

'The ladies of the harem will be given estates and titles. I have no wish to see my uncle's wives go without. Nobody will suffer as part of this... rearrangement.'

Asima settled to a quiet simmer.

'Well at least that's something. We can continue to live appropriately for members of the royal court.'

But there was something about the smile on King Ashar's face that she didn't like.

'I think you'd better take a seat, Asima.'

'I'll stand.'

'Very well,' the King continued, straightening. 'I have just concluded a treaty with the Emperor Darius. He really is a very amenable young man. As well as supplying a sizeable force to help me retake Pelasia, he has given me a number of trade and political concessions and has asked for almost nothing in return; just the return of certain territories claimed by my predecessors.'

Asima frowned.

'You are giving M'Dahz back to the Empire?'

'Yes. It is the least I can do. In fact, it was never worth fighting over in the first place. I suspect it was only ever intended to be a staging post for Ma'ahd's rebellion. Yes, Asima, I am returning M'Dahz to the Empire. I am also making unsought reparations for damage and trouble caused by the presence of Pelasian control. We will supply funds and workers for rebuilding.'

'Can you afford that? You've still got to rebuild parts of Pelasia.'

Ashar raised an eyebrow and Asima was suddenly acutely aware that she had fallen into a very informal mode of speech with a very powerful man. Ashar shrugged.

'The money and workers are coming from the estates of those we have overthrown.'

Asima nodded.

'If my father is alive, would your majesty be kind enough to inform him of my situation and to ask him to come to Akkad?'

Ashar folded his arms.

'That won't be necessary, Asima. I've no doubt you'll see him soon enough.'

He noted the confusion on Asima's face and smiled.

'When I said that the ladies of the harem will be given estates, I was referring to the Pelasian ladies, Asima. You can call yourself whatever you wish, but you are a girl from M'Dahz and as part of the reparations, I intend to send back there anyone who was forcefully taken by Ma'ahd. You're going home, Asima.'

He watched her and gave a light chuckle as he saw her face drain of colour before filling once more with pink as anger replaced the shock.

'You can't!'

Ashar grinned and tapped the circlet on his brow.

'I believe you'll find, Lady Asima, that this says I can. You can go home to your family and friends.'

'But I'm not that person anymore, King Ashar! I'm one of you now. I've been here since I was young. I may have been an Imperial girl, but I'm a Pelasian woman!'

'What you are, Asima, is a dangerous woman. I am mindful of the fact that my uncle was very fond of you and that it is in all probability our fault that you have become this untrustworthy, twisted and self-seeking creature. That is why I intend to send you back in style, with money and a guard. I have no wish to see you suffer Asima, but I also have no wish to see you here any more.'

'What?' Once again, her voice raised a notch as she approached the table and slapped her hands down on the wooden surface opposite the king.

'You are too troublesome and dangerous to keep around, Asima. I do worry a little that setting you loose in Imperial territory probably violates some part of the non-aggression treaty I have just signed, but that's all there is to it. Don't fight me on this, Asima. You're going home. Accept it.'

The strength seemed to go out of Asima and she deflated slightly where she stood.

'Do not make me beg, majesty. I am Pelasian and all I want is to stay. Send me to another city if you must, but do not send me back home. There is nothing in M'Dahz for me.'

'I'm sure your father would be proud to hear you say that, Asima. You must go, for the peace of my realm and the security of my throne. Take some time to go through everything. You may take whatever you wish and have time to say your goodbyes if there is anyone in the palace that you have not manipulated and alienated in your time here. In three days you leave for the border and from that moment on you are forbidden from ever again setting foot on Pelasian soil.'

Ashar eyed Asima's hands on the desk where one had, quietly and unnoticed, begun toying with a letter opener in the shape of a knife.

'Even when you are unaware of your actions, you are dangerous, Asima.'

Reaching across, he took the small knife out from under her fingers and sheathed it.

'Now go and prepare yourself.'

In Calphoris, everything was chaos. Ghassan, captain of the Wind of God, strode through the governor's palace gates, acknowledging the guards as he passed. He was becoming well known to them all now. The Imperial commissioner and his party had arrived yesterday and within an hour the raven flag of the Empire had been raised above the palace, the port and all the city's gates.

Over the last week or so, Ghassan had seen almost nothing of his former captain. Jaral had been busy in his new headquarters building, dishing out orders and charters to captains and mercenaries as though they were at war. Curious really, since Calphoris was currently more at peace than at any time in the last quarter of a century.

He smiled and brushed aside the curl of black hair that made his brow itch. For some reason he never seemed to have time to get his hair cut these days and nothing he tried ever stopped the floppy curls from doing exactly as they pleased. Straightening in a military pose, he strode across the compound, saluted the guards at the palace door and climbed the white marble steps. With practiced ease, he trod the corridors of the great building until he arrived at the audience chamber of the governor.

He stopped at the entrance and waited. One of the guards knocked at the door, opened it when ordered from within, and announced the young captain. Ghassan heard the governor shout him in and, smiling at the guard, ducked past and entered. Jaral stood at the wide desk with the governor and several people he didn't recognise.

As he strode toward them, he sized up the four strangers. One was a thin, reedy man with a large nose, dressed in grey robes; clearly an administrator or bureaucrat from Velutio. Another was a heavy-set, bearded man in uniform; likely the captain of the ship that had brought them here. The other two were a peculiar couple. A young lady, slightly built and heavily pregnant, sat on the governor's chair, while her hand was held by a man with a missing arm and missing eye wearing a uniform, with a tiger pelt over the shoulder, that clearly denoted high rank.

In a very military fashion, Ghassan approached the table, came to a halt and saluted first the governor, then Jaral, and finally the two uniformed strangers.

'Your Excellency sent for me?'

The governor smiled at him.

'Indeed, Captain Ghassan. As I'm sure you've already guessed, this is Minister Fulvis of the Imperial government, here to go through the details of reintegration with me.' Gesturing appropriately, he introduced the others. 'Captain Harald of the "Steel Claw", Marshal Tythias of the southern provinces, and his lovely lady wife, Sathina.'

Ghassan tried not to stare at the Marshal. It could be considered extremely rude, given that this was one of the most powerful men in the Empire. There was something vaguely hypnotic about the network of old scars on the man's face and staring was practically a requirement. He almost heaved a sigh of relief when the scarred commander smiled.

'Captain Ghassan. I hear good things about you. I'm overseeing the reorganisation of the militia in the south. As you may be aware, the Imperial army and navy have been fully reconstituted. I am taking command of all the forces in the southern provinces and intend to set up my headquarters here in Calphoris.'

Ghassan nodded professionally, trying to hide the sheer pleasure of the discovery that the militia were to become part of the Marshal's forces.

'Beneath me, I have Pharus, who is being promoted to general and placed in charge of the Province's ground forces and, on the recommendation of the governor here, I am accepting Jaral as commodore and commander of the navy. All current militia forces, both land and sea, will be reassigned to the appropriate service branches.'

Ghassan nodded once more.

'I understand, sir. I hope we will live up to your requirements.'

Marshal Tythias smiled his strangely warming, broken smile.

'I have no doubt, young master Ghassan. However, you've been sent for specifically for two reasons: firstly, I am reliably informed that you are both the best and the luckiest sailor in Calphoris. I approve of the former, but the latter is just as important. I myself am only alive through the judicious application of luck.'

He took a deep breath.

'And secondly, because of your... affiliations.'

Ghassan frowned, confused. The Marshal sighed.

'Captain, we are trying to get things back to the way they were under the old Imperial bureaucracy. With our position here and new trade treaties with Pelasia, we hope for a significant increase in mercantile activity. And that means the suppression of what has been called a 'plague' of pirates in the waters north of here.'

Ghassan swallowed nervously; trouble was marching his way. The Marshal smiled sadly.

'I am informed that one of the more notorious of the pirate captains is, in fact, your brother. Under normal circumstances, the very last thing I would do is attempt to pit you against him. However, Commodore Jaral assures me that not only will you not allow your filial situation to come between you and duty, but that you are probably the only man capable of both outthinking and out-sailing him.'

'I will not, even as your commander, order you to do this...' the Marshal began.

Ghassan saluted and straightened.

'You don't have to, Marshal. Samir may be my brother, but he needs to be removed. I understand that.'

Tythias nodded.

'Good. Thank you, captain. I will leave the matter in your hands.'

Ghassan saluted again.

'Is there anything else, sirs?'

The governor shook his head, and Ghassan nodded, turned on his heel and strode from the room. It was an unhappy task, but they were absolutely right. Samir had to be taken out of the picture for the good of the Empire.

In which a homecoming is suffered

The eight Pelasian cataphracti in their gleaming fish-scale armour came to a halt, four to either side of the coach. The driver waited, his horses stamping and snorting, while the escort commander approached the gate, requesting permission to enter. Asima leaned out of the window of the coach, glaring at their destination.

Even from here, where she could only make out the basic details of the soldiers, all in Imperial green, she could feel the animosity being projected at the black and steel clad soldiers. The Pelasian military, despite Prince Ashar's excellent relations with the new Emperor, were not a popular sight in beleaguered and oppressed M'Dahz. The people had enjoyed only two weeks of freedom since the Pelasian withdrawal and here were a unit of that land's elite cavalry at the gate. Unpleasant memories would rise, unbidden, to the fore in every citizen who saw them.

There was a brief discussion at the gate and the great wooden portal swung ponderously open. Asima sighed. In her youth, the walls of the town had fallen into disuse due to the uninterrupted centuries of peace. Now, even the gates remained shut.

Irritably, she ducked back inside and pulled across the curtain as the coach began to roll slowly on once again. Throughout the interminable journey across the barren landscape between central Pelasia and the borderlands, she had pondered and thought, planned and schemed. There was no way she would settle back in M'Dahz, but the current situation in Pelasia for her was untenable. Ashar had forbidden her from returning.

And so the plan had been born. It was ambitious; probably Asima's most ambitious plan of all time. It would take a few years and a lot of planning, sprinkled with a judicious topping of luck. But it could work. King Ashar only maintained his hold on power in Pelasia through the respect and fear of the other nobles. The coup of the three satraps had changed things there forever. The ruler was no longer unreachable and immortal, and Ashar knew it.

So she would find a way to return to Pelasia through a different noble house. Half a dozen powerful satraps had lands stretching east toward the Imperial border and Asima knew that, if she had nothing else in the world, her looks and her brains alone could carry her to the top. She would find a way back across the border, entice and entrance one of the powerful nobles and use him to ingratiate her way back into court in Akkad. Ashar would never dare order one of his more powerful satraps to lose a wife.

The first thing to do would be to settle back in M'Dahz and wait for around half a year, living quietly and unobtrusively. She may even change her name; it might be expedient and give her an edge when she broke the rules and returned to Pelasia.

As she pondered, she heard the change in tone when the wheels of the carriage passed from the dusty, rocky sand of the desert road to the flagged streets of M'Dahz. Despite the fact that she no longer considered this flea pit her home and wanted nothing more than to be away from it and back to her beloved Akkad, she would have to spend some time here and had to admit that curiosity was getting the better of her. She pulled back the curtain.

They had passed through the Akkad Gate and were trundling along the main street toward the centre of town and they became the focus of attention to all as they passed. The evidence of M'Dahz's return to Imperial control was everywhere. Imperial banners flew over the towers of the town. The propaganda for the reign of Ma'ahd on the walls to the town was being removed carefully and painstakingly by the citizens. Colour was returning, slowly but surely.

But every face turned as the coach with its escort passed by. Every worker stopped in the middle of their task; every child or mother exiting a side street came to a halt. And every face hardened; every eye took on a look of intense hatred. Asima fumed. She could understand why they felt what they did, but it was so futile. These weren't the same men who'd conquered this town. The man responsible for their misery was dead, by her hands no less. These miserable wretches should be thanking her; throwing petals before her. She had avenged them all!

The more she looked out, the more irritated she became. She had been forced into exile back in this dismal place and the people here were going to hate and resent her. Her anger rose to a climax as they reached the end of the long and level street and turned right, heading up the hill inland. On the corner, between the streets, stood the Pelasian temple with its tower. The building had been a landmark in M'Dahz as long as Asima could remember and had figured in their rooftop chases as children.

At some point in the past few days, revenge for the Pelasian occupation had been carried out on the temple. The white plastered walls were charred where the flames had licked out of windows and doors. The entire building had been gutted, and heavy wooden beams propped up the tower, which was leaning at a precarious angle.

She growled quietly to herself and settled back into her seat. From the directions the coach was taking, they must be heading for the palace complex of the town's governor. Remembering the day she was taken from here, she found herself wondering who was in charge of M'Dahz now. Still grumbling unhappily, Asima sank back into the seat and walked herself through her plans once more as the carriage trundled on up the uneven street.

Several minutes later, she heard the cataphracti rein in their horses and the carriage rolled to a halt. There was conversation nearby and, curiosity getting the best of her, she pulled back the curtains once more. The small party had stopped in the plaza before the gate of the palace complex. The escort captain was speaking to a small group of well-dressed men by the entrance and, from the sound of the rising voices, there seemed to be a problem.

Everything else and now another problem? Asima ground her teeth. She'd been thrown out of this place and sent to an unfamiliar country, only to be then sent back once she'd become so thoroughly native to Pelasia that she would never fit in here again – and now there was *another* problem?

Before she had time to decide whether it was a good idea or not, her anger had driven her to fling open the coach door and storm out into the bright sun, directly toward the group.

The Pelasian captain, his helm clutched beneath one arm while his other hand was busy making argumentative gestures, turned in surprise at the sound, as did the others with him.

'My lady. Please return to the coach. I am dealing with matters.'

Asima snarled at him and turned the most vicious glare she could muster on the tall, thin and elegant man in his silks and satins; clearly the new governor and, from his paler skin tone, just as evidently an Imperial import from across the sea.

'Be quiet, captain. I have had enough of this,' she barked without looking at the soldier.

Ignoring the blustering noises from the startled captain, she narrowed her eyes at the governor.

'I can assure you, Excellency, that I have no more wish to be here than you have for me to be. However, I need a comfortable place to bide my time until I can get out of your hair once again. I will cause you no trouble and stay almost completely unnoticed as long as you can provide me with a few things. Firstly, I need to see my father.'

The governor, far from being taken aback and meekly acquiescing as she'd expected, straightened and looked down his nose at her.

'Young lady, I do not care how you were trained in Pelasia, but here we expect a modicum of manners.'

He watched her intently for a moment and squared his shoulders.

'I checked into matters very thoroughly prior to your arrival and I'm afraid your father passed on a number of years ago of an illness. Secondly, as effectively a foreigner with no familial connections in M'Dahz and no property here, I am not particularly disposed to putting myself out for you. In the spirit of cooperation with King Ashar, I have agreed not to turn you back at the border but, as I'm sure you would soon notice, Pelasians are not well regarded in M'Dahz at the moment and I cannot guarantee your personal safety while in the town.'

Asima frowned. For some reason, the news of her father's passing had hardly touched her at all. She found herself more concentrating on the other focus of the conversation.

'Then may I ask what you intend to do, governor?'

The man folded his arms and nodded.

'You cannot stay here, young lady, and you are clearly not welcome in Pelasia, so I have made alternative arrangements for you.'

Asima's frown deepened and she pursed her lips.

'Other arrangements?'

The governor nodded and gestured to the leader of the cataphract unit.

'Your task is complete, captain. I will take responsibility for your charge now.'

The captain saluted and turned with, to Asima's shrewd eye, just a little too much relief for her liking. She glared at him as he strode to his horse and climbed slowly into the saddle under the weight of the heavy armour. Ignoring the escort as they wheeled their horses and trotted away, she eyed warily the small unit of white-clad gubernatorial guards as they marched out purposefully toward the carriage.

'Explain,' she said flatly. The governor shrugged, unconcerned.

'You are a courtier, so I am sending you to court. In a little less than an hour your ship leaves for Velutio and the Imperial capital. You will be both safe and comfortable there, and may find a number of other Pelasians there at any given time.'

Asima's mouth fell open. She was, for the first time she could remember, completely at a loss for words. Conflicting emotions and ideas raced through her mind. She knew nothing about life in the Imperial court. Certainly they wouldn't have such things as harems and concubines there. And it was cold. They said it was so cold sometimes in Velutio that the rain came down in lumps. Asima hadn't experienced rain in her life until she settled in Akkad and even there it was a gentle, warm and refreshing thing.

Of course, Velutio was, if anything, a more powerful place full of more influential people even than Akkad. There could be possibilities, but it would require a complete readjustment of her thinking, and she would have to start from scratch.

She realised she was standing like an idiot, her mouth flapping open and closed. Angry with herself, she shut it and tried not to grind her teeth. The look in the governor's eye was resolute. She would be on board that ship whether she accepted it or not and so, as had always been her way, she grasped the situation and made it her own.

'Very well, your Excellency. I can see that you have covered every angle and have my safety at heart. Would you ask one of your guards to make sure that my luggage is transferred from carriage to ship carefully? I have a number of breakable things with me.'

The governor nodded.

'I hope that Velutio sits well with you, young lady. I have spent many happy years there and for a young noblewoman with money, there are many entertaining diversions.'

Asima nodded and turned toward her carriage to see a new group of men alongside the governor's guards, busily checking over the carriage. For the second time in as many minutes, Asima's jaw dropped.

'Asima?'

Ghassan blinked.

'Is that really you?'

Asima found that words just wouldn't form on her tongue. She was silent as she stared at the tall, muscular naval officer before her. There could be no doubt that it was him. The floppy black curls that fell over his brow took her straight back to those days of running over rooftops and sneaking into warehouses.

'Ghassan?'

The young man nodded, still staring at her. She suddenly became aware that the governor had stepped forward next to her.

'Captain? You know the Lady Asima?'

Ghassan shook his head in wonder.

'I knew her many years ago, Excellency, yes.'

The governor nodded.

'Then if your ship is ready for the tide, you will have plenty of time to become reacquainted.'

Asima continued to stare as the ghost of her past formed up his men.

In which a journey is undertaken

Asima frowned as her eyes ran up and down Ghassan once more. It was so clearly him, and yet at the same time he had changed so much. The serious, tall, curly haired boy had grown into his look and suited the uniform of a naval officer, for certain. And while she couldn't fathom what series of events had led him from the streets of occupied M'Dahz to captaincy in the Imperial navy at Calphoris, he was obviously born for this life.

He seemed at ease and had acquired that natural rolling gait of the practiced sailor. Moreover, he appeared to know every peg and rope on the ship personally and every man aboard, even those three times his age, looked up to him and treated him with respect and trust.

But then, she would have changed as much to his eyes.

She dropped her gaze to the aperture in the wooden hull and the water rushing past outside and chided herself for even beginning to get sentimental over her childhood friend. They had hardly had a chance to exchange a dozen words in these first few hours out of port, with Ghassan constantly occupied on duty. Now, however, he'd come back to the room set aside for her in the covered housing at the rear of the Wind of God, poured two glasses of high-quality wine and sank into the seat opposite, silently waiting for her to initiate conversation.

The problem was that she just had no idea where to begin; wasn't even sure she wanted to begin. More than half of her life had passed since she had last set eyes on the brothers and she had changed beyond measure. In other circumstances, she might have considered reaffirming an old friendship, but not now.

Digging deep into the well of her being, she was a little surprised to find that the sudden appearance of someone once beloved from her past had almost entirely failed to move her. Once the initial shock had faded, rather than fascination or a desire to catch up, what she found herself wondering was how she could use Ghassan to her advantage?

The greater surprise had been that the realisation that she was truly that shallow and quite possibly now incapable of love, empathy or sympathy had not, in fact given her any cause for concern. Not only had her soul hardened to diamond, cold and impervious, but she was at ease with the fact. Life was a game and needed to be played to win.

Finally, uncomfortably, Ghassan broke the silence.

'I'm so sorry about your father.'

'Mmm?' Asima looked back from the sea, her wandering thoughts sharply reeled in and shut away where they could be contained and protected.

'I asked around and he'd lived well after you left,' Ghassan continued. 'He was looked after, but an illness of the gut settled in and the doctors could do nothing.'

Asima frowned again and shook her head, changing the subject.

'And what of you, Ghassan? Why the navy?'

The tall, curly haired captain shrugged.

'A series of unpredictable choices. Samir and I both vowed to free M'Dahz and kill the satrap, but I think Samir knew we wouldn't agree on how. I went to join the army and then turn them on M'Dahz. Samir left me and ran away into the criminal underbelly of the town.'

He sighed.

'And now M'Dahz is free, and I wasn't even involved. All my plans to launch a rescue for the town and its fate was decided by politicians a thousand miles away. I would feel deflated, but it's just not the all-consuming goal it once was. The military's given me purpose and, now that it's part of the Empire again, it feels like I'm helping to build something.'

Asima nodded sagely while actually only half listening.

'And I've persuaded the governor of Calphoris to request extradition of Satrap Ma'ahd for his unwarranted invasions and executions. Given the alliance between us now and Ma'ahd's involvement in the coup, I'm sure the new king will agree, and then I'll go collect him myself and deal with him in public.'

Asima looked up and was impressed at the cold viciousness she could see in his eyes. Ghassan was about to be sorely disappointed.

'You may have a little trouble there.'

Ghassan narrowed his eyes.

'What?'

'I'm afraid Ma'ahd won't be sent here. He is not imprisoned by Ashar. He never got the chance.'

The young captain stared at her and she sighed, putting on her most sympathetic mask.

'If it's any consolation to you, I can tell you two things. One is that he died horribly. He suffered from beginning to end, and was never buried, but cast from the city walls in Akkad. His remains lay on the rocks by the sea until they were eaten by scavengers.'

She noted a certain satisfaction settle over him. This could easily play to her advantage.

'And secondly, it wasn't during the civil war. He died at my hands in revenge for what he did to all of us. One of us did it, Ghassan. It wasn't you, but it might as well have been.'

She smiled at him as she watched a mixture of disappointment and righteous satisfaction war for control of his face. It was a lie, of course; revenge had not even figured in her motivation. She'd have been quite glad never to set eyes on M'Dahz again, but it would have been a plausible motive, had she any use for morals and nostalgia.

'He died badly then?'

Ghassan's voice sounded almost pleading.

'Very. In fact, if you wait, I have a gift for you.'

The young captain frowned and watched as Asima unfolded her legs and wandered across to her bags. She began to mutter to herself quietly as she delved into one and produced, after much rummaging, a small purple pouch of velvet and gold. Returning to her seat, she sat once more, crossing her legs, and clicked open the catch on the pouch.

Upending the container, she held her hand beneath to catch the two things that fell out, wrapped in silk and tied with a delicate gold ribbon.

Her face grave and serious, Asima passed over the two small parcels, one crimson and one aquamarine. Ghassan frowned at the items in his hand.

'Open them,' Asima urged, pocketing the pouch.

Ghassan chose the smaller of the two parcels, gently untying the ribbon and unwrapping the blue silk. He stared down at the object within the folds of shiny material. A ruby the size of his thumbnail stared back up at him, cut, shaped and immaculate, and representing more than a year's pay for anyone on board.

'What is this?'

Asima smiled and there was something about the expression that Ghassan wasn't sure he liked.

'It's a pommel jewel. I took it from the hilt of Ma'ahd's sword when I'd finished removing his head with it. Call it a keepsake.'

Ghassan stared.

'This is worth a fortune, Asima. You might need this in Velutio.'

She laughed, but the laugh had an edge.

'Ghassan, you really don't know me at all, do you? That is a bauble; a mere bead compared with some of the precious stones I liberated from their imprisonment in Akkad. I could buy this ship with one jewel, and not even the largest one.'

Her smile vanished instantly.

'Though I trust you will honour my wishes and keep their existence a secret?'

Ghassan frowned at her and then nodded.

'I think you'll maybe like the other one more,' she added.

His frown still in evidence, the captain began to unwrap the second parcel and almost dropped the contents as they fell into his hand, causing him to lurch in surprise.

From within the red silk, a gleaming white, fleshless bone finger pointed accusingly at Asima.

'What?' he managed, his voice hoarse.

'Another little souvenir. It's his; Ma'ahd's.'

'You kept his finger?'

Asima laughed and once more Ghassan was unnerved by her expression.

'Better. I kept the whole hand for a while.' She smiled wistfully. 'But I had to trim things down and travel light when I left Akkad, so I just kept a couple of fingers for luck.'

The captain stared at his passenger and then shook his head in a mixture of disbelief and revulsion. He suddenly felt so alone. He'd been looking forward to a chance to talk with Asima; to catch up on the events of so many years and now he found that she was far from the person he remembered. She had hardened; become cold and vicious. He found himself thinking of Samir and his life of crime and murder and wondering how, of the three children that had raced across those dusty rooftops so long ago, he seemed to be the only one that had reached adulthood with a sense of morals and principles of which their parents would be proud.

He frowned again. Asima had not flinched at the news of her father's death. She had not brought up the subject of Samir; not even asked where he was or what he was doing. Ghassan realised with a start that any trust he had in her had evaporated in the past few minutes, and he began to feel for the unsuspecting nobles of

Velutio who were about to have this calculating woman dropped upon them.

'Ghassan?'

He looked up and realised that Asima was watching him.

'I'm sorry, Asima. Thank you for thinking of me, but I don't need these gifts and, I'm afraid, I don't really want them.'

He turned and gestured at her with a waved hand.

'Have you lost touch with who you were so much that your father's death is meaningless? You've not even asked after Samir…'

Asima shrugged.

'I would have got around to it. One thing at a time, Ghassan. To do anything well, you must prioritise.'

She stood and started to walk around the room, waving her hand to accentuate her words.

'I am Asima, Ghassan. Maybe not Asima the poor merchant's daughter from M'Dahz, but the Lady Asima, wife of the former God-King of Pelasia, first woman of the harem and, until recently, the most powerful woman in Pelasia.'

She pointed an accusing finger.

'You expect me not to change in almost twenty years, Ghassan? You have changed, so why not me. I had to survive and, in the name of all that remains, I did so and I did it damned well!' Her voice had dropped to a hiss.

'And Samir? Of course I know about Samir. That ship of his is as infamous in Pelasian waters as it is in yours. And he always did think faster than you, Ghassan. That's why he's still out there. How many times have you tried to corner him? How many times did you think you had him before he slipped out of your grasp like water from a leaky cup.'

She snarled and slapped her hands down on the table.

'I do what I must, Ghassan. So does Samir. Only you are so weak that you hide behind your flags and regulations as you flounder around, unable even to catch your brother with half the world's military power behind you.'

She fell silent, staring down at the table. She appeared to focus on something for a moment and then her mood changed like a sudden squall. She glanced sidelong at the stony face of the now bitterly angry captain; the target of her tirade.

'I'm sorry, Ghassan.' She gave him a weak smile. 'I've had a tough time and life is not very easy for me at the moment. I shouldn't take it out on you. Forgive my harsh words.'

Ghassan continued to glare at her as she returned her gaze to study the map on the table beneath her hands. An interesting archipelago lay between her thumbs and this, if she was reading the map correctly, was looming in her near future. She turned to regard Ghassan again and the captain straightened.

'Thank you for your time, Lady Asima. I shall not disturb you again until the evening meal is prepared. Rest well.'

Without a word, he cast the bones and the jewel onto the bunk and, turning, strode from the room, allowing the door to shut with a loud bang behind him. Asima sighed. Had she gone too far? She needed him distant, but not too distant. New plans… plans within plans. Now, where was that archipelago?

In which Asima makes her presence felt

Asima peered from the viewport in the side of the room. She had been alone most of the time since her 'conversation' with Ghassan when she came aboard, the only interruption being the delivery of her meals by one or other of the crew. Apparently the captain felt disinclined to join her to eat, but that was better for Asima anyway. It had taken around an hour and all of her considerable mental faculties to fathom the arcane naval charts on the table, plot the distance to the archipelago, estimate the ship's speed and therefore how long it would be until they reached the string of small islands. Having embarked on the afternoon tide, the Wind of God should pass the archipelago in the middle of the second night.

The interminable hours alone in a small, bare room were then mostly spent irritably tutting as she went through all her packages. It had been galling enough when she left Akkad stripping so many years of her life's acquisitions down to three large cases. Now she realised it would have to be just one, and preferably the bag, which was easily transportable. Refining what she needed and what she could realistically do without was a task of several hours on its own.

Finally there had been the time spent listening to the orders and the heavy footsteps above and outside, peering out of the door and along the corridor to the deck when she felt she needed more information. To work out routines and schedules by sound alone was a difficult task, but Asima had achieved more during her time in the harem.

The first night had been very informative with respect to the crew's night time schedule. The second morning, she had braced herself and left the room, ostensibly to stretch her legs. Ghassan had glared at her when she appeared on deck and had assigned one of the oarsmen to escort her. She had made a great show of enjoying the sea air, stretching and relaxing, and had shown an interest in the workings of the ship, as she would no doubt be expected to. In fact, she was very interested, but only in certain aspects. How sails were set or oars were stored was of little value to her. Other parts, however…

And then she had retired to her cabin once more to settle in for the day and finalise her plans. The hours had passed tensely for her as the naval vessel bounced lightly across the waves on its journey to the great city that was the centre of the Empire and the start of her life of imposed exile in obscurity.

Now, the moon was bright and shining down on the water, making the waves glitter and dance, which worked both for and against her plan, but then she could hardly control the heavens. Squinting out to the horizon, she confirmed what she thought she saw a minute ago. Marked on the charts, 'Eagle Rock' was one of the standard naval navigation markers and stood at the near end of the closest island in the archipelago. She smiled to herself. Predictably, 'Eagle Rock' was identifiable from here, rising aquiline above a low spit of sand.

That eagle marked the arrival of the archipelago and the departure of one prickly passenger.

Hoisting the heavy bag onto her shoulder, she glanced down at the other two, open on the bed and messy and dishevelled.

With a sigh, she tapped the hilt of the knife in her belt with her free hand and gave a last quick scan of the cabin to make sure she hadn't forgotten anything. She hadn't, of course. Asima was nothing if not thorough.

Nodding with satisfaction, she opened the door of her cabin as quietly as she could, the faint creak going unnoticed among the many other creaks and groans of a ship under sail. It was almost midnight and most of the crew would be asleep. The oarsmen were bedded down in their temporary sleeping rolls in the flat space between the benches in the lower deck, their oars up and locked, out of the water. The ship slipped quietly through the sea, rising and falling gently, carried by a light wind, slowly but continually.

The only crew still active on deck would be two or three of the more senior men above her current position, maintaining course and speed, lookouts in the bow and atop the mast, and two or three ordinary crewmen padding around on watch where the oar benches lay empty overnight. The only light kept aflame was at the rear where the officers worked.

Asima peered out into the corridor from her door at the end. The rear of the ship supported what was, in essence, a partial extra deck. Most of the ship consisted of a hold in the bottom of the hull, with a deck of oar seats and ports above, and then the main deck, with two more rows of oar seats. The centre of the ship, however, boasted a raised timber castle-like structure housing the war machines, while the rear held an enclosed section of cabins with the rudder and command section atop it.

There were only seven rooms in the covered area, five occupied by the most senior officers, one for medical use, and one for dining. Asima had been given the captain's cabin and everyone had shuffled down a room for the duration of the voyage. She frowned at the corridor as she held her breath and listened.

No sound came from the two nearest rooms, while the second door on the left hummed with the sound of gentle snoring. The last cabin and the sick room were silent, but the noise of laughter and activity issued from the dining hall. The door there was slightly ajar, yellow light illuminating the medical bay door opposite. There appeared to be a dice game going on within, along with a lot of drinking.

Taking a deep breath, Asima crept as quietly and quickly as she could down the corridor. Silently, she slipped past the beam of yellow light, catching a momentary glimpse of men at the table within who were paying no attention to the corridor.

Heaving a sigh of relief, she continued on to the end of the corridor. Pausing, she peered out through the doorway. The door itself had been jammed open with a wooden peg, allowing the warm and fresh night time air to circulate in the interior. The sounds of several dozen sleeping sailors rose noisily from the deck below, adding to the creaking and groaning of the ship. If anything, the vessel was actually noisier at night than during the day.

For a brief moment, as she grasped the door frame and prepared to put her plan into action, Asima experienced doubt, a thing that happened so rarely it gave her pause. Was she being foolish? It was possible she could make a comfortable life in Velutio; certainly she would be a great deal more welcome there than in Pelasia or M'Dahz. Could it be that she was choosing the difficult course when she could make a life in the north?

She shook her head, angry at her own weakness. She had no intention of living out her days in exile in a place where the wind chilled the bones and rain was a regular occurrence. And the weather was only a small part of her reasons. The Imperial capital would already be full of people who knew the local game so much better than her. She would stand precious little chance of getting close to the Emperor or his companions and she would likely end her days as some strange, foreign refugee existing on the periphery of court life.

Ashar's ban or not, Pelasia was the place for her. It was in her blood and in what was left of her soul. And the realisation of that in her first few hours aboard had prompted her new scheme. If three satraps; a vicious one, a greedy one and a virtual nomad, could pull off a coup that almost changed Pelasia forever, imagine what she could do. Given a malleable satrap with good connections and a sizeable estate and military, she could put him on the throne within a year; two at the most, and on his own, not as part of some triumvirate.

And Ashar really did have to die. He'd set himself against her and, despite her earlier deluded schemes to ingratiate herself with him, it was clear when she thought about it objectively that he would have to go in order to pave the way to power. Whatever changes to her plans might be caused by unforeseeable events, one thing was certain: she had no desire of a future in the Empire. Pelasia was for her.

Nodding to herself over the correctness of her decision, Asima ducked out of the door and turned a sharp right, around the outer lip of the deck around the cabin section toward the stern. She held her breath once more. The ledge was only a foot wide and a slip here would end in disaster.

Slowly and carefully she edged along the ledge, watching the turbulent waters below with care. Fortunately, the cabins she had passed on this side of the ship had all been silent and apparently empty, so she had no concerns over being seen through a window. It was above her that was the problem. There would be several men on the upper deck busy keeping the ship on course.

Very slowly, she shuffled along the ledge, occasionally feeling her foot slip and grasping the thin rail that ran around the wooden cabin housing as though her life depended upon it, which, of course, it very well could. Every tiny slip sent her thumping heart into her throat and made her want to cry out, though she clenched her teeth and continued on in silence.

A murmur of conversation made her halt and pull herself tightly against the wooden wall. Above her two men approached the railing and stood for a moment discussing something technical that completely bypassed Asima's understanding. She stood perfectly still for long moments, willing the two men away, until they appeared to reach some sort of conclusion and then wandered back to the centre of the deck.

Asima allowed her breath to escape slowly and continued to edge round the ship, reaching the stern rapidly now. She took a peek around the corner and found that what she had seen through the window in her rear cabin was, indeed, the case. The huge rudder that was easily handled by a single man on the top deck was one enormous beam, flattened out at water level to give the strength to guide the vessel. It was attached to the stern by a hinged wooden contraption and safety rope that allowed it to pivot and move freely while remaining firmly under control.

She had studied it for some hours through the window but had been unable to actually reach it from there, hence this night time journey around the dangerous edge of the ship. The Wind of God had been on active service for quite some time since her last sojourn in dock for maintenance, and nowhere was it showing the strain more than here.

'I expect you have to carry a lot of spare parts?' she had asked her escort this afternoon, probing lightly, but he had informed her that they only carried bulk spares of rope, timber and sail cloth. Certainly not anything as complex as the hinged mechanism she now found herself closely examining as she closed on the rudder.

The course had been set as soon as the Eagle Rock had come into view and the rudder locked into position at the top. That needn't matter and, in fact, would prove beneficial, meaning that no sailor would be close enough to the rear rail to notice her work.

Her assessment from her cabin had been correct. The two wooden struts that held the rudder into the hinged mechanism were long past due for replacement. One was white with age and had been seriously attacked by salt and weather. The other had already snapped, though the damage had gone unnoticed as the safety rope continued to hold it together.

However, if the other wooden spar went…

Reaching the mechanism, Asima grasped the shipward end and drew her knife. Inserting it into a natural stress crack in the wood, she began to slowly and carefully work the solid, heavy blade back and forth. She smiled as she felt the wood beginning to give easily under her assault, and small flakes and fragments of ruined timber twanged off and floated down into the water.

She sighed with relief as she realised that this was going to be considerably easier than she had initially estimated. There was a quiet crack and a large piece of the strut disappeared down into the waves. Just a moment longer…

She almost lost the knife as the strut split with the last push, grabbing madly to retrieve it. The effect was more sudden and obvious than she'd expected. Though still attached by the rope, the lack of any solid support had allowed the rudder a great deal more leeway than before. With a crack, it slipped sideways as far as the restraints would allow.

The whole ship lurched and banked with the new direction of control and Asima was almost thrown from the ledge, the starboard side of the ship rising alarmingly. She heard shouts of alarm from above and knew she had only moments.

Flinging caution to the wind, she ran along the narrow ledge, trusting the new raised angle would push her further aboard rather than tipping her over. She reached the corner and flung herself around it, grasping the rail for safety just as the heads of the sailors above appeared at the upper edge, desperately trying to see what had happened to the rudder.

She grinned as she realised she had done it.

The ship's manoeuvrability would suffer badly, and it would not be able to continue across the open sea with the rudder floundering around. By her estimate it would take some serious work with ropes and all the strength of four men to keep the course steady enough to get anywhere to repair it. Ghassan would have no choice but to make for the nearest port which, according to the chart in her cabin, lay some three miles along the island's coast from the Eagle Rock.

The rest should be easy. Once the Wind of God was in dock, she would have the easy task of slipping away into the small town. It would be Pelasian territory and there would be fishermen with sailing boats that could take her from island to island until she found herself on the mainland and away from Ghassan and his principles. Passage would be easy to buy with the riches she carried, as would the silence of anyone involved.

She would shortly return to Pelasia to plan her rise to prominence and Ghassan would have to head back to Calphoris and be disciplined for his failure. Unfortunate for him, but he must be used to failure by now and, besides, he shouldn't have got in her way.

She…

Asima's smile fell as she reached the end of the narrow ledge and turned the corner back toward her cabin and came face to face with a burly sailor.

Momentarily, she considered knifing him and tipping him overboard, but decided against it. Not only did he carry a heavy belaying pin that he may be able to hit her with first but also, if she attacked him and failed, she would compound her guilt in Ghassan's eyes.

Whatever happened, they would still have to put in at the island and she would find a way to leave. Nothing had changed.

In which the reunion is completed

The young captain growled angrily and Asima merely shrugged.

'I could lie to you if it would make you feel any better, Ghassan. Perhaps I heard a dangerous crack from my cabin. Not wishing to disturb the poor, hard-working crew, I risked life and limb to make my way out to the source of the noise and try to help. I barely made it back with my skin intact when the thing gave way just as I approached.'

She smiled with the most unpleasant falseness she could muster, right down to the curl of a sneer on her lip.

'Does that make you feel better, captain?'

Ghassan stood and stared out of her cabin window. The sun had been up for a little more than an hour now. He had refused to order his men to carry out any work in the conditions the previous night, what with the darkness, slippery wood and the ship lurching every few moments. As soon as dawn crested the horizon, though, he had sent three men down to the rudder to completely remove the damaged hinge mechanism and tie the pole tightly in place. The Wind of God bobbed on the calm sea, drifting as the current took it.

'What did you hope to achieve?'

Asima shrugged again.

'I have no wish to visit Velutio and I believe the word you're looking for, Ghassan, is sabotage. You'll have to put in at the nearest island and I will find a way to leave, whatever you do to contain me.'

Ghassan snarled at her.

'You stupid woman! You risked your life and ours because you are so damned spoiled that you will have your own way whatever the cost? Just how selfish have you become, Asima?'

She allowed her sneer to remain while the smile fell from her face.

'Your words mean nothing to me, Ghassan, because you mean nothing to me. I have been mere steps away from becoming one of the most powerful queens the world has ever seen and I will have that again, despite the interference of mindless soldiers.'

Ghassan laughed without a hint of humour.

'Well I'm afraid you've failed this time. I have no intention of putting to port. It will take the best part of a day for my chief carpenter and his men to work up a replacement and a matter of hours to fit it. By this time tomorrow we will be on our way once more.'

He turned and pointed angrily at her.

'In the meantime, you are restricted to your cabin. It will be locked from the outside and your window will be barred, even though I doubt you would fit through it. The only contact you will have with the crew is when Palas brings you your meals and you've never met a more straight-laced and unfriendly man than Palas. He will have none of your charm. Were it not for the fact that you are supposedly a noble guest and I am duty-bound to look after you, I would have you locked in one of the equipment rooms down below in the dark.'

He smiled his least humorous smile.

'And if there is the slightest hint of trouble from you for the rest of the voyage, I will be seriously tempted to tip you over the side in chains and tell the commodore that you leapt to your death. Do I make myself clear?'

Asima flashed him a haughty and disobedient look.

'Just leave me. Your stench will remain in the cabin for days otherwise.'

Ghassan let his glare linger on her for some time and then strode from the room, stopping at the door, removing the key and placing it in the outside. As he shut the door and locked it, he addressed the junior officer in the corridor beyond.

'The Lady Asima is refused permission to leave her room. She will be brought three meals each day and once a day a boy will be sent in to replace her shit-bucket. Clear?'

The young man saluted with a nod and Ghassan strode angrily off down the corridor and out into the light. Eying the inactivity on the deck with frustration, he considered bellowing orders out to the lounging oarsmen to scrub decks or re-coil ropes. No use taking it out on them, though. They worked hard when needed and it was hardly their fault that his childhood friend had turned into a saboteur. What he'd really like to do was to cuff Asima round the ear and try to knock some sense of decency into her.

He turned, grumbling, and climbed the steps to the command deck. Half a dozen carpenters were at work near the rear rail, putting together a replacement mechanism for the rudder. He'd known it was on its way out, but it should have lasted the journey and Velutio had some of the most famous docks and shipwrights in the world. He would have easily replaced it within an hour at the capital.

Now, his men worked tirelessly to form a new one from bare chunks of wood with their saws, chisels and planes. He knew his men and was quietly confident that the new item would be finished and in position before the end of the day, let alone tomorrow.

Calamon, the first officer, nodded at him from the other side of the deck.

'Captain.'

Ghassan strode over to join his second. Calamon was young for the position, much like his captain, but had previously served with distinction and had done an excellent job in the last few weeks on board. The tall, olive-complexioned man was a native of Germalla to the north and spoke with an accent that still occasionally caught Ghassan out.

'Calamon.'

The two men stood, looking down into the calm water as shoals of fish came close enough to investigate the giant thing that had invaded their habitat. The first officer appeared to be a quiet man, possibly a result of the slight language difficulties, but he tended to keep himself away from the crew, often standing alone at the rail.

'You have questioned the princess, captain?'

Ghassan snorted.

'If that's what you wish to call her. She can call herself princess, concubine, queen or Goddess if she wants. What she is is a spoiled brat, and possibly the most dangerous thing we've ever had on board.'

Calamon's face dipped into a frown.

'I thought when she came aboard that you were friends, sir?'

The captain shook his head.

'We were, when we were children in M'Dahz; the two of us and my brother. But while I chose an honourable path and am making a life and serving a greater good, she appears to have spent the last two decades serving only herself and growing to resent everything else. When I was a boy I was always fascinated by tales of the Pelasian satraps and their armies, with elephants and armoured cavalry and their perfumed palaces and so on.'

He sighed.

'But I see now that Pelasia, whatever it is truly like, has ruined Asima; turned her into a spiteful witch.'

With a laugh, he gestured out to the northwest.

'I can only pity the poor bastards in Velutio that are going to get saddled with her for the next few decades. She's been on board for just over a day and she's already ruined my ship.'

Calamon smiled.

'Hardly ruined, captain. Think how much worse her sabotage could have been if she knew the first thing about ships…'

'I suppose.'

Once more the two men fell silent, staring out at the sea.

'Did you lock her in?'

Ghassan turned to regard his first officer.

'Had to. Why?'

'Very unpleasant with no fresh air, sir. Trapped in a room with a slop bucket. It's not as though she could do much during the day with the crew up and about, sir.'

Ghassan shook his head.

'At the very least she could make another run for it. I really wouldn't put it past her to jump overboard in her underwear and swim for the nearest island.'

Calamon opened his mouth to reply with a sly smile, but was interrupted with a call from aloft and his words went unsaid.

'Sail ho!'

The two senior officers snapped their heads back and peered up through the rigging. The boy at the top of the main sail was gesturing desperately out to the east past where the workmen dealt with the damaged rudder and off beyond the stern.

Ghassan and Calamon ran across the deck to the rear rail, hurdling the carpenters who sat cross-legged, working feverishly.

Shading their eyes and squinting into the low morning sun, they could just make out the shape of the ship ploughing toward them on a direct course.

'Tell me there are other naval vessels out this far, Calamon.'

The first officer shook his head.

'I'd seriously doubt it sir. Too close to Pelasian waters for anyone else, unless they're making for Velutio like us.'

'And that's coming from the wrong direction for a Pelasian,' Ghassan grimaced. 'Besides, I think the sail shape's wrong.'

As they watched, Ghassan started in horror to see a sudden flare as a mass of burning material arced up from the other ship and shot toward them across the waves, the orangey-green flare joining the bright glare of the sun for a moment before it crashed down with a splash into the water several hundred yards from the hull.

'How the hell did it get that close without the lookout seeing it earlier, captain.'

Ghassan grumbled.

'It's facing this way and coming out of the sun. We're lucky he noticed it that soon. Whoever that is, they knew we were here and they planned it carefully. And they're testing the range with their artillery, so they have no intention of treating this as a light engagement… they're out for blood.'

Calamon nodded.

'Pirates. Permission to stand the crew and the artillery to and get us moving as best we can?'

'We're barely manoeuvrable, Calamon.'

'Better barely moving than a stationary target, sir. If we sit here and wait, they'll find the range and burn us to cinders.'

Ghassan grumbled. The man was right. They had to at least try and manoeuvre their way into a better position.

'Alright, turn us into them. Use the oars as rudders like they used to do in the old days. Once we're on course, give me ramming speed.'

Calamon blinked.

'Are we not going to try and outrun them, captain?'

'We'd not succeed, Calamon, but at least if we close the gap we make it harder for them to bombard us and it'll come down to a matter of marine versus cutthroat. If we're really lucky, they'll turn as we get close and we'll manage to ram them. I doubt they'll be that stupid, but it's possible. The Wind of God has got a bit of a reputation, after all.'

The first officer nodded, saluted, and ran off to shout orders around the deck.

The oarsmen, woken rudely from their rest, ran to their seats and began very professionally to ship their oars. The engineers clambered into the artillery tower and started to arm, turn and crank their grisly weapons. Marines poured from the doorway below deck and formed up in the centre under their commander's gaze, settling their armour into place and readying their weapons.

'Oars to the water!' Ghassan bellowed. 'Get us moving! Bank to starboard with the steering oars and bring us about!'

Ghassan took a deep breath. As if he didn't have enough to deal with, now there were pirates, too. He stared up to the lookout aloft.

'Can you get any detail?'

'Not sure, sir, but I think it's the Empress!'

Ghassan rolled his eyes and slammed his fist on the rail. Of course it was the bloody Empress. What else could go wrong with this voyage? That at least explained how they'd managed to get into such a position. Samir must have found out they were taking on Asima at M'Dahz and shadowed them until they were in the middle of the open sea.

He slapped his forehead in amazement. Asima must be working with him. She'd effectively crippled the ship just in time for him to bear down on them with his artillery firing as he came.

There was an old superstition that having a woman on board was unlucky.

Certainly this one was.

In which captains clash

Samir frowned at the man in the bow, staring out into the blue.

'And you're sure it's her?'

'Sure as shit, sir.'

The captain of the Dark Empress shook his head in puzzlement.

'Then what the hell are they doing? Ghassan's a good sailor and has uncanny sight. He must have seen us by now, so why are they just wallowing like that?'

The lookout shook his head.

'Can't see anything wrong with her. Maybe they haven't seen us yet?'

'Well I wouldn't want to be accused of being all sneaky, mister Col,' Samir grinned. 'Let's wake 'em up.'

Turning away from the bow, he rushed across to the central artillery castle and pointed at the fire thrower.

'How close can you get to the enemy with that thing without actually hitting her?'

The artillery man shrugged.

'If we wait a few minutes, I can part their hair with it, captain… well, singe it anyway.'

Samir shook his head.

'I want to give him enough warning to face us properly. Fire a few ranging shots as we close.'

The burly engineer frowned.

'What for sir? Surely the less prepared they are, the better?'

'Not in this case. Every chance Ghassan's had to take me on, he's hit us by surprise and tried to trap us. He likes to think he's better than us, because he's working for the government, but we're going to extend him courtesies he wouldn't to us.'

'But why?'

'Because,' Samir grinned, 'when I steal his cargo and sink his ship, I want him to know he had every chance and we were simply better.'

The artillerist shrugged.

'It's your ship, captain.'

Turning away, he issued the commands to his men and the fire thrower was loaded and aimed quickly and efficiently. While they worked, Samir strode back to the bow. How the hell could Ghassan not see them? All right, the Empress had the sun at her back, but Ghassan was better than this, so there must be something else going on. Briefly, Samir wondered if his brother had laid some sort of elaborate trap, but there was nowhere close enough to hide another vessel. The archipelago was just too far away.

Shading his eyes, he peered at the naval ship, drawing ever closer. In minutes they would be on her and she just sat there like a dead fish, floating on the surface.

'Do you think…'

He was interrupted by a wave of the hand from the lookout, who pointed urgently. Focusing on the enemy ship, he saw signs of urgent activity. The deck burst into life and, as he watched, three banks of oars slid out of the sides of the hull and dropped into the water in perfect time.

'Ah. He's seen us. Now we can get this fight underway.'

The yards raced by as the Empress closed on her prey. As they bounced from crest to crest at tremendous speed, Samir smiled and watched the cumbersome ship begin to turn.

'She's coming for us now. For a moment I thought they might run, but Ghassan wants me.'

He blinked as he watched the motion before him.

'They're using the oars to steer. The rudder must be broken… that's why they were just sitting there.'

He turned to the lookout.

'How mean are you feeling, Col?'

The young man grinned.

'I'm always feeling mean as a sack of rats, captain. You know that.'

His captain returned the grin and called over his shoulder to the artillerist.

'Baeso? He's coming at us head on. If you're as good as you reckon, give me a shot along their port side with the heaviest load you've got, at the rear for preference.'

The man nodded without question and, making a few quick mental calculations, adjusted the range and angle of the weapon.

'Ready when you are, sir.'

'By all means, Mr. Baeso. Do some damage.'

The shot was, even for Baeso's high standards, expertly aimed and launched. Samir watched with no small amount of pride as the largest sack of boulders available in the turret was cast up and over the water with a massive thump and a roar. As with all such shots, the bag was designed to hold the ammunition together for only so long. By the time the sack had covered half the distance to the oncoming ship, it had split and the four heavy boulders were now streaking independently toward the Wind of God.

The first boulder hit the rail at the edge of the main deck close to the bow, sending shards of shattered timber and lethal foot-long splinters scything along the deck at waist height and causing a number of horrifying casualties. The second rock disappeared into the sea off the port side with a fountain of roaring foam. The other two boulders, however, ran true. The first hit the top bank of oars midway along the ship, snapping and cracking the wooden shafts and bouncing along the horizontal line of poles, smashing and shattering, until it disappeared with a splash. The last shot arced over, beyond the other three and came down with a crash through the steering oars, smashing them to pieces.

Desperate commands were being shouted over on the other ship, and the hull lurched and veered violently to port, presenting a board target to the Empress.

'This is too easy, Col.'

Turning, he gestured with familiar signals to the artillerist, who nodded and, with the help of his men, loaded another huge sack onto the catapult while another crewman lit the next mass on the fire thrower.

Without bothering to watch them, Samir signalled with his arm for them to fire when ready. There was a straining noise and then a heavy thump. As Samir watched, another expertly-aimed shot sent the bag flying in a high arc, much higher than the last. At its apex, the sack split open and a cluster of iron weights, sharp shards of metal and glass, and rods with pointed ends showered the naval vessel, tearing through the sails, splitting ropes, destroying the rigging and effectively crippling the enemy's ability to make sail.

Simultaneously, the fire thrower launched the ball of flaming material directly at the centre of the enemy ship. As Samir watched the flaming mass bear down on its target, he realised with a start that Ghassan's men had also launched their artillery. Not prepared yet for fire, they had relied on the catapult and the bolt thrower while crewmen presumably fetched the fire ammunition from secure storage. A two foot long iron bolt shot past Samir as he blinked in surprise, went straight through the chest of the junior officer behind him and continued on along the deck with such force that it decapitated another man and impaled a third, lodging itself in his chest and pinning him to the wooden housing at the rear.

It had been a lucky shot. The catapult attack was less so. Unable to get a clear aim with their listing and bucking vessel, the bag of boulders flew past, high above the deck. One of the boulders clipped the main mast while another ripped a section of rigging to shreds, but the damage was minimal.

Pulling himself upright once more in the wake of the assault, Samir noted with satisfaction that the central artillery tower of the naval ship was wreathed in a fire that was beginning to spread up the ropes.

'Heave to!' bellowed Samir and the crew began working like fury to arrest the ship's forward momentum. He nodded. They had to slow now or they would ram the enemy. Ghassan's ship was done for now, and Samir had no intention of allowing the Empress to go down with her.

He winced as he realised what was about to happen and put up his hands to guard himself just in case. As he took a deep breath, the combustible shot that had been brought from storage to the naval ship's artillery section succumbed to the heat of the flames dancing around it.

An explosion burst up like a sickly yellow mushroom at the centre of the enemy ship. Shards of wood flew in every direction and the billowing flames rushed up the edge of the sails as they caught. There was no hope now for Ghassan's ship. Most of his marines had been close to the explosion at the centre of the main deck. Samir would estimate their numbers at perhaps thirty on a standard vessel. A dozen at most made it to the rail, trailing flames and black roiling smoke as they dived over the edge and into the blessed water.

Samir sighed. He hadn't quite meant for that much damage. They would have perhaps five minutes before the vessel sank; certainly not enough time to loot the thing, not that Ghassan would be likely to have much worth taking.

As he stood, his gaze danced nervously around the enemy deck among the flames and the chaos, trying to spot Ghassan. Though he'd not really intended to cause so much death and injury, there was one man on that ship that he particularly did not want to see flaming and sizzling as he tried to reach the safety of the water.

The Empress slowed as she neared the blazing ship and finally came to a halt perhaps thirty yards from the wallowing mess.

Samir sagged and, though he kept his countenance carefully hidden from his own men, a smile of relief crossed his face as he spotted Ghassan stride straight-backed and formal from the cabin doorway.

What he wasn't prepared for was the fact that his brother was dragging another person by the arm; a woman no less. Samir frowned. What in the seven faces of Ha'Rish was a woman doing on board a navy ship? He turned.

'Col? Get two of the lifeboats lowered, have the men be armed and ready and get their survivors aboard as fast as you can.'

Col gave him a look of mixed pride and disapproval and then turned and ran off to pass on his captain's orders. Some of the men would not look kindly on having taken down the most famous ship in the Calphorian navy only to rescue its crew and for no prize. There may be comeback for it later, but Samir was prepared. Part of the Empress' reputation relied on the code of conduct with which they dealt with their prey. Besides, having removed their most relentless hunter from the game should be prize enough.

Samir waved an arm and noticed Ghassan turn at the gesture and drag the woman along the deck until they were at the rail only thirty yards away.

'Ghassan! Get your lifeboats down. I'll give you two of ours as well. Your crew can come aboard for now and they won't be harmed, so long as they surrender their weapons.'

For a long moment, his brother glared at him in silence across the lapping gulf, the roar of flaming sails creating a deafening background.

'Samir!'

The pirate captain frowned as the woman in Ghassan's grip called his name. Who could…

He almost fell over as he realised.

'Asima?'

'Samir! Save me. Ghassan's taking me away!'

Samir blinked and shook his head.

'Get aboard a lifeboat the pair of you, and fast. You've only got minutes!'

Indeed, as he watched, the listing ship was already tipping further as water poured into the oar ports. He bit his lip and watched in silence as Ghassan bellowed the order to abandon ship and the remaining crew ran to the boats, many of them taking a shortcut and diving into the water from the higher side of the dangerously-leaning vessel.

Samir watched with amazement and confusion as his once close childhood friends pushed their boat out away from the sinking ship and some of their companions began to row toward the Empress.

This was going to be interesting.

In which meetings and partings take place

Samir shook his head as he sat back in the chair in his private room on board the Empress. Outside, he could hear the survivors of the naval vessel being disarmed, stripped of valuables, and put under guard. Some of the men would be tempted to take out their frustrations on the men of the Imperial military; certainly most of the captains in Lassos would have simply left the men to drown, or even stripped them of anything worthwhile and then tipped them overboard. Samir, however, was well aware of the role that reputation played in survival as a pirate. The name of the Dark Empress and her captain were spoken with irritation and anger among the military but, with the record of mercy and honour they maintained, many of the ordinary folk felt a measure of approval for Samir. He had heard his name spoken with reverence in the back streets of Calphoris. Better to be loved by half the population than hated by them all.

'Ghassan, I have no intention of killing your men. They will be set adrift in lifeboats with ample room for them all and enough rations to see them all through until they can make landfall near Eagle Rock. Whatever you think of me, you know I am not a monster.'

The taller brother, his curly locks plastered to his forehead and a look of angry misery on his features, stayed silent, his gaze moving occasionally between his two childhood friends and gracing them with equal disdain and disapproval.

'Ghassan, they will be fine. You, on the other hand, will not.'

'You intend to do away with me, then?'

He almost spat out the words and glared at his smaller brother. Samir had to laugh at the ridiculous words.

'Don't be an idiot, Ghassan. In fact, I'm going to help you. If you go back to Calphoris with the rest you'll be at best left ashore to rot in the barracks thanks to the loss of your ship. It's far more likely, in fact, that you'll be disciplined and drummed out of the forces pensionless to go starve on the streets. That's where we came from, Ghassan. You don't want to go back there.'

He thought for a moment and then frowned. 'There is even the possibility that they will try you for your failure and deem you disposable.'

Ghassan grumbled but said nothing. Samir sighed.

'We could use you, Ghassan. You're a born sailor, like me. You had no small reputation yourself, 'til today. Come with us and avoid any unpleasantness at Calphoris.'

The elder brother opened his mouth to speak, his face bleak, but Asima interrupted, launching herself from the chair and slapping the flat of her hand on Samir's desk, crumpling a chart.

'Don't you dare take him on, Samir. This worthless husk that was your brother is a rigid golem following the rules of his foreign superiors without a thought for any of us. He doesn't deserve your mercy!'

'Asima?' Samir seemed genuinely taken aback. 'What are you talking about?'

'This pig was taking me against my will as a gift for some perverse nobleman in the capital. I was to be nothing more than a whore to some fat prince in Velutio. I begged him to turn round; to set me free...'

Ghassan was staring at her as though he'd never seen her before. He opened his mouth and made a croaking sound. Samir matched his expression as he boggled at Asima.

'All I want,' she went on angrily 'is to go home and this creature won't let me. Some superior in the military decided I'd make a nice gift for a friend and Ghassan is hardly going to save a girl he once loved if it means disobeying the order of some fat general half the world away!'

She fell silent and turned to look at Ghassan. With her face now hidden from Samir, she graced Ghassan with a wicked and humourless smile, before allowing an indignant mask to fall across her face once more and turning back to the smaller brother.

Ghassan stared in horror as Samir's expression hardened.

'I still extend my offer, Ghassan. You are my brother and, regardless of anything either of us has done, blood holds true.'

Ghassan blinked.

'You don't believe her?'

Samir shrugged.

'You are the most duty-bound man I've ever met, and you were on direct course for Velutio with Asima on board. Please do not try to deny anything, Ghassan. I would hate to have to listen to you embarrass yourself.'

'But she's lying, Samir. It's all she does. She's not a whore... she's a witch!'

Asima reeled in shock; fake shock, Ghassan was sure, but Samir seemed to be drinking it all in.

'You,' Asima spat, glaring at Ghassan, 'are going to get in the little boats with your crew and drift out into the sea. I would not wish harm on you, for the sake of our old friendship, but I have no wish to see you ever again.'

She turned to Samir.

'If he stays on board with you, then I will go adrift in the boats!'

Ghassan growled.

'You stay here with my precious brother. The pair of you deserve each other and I have no wish to stay on board with either of you. I would rather take my chances with the review board in Calphoris than share a single meal with you.'

Standing, he straightened, cast one unpleasant look at each of them and, turning, opened the door and left the room.

There was an uncomfortable silence after the latch clicked shut. Asima turned her face to Samir slowly, allowing him the full effect as tears welled up in her eyes and she began to shake.

Samir frowned, deep in thought.

'Dry your eyes, Asima. I will not send you to Velutio.'

Noting with interest a small flicker in her eyes, the young pirate captain stood and, reaching out, squeezed her shoulder supportively.

'Wait here. Pour yourself a glass of wine. I'll get the prisoners underway and then be back.'

Without further pause, Samir strode to the door, opened it, and left the room, closing it behind him. Asima took a deep breath. Ghassan was supposed to be the more easily-malleable one…

She poured herself a glass of wine and listened to all the orders being shouted to the prisoners out on deck. Her next move would have to be a good one, but she was sure she could manage it. Samir would take her back.

Outside, the captain blinked in the bright light and spotted Ghassan leaning over the rail, staring down into the waves and waiting for the pirates to finish searching his men and be ready for him.

Samir strode over and leaned on the rail next to him.

'I am truly sorry that it's all come to this, Ghassan.'

The taller brother grunted in reply.

'It was inevitable that one day we would meet and only one would leave. You must have known that; and you also knew that it was always going to be me… but that's a good thing. If you'd won, you'd be obliged to send us all to Calphoris to be hanged. I, on the other hand, am in a position to be magnanimous. I have no wish to harm your men.'

'Apart from the two dozen you burned and crushed in the attack!'

'Ghassan, don't be childish. That's regrettable, but unfortunately inevitable in war, and it's a war we've been in. Don't pretend you'd have done anything different.'

The soldier grunted another answer.

'It doesn't have to end like this, Ghassan. You can still come with us. I have thrown open an invitation to your men and I'm told that a few have accepted. Life at Lassos is good, brother. Better than a dishonourable dismissal from service and starving in a backstreet, for sure. Besides, I have an idea, and it involves you.'

Ghassan turned to Samir and the smaller brother was surprised to see that the look of indignation and anger had been replaced by one of gentle sadness.

'I can't, Samir. You have to understand. I may not always agree with what I'm to do, but I took an oath when I joined up. The only way I can leave the service is honourably and I'm bound to go back and report, whatever they do to me. A part of me would like nothing more than to say "screw it all" and abandon myself to life as a free man.'

He sighed.

'But that wouldn't be me. That's you, Samir. In a way, I envy you your freedom, even if it is a freedom from conscience, but that's not my way. You understand?'

Samir furrowed his brows for a moment.

'I wish there was a way I could persuade you.'

'Perhaps someday,' Ghassan replied sadly. 'But not today. Today I have to complete my duty and take my men home.'

Samir nodded his understanding.

'My offer will remain open should you ever wish to find me.'

He noted the pirates edging closer, waiting respectfully to take Ghassan to his men. With a sigh, he turned away but, as he did, Ghassan grasped his arm.

'Don't take your eye off Asima, brother. Do not believe a word that falls from her mouth. She is not the girl we loved. She has changed immeasurably and, I think, would sell both you and I for animal food if it got her something she wanted. She came damn close to destroying my ship before you even turned up. She'll play you and do the same to the Empress unless you keep her confined.'

Samir stopped and shook his head gently.

'I won't lock her up, Ghassan; not yet. She's not done anything to me yet. But I can see something in her that I don't like. Would you care to tell me the truth about what happened?'

Ghassan shrugged.

'It makes no difference. Just don't trust her. Get rid of her as soon as you can, for the sake of yourself, your ship, and your men.'

Samir watched sadly as his tall, proud brother turned and offered his hands, open and palms up, to the pirate captors. Shaking his head, Samir turned and re-entered his cabin, closing the door on his brother, the crew of the Wind of God and any hope, for now, of reconciliation.

Asima was huddled in her damp clothes by the table on a low bench, a goblet of strong wine clutched tightly in her hands. Samir nodded to himself and walked past her to retake his seat.

'Is there anything you would like to tell me, Asima?'

She blinked, caught by surprise and Samir was satisfied to notice her guard fall for just a fraction of a second. Asima may be good enough to hoodwink the straight-laced Ghassan for a time, but Samir could see how her façade was built and how to cause it to crack so that he could see past it to the real woman beneath. He was genuinely saddened to see what had become of his erstwhile friend.

'Oh it was horrible, Samir,' she sobbed. 'I was a captive in Pelasia where the prince hated me. I think it must have been him, when he became king, who persuaded the governor and the military to send me to exile with some unknown master.'

Samir's expression remained straight and unreadable.

'Hmm. Well, rest assured that I have no intention of taking this ship anywhere near Velutio or even Calphoris.'

Asima gave a little sniffle and threw him a weak, mousey smile.

'Thank you, dear Samir. Will you leave me in M'Dahz alone or will you come back with me?'

The captain of the Empress gave a light laugh.

'M'Dahz?'

He stood, a smile plastered across his face.

'I'm not taking you to M'Dahz, Asima. The next few weeks are going to be a little hot for us around the coast. As soon as the crew of the Wind of God reach any town, you'd be amazed at the speed the news of our victory will spread. Every naval ship afloat, Imperial or Pelasian, along with half of the mercenary warships out there, will all be looking for me.'

He laughed.

'I just sank a legend, Asima. There will be nowhere safe for me for weeks.'

The woman by the table frowned.

'Then what do you intend?'

'Well, I shall have to take you back to Lassos and show you the delights of the pirate island, won't I, Asima?'

She stared at him and he was heartened to see anger and astonishment battling for control of her expression.

'You what?' she screeched.

'Yes, I thought that might bring about an interesting reaction.'

Asima glared at him.

'I have no more intention of spending my life wallowing in the septic pit of a pirate hole than I do of accepting exile in Velutio. You save me from one hell, only to deliver me somewhere worse?'

Samir's smile was irritating her more than she could bear.

'Just drop me on an island somewhere with fishermen and I shall make my own way back, then.'

'Hardly, Asima. You are coming with me. You may be able to play Ghassan with your little games, but I am a match for you, Asima, and you know it. Accept the situation and make the best of it. I have my plans, do not worry.'

Asima fell silent, her glower almost burning into him.

Samir laughed out loud.

'Now are you going to be good, or shall I take Ghassan's advice and have you manacled to the hull now and save a lot of time?'

Slowly, quietly, Asima's breathing slowed and the fire in her eyes receded.

'Lassos then, for now. But be sure, Samir, that I am your passenger and not your prisoner.'

The captain nodded.

We shall see, Asima… we shall see.

In which Asima's beliefs are shaken

Asima, still glowering after days on board, had settled into her solitary life, keeping herself away from the sweaty, coarse crew, and equally from Samir, who seemed to have the uncanny ability to look straight into her mind. She had experimented, on the first day after Ghassan and his crew had been set adrift, with minor issues of rebellion and inconvenience.

The crew had seemed to be aware of her location and her activity at all times and the knife she had secreted in the dining hall had seen her escorted to Samir's cabin, where he had firmly but gently removed it from her and confiscated it. Sailors had stepped up to block her passage to parts of the ship they thought she had no business in. She had tried tantrums, tears and even seduction, all to no avail. In the end, she had resigned herself to making do with her situation until her range of options expanded.

And now, days later, she had at least managed to drum up enough interest in this legendary island to sit in the bow and watch as the landmass approached.

Lassos made the mind reel.

Used to the mainland shores, with their brown dust, heat haze and low rocks, the pirate island seemed alien and strange to Asima. At first sight it had seemed as though a cloud had settled on the water, wearing a dark, shiny skullcap. Closer to, the island was only two miles across at most and consisted almost entirely of precipitous mountain in green and grey. The whole place was enveloped in a thick fog that settled on the water and rose to cover the lower half of the island.

Asima could quite understand that on a day with fog any heavier than this, the entire island could well become invisible and that settled a nagging worry in her mind. Her life had taught her many things, but one of the foremost tenets by which she now lived was a total denial of Gods, magic, fate and anything she could not see, touch or manipulate. Even the idea that something was beyond her control unnerved her, let alone something beyond her understanding. Yes, obviously the legends of this mysterious hidden and vanishing island had been born from the thick enveloping fog that obscured the land unless one was actively seeking it.

And yet, something about the fog still unnerved her.

The ship slowed considerably as they neared the edge of the white blanket that shrouded their destination in damp silence and Asima saw the rocks for the first time.

Rising like jagged and broken fangs from the mist, the glistening black rocks took on a wicked, almost supernatural aspect. The first glimpse was impressive, but a truly breathtaking effect was afforded as the ship first entered the enveloping white. The cloying silence fell over the vessel, muting everything bar the occasional creak and groan of the ship and its rigging; even the crew worked silently. As the prow pushed into the eerie nothingness, it became evident that the reefs that surrounded Lassos were more than the occasional jagged spike. They thickened rapidly, creating a carpet of teeth rising from the dark water in an almost impassable pattern.

Asima drew a sharp breath. She'd had virtually no experience of sailing, despite having spent her entire life by the sea in one place or another, but a single glance at those reefs revealed no safe route between the shards. There was quite simply no hope of passing them, surely. She turned to examine the faces of the men on board. Each expression was one of intense concentration. She noted with fascination that few of the crew looked out at the rocks, keeping their attention locked on their work aboard.

Why would...

Asima blinked and touched her arm in disbelief. Surely this must be some kind of dream?

The closest rock, standing proud of the water, was now home to a figure in wet, grey, ragged robes. As she watched, stunned and vaguely frightened, the sleeves of the robe fell back and two thin, rubbery grey arms reached out imploringly toward the ship. The head rose slightly and two glistening eyes, reminding her of pools of water in the dark of the night, peered out from beneath the dripping hem.

Without intending to, Asima had taken two paces back, away from the railing.

Other figures swam into focus as she watched. One moment they weren't there and the rocks were bare; the next, ragged, wet, grey figures pleaded with her to do something about their horrifying condition.

Her initial shock quickly faded, however. Others, with deeply superstitious minds, may be paralysed with fright, but Asima was made of sterner stuff. Putting aside the natural fear of the unknown, she concentrated on the important things. It was curious... she never saw a figure appear. If she looked at a rock and then looked away and back, there would be a figure on it. But if she concentrated on a rock, nothing happened while she watched.

They could, of course, be some sort of illusion, but that would have to be something that affected everyone, given the reactions of the other sailors, and such a thing was unheard of.

The ship creaked on slowly and, as she watched, Asima realised that there was a channel through the rocks; hidden, complex and almost too narrow to possibly fit a ship through. The rocks with their eerie occupants came closer and ever closer.

No. Not an illusion. It couldn't be in her mind, since it was in everyone else's. Also, given the fact that the figures cast shadows on the rocks and the lapping waves plastered their robes to their ankles, they were solid. They were real. The reefs of the dead, she'd heard them called. But the dead didn't stand up or plead; the dead were lifeless husks returning slowly to the earth. So these were clearly something different that had never been encountered anywhere else and could not yet be adequately explained.

Satisfied with her more rational explanation, and with several minutes to go before the island would be in sight, she turned her attention to the ship itself. The sailors were busy about their tasks, bathed in the eerie silence. The officers...

Interestingly, it appeared that the crew had abandoned the raised command deck to the rear, leaving Samir alone with his first officer. Asima smiled to herself. Samir would be too busy with these rocks to spare time to drive her away. Taking a deep breath, she strode along the deck, paying no heed to the desperate grey figures reaching out to her as they passed.

A couple of the men glanced at her in mild surprise as she passed, though none made a move to stop her until she reached the ladder. She placed her foot on the first rung and a shadow fell across her. Looking up, she saw the shaved and tattooed head of the first officer as he leaned over the ladder from the upper deck.

'Top deck's off limits ta passengers, miss.'

Asima smiled coldly.

'Unless you intend to physically assault me, step out of the way, you painted donkey.'

The man blinked, clearly taken aback, and Asima continued to climb. From somewhere above, she heard Samir's voice.

'Let her up, Ursa. She's a special case.'

The huge pirate, clearly irritated at this suspension of the rules, stepped aside and glared at her as she reached the top and stepped out on to the command deck.

'It's alright, Ursa. I'll be fine. Go deal with the men.'

Again, the second in command grumbled in disapproval and threw an unpleasant look at her before taking the ladder down to the main deck.

'Come, Asima. I'm sure you'll be fascinated.'

Frowning, she approached the rear. Samir was directing the ship with infinitesimally small nudges of the huge rudder, and yet his eyes were affixed on the object in his hands, paying no attention to the ship or its surroundings at all.

'What is that?' she asked, pointing at the object he held.

He smiled and, as she approached, angled it slightly so that she could see clearly.

'This is one of the biggest secrets in the world, Asima.'

In his hands rested a bronze disk, around eight inches across, a flattened container with delicate and smooth glass on the upper surface. Inside, on a central pin, free to spin this way and that, was a human finger, dead and grey, but perfectly preserved within the case. Asima blinked.

'A finger. Your big secret is a finger? For this you keep your crew off the command deck.'

Samir shrugged.

'It's part of the rules laid down by the council of twelve. Only the captain and his first officer are supposed to know about the 'dead man's compass'. I trust my crew implicitly, but rules are rules. On some level, Ghassan was right. Without any rules there would be complete chaos. Even pirates need laws, Asima.'

'And this rotting digit helps you sail?'

Samir grinned.

'This is an almost unique thing. Don't ask me how it works, though. I've asked the cleverest people and studied it for a long time, and there's no reason I can see for it to work. But it does work; the dead man's compass shows me the route... I just align the rudder with this fellow's finger and off we go. I've never seen it fail.'

'Drivel.'

Samir laughed.

'Somehow I thought you might see it like that. But there are unexplainable things, Asima. Have you given up trying to memorize the route through the rocks now then? I presume that was your reason for sitting in the prow. I did that the first few times.'

Asima glared at him.

'The path is fairly clear, if narrow. Let's face it, Samir, as long as I note where the entrance to the passage is, I'd be able to navigate my way out.'

She eyed him slyly.

'Should I wish to leave, of course, that is. But then, you'll be taking me home soon when the sea is safe, so I have no reason to leave at the moment. Nice to know that I can, though; gives me a certain sense of security.'

Samir laughed.

'Is that right?'

The woman beside him frowned.

'You'll not break your word and keep me captive?'

Again, the captain laughed.

'That's not what I mean, Asima. I mean, are you so convinced of your ability to navigate the reefs without the compass?'

Asima shrugged.

'Hardly troublesome, particularly with a smaller vessel.'

Grinning like a naughty schoolboy, Samir pointed out over the rear rail, past the stern. Asima raised her eyes and followed his gesture.

Behind the vessel, a jagged carpet of impassable rocks jutted from the waves in every direction. Pleading grey figures occupied many of them, calling out silently to her. Asima frowned.

'How is that possible?'

'It's not.'

Again, Samir laughed lightly.

'Not everything has an explanation Asima and, since there are only two of these compasses in existence, shared by the pirate captains of Lassos, the island remains about as safe as it's possible for a haven to be. We could be found, but never captured, you see. And don't bother trying to track one of the rocks from the front of the ship to the back as we travel either. I've tried and failed many times. If you follow along the rail and try, it gives you an intense headache.'

His passenger's frown deepened as she looked back and forth between the rocks behind and the compass in his hand.

'And now you must keep me prisoner on Lassos, or kill me.'

'I hardly think so, Asima.'

'But you have told me and showed me your great secret. You have broken your own law. Even if you feel like flaunting the rules, I doubt your peers on the island will see things the same way.'

Samir shrugged nonchalantly.

'Only a few of us know that you know. Frankly, taking you to Lassos at all is going to cause havoc with the council, but they need a little shake up every now and then. You would be best to keep your mouth shut while on the island. I will not kill you, but many would just for knowing some of the things you do, so be careful with your mouth. As for when we leave here… well, let's say that I'm not telling you all of this on a whim. I have my reasons.'

Asima pursed her lips as she took this in.

'Very well, Captain Samir. What do we do now?'

He smiled.

'We're almost through the rocks. Then we dock in Lassos. I will have to report to the council and present you, then I and my crew go about our business. You, on the other hand, will stay on board the ship until I say otherwise. If you do go ashore, you will wait for me or Ursa and go with us.'

Asima frowned.

'Explain?'

'There are a number of very unfriendly individuals on Lassos. Most of my peers are not the gentlemen that I am. For your own safety I would advise extreme caution, but equally, you are my passenger, not my prisoner. You are free to explore the island in the brief time we will have there, but I recommend against it.'

He cleared his throat.

'Lassos can be a dangerous place.'

Ahead, the fog parted as the vessel reached the inner edge of the reefs. Lassos rose like the crown of a stone giant's head cresting the water, clouds clinging to the higher rocks and birds of prey circling.

'Very dangerous.'

In which we are introduced to Lassos

The Dark Empress bumped against the jetty for the final time as it came to a stop, sailors throwing lines and tying them off. Samir strode across to the rail and turned, gesturing at Asima.

'First things first: I need to present you to the council.'

Asima frowned and, shrugging, followed. The captain waited for the plank to be run out to the dock and then trotted lightly down it. His companion eyed it suspiciously and took a tentative step. The plank bowed alarmingly under her weight, a fact which irritated her immeasurably. Gritting her teeth, she hurried as fast as she dared down the board and onto the relative stability of the wet, slippery jetty.

Samir grinned.

'I feel it is important that I explain a few things about Lassos to you. I'm sure my reasons will become apparent in time. It's just as shame that Ghassan isn't here too, but that can't be helped for now.'

Asima frowned.

'You have become cryptic in your old age, Samir.'

He laughed.

'In my position, I am bound to keep some secrets and merely sensible to keep others.'

She grumbled as she carefully picked her way along the drier patches of the wooden jetty until they reached the end and entered the 'town', for want of a better word. The whole community nestled in on the low slope from the port to the point where the hill became more mountainous and rocky and even then other buildings clung to the edge of cliff like the eyries of eagles, with tortuous paths leading to their doors. There were perhaps a hundred buildings in all, of many different styles.

Most of the structures of the port area and the lower town were reminiscent of the architecture Asima was used to from M'Dahz and the borderlands of the desert. As the settlement ambled up the slope, however, the style changed notably. The buildings became larger and grander, and probably older. These would be the earliest remnants of permanent settlement on Lassos. The higher buildings were reminiscent of the architecture she had seen in books on the Empire and its great cities, all bricks and marble and columns and carvings. Others, higher still, hanging over precipices and looking out over the lower town were similar, but grander, with more marble and less brick; eastern, she had a feeling, like Germalla and its surroundings.

'There is nobody in Lassos who is not a pirate,' Samir said as he led her between various stacks of crates and equipment near the dock and toward what he probably considered a street. Asima had grown to adulthood in Akkad, with its clean boulevards. This looked more like the sewers that ran beneath that city but open to the air.

'Then who lives in these buildings?'

Samir shrugged.

'The council of twelve are permanent residents. Also, there are only ever two or three ships out at sea at any time. One of the compasses goes out with them to guide them out and home, while the other stays on Lassos in case of any trouble. Years ago there were three compasses, but one went down with a ship in an

Imperial naval assault. I suspect that there were once ten; one for each finger of whoever donated his hands...'

Asima nodded.

'So the crews of most of the ships live a relatively normal life here and occasionally the population changes when ships come and go? How many ships are there altogether?'

Samir gave her a sidelong glance.

'You sound suspiciously as though you're probing me for information, Asima.'

'Not at all. You suggested this, not me.'

'Very well,' Samir agreed. 'There are actually only a dozen ships at the moment. The number goes up and down, but rarely. New ships and crews have to earn a great deal of respect and trust before they can get close to Lassos, and most of the captains settled here are good enough that the chances of them being caught by the authorities are minimal. So yes, the town is occupied and run by sailors during their shore time.'

Asima frowned.

'Then there are no women here? I am going to be rather conspicuous.'

She was, too. Asima was becoming aware of the stares she was getting from people as they passed, some suspicious, others lusty. Samir grinned.

'Oh, there are women, but they all serve on the one ship. Most captains are very superstitious and don't like a woman on board. Captain Rianna is different, being a woman herself.'

Asima nodded in approval. It was a disgusting life of depravity and danger, living in squalor and filth, but it was good on some level to know that such awfulness was not purely the province of men.

'And you say these pirates are not reasonable like yourself?'

Samir laughed.

'I wouldn't announce that too loudly; some may take offence. There are two captains in Lassos that walk the path of mercy and reason; younger captains too and friends. I live in hope that one day the truly wicked men here will pass away and a new breed of pirate will be able to take control. Khmun, who was my captain, was the first of his peers to consider allowing an enemy crew to leave with their lives intact, but the idea is beginning to take root. Yes, two friends, to whom I shall introduce you presently. The rest you would do well to stay away from. Some of them may even consider rape and murder in public, with a face and body like yours.'

Asima shrugged. She had survived in places much more subtle and dangerous than this.

'I have no intention of letting myself reach that position, yet I would be grateful if you would allow me to carry a knife. I had one for protection, but Ghassan took it from me.'

Samir nodded.

'When we return to the ship in a few hours I will find you a knife, but be careful what you do with it. The murder of anyone on Lassos brings about the death penalty, and even a non-fatal attack will likely see you chained at the bottom of the harbour.'

His companion nodded and fell silent, taking in her surroundings as they climbed the street ever higher, past bristly, sweating men performing menial tasks, who stopped and watched as they passed. As she walked, with Samir reeling off names and facts, her mind wandered; she'd learned what she needed from him for now and had to think quietly.

The problem was that she was at Samir's mercy and that rankled, but she couldn't let it become an issue. Her plans had been shattered repeatedly, and Pelasia was further away than ever, but this was a temporary measure; an alliance of convenience. At least she was no longer bound for the north and Samir would take her back to M'Dahz, of that she was sure. She had to bide her time in the interim, stay low and cause no fuss.

And yet, there was something about the way Samir was acting and talking that made her pause. He was up to something and he was far more subtle and inscrutable than his brother. She would have laid Ghassan's mind open by now, like the entrails of a sacrificial animal, and been picking through his plans and motives. Not so with Samir. In time he would slip, or she would pry the information from him. She may have to sleep with him in time, but it was a small price really for his help and her continued safety.

She turned to him and nodded, focusing once more on his conversation.

'… and the captain of the Sea Witch took the last position on the council, and became the twelfth permanent resident of the island. He lives in that palatial place up there in the cliffs. Brooding, isn't it?'

'It is,' she agreed, nodding as though she'd been listening to his drivel all the way up the slope. To her surprise, Samir stopped. They appeared to have arrived at their destination. A large building in the classic Imperial style, with eight white marble columns fronting a grand portico, this must be the council that he'd spoken of.

With no ceremony, he strode across to the door and pushed it open, stopping and gesturing for Asima to join him. She approached with a little trepidation and followed him through the open door, conscientiously shutting it behind her. She was currently at the mercy of these people and would do well to try and get on their good side.

The hall they entered was impressive, but plain. For some reason, given the architectural style, Asima had expected something more grand and decorative. The hall was constructed of white marble or, as she noted with some satisfaction a crumbled area of wall in one corner showing its core, at least brick with a veneer of thin white marble to give a more noble impression. There was no furniture or decoration in the hall barring a single small wooden chair and desk to one side and a rickety bench by the opposite wall.

She had little time to ponder on the strangely disparate nature of the building, as Samir continued on across the room, gave a smart rap on the opposite door and, opening it, strode through, leaving it agape behind him.

'Masters of Lassos,' she heard him say as she hurried to catch up. 'I return with good news and a request.'

A cracked and ancient voice answered quickly.

'Your requests, captain, are always troublesome.'

Samir was nodding as Asima reached the door and entered, closing it quietly behind her. There were three tables in a 'U' shape here with twelve impressive high-backed chairs at them. The floor space between the tables was occupied with a map of the Sea of Storms and its surrounding lands, constructed painstakingly accurately from different coloured marble and stone. Strange markings had been made in places, presumably noting the location of important vessels or the sites of some great event.

Only three of the chairs were occupied. The speaker, a man of extremely advanced years, was clearly a Pelasian, a fact that took her somewhat by surprise. For some reason she had drawn a mental line that separated Pelasians from these people. The other two occupants were men in their late forties. None of them looked remotely pleased to see Samir or his companion.

'This woman is an old acquaintance of mine and no friend of the Imperial authorities, who was being held captive by them and taken as a slave to the northern cities. I intend to return her to her home in due course and beg leave of the council to allow her to stay on the island until then.'

One of the 'younger' leaders stood and slammed his hands on the table.

'We do not bring outsiders here, Captain Samir. You know the rules. You should have taken her elsewhere before returning. Now we should have her killed.'

'That was not possible, I'm afraid, Master Culin.' Samir smiled. 'She was being held captive on the Wind of God and now that that vessel languishes on the sea bed, it would be foolhardy of me to go to close to the mainland. Half the world's navy will shortly be searching for me. We can't afford to lose a certain item in my possession, after all…'

The three councillors fell silent and the speaker returned to his seat.

'That is good news, Samir. I wouldn't say good enough to offset endangering everyone by bringing her here, but good news nonetheless. The Wind of God was beginning to cause great concern to the council.'

'Do I have permission, then, to allow the Lady Asima to stay in Lassos?'

The councillors shared hidden looks and the elder rumbled for a moment before looking down his nose at them.

'She may stay on board your ship until the full council meets tomorrow. We will then decide her fate and consider yours. You are foolhardy, Captain Samir. Khmun paid the price for your adventures, but rest assured that we will not fall in with your lunacy. Return to your ship and wait there until we send for you.'

Samir bowed and, turning, grasped Asima by the arm, guiding her from the room. As the door shut behind them, she regarded Samir levelly.

'Not over-friendly. I fear they will weigh down against me and you will pay the price for bringing me here. We may both die tomorrow'

Samir shrugged.

'There are events set in motion, Asima, of which you know nothing. The council will almost certainly sentence you to death and exile me. These things needed to be done. Now we must stop in and see a few friends before we return to the Empress and I need you to be as charming as possible and preferably drop a few hints that you are full of very useful information. I am far from foolhardy. There are reasons for everything I do.'

Asima narrowed her eyes. She was sure of that... oh yes.

In which the Empress breaks out

Asima woke with a start. She hadn't meant to fall asleep at all, let alone as deep as that, but the hours spent at Captain Faerus' lodging had been warm and inviting and she had been 'encouraged' to drink considerably more wine than was good for her. It had taken every ounce of her self-control to hold her tongue and keep her secrets while playing the part Samir had asked of her.

The house had been prepared to celebrate the return of Samir. As soon as the Empress had appeared at the dock, Faerus had begun to crack the barrels of drink and sent one of his men out to gather their compatriots together. By the time Samir had arrived with Asima and a few chosen crewmates in tow, the alcohol was already flowing and more than a dozen men were laughing and singing.

The reaction to her presence was curious, with initial surprise giving way to suspicion. Then Samir had explained who she was, embellishing certain aspects of her history, such as her repeated captivity and her dislike of Imperial authorities. In Samir's words, she appeared to be a troubled rebel repeatedly surviving the hardships brought down by one government or another. Asima was once again impressed at the subtle ways the young captain's mind worked. When she thought about it, he had told no lies and left out few facts, while bending the truth to appear as he needed it.

To the other occupants of the room, she quickly became a figure of respect and would appear to have knowledge of the Pelasian navy and access to people in higher positions both there and in the Empire.

It had taken only moments for her to realise what he was doing. In the morning, the council would meet and Asima would be condemned to a watery grave as a danger to the security of Lassos. Samir may receive the same punishment or, at the very least, would be exiled from the island. However, by the time these decisions were announced, those who were already sympathetic with Samir and his politics would be aware that he had heroically removed the single greatest threat to the captains and their ships: the Wind of God. He would be a hero to them, which means the council would be condemning a hero to death.

Moreover, Asima was now known to have helped take down the ship by crippling her rudder. When combined with the impression that she was herself an outlaw with information that could be of great use to the folk of Lassos, the death sentence pronounced on her would likely create equal outrage.

Samir had used her to turn some of them against their own leaders. It was a masterly stroke, along the lines of things Asima had done herself.

The downside, of course, was that those who were outraged by all of this would still be vastly outnumbered by those who were loyal to the council and no great friend of Samir. He may have turned some pirates to his cause, but not enough to prevent their death once the announcements were made.

And that was obviously why mister Ursa, the bald and tattooed first officer, was gently shaking her awake now.

'Captain wants ya on the command deck, miss.'

Asima blinked wearily. This hardly seemed the same man who had glared and grumbled at her as they had first arrived yesterday afternoon. But then, Ursa had been present last night; had learned what the others had of her somewhat exaggerated past. By the middle of the evening he had begun to smile when he looked at her and, by the end, he'd been the worst of all culprits for force-feeding her the strong wine.

She had tried to tell Samir that all this alcohol was a bad idea, but he had insisted that it would be abnormal and unseemly to reject Faerus' hospitality.

Rubbing her bleary eyes and trying to ignore the insistent thumping in her skull, Asima stood and stretched. With a grin, Ursa draped a blanket over her shoulders.

'Cold out there, miss. Fog's in thick tonight.'

With a nod, Asima grasped the blanket and, pulling it tight around her, exited the cabin and walked the short distance to the ladder that led to the command deck.

She frowned as she eyed the deck.

There was a more activity that she thought there should be at night. The few visible crewmen moved silently, in much the same way as they had through the rocks. Ropes were being coiled and crates lifted aboard. The sight was made all the more eerie by the thickness of the fog that enveloped them all. She could barely see the bow of the ship, let alone the town. The jetty marched away on legs of oak into the blanket of white.

Turning, she climbed the ladder. Samir sat on a low wooden bench near the rudder.

'Ah, Asima.' His voice was soft, almost lost in the fog that settled creepily around the ship. 'It would seem that the Gods of weather are feeling kind.'

She tried to keep the sneer from her face and was only partially successful.

'You need fog?'

Samir smiled.

'It wasn't a necessity, but very useful, nonetheless. Makes things considerably easier'

Asima frowned, turned and cast her eyes across the rail. Sure enough, the jetty was slowly slipping away from them. Even in the moment she watched, she saw the end, jutting out welcomingly, disappearing into the all-consuming white.

'We're underway? I never heard a thing!'

Samir smiled.

'Just ten oars. Enough to get us moving but not enough to make a loud noise, particularly in the fog. With any luck, we'll be almost out of the harbour before we're noticed.'

Asima shook her head.

'What are you doing, Samir?'

The young captain smiled.

'Saving your neck, among other things. As I keep saying, plans are in motion. Well, I've now turned a corner and burned another bridge, to mix my metaphors.'

He noted the look of distrustful uncertainty on her face and his grin widened.

'The few members of my crew of whom I have never been entirely sure are back in Lassos, hopefully still drunk and unaware. The Empress now has a totally loyal crew. We will have a bounty placed on our head by the council as soon as they find out we've left, particularly when they realise that I've had to take one of the two compasses with me. But the leaders will lose a great deal of their support. I have friends in Lassos, Asima. The time of the council of twelve is coming to an end. Soon there will be only one ruler of Lassos.'

Asima nodded. Though he still had his secrets, some of his motives and plans were beginning to unfold and she could easily put herself in his position. Samir was more like her than she had ever imagined. Just as she planned and aspired to become an Empress in her own right, Samir had his sights set on total rule of

Lassos. Even now he was undermining the council and building a power base.

She smiled.

'You may just be the absolute opposite of your brother, Samir.'

For a moment, she pulled back as something dark and dangerous passed across the young captain's face.

'I wouldn't say that, Asima. Ghassan may be a little more law-abiding and strict than I, but we both have our ethics and codes of conduct. I recognise that there is some small similarity in the way our minds work, but I would advise against considering yourself my peer in any way. You are useful and our paths currently coincide, but make no mistake… I trust you less than any occupant of Lassos. They may by murderers, thieves and rapists, but they make no attempt to hide what they are. You can wrap yourself in as many layers of respectability as you wish, but I know what you are.'

He frowned.

'And you apparently bring out the worst in me, too. I brought you up here for two reasons. Firstly, you deserve to know what's happening, in case we are caught and captured or sunk.'

She nodded, her own eyes now flashing darkly. There was a tension on deck that could not be settled right now.

'Secondly,' he went on, 'I am now down by almost two dozen crewmen. I need lookouts. Take position over by the rear rail on the port side. As we leave harbour, any minute now, we'll have to pass beneath the rocks and I need you to warn me if we get too close. I can angle the bow correctly, but the current here pulls ships into a drift and if you're not careful the stern is turned into the cliff.'

Asima continued to glare at Samir through narrowed eyes for a moment longer, then turned and approached the rail, taking up position and peering into the white. The situation was as strange and unreal as any she could remember. The blanket of fleecy fog was so thick she could hardly see the water below the rail unless she concentrated extremely hard. The silence was oppressive, with the only sound the occasional creak of timber or splash of oar, and even that had to be listened for. Somewhere along the ship, a sailor coughed as quietly as possible; so quiet it should hardly be audible, but in this strange otherworld it seemed deafening.

And then the rocks were lunging at her through the fog and Asima had to summon all of her self-control not to cry out a warning. Turning sharply, she hissed through her teeth and pointed down toward the glistening black shard that marked the edge of the cliff and was drifting toward the hull at an alarming rate.

Samir's head snapped toward her and reacted instinctively without seeing the rocks, turning the rudder so that the Empress changed course slightly but rapidly. The rocks that had seemed so threatening a moment ago drifted past alongside the rear rail and Asima heaved a deep but quiet sigh of relief.

The heavy silence was suddenly torn apart by the sound of a horn from astern. Asima's heart leapt into her throat.

'Oars!' Samir bellowed, removing any doubt in Asima's mind as to what the blast meant. The silence exploded into noisy activity as dozens more oars slid out of the hull and dipped into the water, seeming momentarily disorganised until they managed to match the stroke. Asima stood rigid, wondering whether to go below again, when Samir turned to her.

'Keep an eye on the rocks… we've got to get closer.'

'Closer?' Asima said, astonished. It looked as though the oars would scrape the cliff any moment as they were.

'We have to hug the cliffs, turning to port until we're out of 'sight', so to speak, of the port. Then we strike out for the reefs, and we can get a few yards closer to them yet. Watch the oars and the cliff and when you see the spray from the oars touch the rocks we're close enough.'

Asima blinked as Samir yanked on the rudder and sent them banking left and back toward the cliff they had just rounded.

'That's crazy!'

Samir shrugged.

'That's the way it is. Any further out in the open water and… wait for it…'

As if on cue, somewhere above them there was a dull thud, followed by several more in sharp succession. Out to starboard, away from the cliffs and hidden by the fog, came the sound of a number of very heavy objects plunging into the deep water. After the first couple of huge rocks hit, Asima found she was wincing with each splash. Somewhere at the top of that cliff must be a defensive artillery platform. Their view was totally obscured but, given a wide enough spread of shot, there was always the possibility of a lucky shot... unless they stayed so close to the rock that the artillerists couldn't get a range.

She almost jumped as a flaming green-yellow ball of flaming matter arced over the ship from high above and plunged into the water with a splash and a hiss.

Suddenly, Asima realised that Samir was watching her intently. Turning her eyes back to the cliff, she realised that the water thrown up by the oars was already spraying across the slick black rock. In a panic, she turned and waved her arm in what she hoped was an appropriate gesture.

For a moment, as the ship continued to near the cliff and she was sure the oars must strike home and snap, she realised she was, right now, more nervous than at any point since those days of being young in M'Dahz, and possibly more so than even then. She was not by nature a nervous person and these days little frightened her, but this was something different. She was in an unfamiliar situation and with no power over events. Helpless and with no experience or knowledge of sailing, she was completely at the mercy of others and nothing she could do would allow her to take control of the situation. And Samir was using her and seemed to hold her in as little regard as she truly held him.

Blessed anger began to filter through her, smothering the fear, bringing control with it.

Samir would suffer for putting her through this.

Splash!

Well, once they were out away from the island and safe, he would, anyway. Tensely, she watched as the cliffs slid slowly past. Now there were more horns from behind; great activity in the harbour, which likely meant other ships weighing anchor to chase them down. The rocks of the reef would be moments away now and, once they were in there...'

She blinked as she realised that didn't exactly mean safety. The captains in pursuit would have the other compass and could navigate the reefs too, so it would come down to Samir's ability as a captain in the end.

Oh, he would suffer, but not yet, she thought as she saw Samir take out the disc and align the rudder with the disembodied finger within.

Just let her get away from here first.

In which Ghassan drifts

The six boats bobbed along quietly. There had been talking like this during those first few hours. Most of it, though, had been violent threats against the captain and crew of the Dark Empress, curses or oaths of vengeance. Others had been more consumed with the fear or drowning, starving to death, or even falling prey to the sharks that sometimes made their way toward the south coast, and praying to whichever God they most favoured. It had taken an hour of listening to the chatter before Ghassan had snapped and barked at his crew to shut up.

'Do you have any idea what just happened?' he had bellowed at them.

The boats had fallen silent as the crew of the Wind of God had turned as one to stare at their captain.

'Samir let you go! All of you... us! Let all of us go. We've got boats, enough food and water to last two days, which we shouldn't need, as we're only a day from land. None of us were harmed. You've lost the ship and a few valuables, but you're alive!'

The message he was trying to put over began to filter through their anger and despair.

'If we had caught them in the same state, they'd be in chains below deck, on their way to be tried and executed. Do you think they had to be merciful? Do you even think that many of them wanted to? Their captain saved your lives because, despite anything else we can say about him, he has mercy in his heart!'

After that, the conversation had become quieter and a little more thankful and positive.

But by the afternoon, even the most vociferous of the crew had run out of things to say and a silence had settled over them. Their ship had drifted during the night and early morning and the action had taken place far enough from the archipelago that the islands were out of sight, even the landmarks they all sought.

But they had not really moved far beyond them, and the direction of land was clear enough to them all. In the late afternoon they had spotted Eagle Rock and there had been a collective sigh of relief. The current had begun to pull them toward the island and the crew had taken the opportunity to boat oars and let the sea do the work for them.

While the chatter resumed among the crew, Ghassan kept his peace and concentrated on the glinting water as it washed past.

The men would be fine. When they finally got back to Calphoris, they would be shore-bound for a while, but would eventually be assigned to another vessel. Ghassan, on the other hand, would be disciplined very heavily for his actions. In ordinary circumstances, he would probably be retired from service. There were, after all, extenuating circumstances; the crew would be able to confirm that the ship had been sabotaged by Asima prior to the Dark Empress' arrival, but that would not be enough now. The Imperial navy was new here. It had been decades since the Empire had had control over the ships of Calphoris and now, within a few weeks of the transfer of power, Ghassan had lost their most notable vessel, more or less the flagship of the Calphorian fleet. Moreover, he had lost it to the very man he had been assigned to hunt down and remove and in the process he had lost a cargo that the lesser governor in M'Dahz had entrusted to him.

No, things would not go well for Ghassan.

He watched the low, sandy coast of the island slide toward him. Pelasian territory. This would be the first time in his life he had set foot on Pelasian soil, though he had brought destruction to their navy for many years. How did the Pelasians feel toward the Imperial military now? They had no reason to feel animosity, but that hardly mattered.

They would have to argue, persuade, beg, and possibly even barter, transport on Pelasian fishing boats to get to the mainland; to attempt to row that far in the lifeboats was unthinkable madness. Failure would mean being trapped on an island in Pelasia indefinitely, at which point they might as well settle there and fish for a living.

For a moment the need to fulfil his duty wavered in the face of the attractive proposition of a quiet life of fishing on an island far from what he considered 'civilisation'. It had a lure, he had to admit.

He took a deep breath. Even if they could make their way from settlement to settlement along the chain of islands, they would arrive in Pelasian territory and have to make their way along the coast back to Imperial lands. The journey would take weeks at best, more likely months… and, of course, it was entirely possible they would never make it back.

His mind latched on to M'Dahz for a moment. Every time he went to the town of his birth it was a disaster. Their youth had seen earth-shaking events that had almost broken them all. Then, after decades away, he had returned with a naval commission, only to take on a cargo that had ruined his career and almost cost him his life.

But now, if he managed to get back to Imperial territory, he would have to stop there first to inform the local governor that Asima had been taken by pirates. Even though the governor knew little of her and probably cared less, the news would not likely be welcome.

Sighing, he turned to the sailors under his command.

'Alright, men. We've no ship and we're refugees in foreign waters right now, but remember that you're men of the Imperial navy, and the Pelasians are now our allies. When we land, you will treat anyone you should meet with respect and we will maintain military order. Once we reach the shore, beach the boats, carry all the goods we have ashore and make an equipment store. I want two foraging parties to search out fruit, game and fresh water.'

He straightened, the familiar mode of speech of a captain in command returning to him.

'Everyone else needs to set up camp just back from the beach. We'll need to gather wood and get a fire going, and construct some sort of shelter. We may be there a few days before we can move on.'

He cast his eyes across the crew, wishing Samir had left them a few weapons.

'As soon as we've landed I will take a small party with me along the coast until we find the nearest village, and try to negotiate passage toward the mainland. Is that all clear?'

There was a low murmur among the crew.

'Did I hear something?' Ghassan barked. 'Are my orders clear?'

Silence reigned.

Ghassan glowered at the men in his boat.

'Does anyone have something to say?'

The was a pregnant pause, and then a burly man squared his shoulders. Ghassan eyed him thoughtfully. Caro, his name; an oarsman who had been on that bank of oars that Samir's artillery had targeted. While there were no marks on him, he had likely been sat in the centre of hell this morning as men burned and were smashed to pieces around him.

Ghassan was surprised that he hadn't seen this coming, but then he'd had rather a lot on his mind. There was a word for this in the navy.

'Mutiny, mister Caro? Is that it?'

'You c'n call it that sir, if you want. But the way I look at it, we've no ship and we ain't in Imperial waters. I ain't in the mood to take orders, right now, see sir? And I don't think many of the lads are neither.'

Ghassan nodded.

'So what's this to be? A direct takeover? Will you be the new captain or is this to be a democracy? If the former, I hope you have your plans ready.'

Caro growled.

''S not funny, cap'n. As of now we ain't navy no more. No one'll hurt you, long as you sit there quietly and don't get in the way.'

Ghassan gazed levelly at the man. He was an oarsman, not a marine; burly and big but not trained to fight. Ghassan, on the other hand, had had more than his share of brawls.

'It doesn't matter whether we're floating on a tray in the underworld, you're still a sailor in the Imperial navy, Caro. Sit back, grab the oar and get ready to row and I'll forget I ever heard the word mutiny.'

Ghassan almost laughed as the other twenty or so occupants of the large boat shuffled backwards as much as possible to be out of the way of this potential clash. There was precious little room to stretch in here, and yet somehow they managed to open a clear passage between the two men. Duty brought responsibility… and one responsibility was to keep the crew together and under the chain of command.

Caro leaned forward and cracked his knuckles.

'Don't push it, cap'n. We don't wanna hurt you. Just sit quiet and relax.'

Ghassan straightened.

'Very well, Mister Caro. I hereby officially charge you with attempted mutiny and have no choice but to bring you before the authorities on our return, if you survive that long.'

The oarsman rumbled deep in his throat.

'I ought to…'

Ghassan cut him off with a shout.

'You ought to what, mister Caro?'

He nodded inwardly as he watched the man reach down to one of the supply crates wallowing in the bottom of the boat. Predictably, Caro wrenched at the crate's lid and tore a short length of wood from it, gripping it tight enough that his knuckles whitened.

Ghassan treated him to a smile. This was a critical moment. To lose now was to lose everything, but to win in the wrong way would be to cause anger and resentment and to invite further challenges. He sized the man up. Caro was big and strong, and any blow by the man would hurt tremendously, but would be wild and fuelled by frustration and anger. Ghassan had the luxury of already knowing what he needed to do and how to bring that about. He smiled as he looked at the man's face, those dark eyes glowering under a heavy brow. The oarsman's hair was short, as was his beard, but one eyebrow ran along the ridge above his nose… a nice, straight nose.

He hated to lose people, but better one than all.

'Why're you smilin'?' the man asked uncertainly.

'Because I know something that I believe you do not, mister Caro. And because of that, I give you one free shot. Make it count, as, if you can put me down with that shot, the crew is yours.'

As he finished speaking, he shuffled forward into the space between the crew and held his arms out level from his shoulders. Caro stared at him.

'Changed your mind, sailor?' Ghassan asked lightly.

The man flared for a moment and launched his attack, just as Ghassan had hoped. He had goaded the man into wasting his opportunity. The blow was heavy, as Caro swung the plank, angling the makeshift weapon so that it landed with the edge rather than the flat. Ghassan felt bones break: probably two ribs, but maybe even three. This had better settle things, as he'd be in a bad state to deal with anyone else afterwards.

He collapsed to the bottom of the boat, hurled to one side by the force, the wind knocked from him. Caro had stood and, as Ghassan pulled himself back from the floor, he realised how stupid the man must be to get to his feet in a rowing boat. Indeed, he'd just made Ghassan's job harder. If he did this wrong now, the sailor would end up in the water, swimming around and waiting to come back for the next shot.

Slowly, he pulled himself upright, grunting at the excruciating pain in his side. Caro was grinning at him.

'C'mon cap'n. Stay down so I don't have to really hurt you.'

Still grunting and with heaving breaths, Ghassan stood straight. If Caro stood, he would have to as well.

'My turn', the captain said, flexing his fingers.

Caro gave a deep belly laugh.

'Come on then, cap'n. I'll give you a freebie too, but then I's gonna have to put you down hard.'

Ghassan nodded as the sailor mimicked his earlier stance, arms held out to the sides.

'Fair enough.'

There were certain things he'd learned from his uncle, but they involved fighting like a soldier, with weapons and there were others that he'd picked up when he headed a boarding party. Then there were a few things he'd learned when still a boy on board, serving in whatever lowly position was required. In those days, he'd been careful to pick up anything anyone would teach him. And throughout his life, he had come to the inescapable conclusion that strength and endurance were no match for planning and accuracy.

With a lightning-quick blow like the attack of a coiled snake, Ghassan lunged out with his right arm, palm open and fingers up as he straightened the limb into the blow. The heel of his hand connected with Caro at the upper lip and carried through, driving the mutineer's nose bone deep into his brain and exploding the man's face in a shower of blood.

Ignoring the shocked silence that fell around him, Ghassan stared into the surprised and suddenly lifeless eyes of his opponent and then reached out and grasped him by the shoulder before he fell overboard. Gently, in the stunned quiet, he lowered the body to the seat once more and left him to loll there, flopping to the left to end up draped across a horrified sailor.

'He'll need a proper burial when we beach, so I'll also need a burial party. Am I clear?'

The chorus of affirmative voices brought a wave of relief to the captain and he sat heavily in the bow once more and tentatively prodded his side.

That was going to take a long time to heal.

Fortunately, time was not something he was currently lacking.

In which new plans are laid

Asima tapped her fingers irritably on the rail at the stern of the Empress. Samir seemed to be largely unconcerned and whistled quietly as he made minute adjustments in course according to the compass in his hands. As seemed to be always the case these days, what irritated Asima was the lack of control she felt; helpless to direct her own destiny and Samir's irritatingly smug calm in the face of danger merely heightened the aggravation she felt.

'You're supposed to be a remarkable sailor, Samir, so why are we going as slowly as those following us? Can you not find a tiny turn of extra speed and put us further ahead of them?'

Samir laughed.

'Asima, these rocks are extremely dangerous and unpredictable. I go at whatever speed safe passage affords; no more and no less.'

'But as soon as we get past the reefs, those other ships will be virtually on top of us. Can you really outrun them all when we hit open sea?'

'Perhaps... probably not. We could outrun most ships, but we're short a number of oarsmen, so we'll be lucky to stay ahead of them at all.'

His passenger ground her teeth audibly.

'So why are you looking so pleased with yourself?'

'Because I rarely leave anything to chance these days, Asima. You should appreciate that. I have a feeling you live by similar rules... if different ethics.'

'I hope you're right and not merely being smug and self-aggrandising.'

'Ha.'

She gritted her teeth as Samir narrowed his eyes and peered past the masts toward the front of the ship.

'What now?' she barked angrily, not taking her eyes from the vague shapes behind them. The fog had thinned a little as they left the clinging, steamy vegetation of the island. There was still a blanket of white but, since they had been among the reefs, she had begun to see their pursuers more clearly, though it had taken an effort of will to keep her attention from wandering repeatedly to the desperate and gloomy figures occupying the rocks. She had counted at least three vessels but had a feeling there were four or five back there in the mist, following their own directions from the other 'dead man's compass' on the lead ship.

'Almost out of the reefs. I can see open water ahead and the mist's almost clear. That'll be a relief. I'm starting to miss the sight of the stars and that wonderful white moonlight.'

'A relief?'

Asima fell angrily silent for a moment. Clearly Samir was unconcerned and unwilling to explain himself to her so it was time to plan ahead on the assumption that he knew what he was doing and change the subject.

'I'm still very much in the dark as to what you intend now, Samir?'

'Hmm?' he prompted, concentrating on his rudder.

'Well, you're in the same position you were before you dragged me to Lassos, but now you've got pirates chasing us as well. You said you couldn't go near the coast as they'd be looking for you.'

Samir smiled.

'I've got a day or two at the least until news reaches anyone. Pelasia will learn about it first. Ghassan will have landed there and news travels fast there, as you'll know. Can't go to Calphoris though, as they've got it in for me anyway. So I shall make for M'Dahz, but by a roundabout route.'

Asima rounded on him angrily.

'What? Then you could have taken me there first!'

'Asima, calm down. I was unable to do so before, but things have now changed. I shall take you to M'Dahz in due course. First thing's first, though. Got to get clear of pursuit. I can't just breeze into M'Dahz on board one of the most notorious vessels afloat and drop you on the dock. Be sensible. So we need to disappear altogether for a while.'

'You're being needlessly cryptic again.'

Samir laughed.

'We've taken on some cargo during the night at Lassos. As soon as we're out of sight of other vessels, our colours change, as do our clothes and even the name on the ship. Given about an hour, we will no longer be the Dark Empress, but the Spirit of Redemption, a private Imperial merchant out of Serfium.'

'You're going to pretend to be another ship?' she blinked in surprise.

'Certainly,' Samir smiled. 'How else do you think we've ever got into Calphoris or M'Dahz? It's dangerous, so I don't like to do it unless it's imperative, but there are odd occasions when we have to go places that are really way too dangerous for us.'

Asima shook her head in disbelief.

'So you change your flag and your shirt and then drop into M'Dahz? That's ridiculous. Don't they check you or anything?'

'Of course they do. That's why we're not going there straight away. There are half a dozen convenient small towns along the archipelago and on the coast of both Pelasia and the Empire that we can trade our goods in and even make a little money en-route. Then, when we get to M'Dahz and they check our manifest we'll have plenty of supporting evidence for our story.'

He raised an eyebrow as he noted the speculative look on Asima's face.

'I cannot fathom what that dangerous mind of yours is cooking up now, but I would recommend against it.'

With an angry flash in her eyes, Asima turned once more to gaze into the rapidly thinning fog behind them. Four vessels, moving painstakingly slowly through the reefs, each captain relaying the orders from the leading ship. What was Samir up to?

The last of the rocks drifted past, an old man with hopeless eyes in a drenched grey robe fixing her with an accusative stare as he slid by. Again, in spite of herself, Asima found herself shuddering.

'Very well, Samir. We're in open water. What now?'

'Now', he replied with a grin 'we set as good a pace as we can out into the open sea, bearing south west.'

'I meant about our pursuers!'

'Watch and enjoy, Asima.'

Aggravated as always by his slightly smug silence, she turned and watched as their pursuers came on relentlessly, a line of vessels in perfect coordination, echoing one another's movements like…

She blinked. Something was clearly wrong out there. The lead ship had turned to port… no wait… to starboard; her port. She would never get the hang of sailing. The vessels following closely, however, seemed to have received incorrect information. There were sudden bellows of alarm. The front ship quickly slewed to a halt almost side on, stuck between rocks that prevented further passage. Behind them, chaos ensued as ships desperately came to a stop, receiving either no instructions or incorrect ones from the leading vessel.

Asima narrowed her eyes.

'That wasn't an accident, but I don't see how you could have done it?'

Samir smiled.

'Every gambler worth his salt has a card up his sleeve.'

'But you haven't been on board their ship. You couldn't even have known whether they'd follow us at all, let alone who it would be? And you haven't had the opportunity to lay a trap. So what happened?'

Samir tapped the side of his nose and smiled at her, before cupping his free hand round his mouth and shouting out the order for full speed, both sail and oars. Behind him, Asima grumbled and glared at him. Why would he continually reveal everything he did to her, despite his professed lack of trust, and yet withhold what seemed to be a small detail.

She narrowed her eyes again. There was something going on here. Samir had plans, for sure. He'd said as much to her; and they appeared to involve his designs on rule in Lassos, which she could heartily understand. But he was using her somehow and it infuriated her that she could see that and could feel it happening, but had no idea how it was happening.

Well, she'd been thinking too and it was time for the lady Asima, former consort of the King of Pelasia, to begin working her way back to power. For some time since being taken from Ghassan's ship, she had pondered on her best course of action once she returned to the mainland. When the Wind of God had disappeared beneath the waves, it had taken most of her belongings with it. She had saved the most important and the most valuable items about her person, yet with diminished funds it would be all the more difficult to set herself up as an eligible widow, beautiful and young, to trap a high lord of the Pelasian court.

But now funds would be largely irrelevant. Samir had used her as part of some plan she could not fathom, and a plan that was clearly still in progress, but it would never come to fruition.

Asima smiled inwardly as the true value of her situation dawned on her.

Lords and officials, both Imperial and Pelasian, would practically deify her if she could deliver them Samir into captivity. Moreover she had seen Lassos; knew its occupants, its layout and military strength, and even the secret method of navigation through the reefs. When she reached M'Dahz with Samir and that knowledge, she would find herself in probably the strongest bargaining position of her life.

She realised that she was smiling openly as she noticed Samir watching her with interest.

'Something funny, Asima?'

She laughed lightly.

'Care to share with me how you chased those ships off?' she asked with a cheeky grin.

'I think I'll hold on to that for a while. Never know when I might need a little trick or two of my own.'

'Then yes, there is something funny, but I alone shall laugh at it.'

Samir shrugged.

'As you wish. For now, however, I think you ought to go below and catch up on a bit more sleep. The moon's almost down and dawn won't be far off. I'll want you fully alert and ready to lend a hand when daylight strikes.'

Asima shook her head.

'I haul ropes for no one, Samir.'

'Ha. I realise that. In the morning, the Empress will be barely recognisable and we'll have Imperial clothing, colours and name. You will be a wealthy passenger on her way to M'Dahz; it's basically true anyway, but I need you to play the noblewoman. Some of the people we will be dealing with in the ports on the way are more inclined to give us favourable deals if they think it will curry favour with a courtier of note.'

Asima nodded thoughtfully.

'Then I shall need to be attired and addressed appropriately, of course.'

'Of course. So get some rest. For the next couple of weeks, you are a rich passenger on board the Spirit of Redemption.'

In which Ghassan goes home.

It had been a strange journey, Ghassan sighed, as he stepped down from the Pelasian daram; strange but quick. From their initial beaching near Eagle Rock, they had found the local Pelasian fishermen to be extremely helpful and accommodating. The first three days had seen the sailors escorted by one fisherman or another between islands, the locals going out of their way to help and delivering the refugees to their destination before going about their ordinary daily business.

Then, on the fourth day, they had all been surprised to see the next settlement in the chain that led them home. Arhab was somewhat different from the other fishing towns and villages they had seen. This was a new settlement, only a few years old and purpose-built as a shipyard for the navy of the local satrap, whom they learned was a man named Khalad, and who shared the dual distinctions of being the controller of the most land at the Pelasian court, ruling a sizeable portion of the coast as well as the entire archipelago, while also holding the exalted position of commander of the royal fleet at Akkad.

In the spirit of cooperation between the two governments, the Pelasian admiral in command of the Arhab shipyard immediately had one of their newest daram put at the disposal of Ghassan and his men, to ferry them wherever they wished to go.

While the repeated aid of helpful fishermen had brought them a surprising distance in only three days, the powerful military daram of the Pelasian navy was capable of astounding speed. Ghassan had almost forgotten the awful situation into which they were heading as he spent the next two days strolling around the ship and investigating it; comparing it to his own lost vessel. If anything, this new Pelasian warship would be faster than his had been, though less effective in direct battle. He was suitably impressed by both ship and crew and had found that he was beginning to enjoy himself a little for a time.

Real life had impressed itself on him once more this morning, however, when he had been called up on deck by the captain, to see the smudge that was M'Dahz on the horizon.

He had gathered his men on deck and given them his instructions. While the crew settled in to wait in one of the military bunkhouses of the docks, he would report to the local governor. They had finally docked mid-morning and, with no small amount of trepidation, Ghassan had descended the gang plank.

M'Dahz hadn't seemed to change much. It had when he had been growing up, though. What he'd remembered from his childhood as a happy, noisy, busy place had become quiet, depressed and almost dead in the years of the rule of Ma'ahd. He'd been sure M'Dahz had changed fully, never to recover.

Yet in the short time the town had been once more controlled by the factors of the Empire, the failing settlement had experienced a rebirth. Clearly hope had never died and, with the removal of the oppressive ruler, M'Dahz had begun to flower once more. People who had fled to Calphoris had returned, as had traders from the desert and overseas. The port bustled and was filled with voices in a dozen accents. Bright carpets and hangings were in evidence in the streets once more and many of the buildings had been given a fresh coat of white.

And yet all this positive attitude that seemed to flood out of the very stones of M'Dahz could do little to lighten Ghassan's mood. Taking a deep breath, he turned and cast one long look at his crew, some of whom had been veteran sailors on board the Wind of God when he had come aboard as a boy. He couldn't fight off the impression that he had failed them all.

With a sigh, he strode through the organised chaos of the dock, between coiled ropes, lobster pots, crates and junk, toward the main street that climbed the hill to the top of the town. Even with his uniform dirty and torn and showing signs of the awful events it had witnessed, the people of M'Dahz parted as he passed, many nodding their respect to him, an act that merely heightened his unhappiness.

He passed through the main square where they had burned Pelasian flags so long ago, crossing diagonally and continuing up the slope as it steepened. The searing sun was hidden in these streets by the age-old means of stringing blankets and rugs across between the upper storeys.

His heart sank like an anchor in the sea of his soul as he reached the end of the long street and strode out at a military march into the plaza before the governor's compound. Despite their childhood vow to climb the roofs of these buildings, Ghassan had never stepped foot inside the compound yet, the closest being when he had collected Asima a week or more ago. Even then, he'd only spent an hour or two in the town.

The thought of his childhood friend – love? – darkened his mood further, if that were at all possible. Grinding his teeth, he approached the gate. Two white-uniformed guards stepped forward, their spears and shields reflecting the brilliant sunlight and creating random spots of dazzling white that danced around the shadows as they moved.

'Captain Ghassan of the Wind of God, to see the governor.'

'You have an appointment?' asked one of the soldiers, his northern accent thick.

'No, but it is imperative that I see him urgently and, I fear, he will want to see me.'

The guard nodded and then conferred with his companion in his own language for a moment before turning back.

'Wait here.'

Ghassan nodded and stood silently, his gaze wandering over the buildings both inside the compound and out as he waited for what seemed an eternity. The white-clad guard effectively ignored him, standing stiff and proud by the gate.

With relief, perhaps five minutes later, Ghassan saw the guard emerge from a door on the far side of the compound and gesture, calling out. The guard in front of him gestured.

'You go in now.'

Ghassan saluted and marched across the compound. He had always hoped to see the inside of this place and now he found he couldn't wait to get out of it. The closer he came to his meeting with the governor, the more convinced he became of the bleakness of the fate that awaited him. The new local governor in M'Dahz had seemed very straight and humourless at their last, brief meeting. Ghassan's future career, livelihood, and even life, may well depend upon the decision or recommendation of this man. Ghassan realised he didn't know the political structure enough to know how much power this lesser governor had when compared with that of the provincial governor in Calphoris or his military commanders.

His heart pounding, Ghassan reached the doorway and was ushered inside by the guard, who escorted him in silence up one of the flights of stairs that framed the main hall.

The governor's door was open and, as they approached, the white-clad guard gestured to him to enter. Making a futile gesture to tame the tangle of black curls on his head and straighten his jacket, Ghassan cleared his throat and entered the room.

The occupant was a tall and well-dressed man with a long nose and piercing eyes, a foreigner, sent from Velutio to take control of M'Dahz. He also had a dangerous look. Ghassan swallowed nervously.

'Sir.' He came to attention and saluted.

The governor turned and stood against his desk, crossing his legs as he leaned back and folding his arms.

'Captain. I presume the news you bring is not good?'

Ghassan shook his head and had to fight for the words, momentarily wishing he'd taken Samir up on his offer. Duty must be done, though.

'I beg to report, my lord, the loss of the Wind of God and a small portion of her crew. Most of the men returned with me and await further instructions at the docks.'

The governor tapped his finger on his lips.

'I felt certain you had not made it to Velutio and back in this short time. Pray tell me what happened to the most renowned vessel in the Calphorian fleet and where your charge, the Lady Asima, is at this time?'

Ghassan swallowed again. There was an edge to the man's voice that spoke volumes, regardless of his almost casual words.

'Regretfully, sir, we fell prey to pirates.'

He winced. This was a moment of defining character, he realised. Did he take on the full responsibility himself? The situation had been unfortunate and largely beyond his control. The truth was less noble and considerably less believable. But then, Asima deserved anything that life threw at her now… or that Ghassan threw.

'The Lady Asima, in an effort to prevent us achieving our mission, sabotaged the ship and left us unable to manoeuvre when the pirates appeared. We were not in a position to take them on, sir.'

'And may I ask if you identified your attackers?'

Ghassan sighed.

'Yes, sir. It was Captain Samir of the Dark Empress.'

The governor nodded knowingly.

'I'm sure you realise just how irregular all of this appears, Captain Ghassan. I would normally have to decide between disciplinary courses of action to take against you for the loss of a ship and an important passenger. However, given that both said passenger and the captain of your attackers are old acquaintances of yours, other questions are raised and I fear that we have now surpassed my jurisdiction.'

Ghassan nodded professionally.

'I can see how this must appear, my lord…'

'Be silent!' the governor hissed. 'You will be very lucky to escape this debacle with your head on your shoulders, captain. At any rate, I will pass along my recommendation to my superiors in

Calphoris that you be dishonourably discharged from the force without pay or benefits and possibly banished from the province.'

Ghassan shook slightly, trying to hold himself straight.

'Sir…'

'That is all, Captain Ghassan and be grateful that I am a merciful man. The lord who trained me in Velutio would have recommended execution for such a failure, given the dubious circumstances surrounding it.'

Ghassan straightened and saluted.

'Yes sir.'

The governor glared at him.

'You have family in M'Dahz I believe? A home here? I'm sure I've seen it in the records.'

Ghassan blinked for a moment, unsure of the answer.

'There is a house that belonged to my mother, if it still stands, sir. None of my family survived the occupation.'

'Very well. We'll have the address on file, no doubt. Go there and stay until you are ordered otherwise. I will send a courier to Calphoris with the news and ask for the Marshal's recommendation. When it is given, I will send for you.'

'Sir.'

'And do not think about leaving the city. Your name and description will be given to the army and the port authorities. I am releasing you on your honour on the understanding that you are still currently a serving officer and that no decision has yet been made. Stay out of trouble until you are sent for.'

Ghassan nodded and saluted.

'Now go.'

With a final salute, Ghassan turned on his heel and strode from the room. Without pausing or looking back, he marched down the stairs and across the hall; out through the doors and across the compound, into the plaza.

Those occupants of M'Dahz he passed shied out of the way of his fierce gaze and gritted teeth. Depression and despair had given way to something else as Ghassan left the compound: angry determination and a cold certainty.

There was only one way to make this right with his superiors. He would have to give them Samir on a platter and return Asima, unscathed, to answer for her own crimes.

The baking sun hung suspended above M'Dahz and shone down on a town in flux. The end of a regime had lifted the spirits of the people and had brought back trade and life. Things were changing in M'Dahz and many of its lost children had returned home.

And now, three of those children, repeatedly torn away from one another and thrown back together, changed beyond measure from the boys and girl who raced across the hot rooftops a lifetime ago, converged on their childhood playground.

The pirate, the soldier and the princess were coming home, bringing schemes and plans with them.

Part Four:

My Enemy's Enemy

In which Samir goes home (part one)

M'Dahz looked just as it always had from the sea: a sprawl of tangled narrow streets and alleyways winding their way among white blocks as they snaked up the slope to the crest, where the walls and towers of the governor's palace complex stood proud of the lower roofs. Though in truth all they could smell on board the 'Spirit of Redemption' was the fresh, if salty, air of the sea, the mind filtered in the mixed aroma of spice and dung that they remembered from their youth.

Samir sighed. They had been at sea for more than two weeks, including the occasional stopovers in one port or another. Much as he hated to admit it, Samir found he rather liked the life of a legitimate merchant. While it was less exciting on a physical basis, the challenges inherent in business gave his mind something to work on even in quiet restful periods. Moreover, Asima played the Imperial noblewoman so well that she had charmed and impressed many otherwise shrewd traders into extremely favourable deals.

It was no real surprise to Samir that his lady passenger was capable of taking on a role and playing it with no slip or hiccup, but on these occasions, her devious mind and slippery morals had played to the advantage of all concerned.

And yet, with every hop between ports bringing them closer to their destination, Samir found that a cloud hung over his mood and darkened with every league they passed. Not only was a trip to M'Dahz not the most pleasant on his list of things to do, but this was where everything would change and each detail had to go well. He hoped in the name of whatever Gods were still interested in watching his hometown that he had not underestimated Asima. He doubted he had, but there was still a nagging doubt. He could nudge her in the right direction, but she was almost as subtle as he, and she might just notice that.

He turned and looked along the rail upon which they leaned, casting a non-committal glance at his passenger in her expensive northern-style dress. He had to admit that not only did she look the part, but she was extraordinarily alluring.

'I'm never entirely happy coming back here,' he said sadly.

'It is a stinking hole,' Asima nodded absently.

'That's not what I meant!' Samir snapped at her. 'I feel happy, sad, disappointed and angry all at once when I even look at the place. It tears me in too many directions at the same time. And, of course, with the path that I follow these days, I can never truly let my guard down when I'm here, so I'm also tense and jumpy.'

'How long til we dock?' she asked.

'Five minutes.'

The woman nodded.

'What will you do now?' Samir enquired.

'I will sell on my few expensive items and find myself safe passage back to Pelasia. I shall have to avoid any contact with the governor or the military, though, as they're the ones who sent me into exile across the sea. I expect I can find the right sort of people given a few hours.'

'I have a little money put aside for you. You made us rather a good profit on the voyage, my lady of Velutio, so I thought a small token of our thanks might help you find your way safely to where you're going as fast as possible.'

Asima smiled.

'Thank you, Samir. I will have to stay at least one night in the town, though. My father passed away a few years back and I've never had a chance to visit his grave, so I think I ought to take the opportunity while I'm here.'

'Indeed. I considered visiting our old neighbourhood, but there are too many people in M'Dahz that might know or recognise me. Safer that I spend the night on board and venture no further than the docks. If you're spending time in the town, perhaps you would look in at my mother's house and pass on my regards to her ghost?'

Asima nodded.

'Of course.'

The pair fell silent and watched the sprawl of M'Dahz drifting toward them. Minutes passed as the two, deep in thought, leaned on the rail, their eyes locked on their destination.

'Prepare for docking!' a voice from the command deck called.

Samir looked back up at his first officer who was also concentrating on the town ahead. The crew moved around them, preparing the mooring ropes, taking seats with the oars and furling sails. Samir barely paid them any attention, still carefully concentrating on figuring Asima's likely activities.

Straightening, he adjusted the tight and itchy Imperial green jacket and flattened his hair for neatness. Reaching down beside him, he undid the bag he'd brought out from his cabin, removed a leather wallet and then slung the bag over his shoulder.

'Don't let your act slip now, Asima.'

She nodded and allowed her face to fall into the grave and serious mask she had worn so often over recent weeks. A few moments later, the ship came slowly alongside the jetty, the oars retreating within the hull and being set down as other sailors threw out the lines. Samir glanced along the wooden walkway to the small group awaiting them. Two of the town guard stood at the shoulders of a small, weasel-like man with a tablet and stylus, who was frowning at the new arrival.

Carefully and diplomatically, Samir waited until the ship had come to a complete stop and the lines were being tied and then took Asima's arm in a respectful fashion. As the sailors ran out the gangplank and lowered it to the jetty, Samir and his passenger stepped across to it. In the age-old manner of a captain with an honoured guest, he bowed to her and then slowly backed down the plank, holding his arm out before him for the lady to grasp.

The board was slippery and Asima made a point of skittering once in her expensive slippers, just for the look of the thing. Samir almost smiled at that. Attention to detail; that was what made her good. It was also what made her dangerous.

They alighted on the walkway and he escorted her forward, her hand on his arm, until they came to a halt before the group of men. Samir nodded his head professionally while Asima graced them with a superior smile.

'Good morning captain… lady.'

Samir smiled.

'Good morning, officer. May I present the Lady Lyria, once of Calphoris and lately of Velutio.'

The port official bowed seriously and then gestured at the ship with his stylus.

'Your name, cargo and destination, as well as port of origin, captain?'

Professionally, Samir nodded and passed the leather folder over. The official opened it, glanced briefly at the documents and turned the page to check the one below. Nodding, he passed it back and gestured with his stylus to go on.

'Captain Halvus of the Spirit of Redemption, out of Velutio these past four weeks,' Samir announced. 'Varied cargo, mostly of fabrics and grain. Nothing restricted. We're simply on one leg of our journey. From here we head for Calphoris in a day or two, then the ports of the east coast and up to Germalla before returning to Velutio.'

As he spoke, the official nodded and made marks on his tablet.

'Long journey, captain.'

'Roundabout trip, keeping to coastlines for safety. Too many stories of pirates in your waters, I'm afraid, officer.'

The official shot him a miserable look and then returned to his marking.

'Sadly, you're not the first to say that. At least you came, though. Many keep away altogether.'

'Will you be wanting to do a search of the hold? No trouble, if so, but the lady will be staying on in M'Dahz for a few days to visit an acquaintance and I would like to have her escorted to meet her friends before we begin, so as not to inconvenience her too much.'

The official looked Samir up and down and then smiled superciliously at Asima.

'Everything appears to be in order, captain, so I think we can forgo such formalities. Welcome to M'Dahz, my lady. I hope you enjoy your time here. The town is in a state of extreme busyness at the moment. We are preparing for the first full-week festival since the city was freed and it will be rather a large celebration. I hope you can stay for it.'

Asima smiled a dazzling smile at the man.

'I shall make every effort to attend, sir.'

He smiled at her once more and then lowered his face respectfully as he stepped aside. The two guardsmen bowed slightly and parted to clear the jetty.

'Please, captain, after you.'

Samir nodded and, arm still held out for Asima to grip, strode from the jetty onto dry land. Once they were safely out of earshot, Asima took a deep breath.

'Dangerous, offering your hold to search.'

'Openness and honesty is often rewarded, even if it's faked. Much more dangerous to appear cagey and unwilling.'

'Well,' she said, squaring her shoulders, 'I think you can safely leave me here, Samir. You don't want to go too far into the city.'

Samir shrugged.

'I'll escort you to the edge of the docks and to the town itself. Such would be expected of your escort.'

The pair strode on for another minute, he leading her through the port as though she were unfamiliar with it, rather than knowing each stone and plank from youthful games. Presently, they reached the edge of the docks, where a delimiting stockade marked the beginning of the town proper. The gate stood open jammed with crates and was apparently rarely closed now, even at night. The pair of guards standing to either side of the gateway appeared bored to the point of stupefaction.

Samir smiled. He had no intention of spending his time in M'Dahz lounging around on the ship, but what he was going to do depended at least partially on Asima's next course of action.

As they approached the gate, Samir fished in his jacket and withdrew a small pouch.

'Here. Take this. It'll hardly buy you a palace, but it'll make your journey considerably easier.'

Asima smiled and stopped, reaching out and grasping and pocketing the pouch.

'Thank you, captain. I hope all goes well for you here and that when you return to your home port you achieve everything you dream of.'

'I'm sure I shall, lady. Perhaps our paths will cross once again someday.'

'Perhaps.'

She gave him a warm and very forced smile, showing just a little hint of her desperation to depart.

'Until then…'

'Yes ma'am.'

Samir touched his forehead respectfully and had to hide his smile at the vaguely lustful glances the two bored guards cast at the retreating beauty as she turned and wandered up the road.

'Trust me, lads. You couldn't afford that one.'

One of the guards laughed and then returned to his languid pose.

Tapping his foot impatiently, Samir watched Asima trot up the street. Too soon. Wait just a little longer…

He blinked as she disappeared down a side street. Damn it. Could she possibly be doing something else? Where was she going? He'd assumed she would go straight up to the governor's complex to announce the presence and location of the Dark Empress and its captain. Could she actually have been telling the truth? Was she just going to disappear?

No.

Samir chuckled, raising interest from one of the guards. Ignoring the man, he set off up the street at a fast walk. No… she would betray him; it was in her nature. She was just going somewhere else on the way to the governor's. Could she be heading to her father's old house? Maybe…

He slapped his forehead as he picked up his pace to reach the side street.

Of course! He'd asked her to check on his mother's house. He hadn't expected her to actually do it, but perhaps he had piqued her interest enough that she could spare the time to go and check. After all, as far as she was aware, she was in no rush. She may even go and visit her father's grave too after all.

With a frown, he strode along the busy street. The port official had been right. There was so much activity one could hardly imagine this was the same town that had suffered and almost died beneath the rule of a harsh foreign invader. Colour and noise abounded and the narrow road was so crowded that Samir was forced at times to pause and wait for a gap to open up or to push through a resistant and inattentive bunch of ditherers.

He had lost sight of Asima as soon as she had turned into the side street but now, convinced of her destination, he knew exactly where to go. Gritting his teeth as he pushed his way between half a dozen burly men with a ladder and roll of banners, he shook his head.

Would their mother's house still be standing?

Moreover, did he really want to go there and dredge up all those old memories and feelings? There wasn't much choice, though. He needed to be sure of Asima's betrayal to adjust his own plans accordingly, so even if she walked into the jaws of hell, at this point he'd follow her.

Taking a deep breath, Samir headed home.

In which Samir goes home (part two)

The house looked the same. Somehow, Samir had expected either years of abandonment and neglect to have taken their toll and left a ruinous shell of a building, or for someone to have taken up residence and changed the place.

And yet he suddenly felt eight years old, returning from buying juicy watermelon at the market to wait for the noon meal.

Clearly someone had taken up residence, though. He could see a blanket and some clothes hanging out of an upper window; men's clothes too. Asima either had not noticed this or did not care, though, for, as Samir finally came within sight of the front door, the crowd parting as he reached the outskirts and streets that were less busy, he spotted Asima. He'd almost caught up with her, and she stood looking at the door of the building with her head on one side before shrugging and reaching for the handle.

Samir hurried along the street, keeping to the side and obscured from sight by a couple playing noisily with a dog. He ducked and, keeping his head low, waited until she had pushed open the door and entered before rushing along the buildings and pushing himself up against the wall of the house.

It felt exceedingly odd to be sneaking up on the only permanent home he had ever known, the place that held the memories of his mother, brother, father and uncle. He heard a call of alarm in a woman's voice, muffled by the thick, cooling walls of the building. He couldn't be certain, but was reasonably convinced the voice would be Asima's.

Judging the location of the occupants from the level of muffling of the voice and his flawless memories of the building's layout, Samir ducked into a side alley that led up the slope between the houses to a higher road beyond and hurried up the steps to one of the small rear windows of the building.

The aperture, partially obscured by a damaged blind that had been in that state as long as Samir could remember, led into the kitchen where he and Ghassan used to help their mother prepare meals.

Now there were two voices, becoming clearer as he approached the window; one male and one female.

Stooping slightly, he put his eye to one of the small gaps in the blind and blinked in surprise. Ghassan stood at a ruined table in the kitchen, propped up on a broken chair. He looked tired, scruffy and badly-shaven. Samir nodded to himself. His brother must have been discharged from the navy. They wouldn't countenance an officer in that state. As he watched, Ghassan flung his arms wide in an angry gesture as he fixed his gaze on Asima, standing in the doorway. To Samir's surprise there was a bottle in his brother's hand; one of the powerful spirits distilled by the northern tribes and quite hard to buy for a reasonable price this far south.

'I don't care what you're doing here, Asima. Get the hell out of this house. You're cheapening mother's memory with your stink!'

Again Samir blinked. Ghassan was taking it hard, but then the taller brother had always been the more sensitive, and the pungent brew would not be helping. Asima's betrayals and deceit were easy enough for Samir to brush off, but Ghassan would feel wounded every time he saw her.

For a moment, Samir's heart went out to his broken brother.

'Things will be better, Samir...' The words Ghassan had spoken to him on that day when so many innocent people had been cast to their death from the town wall. And right now, things were better for Samir. Not so for Ghassan, but then, the taller brother was unaware of Samir's plans for the future.

The small, handsome brother smiled at the window.

'Things will be better, Ghassan,' he said under his breath.

Asima had entered the room now and levelled a finger at Ghassan across the table.

'Don't be blind and petty, Ghassan. If you don't listen to what I have to say, you'll sit here and wallow in your own filth and drink yourself to death, and nothing good will come of this for either of us.'

'Go away!'

Samir was surprised once again as Asima rounded the table and grasped Ghassan by the forearms. The bottle fell to the surface, where it tipped onto its side and began to spill its expensive and corrosive contents onto the wood. He hadn't realised how bad things had become. His brother was either truly drunk or a broken man.

'Ghassan, you have a chance here to make everything right and I ask for very little in return!'

'Whatever it is, Asima, the price is too high. Whose life or liberty are you selling now?'

Asima smiled and Samir couldn't believe how horribly feral that face had become.

'I can give you your honour and your career again. How much is that worth to you?'

'Less than it'll cost.'

Asima pushed Ghassan and the slightly inebriated soldier fell back into the chair behind him.

'Wake up, you idiot. Samir's in M'Dahz. He's brought me back and he's in port as I speak.'

Ghassan sat up straight and Samir suddenly wished he could see his brother's expression.

'Samir's days of piracy are numbered,' she went on, jabbing an angry finger at the seated man. 'I was on my way to turn him in to the governor but I made a side trip out of curiosity.'

Despite everything, Samir had to smile to himself. There was a certain point of untrustworthiness and deviousness where a person became as predictable as a straight and law-abiding citizen. He peered down at them. Ghassan was shaking his head.

'What have you got against Samir? I thought your quarrel was with me, Asima.'

Samir raised his eyes to the heavens. It wasn't that Ghassan was slow or stupid, but he had trouble seeing the dubious side of anything, even of Asima. The alcohol had likely blinkered him a little too.

'Ghassan! I need to return to Pelasia, and I prefer to do it legitimately, with power and finance. A good step to doing that would be to have the governor on my side, and possibly even a reward.'

'Then why come to me?'

Asima laughed.

'Happy accident, Ghassan. I came here on a whim at Samir's suggestion, just to see if the building still stood. But there are advantages to coming to you rather than the governor.'

The seated man greeted this with an empty silence, so Asima shrugged.

'The governor may not agree to see me… I'm not precisely in his favour, as he only wanted to send me away. Even if I do get to see him, he may not believe me, and that just leaves too many uncertainties for me. Then there's the practicalities too. If the governor sends troops to the port to take him in, Samir may well get away with his ship before they can board. If not, it'll likely end in a fight and, again, the outcome's too uncertain for my liking. No, we need to capture him alone, and I can't really do that on my own.'

Ghassan nodded and cleared his throat.

'It so happens that the notion of the capture of Samir and his ship has been knocking around in my head for a while now. I've not had my judgment decided by the provincial governor yet, but if

I can deliver Samir, it would go a long way to solving my problems.'

He stood once more, with only a slight wobble.

'I am not happy at all with working alongside you, Asima, but if you can deliver Samir to me I give you my word that I shall speak to the governor and ask him to grant you permission to stay, and at least a portion of the reward.'

Asima smiled.

'Just what I had in mind.'

'And then I never want to set eyes on you again, for as long as either of us lives. Is that clear?'

Asima nodded with a nonchalant shrug.

'Once I am on the road back to the Pelasian throne, I care not a jot for what you do, Ghassan.'

Samir listened for a moment to them finalising their deal and then stole away from the wall. He would have to see where she went from here: the governor's compound or the port? The pirate captain was sure of three things.

Firstly, he knew that Asima would not leave Ghassan to glean most of the glory and profit from this. She was spiteful and greedy and would want everything for herself. She needed every ounce of support if she was to try and return to her place in Pelasia.

Secondly, Ghassan had no intention of letting Asima take her portion of the glory. She had dishonoured him, committed crimes against the navy and the Empire, at which the tall captain would take great offence, and had personally betrayed and insulted him. Samir was convinced his brother would turn her over after they succeeded.

Finally, he was also sure that neither of these things would come to pass. Asima must be stopped for the good of the world at large, and that of the brothers specifically. Under no circumstances should a woman with that kind of mind be any closer to power than she was now. Moreover, Ghassan had to be made to realise that he was wallowing and drifting when he should be working with Samir, and Asima would have to betray them for him to have any hope of convincing Ghassan.

Samir suddenly ducked back into the shadow of a wall as Asima strode from the front door of his former home. He held his breath as she looked up and down the street and then walked off down the slope from whence she'd come. Nodding to himself, Samir disappeared into the crowd and rushed ahead until he reached the point where this street joined the main thoroughfare up the hill through the town. There he waited in a doorway, watching.

A minute later he caught sight of Asima's face among the crowd as she reached the main street. Again he held his breath as she looked up and down the hill.

Governor or port?

Squaring her shoulders, she turned, a determined look about her, and strode back down the hill.

Nodding, Samir moved off ahead of her among the crowd, making directly for the port gates as fast as he could. She'd not been to see the governor, then. What on earth was she up to? He needed her to do something wicked to help him with Ghassan.

Sighing, he made his way down the hill, through the docks and up the plank to the ship that wallowed in the water by the jetty. Two of his men nodded respectfully at him as he came aboard. Quickly, he looked himself up and down; a little dusty, but fine, really. He brushed himself down and strode across to his cabin, entered, poured a drink and waited for his visitor, relaxing in the chair.

The wait was not long. He had counted two minutes when there was a knock at the door and it opened a little.

'The lady's back sir, and asking permission to come aboard.'

Samir nodded.

'By all means. Show her in.'

He smiled as he took a sip of the good wine he kept in his cabinet and then looked up, feigning mild surprise, as Asima entered and the sailor shut the door behind her.

'Asima? Back so soon? I thought you'd be on your way to Akkad by now?'

She shook her head. There was a look of despair, or possibly sadness, on her face. Both expressions seemed so alien in that environment that Samir had trouble identifying it. What was she up to?

'Samir... I don't know how to tell you this...'

He frowned.

'What are you talking about, Asima?'

She fell silent. A tear rolled down her cheek and a slight wobble began to affect her lip. Samir didn't know whether to laugh or be impressed. The show was well and truly underway.

'Samir, it's your brother...'

Got to play it right, he thought, as he threw the most perplexed and cautious expression he could manage across his features.

'Ghassan? He's here?'

'After a fashion...'

'Asima?'

More tears now. It really was quite impressive how she did that.

'He's dead, Samir!'

There was a momentary hoarse catch in her throat and then she threw her hands up to her face and began to sob. Samir blinked in shock and stood suddenly, clambering wildly round the desk to grab her by the shoulders. Gritting his teeth, he shook her a little so that her head jolted back.

'What are you talking about?'

She burbled and wiped her eyes.

'I went to your mother's house to see if it still stood. It was empty and quiet, so I went in to have a look, and there he was... oh, Samir. It's horrible.'

Samir frowned. She was good. How could he resist this?

'What happened, Asima?' he barked, his voice on the edge of feigned panic.

'He... oh, Samir. He's been attacked... beaten... knifed.'

Samir smiled inwardly. It was perfect, but now he had to play his part in the drama with equal skill. Settling his features into a grim determination, Samir addressed her through clenched teeth.

'Take me there!'

In which plans are laid and undone

Samir followed Asima through the crowded dock. He wondered for a moment whether he should have suggested taking a few sailors with him. It would be inconvenient, though a natural thing to do, but in the end he decided to forgo that and head out with her alone, trusting she would put any lack of caution down to shock or the necessity of speed.

They passed through the dock at a fast walk; a run would attract far too much attention for either of them and, at the far side, Samir almost walked into Asima's back as she slowed near the port gate. What was she up to?

Surreptitiously, while keeping his head lowered, Samir scanned the area and almost smiled as he noticed the gate guards. The military were not noted for their subtlety and these two were no exception. One kept his eyes averted from the pair of them while the other gave a barely-perceptible nod to Asima. Samir's eyes strayed a little and noted that the man's grip on his spear tightened, the knuckles whitening.

That was it then. She'd not needed to go to the governor because she'd already sold them out to the town guard. It was a dangerous play, given the likelihood that the guard might just be eager enough to capture him that they'd go ahead and ruin whatever plans she had.

He frowned as they passed the guards and entered the street leading up the hill, repeating their earlier journey precisely. The soldiers weren't trying to take him at the gate, so she must have told them to come to the house. It would have been easier to capture him here, so they must be intending to take Ghassan at the same time. But why? Separately would have been so much easier for them.

Quickly, they hurried up the street toward the turning that led toward the west gate and their house. Samir worked through every conceivable angle and motive as he rushed along behind her. They were trying to get both brothers together and that meant that some extra evidence was afforded by them being in the same place.

He almost slapped his head as he realised.

Ghassan could very easily be accused of complicity in the whole affair. From a legal standpoint it was not unrealistic to assume that the naval officer had delivered both Asima and his ship to his brother for a cut of the profit, through some familial obligation, or myriad other possibilities. To find Ghassan in apparent collusion with Samir would likely damn them both and leave Asima with a cloak of innocence.

Once more, Samir considered just how dangerous Asima could be if she managed to get her hands on real power. She was more trouble than a thousand Pelasian invaders.

Casually, he turned his head and cast his gaze behind them down the street. Sure enough, pairs of guards were filtering through the crowd, converging slowly and subtly. Likewise, up the hill ahead of them, he could see the uniforms of other soldiers scattered among the people, moving down the hill. There would likely be more guards moving in from the other end of the street upon which the house stood.

No time to worry about that now, though. Both he and Ghassan had spent their life getting out of trouble in one situation or another and the pirate captain was sure they would be able to do so again. Escape was not the highest priority right now. Top of the list was to meet Ghassan, to make it clear to him what a lying, deceitful woman Asima was, and to get him on the same side.

They turned the corner into the narrower street and hurried along. Samir glanced back to see that the pursuing guards had slowed as they converged at the end of the road. They were having trouble, now in larger groups, remaining inconspicuous and had wisely chosen to hang back.

He bit his lip as they approached the old neighbourhood. He couldn't act to try and recruit Ghassan until Asima had revealed her treachery. He could only hope that she wasn't going to similarly wait on them, but then she couldn't, really. As soon as Samir officially discovered that Ghassan was alive and well, she would have to act.

With a smile, he realised that without even concentrating on it, his ever-frantic mind had already planned out his escape. Good thing, really, since they were approaching the door and there would be very little time to pull this off. With a last glance up and down the street, he could see the guards at both ends now, tightening the net. In a minute they could be on him.

Here goes.

As Asima approached the door, she stopped, covered her face with a hand and turned to him.

'I… I just can't. Not again, Samir.'

He had to stifle an inward laugh. Well played, Asima.

'That's alright Asima,' he said, his face straight and grim. 'You wait here.'

Turning his back on her, he pulled on the handle and entered the house, allowing the door to swing almost closed behind him. The common room was very much how he remembered it, though dirty and dusty. The furniture was mostly gone or broken, but the small low table in the centre remained, a reminder of family meals long ago. Though he knew the layout of the building intimately, his mind had already checked out and catalogued the exits regardless: doorway to kitchen with climbable window to steps out back; doorway to corridor that led to latrine… no exit that way; stairs to rooms above… mother's room with window onto street or their old room with the only clear exit. Samir smiled.

Ghassan stepped out from the kitchen into the doorway.

'Samir.'

The pirate captain smiled at his tall brother.

'Ghassan. I'd like to say you look well. Better than Asima tells me, anyway?'

The taller brother laughed darkly.

'I had a feeling you'd be less gullible than she believed. I'm rather sorry that I have to do this, Samir. Even though it pains me to aid Asima over you, I just have to try and rebuild my life. I am sorry.'

'Not as sorry as I am, and not as sorry as you will be in a few minutes.'

Ghassan frowned and tilted his head.

'Explain?'

Samir sighed.

'I really wanted to provide you with the evidence before I explained all this, but here goes…'

He took a deep breath.

'Asima is outside with several dozen of the town guard. She doesn't need you at all, Ghassan. She knows that turning over a notorious pirate captain would likely garner her the governor's support, but not as much as she would get if she also provided at least circumstantial evidence that you were in league with me and had sold out your own navy. Imagine what the governor would do for her then.'

Ghassan blinked.

'I know she can't be trusted, Samir, but are you sure about all of this?'

'You can either believe me and we can get the hell out of here and somewhere safe, or you can wait a couple of minutes for hard evidence to turn up and take you into custody. I told you a few weeks ago that my offer would remain open. You've done your duty Ghassan; all there is left now is punishment and ignominy. Come with me and we can work it all out.'

'I'm not cut out for piracy, Samir,' Ghassan replied, shaking his head. 'You know that.'

His brother rolled his eyes.

'Are you cut out for jail, beatings and executions? Come on.'

For a moment, Ghassan dithered, staring at his brother and then, taking a deep breath, he strode across to the door, still standing ajar. Ducking to one side, he peered through the gap. A number of uniformed figures lurked by the doorways opposite.

'She sinks to a new low every time I see her. What are they waiting for, Samir?'

'Either they're not all here yet, or they're waiting on a signal from Asima or, more likely, they're waiting for their men to block all the alleys and streets leading away from here. They've got to seal us in.'

Ghassan nodded.

'I'm assuming you have a plan?'

'I used to put together all the most complicated roof races, didn't I?' Samir smiled.

'You almost got us killed so many times.'

'Yes, but we're bigger and stronger now, Ghassan. And no guard in M'Dahz knows the roofs like we do. How's your memory?'

Ghassan shrugged as he bent and stuffed the various items he had on the nearby cupboard into a bag.

'Depends where you're thinking of heading?'

'My ship's going to be in trouble. Either it's already under the control of the guard and the men are in custody or the crew have taken her out to sea to be safe. Either way, though, we're going to have to get to the port and find out.'

Ghassan shrugged.

'Then we need to take "Four Temples", cross by the dye factory, turn once we're over "Broken Promises", down into "Coppersmiths" and across the five warehouses. That'll bring us to the port on the west, away from the gate.'

Samir laughed.

'You see, I would have foregone "Coppersmiths" and taken the long jump over "Seven Gables". Quicker.'

Ghassan reached out and squeezed his brother's shoulder.

'You keep coming back for me, Samir. I do nothing but try to take you in, and yet you come to my aid every time. How can I be worth all the effort? I'm no better than Asima, in some ways.'

The smaller brother shook his head.

'You've always done what you thought was right, even when it hurt you. You're in no way the same as Asima and you know it. Now come on.'

Ghassan grabbed his bag and nodded as the two men turned and made for the small staircase in the corner of the room. At the foot, Samir stopped and stepped aside, gesturing for Ghassan to go first. The taller brother frowned, but took a step upwards and suddenly cried out.

Samir blinked and reached out to grab his brother as the taller man fell back from the stairs, a knife protruding from his thigh. The two men staggered back against the wall, Ghassan's leg unable to take the weight with the painful wound.

'Leaving so soon, boys?'

They looked back to the door to see Asima standing in the open archway, her hand still raised from throwing the weapon.

'No rooftop races, today, gentlemen. You're my ticket back to Pelasia, so I'm afraid I can't let you leave.'

Ghassan clenched his teeth as he reached down and pulled the knife from his leg with a grunt. A spurt of blood gushed out and down his leg.

'Asima? You going to keep two of my fingers to give the governor as a gift?'

Samir frowned.

'Forget her. Come on.'

The sound of metal outside testified to the closing presence of the guards. They only had seconds.

'Go, Samir.'

The pirate stared at his brother, who was wincing from the pain in his leg.

'I'm not leaving you again, Ghassan.'

'Yes you are. I'm yours, Samir. You already knew that somehow, and now so do I, but not at the moment. Come back for me when you're safe.'

For a long moment, Samir stared at his brother, but finally nodded.

'No, no, no…' came a voice from across the room

Asima was already rushing past the low table and, as she moved, she drew another knife from her belt. Samir shook his head, but Ghassan turned and pushed him into the stairwell and urging him to go before turning back to meet the assault of their childhood friend. Asima lunged like a wild animal, snarling as she swiped the sharp blade back and forth at Ghassan's face.

She was untrained. She may be angry and dangerous, but Ghassan had dealt with killers his whole adult life. Gritting his teeth against the pain in his leg, he twisted and threw up his arm inside her last swing, blocking her attack. Reaching up, he grasped her wrist so hard that he feared he may break it. Asima's fingers loosened and the knife fell from her hand, but there was no easing of her vicious attack, as she leaned forward and sank her teeth into his hand, the incisors meeting between his thumb and forefinger.

He howled and, reaching back, delivered her a stinging backhanded slap with his free arm.

Asima fell away to the floor, stunned, and Ghassan looked up, blood running down his hand and arm and dripping into the growing pool below him on the floor. Half a dozen guards stood in the entrance to the room. He smiled weakly.

'I don't suppose any of you gentlemen thought to bring a bandage?'

Sighing, he sank to his knees as the guards fanned out around him, weapons at the ready.

In which old games are revived

Samir clambered through the open window and dropped to the dusty rooftop below. Behind, he could still hear the activity in the main room and was suddenly faced with a problem. He needed to know where Ghassan and Asima were bound, but within moments there would be guards pouring up the stairs in pursuit of this infamous pirate captain, while their fellows already occupied the nearby streets and would see him jump between roofs if they were paying attention. Problems... and very little time to decide on a course of action.

He bit his lip.

Asima could only reasonably be going one place from here: the governor's complex, and she would be in no hurry. Possibly the most senior of the guards would escort her there, as he'd want to glean a share of the glory for the catch... or perhaps he wouldn't, since they'd failed to catch Samir. He briefly wondered whether Asima would give chase. No; she'd tell the guards where to look and then she'd go see the governor.

The larger question was over Ghassan. Would they take him to the governor too? Or perhaps to the guard house in the main square that stood behind the civic hall? Then there was also the prison that occupied the north-western-most tower of the city walls, hanging above the sea and separated from the town itself by a hundred yards of scree slope. And finally, there was the possibility that they would just strap him into a wagon or onto a horse and take him to Calphoris to his superiors.

Shaking his head, Samir realised he could hear the thunder of footsteps in the house below. The guards were coming and there was no time to plan now. He knew where Asima was going as soon as she had the chance, and Ghassan would likely remain in the city, in one place or another.

Dropping to a crouch, Samir smiled. In a curious way, this was refreshing; a hint of his long-gone youth. If it weren't for the circumstances, he could really enjoy a good chase. Closing his eyes, he took a deep breath. Below, a voice called out.

'The window!'

Grinning, Samir set off with the crunch of gravel on the rooftop and a cloud of choking white dust. By the time the first guard's face appeared at the window, the lithe pirate had already reached the far end of the roof and, with practiced ease, leapt across the gap without even glancing down.

As the first guard dropped down from the window to the roof, blinking in the dust and adjusting his armour, the second appeared behind him, staring across the roof.

'Shit, he's fast!'

The front guardsman nodded unhappily.

'I'll never make it across there; not in armour anyway.'

As the second man dropped down, a third appeared behind them, wearing the crest and insignia of an officer.

'Stop pissing about and get after him!'

'Sir, we can't jump over streets! We'll die.'

The officer clenched his teeth.

'If you don't get after him, I'll gut you myself.'

The second guard, a tall and muscular man with the colouring of a desert nomad, heaved off his mail shirt, his helmet falling to the roof unnoticed.

'I'll get him, sir.'

As the armour fell to the floor with a heavy 'chink', he dropped to a crouch and then set off like one of the dusky hounds the desert folk raced at the oases. The officer nodded appreciatively, while the first, shorter, guard stooped to collect the discarded armour. It was a hot day, even for a M'Dahz summer, and the armour was already hot to the touch.

'He's good,' the officer mused.

'Used to run in the Five Gods Games at Calphoris, sir. You've never seen anything like it.'

'He'd better be good. I need that piece of shit brought to justice.'

They stared off into the distance as the dust clouds settled. There was no sign of the pirate, but Jûn of the M'Dahz guard had already cleared the first street and was heading for a corner, his quarry's path revealed by the trail of settling dust.

Streets away and several minutes later, Samir puffed as he ran. The guard that had decided to follow him was so damn fast! He could have no experience of the rooftops, while Samir knew every nook and cranny, and yet still the man gained on him. It was astounding and, more importantly, it was putting Samir under pressure he could ill afford. With guards rushing through the streets below and trying to keep level with their quarry, shouting instructions across the intervening buildings, and this hound-like man hot on his heels, he had so far had precious little time to plan his route, relying instead on instinct and his memories of old races.

This was no good... without a plan, he would just keep racing until he was caught or cornered. He'd assumed that once he was out on the rooftops he'd be able to lose them easily. He needed to give his pursuers the slip and vanish, but that meant dealing with the guard chasing him.

The problem was that he had nothing against the man. Indeed, this dogged pursuer was the sort of man that, in his youth, Samir had yearned to be, that reminded him in many ways of uncle Faraj.

He shook his head. His life hung in the balance here, as did Ghassan's liberty and the only opportunity he might ever get to curb Asima's lust for power, and that outweighed one guard, no matter how innocent he might be.

With a fierce resolve flooding through him, Samir glanced left and right. The roof garden of the temple-hospital of Belapraxis was only two jumps away and the most dangerous route he'd ever planned passed by there. Time for a change of plan. He couldn't outrun this man, and he wouldn't have time to hide, so he had to outthink and outmanoeuvre him.

Veering off to his right, Samir made for the jutting outline of the temple's upper level, feeling a little bad for the poor man following him. Risking a quick glance over his shoulder, he could see his pursuer in enough detail now that he could make out the determination on the man's face. Of course, the man's career might well ride on this moment, if not his life, but that couldn't be Samir's concern right now. With another deep breath, he made the last small jump to the temple's main roof.

His nemesis close on his heels, Samir ducked out of sight around the wall surrounding the roof garden and made for the water-bearing pipe that crossed the street. Relief washed across him as he laid his eyes on the blessed escape-route. He hadn't had the time and leisure to contemplate the possibility that in the decades since he'd run these roofs the pipe had been moved or replaced, or had simply corroded and fallen away.

But it was there, precarious as ever.

A single beam, dusty and narrow, crossed one of the widest streets he had ever used in his routes. In the old days, blanket ceilings in the street had created a possible safety net around fifteen feet below the beam, but such was no longer the case. As Samir came to a halt at the roof's edge and bit his lip, he could see three storeys down to the sloping cobbled street. A few people milled about below, unaware of the drama unfolding on the rooftops above them but, as yet, no guards had reached this point. It wouldn't be long, though, given the shouted orders he could hear nearby.

At almost forty feet long, the beam was a nightmare in unfinished ash, worn smooth by the elements over the years and far from even. The only grip provided anywhere along the distance was the iron clamps that held the searing-hot metal guttering pipe that carried the water across the street, and those could only be trodden quickly and lightly in passing, for fear of burning the feet even through shoes.

Asima used to call him mad for planning runs like this. Funny how everything Samir had done in his life had seemed to contribute to his present liberty and health. With a smile of gratitude, he gave a brief nod of acknowledgement in the direction of the temple and, holding his breath, began to walk across the beam, keeping his eyes carefully locked on the wooden surface stretching out before him.

He was concentrating hard and his first distraction came when he was almost a third of the way across, as he heard the guard reach the end of the beam behind him and draw a deep breath. Without taking his eyes off the route ahead, Samir called out to his pursuer.

'You should stop there.'

'I imagine that would suit you,' replied the man and Samir was surprised and pleased to note a hint of wry humour to the voice.

'You really are very good. Where did you learn to run so fast and jump so well?'

He smiled, his tongue stuck out of the corner of his mouth in concentration.

'I used to run in the games, pirate.'

'Call me Samir. And you are?'

'Getting tired of chasing you. I will make it across and I will catch you. If you stop at the other side, I'll make sure the captain goes easy on you, though.'

Samir laughed. Two-thirds of the way across now. He'd had a couple of moments where he'd had to readjust his footing and his heart had skipped a beat, but he was sure of his abilities; knew himself and this beam very well.

'I'm afraid I can't do that, officer. You see, I have obligations to help people and I can't do it while your captain uses me to blunt his knuckles.'

He laughed again.

'Gods, I wish you were on my crew. I could use a man like you.'

'I'm sure the same could be said the other way around but, sadly, things are what they are, captain. Now... whoa!'

Samir bit his cheek and stopped for a moment, taking the dangerous opportunity to glance over his shoulder. The guard had almost slipped and was wobbling back and forth, regaining his balance.

'That was close, my friend. I have no wish to see you shattered on the cobbles, so do be careful.'

'Thanks,' came the dry reply, and the two men began to step forward again. Samir sighed. He hated this with a passion, but there was no choice. He couldn't allow the guard to follow him beyond the beam. There would be nowhere better than this to halt the pursuit.

He clenched his teeth as he stepped from the end of the beam onto the edge of the flat rooftop, where the water channel continued to run in a narrow gutter and turned to face his pursuer. The guard really was good and had made it almost three quarters of the way across.

'This is my last offer. Turn round and go back, officer. I can't have you following me.'

The guard shook his head.

'You know I can't do that, Captain Samir.'

'Then I apologise for what I have to do now.'

Reaching down, Samir cupped his hands and collected a scoop of gritty, dirty water, swinging his arms forward and flinging the liquid across the beam. With a splash, the water covered the wood, becoming slick and reflecting the tiny, scudding fleecy clouds in the otherwise clear sapphire sky. As the guard frowned and slowed, reaching the edge of the slippery section, Samir bent and repeated the process twice more, soaking the beam thoroughly.

'Turn round, for Gods' sake. You can't safely cross.'

'I wouldn't say I can turn round safely either. Get running. I won't let a little water stop me.'

'For fuck's sake, turn round.'

He grimaced as the guard took a step into the water, shaking slightly and wobbling back and forth. Another step. The man was managing to maintain his balance, but there was a long way to go yet. He'd never make it. Samir shook his head sadly.

'Listen... I'm not a bad man and I don't really want your death on my hands.'

Another step and suddenly a slight slip to one side left the man teetering. Samir watched with dismay as the man rocked back and forth, picking up momentum. He was about to go.

'Jump for the roof!'

But before the man could get enough purchase, he slipped. Samir watched for only a fraction of a second before leaping into action, quite literally. As the man slipped, he did his best to push himself forward, his flailing arm launching him out from the beam at an angle. As he did so, Samir crouched, grasped the iron clamp at the very end of the beam, the searing heat here only slightly tempered by the water that flowed by and over it and the soaking he had just given it. As he vaulted out over the open space, feeling his shoulder jerk, he clenched the hot iron tightly. His other hand caught the falling man by the arm and the pair of them seemed to hang, suspended in the air for an eternity before the pull to ground began to assert itself.

With agonising force, the pair swung down against the wall, Samir's arm almost breaking where it held the clamp and carried the weight of two men. Below him, the guard slipped from Samir's wet grip and, eyes wide, grabbed desperately onto the pirate's leg, gripping tightly. Samir grunted, the pain intense.

'I'm going to try and pull myself up. If you can find any purchase on the wall to take some weight, it would be a great help!'

The guard nodded vigorously and began to scour the plaster wall quickly. There were pits here and there; nothing that could be considered a handhold but, with some effort, he got his toes into one and pushed up.

Samir felt a slight relief in the extraordinary weight of the big man below him. Gritting his teeth, he swung his free arm up and grasped the really rather hot iron clamp with both hands. Groaning with the strain and tearing muscles painfully, he slowly hauled the pair of them up to roof level.

After a minute that seemed like hours he managed to get his elbows over the edge and used his powerful shoulder muscles to haul himself the last stretch. Once his torso was flat on the roof, his legs still hanging, he shouted down to the unseen guard.

'Can you grab the edge of the roof now? There's a very slight lip; it's not much but it should be enough if you're strong.'

The man made an affirmative grunt and, clinging to Samir's leg with one arm, began to search out a hold with the fingertips of his other. Samir watched with relief as the fingers gripped the edge and he felt a sudden release on his leg. Two hands now gripped the roof.

Swinging his legs up and around, Samir climbed wearily to his feet and walked across to the dangling man.

'Are you alright?'

'I've been better, but I could be a hell of a lot worse.'

Samir laughed.

'I'm afraid I have to leave you now. I hope you manage to climb, but you'll understand that I can't afford to hang around.'

The guard looked up at him.

'Be assured that when I climb up, I'll be after you again… but I think I may have twisted my leg in the fall, so I might be a little slower now.'

Samir grinned down at him.

'Get drunk tonight, officer. I think you deserve it.'

'Jûn'

'What?'

'That's my name: Jûn.'

'I'll remember that next time I get to the races,' Samir laughed.

With a nod, he turned and ran off across the rooftops toward the palace complex.

In which Asima seals a deal

Samir took another deep breath as he made the penultimate jump. Many times and many years ago, he'd sat on this slight incline and stared across the gap at the walled complex opposite. He'd always meant to walk those roofs, but had never expected it to be under such circumstances.

From here the building that faced him was the residence of the local governor himself, or, at least, it had been when they were children. He had seen governor Talus standing at the ornate windows several times in the past. It was quite possible that the new governor had taken other quarters, but the chances were against it. These would be the best appointed of all the rooms in the complex.

So long ago he had spent time studying the complex and, while he'd never had the opportunity to put his observations to use then, now would seem to be the time.

There was only one possible route to the roofs of the complex. It had made him too nervous as a child to even contemplate trying it, but he was a great deal faster and stronger these days. Of course, it was still life-threatening and a ridiculous proposition even for a grown man, but it was the only option if he wanted to get a step ahead once more.

He watched for several minutes. There were figures moving around in the room, but they staying deep in the room and never came close to the window. One was tall and well dressed and Samir was prepared to put money on that being the governor. There were two or three other shapes that he could make out, but they were too distant and shadowy to identify. He couldn't even tell what gender they were.

Still, he had to try, and that was the only window that seemed likely.

Gritting his teeth, he offered up a quick prayer to whichever of Ha'Rish's faces was currently keeping an eye on him and crossed the roof to the small, low pile of rubble in the corner. It had been over twenty years. Of course, rope didn't rot and iron didn't rust in the M'Dahz climate, but it could easily have been found and moved.

Fumbling in the dusty rubble, he sighed with relief as his fingers closed on the curved iron. Moving a few of the heavier blocks aside, he extricated the grapple that he had 'liberated' from the docks more than two decades ago. Time had been kind to his little prize. The grapple, along with the thirty feet of thin cable coiled behind it, had lain in secret all these years, awaiting the day when Samir plucked up the courage to actually execute his plan.

He frowned at the rope. Long ago he'd selected this specific rope as being light enough to carry across the rooftops when coiled, while long enough to cross the gap and strong enough to hold his weight. Now, as an adult with a slightly more discerning eye, he was beginning to doubt whether thirty feet would be quite enough and whether the thin rope would hold his adult weight.

Turning, he glanced over the low walled parapet. There was less than thirty feet between him and the building, but only just. Ah well…

Carefully scanning the outer wall of the palace, he took in every window within his target area. None were occupied that he could see, though people could easily be close by within the shadowed interiors. The governor, if that was who he was, was occupied with his activity in the room. Of equal importance to him, the street was empty below. There would never be a better time… there may, indeed, never be another opportunity at all.

Crouching, he located the heavy pitons that had been driven into the parapet long ago, onto which a huge cover could be hooked to provide shade on the flat roof, in the days when this building had been a more elegant residence. Nodding to himself, he tied the end of the rope to the piton, though not too tight.

Standing, he took a deep breath, made sure the coiled rope was untangled, took the iron grapple in hand, and let the grapple slide slowly from his grasp until he gripped the rope around four feet from the metal. Starting small and slow, he began to swing the grapple, slowly picking up pace as the heavy object whirred past him ponderously. Gradually, as the speed of the spinning item increased, he let the rope slip out, inch by inch. Years of boarding actions aboard the Empress had trained him well.

Finally, when he judged the swing was right, he clenched his teeth and let go, uttering a small prayer under his breath as he watched the grapple arc out over the gap. His heart skipped a beat as he watched it strike home against the wall opposite, close to the governor's window, and then tumble toward the street. Grumbling, Samir hurriedly began to haul the rope back in.

After a nervous moment, he had the grapple once more and squinted across the street. No one had appeared at a window. Lucky. Coiling the rope once again, he prepared for a second attempt. At least his failure had ascertained that the rope was, indeed, long enough to reach.

Again, starting small, he began to swing, letting the speed build as he let the rope out slightly. Metal thrumming past his ear, he reached the optimal moment and released, watching with trepidation. The aim was true this time, though, and the grapple disappeared into the opening of the window to the left of the governor's.

Tense, Samir ducked behind the low parapet and watched for almost a minute. There was no sign of activity and, slowly, he released the breath he hadn't realised he was holding. Reaching down, he untied the end of the rope from the piton and began to pull slowly. The rope came in by almost three feet and then jammed tight. Just to be sure, he hauled on it a few times. It was solidly fastened and he nodded approvingly as he tied it once more, much tighter this time.

'Here goes,' he said quietly to himself, as he made a last check of the façade opposite, the complex's outer wall presenting an aperture-free surface for fifteen feet, with the palace windows above, surmounted by a gabled roof. In the old days it was that roof that had fascinated him. Not so, now.

Gripping the rope, he slowly lowered himself over the parapet, wincing. The rope held so far. Offering up his third prayer of the hour, an activity he had long foregone, he began carefully and smoothly to cross the gap, hand over hand along the thin rope, his lower lip between his teeth as he went.

There was an alarming moment almost half way across when the rope gave just a little; perhaps a foot. Possibly the grapple had attached itself to something badly-secured in the room. Samir shifted a little from his slow and careful technique, picking up speed to cross as fast as he could. The fall from here may not kill him but, if not, it would seriously injure him and almost certainly lead to a life of imprisonment or a death sentence.

The notion of swinging bulge-eyed before the public at the port as a warning to would-be pirates spurred in him an extra turn of speed, and he crossed the remaining length of rope at an almost dangerously unsafe speed.

Finally, blessedly, he reached the window and slowly pulled himself up to the lintel to look inside. The room was empty and, while reasonably decorative, devoid of furniture. Some kind of ante-chamber, it seemed.

Glancing left, he smiled. The wall here was decorative and the rows of bonding tiles jutted out slightly, making a handy ledge for both fingers and toes. Holding his breath, he shuffled along, edging ever closer to the window of the next room.

Over the general background noise of M'Dahz, he could hear voices in the next room. Concentrating as he shuffled slowly closer, he tried to block out the ambient sound and pay attention to the activity in the room. One of the voices was female and he would be willing to bet that it was Asima, particularly given the dark and unpleasant tone of the man's voice. Asima seemed to have that effect on people these days.

Hurrying as much as he could, Samir closed on the window and finally, as he reached it, grasped the lintel with his fingers and drew himself close enough to peer over the edge.

There were four people in the room. The governor was clear, a tall man with a sour face, dressed in neat and expensive clothes. The other two men were clearly a senior officer in the town guard and some sort of advisor. The last, of course: Asima. He was momentarily disheartened to see that he was too late. The woman was leaving. As he watched, she nodded to the governor and, turning, walked from the room.

Samir wondered momentarily whether he should give this up now and move onto the next step, but shook his head slightly. This was important. He had to know what she'd done.

As the door closed with a click, the other two men approached the governor's desk and he sat back heavily.

'What do you think, gentlemen?'

'She's telling the truth, as far as we can confirm. Ghassan is in custody and is being taken to the tower now, awaiting your decision. Samir is definitely somewhere in M'Dahz, but the men lost track of him on the rooftops. All the gates are being watched, as is the port. His ship's been taken and is under guard and a part of his crew are being detained in the guard station at the docks. Whatever Samir plans, he can't escape and we have his ship.'

The governor nodded and Samir mentally urged them on in the silence that followed. How far had she gone and what had they granted her?

'Do we stop her at the gate, or are you really intending to let her go, Excellency?'

The governor shrugged.

'She's Pelasia's problem now. Her information is well worth the fee she asked and the issue Prince Ashar will raise with me. The important thing now is to find Captain Samir and drag out of him the location of this 'compass' thing. Then we can put an end to Lassos and the pirate threat. Ashar will forgive a great deal for that… the pirates prey on his ships too.'

Samir heaved a sigh of relief, grateful that he'd not overestimated her.

'Perhaps we could start hanging his men until he shows up?' the aide offered hopefully. He was greeted with a cold stare from the governor.

'Coro, we are civilised people. The crew will get a trial and, if they are to be hanged, it will be with the knowledge that it is for the good of the people, and not out of anger, revenge, or deceit. Samir cannot stay here forever. Sooner or later he will make a move and we will catch him. Likely it will involve his brother, his men or his ship, so have the guard pay a great deal of attention in the next few days. I want Samir.'

Nodding with satisfaction, Samir glanced around. This trip had served a second purpose that he'd also hoped for: he now knew what the governor looked like and what sort of man he was and he appeared to be a reasonable man, which would be very useful shortly, when the time came to take the next step.

Smiling, he noted that a couple of ladies were standing chatting thirty feet below him. He contemplated just dropping from here, but a broken leg would seriously ruin his plans. Instead, he lowered himself slowly and carefully down the wall below the window, using the small hand- and footholds he could find until he reached the bare surface of the defensive perimeter wall. With a smile, he let go and fell the last fifteen feet, landing lightly with bent knees.

The two women turned in surprise and stared at the strange visitor that had appeared from nowhere.

'Ladies,' Samir addressed them, touching his forehead respectfully and with a smile, before turning and running off into the city.

In which castles crumble

The harbour's military quartermaster glared at the guard as the first light of the sun crested the horizon and picked out the decoration on the tip of the building's roof.

'How the hell do you misplace stock like that?'

The soldier winced. He'd been on guard all night, from sundown til sunrise. It had been excruciatingly dull, and it was understood among the naval guards stationed in M'Dahz's port that nothing ever really happened. It was almost expected of one to drop off to sleep for a while – so that you were fresh, so to speak. It just had to be the unluckiest day of his life for him to doze off without locking the door to the ammunition store. And he could hardly own up to that last part, else he'd be swinging in the wind by the end of the day.

'I just can't account for it, sir. When I did the pre-dawn check this morning there were three items missing. I can't vouch for the evening check, coz it was before I came on duty so maybe the previous count was wrong?'

The officer narrowed his eyes.

'If I find out that you sold stock to supplement your dice habit, I will skin you and wear you like a cloak, do you understand?'

'Sir, I didn't do nothing!'

'Then where the hell did three fire pots half the size of a grown man...'

The quartermaster's voice tailed off as the air thrummed to the sound of an explosion so powerful that the very wall vibrated where he leaned on it.

Samir's head rose from the rock behind which he had sheltered, his eyes wide. This, of course, was why all good warships had very careful and well-trained artillery masters. Novices playing around with liquid fire pots was clearly a bad idea.

He'd stolen them from the armoury in the port in the middle of the night, with considerably more ease than he'd expected, given the laxness of the guards. An hour's journey through the dark streets had been unobserved as the cart rattled up the slope toward the west with its heavy load of explosive pots.

The donkey and cart had managed the slope well, bringing Samir and his ammunition within ten yards of the wall. Manhandling the heavy earthenware pots, however, each more than two feet in diameter and packed with deadly combustible material, from the cart to the tower was a whole different matter.

He'd originally intended to perform his miracle breakout in middle of the night, but had seriously underestimated the time it would take to get the three great pots up to the base of the tower.

On the other hand, he was forced to admit as he watched chunks of stone rain down over the port and splash into the sea, he may had overestimated the quantity of explosives he needed just a tad.

His head ringing like the inside of a bell and his ears making a horrible whining noise, Samir peered into the smoke and dust to assess the damage.

He had assumed that if he placed the pots far enough apart they would detonate in a chain, as per his fuses. What he hadn't counted on was that the force of the first blast was enough to detonate the other two instantly. Consequently, the explosion that was supposed to be contained and sensible and to produce a hole in the tower's lower wall large enough to climb through had, in fact, obliterated a portion of the foundations on the eastern side and blown much of the lower wall on that side out and over the bay and the port district. The exact damage was hard to assess, given the huge cloud of grey dust and the falling fragments.

His breath caught as he realised that there was more than a vague possibility that his reckless actions had actually killed Ghassan and others along with him. Probably not, though. From what his sources had told him last night, the lower levels were mostly given over to storage, the prisoners being kept in cells at the centre of the tower where there were no windows. It was possible that he'd caught one or more guards in the blast, but he was hopeful that wasn't the case. The night shift of guards was a 'skeleton staff' and they would mostly be on patrol at the top.

Samir shook his head, his ears still throbbing and whining. It was no good panicking about it now.

Taking a deep breath, he tied a scarf around his lower face for protection against the dust and left his shelter as the last of the debris rolled down the slope from the ruined wall. While he climbed the scree as fast as he could manage, taking care to avoid the chunks of masonry that were still sliding down toward the town below, he peered, blinking, through the grey cloud and picked out as much detail as he could.

Relief flooded over him as he closed on the structure and the cloud began to dissipate. The damage was not as bad as he'd initially believed. The tower was still structurally sound. The hole that had produced so much falling rubble was perhaps fifteen feet in each direction. It revealed the lowest floor and a little of the one above, and had done considerable damage to the interior walls on this side, but not enough to penetrate higher into the tower. Unless anyone happened to be in the ruined lower storeroom or the outer chambers of the next floor up, they would be fine. They may spend the rest of their life with whistling ears if Samir's were anything to go by, but that could hardly be helped.

Reaching the bottom of the tower, Samir gingerly pulled at the edge of the aperture. Stone fell away under his grip, but the core was sound. Taking another deep breath, he clambered across the ruinous threshold and into the storeroom. Stopping for a moment to get his bearings, he tried to superimpose the mental map he had constructed from the information he'd gathered last night over the building around him. Nodding, he calculated both the quickest and the safest route to the prison area on the third level and weighed them for a moment before shrugging and deciding on speed over safety. It wouldn't even be the first stupid thing he'd done this morning, he grinned.

Gritting his teeth, he grasped the ruined wall and began to climb the mangled stonework toward the open floor above. The climb was difficult and dangerous, as illustrated amply by the amount of stonework that came away in his hands and skittered off down the slope. Still, Samir was lithe and determined and, in a little more than a minute, he stepped gingerly onto the flagged floor of the second level. There was an ominous creak as he put his weight down and he quickly hurried away from the ruined edge and toward the middle of the tower.

The town walls and their towers were mostly of Pelasian construction and relatively recent, given that the original walls of M'Dahz were already ruinous when Ma'ahd invaded and had to be rebuilt for his new conquest. The Pelasians loved symmetry in everything they did, so the huge drum tower that marked the north-western end of the town walls was five floors in height and organised like the spokes of a wheel. A central spiral stairwell opened on each floor into a circular inner corridor with rooms off it. At intervals, however, passageways led between the rooms to another outer corridor that circled at the edge and from which doors led inward to more rooms.

Slowly and, he hoped, quietly, Samir drew his sword. Listening at the door was a waste of time in the circumstances and steadying himself, he flung the door open and jumped inside. The stair well had escaped the blast, even at the lower levels, and fresh, clean air blew down from above. There was no sign of movement and Samir began to leap up the stairs, two at a time.

The next level's door stood open and Samir approached with caution. Ducking his head round the door, he quickly drew himself back, but not before having noted in the flash of an eye what lay beyond. This was most definitely the prison level. The doors leading off the inner corridor were heavy and iron banded, each with a grille at face height and a locking bar across the outside, all lit only by oil lamps burning on ledges at intervals in the corridor.

The guard he'd seen just inside the door had worn an expression of utter confusion and shock. His helmet lay on the floor alongside his sword, while he stood with his head at an angle, poking at his ear with a gloved finger.

Samir smiled; Ha'Rish was working hard to help him today. Without delay, the pirate captain strode into the circular corridor, stepped up behind the guard, raised his sword above the man and brought the pommel down hard on his skull. There was a crack and a groan and the man sank to the floor, his eyes rolling up into his head.

For a moment, Samir considered shouting out Ghassan's name in an effort to identify which cell he needed, but the futility of that struck him immediately: there was no hope of anyone hearing anything in here. His own hearing had gone and he'd been outside the tower in the open air, let alone trapped inside with the explosion ringing echoes around the hall.

Instead, he ran to the nearest door and peered into the grille. Speed was now of the essence. As soon as the town guard realised what had just happened, this place would be flooded with uniforms and he had to get Ghassan out of the tower before then.

The first cell appeared to be empty. Despite his urgency, Samir spent a moment casting his eyes left and right to be sure there was no figure lurking in the darkness, his vision largely impeded by the low, dancing light, the shadow cast by his own body, and the dim conditions within. Shaking his head, he moved on to the next door. Careful peering around within revealed finally a thin old man hunched over by the far wall.

This was ridiculous! He could search for half an hour and still not find his brother. Samir stopped and scratched his head as he pondered. A moment passed as the whining in his ear continued to insist on his thoughts and then he slapped his forehead in irritation at his own short-sightedness. The solution was simple. Returning to the first door with a determined expression, Samir drew back the locking bar and threw the door open.

'Let's give them a crowd of escaped criminals to keep them busy,' he said to himself as he rushed to the old man's cell, grinning, and slid the bar, swinging open the portal.

On he rushed from cell to cell, throwing back bars and opening doors, taking only the briefest glimpse within as he did so. Behind him, prisoners emerged, blinking, into the lamp light, some clearly having spent years inside; others more recent additions to the captive population.

He was so surprised when Ghassan appeared at one of the doors and reached out to him that he was already moving on to the next door. He stopped, turning, and grinned at his brother. The taller sibling was dirty but had not been mistreated, his leg wound now tended and bound, along with the bite wound on his hand.

Ghassan grasped him by the forearms and said something, his lips moving rapidly, excitement clear on his face. Samir shrugged and pointed to his ears. Ghassan laughed and mimicked the gesture before pointing at the stairwell. The smaller brother nodded and, leaving the half dozen confused prisoners milling about in the hallway, Samir led Ghassan back round the curved wall to the door.

As the pair dashed out into the cool stairwell, slowed only a little by the taller brother's limp, Ghassan initially turned upwards, there having been no exit at the lower levels prior to the explosion. Samir grasped him by the wrist, pointing at shadows cast on the wall. Though neither of them could hear a thing, the shade puppets moving against the torchlight from above clearly announced the approach of the tower's guards from the higher levels.

The two men moved down the stairs to the next level as fast as they could. Samir had considered leaving the stairs on the ground floor, but the destruction of the store's contents would make it slow and difficult to pick their way out. Ghassan blinked in astonishment as they reached the lower level and stepped out into the light admitted by the enormous gaping hole in the outer wall. The taller brother frowned, pointed at the huge opening and then at

Samir, a question in his expression. Samir grinned and nodded as he beckoned and ran over to the edge.

Once again the floor creaked alarmingly as the pair approached the hole, and he slowed as he reached the drop. Ghassan's wounds seemed hardly to hamper his movement at all as the pair made light work of climbing out onto the ruined wall and down to ground level, the taller brother slipping only once as his bad leg gave way. As they alighted on the scree, he mimed a question to Samir over their next move.

The smaller brother beckoned once again and led his sibling over to a small knot of scrub bushes. There was no hope of the two men escaping down the scree without being spotted and guards from the port area would even now be approaching the bottom of the slope. There was nowhere they could safely go, and nowhere to hide, but Samir had counted on this being the case. As he and Ghassan disappeared into the cover of the greenery, he reached down to a small bag hidden under leaves and withdrew two neatly folded guard tunics and cloaks. Helmets, chain mail and gloves sat ready next to the bag.

Ghassan grinned and quickly began to don his uniform as his brother did the same.

No matter what the rest of the day might hold, even amid a hundred enemies and with a horrible whistling in his ears, it was good to be working with Samir. His smaller brother was a force of nature and it seemed there was just no stopping him.

Ghassan couldn't help but smile.

In which brothers escape

The brothers looked at one another, took a deep breath, and strode out from behind the ruined wall of the tower where they had been lurking as they watched the guards approaching up the scree bank. Ghassan kept his head slightly lowered, shaking it as if to clear his hearing. In fact his hearing was returning slowly; he could make out noise from the men as they climbed. Samir strode boldly out next to him, squaring his shoulders.

'Ha'Rish watch over me now.'

Ghassan smiled at his brother, not entirely sure of what he'd just said, but aware of the feeling behind it from the tenseness in Samir's expression.

'You!'

One of the unit of town guard climbing the slope and wearing a commander's uniform pointed at the pair of them as he reached the top and came to a halt before them.

'What the hell happened here?'

Ghassan furrowed his brow and pointed to his ears. Samir caught the gesture out of the corner of his eye and took the lead.

'SOMEONE BLEW UP THE TOWER!' he shouted in an exaggerated fashion.

'Lower your voice,' replied the commander, grimacing at him.

'WHAT, SIR?'

The commander turned to a lesser officer next to him.

'These two need to see a medic about their hearing. They must have been too close to the blast. Have someone help them back down.'

The junior nodded and waved at the brothers, pointing down the slope.

'Cavis... help these two back to the barracks and get the company medic to check their ears.'

A young guard saluted and ran forward to the two dusty men. He opened his mouth to speak and then shut it and shook his head, instead gesturing down the slope with his thumb.

Samir nodded and began to move slowly and carefully down the gravelly slope, trying not to slide and lose his footing as they followed the young soldier. Moments passed as they moved ever closer to the town and further away from the unit of guards.

Somewhere around half way down the slope, Samir risked a look about him to check the situation. The guards had converged with three other units coming up the slope and along the wall. Any minute now the real problem would become apparent to them and then the fugitive pair would become very highly sought after. The young guard, Cavis, was several yards ahead of them.

Frowning, he leaned across to Ghassan as they picked their way down, slowing slightly in order to increase the distance between them and their escort. Quietly, he cupped his hand around his mouth and leaned into his brother's ear.

'Is your hearing returning yet?' he said quietly.

Ghassan nodded.

'It's a bit whiney and there's a constant whistle, but I can hear you if I concentrate.'

Samir smiled.

'Mine's better, but then I wasn't trapped with the blast.'

Turning back, he studied the young soldier. They'd said nothing untoward yet, but the guard wasn't listening anyway, concentrating on his footing on the treacherous slope.

'Any minute now they're going to discover that you've gone and questions will be raised. As soon as they know that all the guards are still accounted for up there every uniform in M'Dahz will be searching for us, so we need to get out of sight as quick as possible.'

Ghassan nodded.

'We'll have to deal with Cavis over there.'

'Yes, and now, really.'

Ghassan nodded and shrugged.

'Nothing we can do til we reach the bottom, though. Too open here to be busy beating up a guard. You can be seen from every direction. Anyway, we're in a hurry. Leave him to me... I have an idea.'

Samir nodded, frowning, and almost called out when Ghassan, grinning, threw himself into a forward roll, bouncing down the slope and plummeting past the guard. The smaller brother smiled as his sibling tightly clutched his head, protecting himself from serious damage, and ended sliding down the last part of the slope and coming to rest on his back near a low wall at the rear of a house, carefully located out of sight of almost everywhere.

Cavis squawked in alarm and ran off precariously down the slope after his charge, dropping to a crouch at the bottom and hovering over Ghassan, examining him closely. The young man realised at such close quarters that this tall, swarthy man had longish, curly locks, was badly-shaven and smelled stale. Most unlike one of the town guard.

'Hey…'

Samir watched with interest as his brother burst into activity. Reaching up to the young guard above him, one hand went over the mouth, preventing any cry for help, while the other reached round and clamped on the side of the guard's neck. As the young man's arms flailed, Ghassan rolled over, pinning his victim beneath him while he maintained his hold. As Samir slithered down the last of the slope, his brow furrowed. Ghassan was pressing into the young man's neck in a very precise manner and holding him tight now as he struggled. Cavis' eyes widened a moment and slowly he went limp until he sagged beneath his assailant.

Sighing, Ghassan rolled away from the boy, patted him on the cheek in a friendly fashion, and stood, tenderly touching a few grazes from his controlled fall.

'You've picked up some interesting tricks,' Samir noted as the brothers gave Cavis a last glance to make sure his chest was rising and falling safely before disappearing around the wall and into an alley. Just as they vanished from sight, the warning blast rang out from the tower above and the top of the slope blossomed with sudden activity.

Ghassan shrugged as they strode along the narrow alley.

'One of my old marine sergeants used to fight in the pits in Rilva. He knew all sorts of fascinating things. Most of them are deadly, but this one just renders someone unconscious for a while.'

Samir nodded, impressed.

'So what now?' Ghassan asked. 'I presume you've planned beyond this, since we're both wanted men, trapped in M'Dahz with no way out?'

'I've the bare bones of a plan. Sadly, I need you to put a bit of meat on them.'

He stopped and turned to Ghassan.

'You see, I need to go take care of something, so I'm going to have to leave it in your capable hands.'

Ghassan frowned.

'Last time you did that, I left to join the army and you abandoned me and became a criminal.'

The smaller man laughed and grasped his sibling's shoulder.

'Ah, but now we're both criminals, my brother. The problem is that I have a much grander plan than you could know, but the timing is running very tight and I need to go now or I'll miss my opportunity. I will be back for you... or rather, I hope you'll be back for me.'

Ghassan frowned.

'Alright. What's your plan, then?'

'There's a tavern in the docks called the Laughing Mermaid. Remember it?'

'Yes.'

'Only around a small portion of my crew will have been on board the Empress when they impounded her. The rest I told to go ashore, realising that Asima was going to turn us in. The ones who stayed behind volunteered to maintain the fiction that the ship was occupied.'

Samir squared his shoulders.

'I'm sorry to land you with the big job, but there's no one else I could trust to do it. You need to go find my crew and gather them together. Then get them to help you break the rest of the men out of the stockade in the port; they may have volunteered, but that doesn't mean we should leave them to rot.'

Ghassan whistled through his teeth.

'Good grief. And then you'll join us?'

'Not exactly. Then comes the hard bit: you'll have to lead my crew down to the secure dock, take on the town guard and cut out the Empress and get safely away out to sea. That's going to be the tough bit, particularly since I presume you'll try to do it with the minimum possible casualties.'

'That's a tall order, Samir. I'm not convinced we could achieve that together, let alone me on my own.'

'Yes you can, Ghassan. When you meet at the Mermaid, speak to my first officer, a man called Ursa, and make sure he still has my bag. There's something in there we can't afford to lose.'

'Anything else?' Ghassan asked in exasperation.

'Just this: Once you're out of port and safe, head for Pelasian waters. Right on the border, about six miles away, is a coastal village called Khediv. Anchor offshore and wait for me there. I'll be with you as soon as I can.'

Ghassan narrowed his eyes.

'Don't you think it might be handy for me to have at least a clue as to your plan? What are you up to, Samir?'

The smaller brother laughed and scratched his head.

'Just saving the world, Ghassan. Can you do all this? And meet me at Khediv?'

The taller man brushed his errant curl from his forehead and nodded.

'I'll manage somehow, so long as your crew don't try to kill me on sight. I can't imagine I'm their favourite person.'

'You'd be surprised, Ghassan. Speak to Ursa. Go safe and be lucky, and I'll see you hopefully tomorrow morning.'

His brother furrowed his brow once again and then shrugged and sighed.

'Alright. Get going on your mysterious errand and we'll see you at the border.'

He watched with a mixed sense of gratitude and worry as Samir ran off through the tangled streets up the slope of M'Dahz, removing his guard uniform and discarding it as he ran. It would be awful to have finally reconciled his differences with Samir only to lose him once again. The little devil was too secretive and devious for his own good, sometimes. With a smile, Ghassan turned and made for the port at a quick walk, removing the guard cloak and tunic as he went.

As he descended the widening street toward the port he was relieved to note that the gate remained wide open as usual although now, rather than being guarded by two bored men, half a dozen soldiers stood alert, eyeing up everyone who entered or left the port. Presumably they were mostly on the lookout for Samir; they wouldn't know of Ghassan's escape yet and probably didn't have his description. Still, it was better to be safe than sorry.

Ducking into a shadowed alleyway that hadn't yet been graced with the dawn light, Ghassan looked up and down the street. It was still early and there were few enough people around that he would be observed as he entered the port, and that might raise questions. His attire, condition and grazes might attract just too much attention. With a smile, he turned and jogged down the dark passage.

Sure enough, it met another tiny alley, too narrow for animals or vehicles. Clean washing hung on lines at the rear of residences. If he remembered this area correctly...

Yes, there it was: the rear entrance of the stables that fronted onto Khaz Gharda Street, and just inside the gate stood a huge stone trough, half full of water. Later it would be filled for the horses. Grinning, Ghassan pulled himself easily up and over the low wall, grunting at the pain in his leg as he dropped to the stone within. Removing the chain mail and gloves, along with his tunic, breeches and boots, he dropped them one after the other onto the floor beside the trough until he was standing naked. He grinned. That would give the stable master a shock if he came out now.

As quickly as he could, he climbed into the trough, immersing himself in the cold water that had chilled overnight and was yet to see warming sunlight. There was barely enough water to cover him but, ignoring the goose bumps that rose on his skin, he quickly washed himself down as best he could to remove the odour of the jail cell and sweat and plastered his unruly hair back down to his scalp.

Shivering, he climbed back out into the early sunlight, paused for a moment as he decided what to do with his armour and finally, shrugging, left it where it lay and climbed, naked, over the wall and back into the narrow alley. Minutes later, he was in the back yard of a house, selecting unremarkable garments of an average quality, and dressing as speedily as he could.

By the time he returned to the main road, there were noticeably more people about. With a frown, he perused the population. The best way... yes, there was his ticket into the port unmolested.

Down the street came a teamster with a cartload of bags and sacks, partially covered with a thick blanket. The donkey pulling the cart rolled its eyes in a bad tempered fashion and snorted. Ghassan chuckled.

'I know how you feel.'

Waiting for just the right moment, he walked out of the alleyway just as the cart rolled past and ambled quietly along on the opposite side of the street, keeping pace with the carter. Slowly, they rolled on toward the port and, after a few tense minutes, Ghassan let the carter pull slightly ahead. As the donkey reached the gate, guards stepped across to block passage. The man reined his beast in and the wheels rolled slowly to a halt, while the soldiers on duty began to go through the cart's load, prodding with the buts of their spears.

Keeping his expression carefully neutral, Ghassan walked calmly on past the activity and through the open archway into the port district with only the most cursory of glances from one of the free guards.

He smiled. Being totally unremarkable was always the best way to remain unnoticed.

Now to find the Laughing Mermaid.

In which Ghassan instils order

The tavern was noisy, smelly, and absolutely full of life, exactly as Ghassan remembered it from the many times he had passed by during his youth, as well as the more recent occasions when the Wind of God was docked here. However, despite his familiarity with the building, he had never before set foot inside it.

The interior was murky, reeking of the root cultivated by the desert nomads that was burned and smoked in clay pipes, mixed with the smell of sweat and that curious salty odour that only a lifetime sailor could cultivate. Squinting, Ghassan cast his gaze left and right. The tavern population seemed to polarise, with certain types gathering in small groups. There were several likely-looking groups that could represent the crew of the Empress and for a moment the fugitive officer chided himself for not asking more detail of his brother.

Through the crowds, as he clicked his tongue irritably, he spotted a heavy-set man with a design of whorls and spines tattooed across his scalp. Smiling, he realised that was probably why Samir had directed him to the first officer. Ghassan remembered that scalp from his brief time on board. Ursa was rather hard to miss.

Taking a deep breath, the tall man straightened and strode across the room, coming to a halt before the group who were spread across four tables at one end of the room. He almost laughed when the whole bunch fell silent, to a man, as he approached them. It was like something from an old comedy tale.

'Ursa, yes? I'm sure I remember you.'

The big man turned an angry face on him and his eyes flashed dangerously.

'Only if you'd like me to shout out your name, captain.'

Ghassan nodded.

'Agreed. Indiscreet of me. My apologies. I'm here at the request of my brother.'

Ursa nodded.

'He warned me. You're to help us cut out the Empress and meet him later?'

'Yes, but more than that,' Ghassan said, gesturing at a chair and raising his eyebrow.

The big first officer nodded and, as they sat, Ghassan noted with a mix of humour and discomfort the unpleasant looks many of the pirates were directing at him. He couldn't entirely blame them, of course. He had been their most ardent adversary for many years and, were the roles reversed, he might well have tried to kill them by now.

'My brother is unwilling to leave even a part of his crew, and I tend to agree. We're to free your shipmates and then take the ship. But before we make any sort of move, I need to be sure that you're with me and I have a feeling some of you are struggling with that?'

Ursa shrugged.

'You're no one's favourite here. Can't say as I'd have time for you myself, if it weren't for the law having been laid down by the boss; he threatened to gut anyone who laid a finger on you. Most of the lads would never dream of disobeying the cap'n, but there might be the odd man who thinks it would be worth it just to watch you bleed out.'

Ghassan nodded and turned to smile at the other men, who were still glowering at him.

'Anyone here have an issue with taking orders from me in your captain's absence?'

There was a tight silence, though the level of apprehension around the table increased noticeably.

'Let me put it another way: I release every man here from their oath to my brother. I can't do anything with a crew that are only with me because they've been told to be. So… given that you're all free to knife me, with Ursa as a witness to my promise, who wants a go?'

Smiling, he pushed his seat back from the table, remaining firmly in it.

There was an uncomfortable pause as two men opposite him looked at one another and shuffled in their seat. The threat of displeasing Samir apparently still held them back. He smiled.

'No one at all?'

Ursa, next to him, leaned close for a moment.

'Don't do this, sir. The cap'n will kill me if I let the men hurt you.'

Ghassan smiled and nodded.

'I'll take my chances, Ursa. You take yours.'

Noting the man opposite who was almost out of his seat, his knuckles whitening on the seat arms with strain, Ghassan sized him up. These men were brutal and dangerous, but they would be honourable at some level, or Samir wouldn't have them. It would be a shame to hurt them, but an example was worth a thousand speeches.

'Well?'

He took a preparatory breath as the man launched himself from the seat, pushing the table out of the way as he rose. Ghassan continued to sit and smile.

Stepping closer, the man clenched his fists and leapt in. Ghassan, having apparently goaded the biggest of the opposition and therefore most likely the slowest, waited until the first swing came. Lunging forward out of his chair, he rose immediately in front of his target, so close he was already inside the man's swinging arm.

Ducking his head as he rose, he jabbed out with both hands. His left, formed into a shape resembling a dog's paw, jabbed hard into the inner elbow of the swinging limb, his aim accurate. Simultaneously, his other hand homed in on the man's free arm, which was reaching toward the sheathed dagger at his waist. Ghassan's thumb and forefinger shaped into a pincer, he grasped the man's wrist on the inside, just up from the heel of the hand, and squeezed hard.

As the man stumbled forward, blinking, his right arm dead from the elbow down and his left hand frozen in a claw of pain, Ghassan sighed and stepped back.

'I've always accorded myself a man of principle and honour and, as such I need everyone here to be completely open with me and I'll extend you the same courtesy.'

He smiled as he gently pushed his assailant back upright.

'This man was going for his knife with the plain intent to kill. At least he's let me know where he stands with this… or rather, where he falls…'

Still smiling warmly, he took a single step forward to stand inches from the nose of the stunned attacker, who was staring at his own lifeless hands in astonishment. Tilting his head to one side, Ghassan reached out and tapped the man in the temple with his forefinger. With a sigh, the large pirate folded, his eyes rolling upwards as he collapsed to the floor.

'See…' Ghassan said, stepping back away from the shuddering heap, 'I don't really want to hurt any of you but I'm going to need every man tonight, and I can't have anyone with me who isn't totally committed to the goal. Anyone else have any issue?'

He held his smile as he looked around the assembled stunned faces. Ursa blinked at him.

'How the hell did you do that?'

Ghassan turned to him.

'I'm a man of hidden talents, Ursa. Now, shall we get on with this?'

With a nod, the heavy-set, tattooed man sank into his seat and pulled it up to the table. Ghassan nodded to himself and returned to his own seat, pulling it forward next to the unconscious form of his victim, and leaning with his elbows on the table conspiratorially.

'I've no idea what your captain's grand plan is, but I am with him now, entirely. My duty is done and I am committed to helping get your crew and your ship out. I don't want to have to perform any more demonstrations so, if anyone is still unsure, leave the tavern now.

He waited for a moment. There was silence and a great number of meaningful looks were exchanged, but nobody stood.

'Good. This is going to be hard enough even if we're all reading from the same scroll, if you get my drift. Now... are we safe enough to talk here, so long as we keep our voices down?'

Ursa nodded.

'Lot of friends of the Empress here, sir, so no problem as long as you're quiet.'

'Good. The way I see it, we've two distinct goals here, and they each have their problems. Firstly, we've got to get your shipmates out of the stockade, and secondly we've got to get on board the Empress and get her underway before anyone raises the alarm.'

The man across the table next to the recently vacated seat, who had clearly been verging on attacking Ghassan himself, leaned back, his brow furrowed.

'I've been in that stockade, drunk and detained. There's no easy way in or out. There's a compound with three huts for the port guard: guard house, armament store, and bunk house. The compound's walled and patrolled, with only one gate. The stockade is inside that, and has its own permanent guard. I'm not even going to go into how hard it'll be to get the Empress out...'

Ursa nodded.

'I helped the cap'n get the big liquid fire pots from the store, but that was easy. The ammunition store backs onto the perimeter wall. The stockade's inside, though; much more difficult.'

Ghassan frowned.

'There are only eight guards in the compound at night on a normal night. Given the current situation with them looking for myself and my brother, I would expect them to double the guard, and they'll be more alert than usual. So we're looking at perhaps sixteen guards.'

He raised an eyebrow.

'You say you got into the armament store?'

'Yes,' Ursa replied, shrugging. 'It backs onto the outer wall. The cap'n and I went over the wall onto the roof of the place and just took some of the tiles away and climbed in. That was easy, coz the man on the door was asleep. Tonight'll be different, though. They won't be asleep, there'll be more of them, and you'll need to get past that and across the compound.'

Ghassan grinned.

'I think I have an idea how we can do this. In fact, if I've got this worked out right, it'll help with getting the Empress away too.'

The crew collectively frowned, but they were used to such tight-lipped confidence from their own captain, so this was nothing new.

'I give you my word,' Ghassan said, his face straight, 'and my word is not given lightly, that I am in allegiance with my brother and I intend to do everything I can to get the Empress and her crew out of M'Dahz. Do I have your word that you won't make stupid attempts to knife me in the back as soon as I turn it?'

There was a general murmur of assent, though Ghassan would have liked a little more vehemence about it. Ursa leaned on the table and gestured at him with a finger.

'We're all honest men, cap'n… or at least as honest as ever trod on Lassos. The boss carefully chose every man here over years, shipping out crewmen he didn't trust or that didn't have the right sort of character for him, if'n you know what I mean. You'll have no trouble from us, but every man here, me included, wants to know why you're doing this, you being a naval man and all?'

Ghassan raised his brow and nodded slowly.

'That's a fair question. Firstly, I am not turning against my former comrades... that would be unthinkable. Consequently, I will not attack a naval ship or crewman without just cause.'

He sat back heavily.

'But I know my brother. He is not a bloodthirsty maniac and, despite appearances, he is as noble and honourable as I. He has some grand plan that he's not shared with any of us yet, but I've seen for decades how his mind works, and he's cleverer than any of us.'

The frowning man beside the empty chair narrowed his eyes.

'That's half an answer. You've spent years hunting your brother down and now you want to join him? There's got to be more to it than that.'

Ghassan nodded.

'Truly, I wouldn't be here by pure choice. Unfortunately, when the woman responsible for all of this sold your captain out to the governor, she also blackened my name and made me a traitor in the eyes of my superiors. Had I stayed in the tower, I would be dead within the week. My brother offered me the chance to free myself and clear my name.'

The other pirate laughed.

'Strange directions the fates take you, captain, when you have to join pirates to clear your name.'

Ghassan laughed. 'Strange, indeed; but nothing that involves my brother is ever what it seems at first to be. Come on. Let's wake your friend here and get to serious planning.'

In which Ghassan's scheme goes into action

Ghassan raised an eyebrow questioningly in the shadow of the wall.

'S'alright cap'n. I can manage.'

Nodding at Ursa, Ghassan turned away from the first officer and his three companions and crept along the edge of the building until he rounded the corner to join the rest of the crew once more, disappearing from sight.

Ursa heaved a sigh, though he wasn't sure that it was one of relief. It was entirely possible that this brother was crazier than their own captain. However, the big man had to admit, there was enough innovation and general brilliance about the man's thinking that it was not hard to see how the Wind of God had been such a hazard to them over the years. Ghassan and Samir were certainly of a kind.

Stretching, he gestured to the men with him to pay attention to their surroundings. Was he equally insane to agree to such a dangerous mission with so few men? He almost laughed out loud.

Returning to his tense waiting, he cast his eyes round at his companions once more. Hidden within the shadow cast by the L-shaped exterior of one of the port's many warehouses, the four pirates crouched, hidden and watching the complex opposite intently. The only positive thing that Ursa could really say about the plan was that they would be unlikely to bump into folk here. This area was a long way from the taverns and populated areas. Here, the guards' compound stood out starkly among jumbled clusters of warehouses and few people would tread at night, the legitimate folk of M'Dahz having no reason to be here and the less savoury staying a good distance from the centre of the town guard's control.

Funny really, how the presence of the law was the thing that kept the streets empty enough for the criminals and fugitives to move around safely and unobserved.

Ursa grinned. Two decades ago, as a young man, he'd been part of the M'Dahz militia based in this very port, and in those days the buildings across the road and their perimeter wall had been his home. Then had come the Empire's collapse and Ursa, like so many others, had been driven to piracy to sustain himself. Having served as an oarsman and then commander of a boarding party on the Gorgon's Revenge, he'd come to the Dark Empress under Captain Khmun as a solid officer with a good reputation.

There, after years of sliding into the depravity that went with the life of a resident of Lassos, he had begun to reclaim both his self-respect and his sense of right under the man that he had considered the best captain the sea had to offer... until Samir. What Khmun had begun by instilling a sense of honour and mercy into his crew, Samir had completed by systematically weeding out those who he considered unfit for his crew. It was almost laughable to Ursa that he would take the word and honour of any man on board the Empress before that of the legitimate navy, and yet it was this that kept him loyally with Samir.

Since Imperial power had been reinstated in the Sea of Storms, the activities of most of the captains of Lassos had become more and more brutal in the constant struggle to stay ahead of the increasingly powerful navy. And yet the Empress had, in this time, somehow maintained her reputation while actually reducing their activity. Likely most of the pirates, even of his own crew, had been oblivious to this, but Ursa was an old hand, and he noticed how his captain was going out of his way to improve their reputation among the ordinary folk and to draw ever further from the twisted authorities in Lassos.

Something was afoot. Samir's plan was continually picking up pace; Ursa could feel it happening without being able to identify any specific move in the game. The young captain was so damn subtle it was hard just working out what he'd already done, let alone what he was going to do.

The first bell of the midnight watch rang out.

Clang.

'Steady, lads.'

Clang.

And now their former nemesis was with them, professing loyalty and deeply involved in Samir's plan without knowing himself what he was working toward.

Clang.

Yet there was no accident to this, Ursa was sure. If Ghassan was with them now, it had been in Samir's mind for a long time and was yet another thread woven into the plot.

Clang.

And it had to be said that this man, for all his history of mindless subservience to the navy, seemed to have a similar mind to his brother. Amazing, really. Should these brothers truly work together, there would be little they couldn't achieve.

Clang.

Ursa frowned. How many was that? Damn it, he must stop getting side-tracked. Nodding, he put thoughts of his two commanders and their relationship aside and concentrated.

Clang.

That must be the sixth? Yes, the sixth.

Clang.

'Ready lads?' he whispered. 'Know where you're all going?'

Clang.

There was a low murmur of affirmative noises.

Clang.

Good. Ursa tensed.

Clang.

'Ready…'

Clang.

'Go!'

As the last bell tolled, the four men hurtled out of the shadows like cockroaches in sudden light. The perimeter wall of the compound was thick and solid and around eight feet high, but not wide enough for a walkway. Broken sherds of pot had been cemented into the top to prevent easy access and the guards patrolled around the inside edge every few minutes.

Ursa and his companion made straight across from the shadows and to the wall opposite, behind which he could just make out the apex of the tile roof. The other two men veered off to the right, heading toward their second phase.

As the big man reached the wall, counting slowly under his breath in order to keep the perfect timing this would need, he crouched and cradled his hands. The second man reached him, put his foot in that huge grip, and launched himself up and onto the wall. The heavy leather bracers he wore on his forearms were a last minute idea, but proved invaluable as he landed on the sharp pottery tips and struggled quietly across onto the roof.

Turning, he threw the heavy blanket from his shoulder over the sherds and reached down, quickly hauling the heavy first officer up after him.

Ursa tipped over onto the roof as quietly as he could. From here they could see the entire compound and therefore could be seen from it. However, the guard changed at midnight and the two men now on patrol were at the far side, hidden from this angle by both the bunk house and the stockade. They would have little more than a minute before the two guards emerged from either end of the buildings, heading round the periphery to converge on this spot before crossing paths and continuing on their way. There would be a man at the door to the shed, but he would be looking out the other way across the compound and should remain unaware of their presence, given the crackling of the brazier next to which he stood, so long as they were quiet enough.

The first officer, familiar with the layout of the ammunition shed from the previous night, gestured to the man with him and the two began to hurriedly lift the tiles from the roof, placing them quietly nearby.

As the covering gradually disappeared and a hole formed, the room below obscured only partially by the supporting beams, Ursa pointed down and grinned.

Directly below them, wooden shelves contained small pots of liquid fire for use as grenades in ship to ship combat. The two men smiled and nodded at one another, reaching into their jackets. With a deep breath, they withdrew two ceramic flasks each, marked with the strange language of the northern barbarians. It broke Ursa's heart to discard such rare and expensive liquor this way, but when needs must…

With a deep breath, the two men uncorked the flasks and liberally emptied their contents through the hole onto the pots below and the straw and wood shelving beneath them. As the last few drops fell and they carefully placed the flasks on the roof, Ursa clenched his teeth and removed the bundle of sticks and wadding from his jacket. Retrieving flint and steel, he began to strike as quietly as he could, praying devoutly until the showing sparks finally caught on the bundle.

61… Timing was getting too tight for comfort.

With a deeper breath, he dropped the flaming mass into the hole and the two men slid down the tiles and off the edge. They dropped the eight feet from the roof onto the soft gravel with a crunch that was altogether too loud for Ursa's liking. Here, the two men stood, hunched into the corner formed by the meeting of the perimeter wall with the ammunition shed. The main light within this area of the compound: the brazier in front of this very building, cast a deep shadow here and the two men held their breath.

Across the compound, the patrolling guards emerged from behind the other buildings. This would only work if the timing was right…

Suddenly, the wall behind the big man seemed to actually bulge and buckle for a moment, trying to contain the pressure from within. There was a series of deep thumps from within as several of the pots exploded. The interior of the ammunition store would now be wreathed in fire, but the building had been constructed with this possibility in mind. The heavy walls contained it, and the huge pots would survive intact, so long as the fire was put out quick enough.

A cry of alarm issued from round the corner at the front of the building as the guard by the door realised what had happened. Sure enough, just as Ursa had expected, the two soldiers on patrol came hurtling directly across the compound toward the building as the guard struggled with his keys to open the door. There were several more bangs from within and flames were now issuing from the roof in an impressive column. As the approaching guards reached the front of the shed, occupied with the fire and the noise, distracted by the dancing flames within, Ursa and his companion took the opportunity to run along the wall, heading toward the compound gates.

They were only halfway there when the ox cart that marked phase two burst through the wooden portal, shattering the beam that held the gate fast and coming on unstoppably.

Briefly, Ursa had to feel for the oxen. They were huge and strong creatures, but to be driven directly into the gate must have been excruciating for them. The heavy cart thundered into the compound, the two drivers turning slightly and heading for the next gate; the one in the stockade.

Behind the cart, Ursa and his companion ran to keep up.

All hell was now breaking loose in the compound. Most of the soldiers were holed up either asleep in the bunkhouse or drinking and sheltering in the guard room. Men emerged from the doors, expressions of shock and surprise plastered across their faces; many of them unarmed and unarmoured, caught in an off-duty state.

Confusion reigned and the newly-arrived guards panicked, most of them rushing off toward the burning ammunition store. They would have to get the flames under control before the larger pots caught or they could lose a lot of the warehouse district to fire in the night. A few men who could see beyond this immediate danger turned and ran for the cart. The first, stupidly, tried to grab the reins of the oxen as they thundered past. There was no hope of stopping the huge bovines with this amount of momentum, and the unfortunate man was dragged beneath and trampled to a bloody pulp.

As others tried to keep pace with the heavy, unstoppable cart, Ursa caught up with it, panting and running along behind with his companion, moments before the vehicle hit and burst through the stockade gate.

Screams and shouts of alarm issued from within as the captive pirates and other criminals threw themselves out of the way of the rolling nightmare. As they passed the threshold, the two pirate drivers threw themselves from the cart and rolled to their feet.

Ever-prepared, the men of the Dark Empress began to emerge from the stockade at a run. Ursa heaved a deep breath and bellowed 'To the Empress!'

The pursuing guards pulled up sharply as previously-caged criminals of numerous varieties poured out of the stockade with a taste for freedom – and many, a grudge against their wardens.

As the two dozen men of the Empress ran toward the gate, Ursa shook his head sympathetically at the plight of the guardsmen around him as they struggled amid the wreckage of shattered stockades and gates to control the ever increasing fire at the ammunition store that threatened the whole district, while several dozen vicious criminals took the opportunity to either flee or exact their vengeance on any figure of authority they spotted.

Ghassan had been explicit that he wanted the body-count kept as low as prudence allowed; preferably nil. To Ursa's knowledge, the only direct casualty had been the man beneath the oxen but, he thought sadly as he ran toward the jetties with his shipmates, the number of deaths caused by fire and escaping prisoners could yet be appalling.

Nothing he could do about that, now, though. His duty was to the Dark Empress, her crew and her captain, wherever he might be.

In which there is a night time visit

The rope had been removed, of course. Samir wondered how long it had taken before the more observant of the palace guards had spotted it arcing out across the street. Likely the entire compound had been searched down to the last cupboard for some kind of interloper. They'd been sadly disappointed. Briefly, the fugitive pirate captain considered walking up to the main gate, bold as brass, and demanding entrance. The shock value of such a move appealed tremendously. However, in all likelihood he would end up chained in the remaining half of the prison tower without ever setting foot in the compound that way.

He glanced up and down the street. The sun had gone down hours ago and, while he had no idea how Ghassan was going to break out the rest of the men and free the ship, he knew two things for certain: that his brother would succeed, and that something spectacular would be involved.

And so he'd stood on one of the highest roofs in this the upper part of the town where he had a magnificent panoramic view of the docks way below at the other end of M'Dahz. He'd not known exactly what he was waiting for, but he felt sure he would recognise a sign of action and he didn't really want to make his next move until he was sure Ghassan was getting underway.

The wait had been long and dull and Samir had sat on the roof, cutting slices of peach with his pocket knife and snacking as he watched the dark district far below. And then, just after the midnight bells rang out in the town's temples, he'd spotted what he'd been waiting for. There had been a flash and a column of flame had burst through a roof. He'd have put that down to Ghassan regardless of where it happened, but there was no doubt that the flames were rising from the ammunition store in the guard compound. The colour of the flames and the roiling smoke rising to the stars above was testament to that.

'Good.'

And so he'd turned and made his way down to the street where he now stood, frowning at the palace compound wall. This time he was here on his own schedule and, while he couldn't afford to waste hours, it was dark and the streets were empty, giving him plenty of space to work.

Looking up, the fifteen feet of sheer-faced boundary wall revealed no possible hand or foot holds but the construction, while cored with solid stone, offered a mud-brick and plaster outer as was common in architecture from the poorer days of M'Dahz.

Gritting his teeth and frowning in concentration, Samir drew two weapons from his belt; utilitarian knives, rather than fighting blades, these were thick and strong. His tongue protruding slightly as he worked, it took only half a minute to dig out a chunk of the wall's surface at waist height. Smiling, he made another hole at head height with equal ease.

Slowly, he began to climb, using his freshly-excavated hand holds and carving out new ones as he rose. In less than ten minutes, he reached up and for the first time his fingers touched the tile bonding-layers in the wall of the main building itself. With a smile, Samir hauled himself up to the layer and put his knives away carefully, clinging on to the narrow holds and trying not to look down.

Slowly, he pulled himself up to the next available grip and made his way diagonally toward the window of the governor's office. There had been no light or sign of life in the room when he'd checked from the building opposite, so it was a good place to start. With a grunt and a last heave, he grasped the lintel and pulled himself up and inside, dropping lightly to the floor in a crouch and glancing around sharply.

There was no sound or movement; the office was dark and quiet. Standing, Samir examined the exits. The main door at the far end would lead to the main hallway, probably with a stairwell. That would be the way people entered the governor's reception room, which this clearly was. Likely, though, the governor would have a second entrance so that he could move between his private apartments and this room without passing a more open, public space.

There were two doors leading off in addition to the main exit, one on each side. Closing his eyes, Samir summoned up a mental picture of the outer façade of the palace from the roof across the street. The two rooms to the left, as one faced the wall, had been busy during the daytime when he'd sneaked here to eavesdrop on Asima. That meant they were almost certainly administrative or business areas. He couldn't remember seeing any movement in the rooms to the right, however. They had been empty and silent during the middle of the day.

Nodding with satisfaction, he stepped lightly across the office toward the door, stopping suddenly as he passed the heavy wooden table of dark, northern oak.

Papers scattered around amid ledgers and maps appeared to be random and messy, and Samir leaned heavily on the edge of the table and squinted, trying to make out as much as possible in the scant moonlight afforded by the window.

He smiled and rounded the table to the governor's chair, where he grasped a particular unfinished letter and sat back, smiling, in the seat, holding up the missive to take maximum advantage of the low, silvery light.

To his majestic highness, Ashar Parishid, high King of Pelasia…

Samir's smile intensified as he read on, through the governor's carefully worded explanation of his actions regarding Asima; not quite an apology for turning her back to him, but close enough. It would appear from the letter that Asima was less popular even with the King of Pelasia than with the folk of the Empire. He grinned and cast his eyes across the table.

Reaching out, he grasped a stylus and concentrated as he hunched over the letter. He'd learned to read and write, but it required concentration if he wanted it to look good.

At the bottom of the half-finished letter, he finished a note with a flourish.

Do not send this.

The grin still on his face, Samir dropped the pen, scanned the desk and, finding nothing else that particularly attracted his attention, he left and returned to his original goal: the side door.

As he approached, he leaned close and put his ear to the wood. This was an interior door of no great substance and there was no sound from the other side. Clenching his teeth, he slowly twisted the handle; the door remained steadfastly shut. Locked. He'd assumed for some reason that the main door to the office/reception room would be locked, but the separating interior doors would not be. Plainly this governor placed a high value on security.

Smiling, he crouched. Never let it be said that something as simple as a lock had got in the way of his plans.

His tongue working around his teeth as he concentrated, Samir withdrew a leather wallet from his belt, opened it, selected a specific narrow, metal prong with a curious tip, and began to work it slowly, gently, and quietly, in the lock.

After a few seconds there was a gentle click and he held his breath as he leaned back. Chances were that even someone awake in the room beyond hadn't noticed the tiny noise, but this was no time to blunder. Silence reigned as he put the lockpick away and tucked away the wallet at his belt.

Slowly, he exhaled. So much would fail if he messed up and guards were called. He would be carted off to his doom without the opportunity to carry out his mission.

Slowly, wincing with each miniscule whinge of the mechanism, he turned the door handle and pushed gently. The door swung quietly open a few inches. Samir smiled. Somehow he'd known that the door wouldn't squeak. The sort of man that locked his interconnecting doors was the sort of man that would keep them oiled and in good order.

Standing once again, he leaned closer and put his eye to the crack. The room beyond was some sort of sun room or lounge, filled with low tables and seats. Very comfortable; a more private meeting room, where the governor would socialise with friends or well-known dignitaries. Good. That meant he was in the man's apartments now. Once more, two other doors led off from here. One, at the far end of the room, opposite the window, must lead to a lobby, given the length of this room compared with that next door. That lobby, in turn, would have several doors and a main entrance from the stairwell. The other exit, opposite the one through which he'd entered, was likely the one he required.

Smiling, he strode across the room, quietly but quickly, and grasped the handle of the other door. Turning it lightly, the portal gave easily. Of course... no need to lock the door between private lounge and private bedchamber.

The interior was dark as the deepest cave, the windows closed in with shutters and drapes to keep out the bright moon and starlight. Samir quickly nipped around the door and pushed it closed behind him. The dim light that he'd cast into the room when he opened the door would shine out like a beacon to anyone awake in here.

Holding his breath again, he stood just inside the door in the darkness and waited. Slowly, his eyes adjusted a little while he listened for a challenge that never came. Very gently, he could hear the deep breaths of the governor, asleep in what must be a large bed at the room's far side. Samir concentrated for a moment, trying to identify more than one breathing pattern; after all, the governor may well be married. Nothing, though. Just the one.

Smiling, Samir padded silently across to a shelf on the wall where an oil lamp stood with flint and steel. For a moment, he considered lighting that, but it would take too long and be noisy and trying. Shrugging, he walked on past the shelf until he reached the large windows. Slowly, and quietly, he drew back the drapes. Tiny dots and points of silver light picked their way through the cracks and joints in the shutters. Taking a deep breath, Samir threw open the shutters, admitting bright moonlight and bathing the room in a silvery glow.

He turned to address the governor, hoping the light had at least woken him.

Samir was astonished, though he kept his composure and hid his surprise well, to see the governor sitting up calmly in his bed, a small hand bow aimed at him. It was one of the torsion-based personal weapons that Pelasian assassins used; deadly and accurate. Samir smiled.

'Excellency... you are apparently a remarkable man.'

'As are you, Captain Samir.'

The pirate stretched, silhouetted against the window and presenting a clear target for the governor's weapon.

'May I ask why you have not simply shot me or called for the guards, Excellency?'

The governor shrugged.

'I have the upper hand, captain. Moreover, had you the intention to do me harm, you would hardly have sneaked around the room and opened the window first.'

'I could be wanting to intimidate and torture you, first?'

The governor, a serious looking man, shook his head, his aim remaining steadfast.

'Hardly your reputation, captain. Now what can I do for you?'

Samir smiled and strode across to sink into a seat opposite the bed, lit by the white square from the window.

'I have a proposition for you, governor.'

'Go on...'

'I am aware that you know a certain young lady by the name of Asima?'

'Of course.'

'Asima is, as you may or may not know by now, one of the most clever, deceitful and generally wicked people you may ever set eyes on. I know her of old.'

The governor nodded; no sign of surprise or denial. Once again, Samir was impressed by this man.

'Well,' he went on, 'her accusations regarding my brother are entirely fictional. I am quite openly, and even proudly, responsible for the sinking of the Wind of God. I was aided in the most unexpected way by that same young lady, when she sabotaged Ghassan's rudder and left him helpless.'

He grinned.

'I apologise for the mess I made of your town walls yesterday, but my brother is innocent and, moreover, I need him for a while.'

The governor frowned.

'This is all very well. I can't confirm or deny any of it, of course, although I'm sure you're right. But this information is currently valueless. Asima is gone from here on her way back to Pelasia, with a purse of my money and an escort until she's safely at the first royal way station in their country and as far as possible from me. Ghassan, on the other hand, is now with you, as we're well aware. So what in the name of the Imperial raven is your proposition? What could you possibly offer that would be worth more than me, as you so succinctly put it, "simply shooting you or calling for the guards"?'

Samir laughed lightly and reached into his tunic.

'I'm afraid I have no intention of staying right now. I have so many things to do and so little time, you see. If you listen very carefully, your Excellency, you'll hear the commotion down at the docks where my crew have been freed. I'm fairly certain that by now the Empress will be back at sea and making for open water. You'll have your hands full in the morning, if you intend to take us again.'

He withdrew a folded and tied paper from his tunic and tossed it across to the bed, where it landed on the governor's knee. The older man glanced down at it with interest, though his hand never wavered and his aim remained true. He looked up at Samir again with a raised eyebrow.

'That's my offer; my proposal. I don't expect an answer right now. You'll have to think it over and you may even need to consult with your superiors. I give you my word, though, Excellency, that until we meet again and I have your answer, I will forego any opportunity to take on one of your ships. I believe that's as plain and as fair as I can make it.'

The governor smiled.

'I have to admit that I'm intrigued. I'm just not sure whether I'm intrigued enough to let you go, rather than having you taken into custody first and then perusing your proposal.'

Samir answered with a grin of his own.

'Then I will just have to take my chances, Excellency. I'm on a tight schedule, you see.'

Standing and noting how the governor's weapon kept track of his movements even while the man gazed down at the paper in his lap, Samir turned his back, strode across to the window and began to climb out.

'I shall see you soon, sir. Have a good night.'

With a last smile, Samir clambered down from the window, climbed as far as the end of the bonding-tile layers, and then dropped lightly to the street.

In the dark room, the governor put down the weapon and, standing, wrapped his robe tightly around him. Taking the paper and untying the ribbon, he placed it on the shelf while he lit the oil lamp and then retrieved and unfolded the note, and began to read.

As he neared the bottom of the text, his eyes sparkled.

The guard on duty outside the governor's apartment started in surprise at the sound of deep laughter ringing out from his Excellency's chamber in the middle of the night.

In which another journey begins

Asima stopped at the gate and listened to the midnight bells echo away.

'Move along, miss,' the cavalry sergeant said quietly.

'Just a moment.' She turned and looked back up at the town gate, with its heavy towers to either side and battlements above. She was outside once more, away from the narrow, teeming streets in which she had grown up. M'Dahz should feel like home really, or at least it should have some vague connection for her. Instead, as she looked at it, the town of her birth, home to her father's grave elicited no emotion from her at all.

With a raised eyebrow, she realised she'd not gone to see his last resting place after all. She'd left her father there so long ago in the knowledge that, by going to Pelasia for the satrap, her father would be safe. Curious how she'd hardly even thought of him after that. Had she always been this way, or had Pelasia changed her?

The sergeant, commander of the unit of a dozen Imperial cavalry that were to escort her back to the neighbouring kingdom, cleared his throat and smiled sympathetically.

'Sad to be leaving, miss?'

'Hardly!'

With a sneer, she spat once in the direction of the town and turned her back on it, hopefully for the last time, this time.

The guard stepped away, taken aback a little by her display. His face hardened and he gestured forcefully to the staging post a few hundred yards ahead where the coach, along with the baggage cart and the horses, waited, tended by her cavalry escort.

'Get in the coach, miss, and we'll get you away from here.'

Asima nodded sourly as she strode over toward the small settlement. Staging posts now existed outside each of the city's gates, growing gradually into villages in their own right. The new governor had banned unlicensed work animals and vehicles from the town. The administration claimed that it lowered the chance of accidents and trouble in the steep and narrow streets and made the city cleaner and safer. This was certainly true, though the more cynical also noted that the licenses were a good source of revenue also.

And so these small settlements were springing up; corrals with animal traders and stabling facilities to take advantage of the new laws, traders to take advantage of the high turnover of travellers, desert nomads come close to the city to sell their own wares and purchase goods unavailable in the hot sands, and finally the inevitable beggars, homeless and hopeless.

The coach and its escort stood at the edge of the small settlement, the guards keeping a watchful eye over the vagrants and nomads in their makeshift shelters nearby. Asima barely noticed them as she strode past, her nose wrinkling at the smell, toward her transport to Pelasia.

A few yards from the coach, one of the scarecrows in tattered black, lounging cross-legged beside a dancing fire, stood, her curved back giving her a slight stoop, and shuffled toward them on a course of interception. The sergeant began to steer Asima to the side away from the woman, gaunt and dark and haggard, but the desert-dweller changed direction and homed in on them once again.

Asima's sneer was still in full effect and the old woman cackled, grinning, as she approached.

'Want to hear your fortune, lady?'

Asima shook her head, irritably.

'A toothless desert hag has less idea of my future than the stars, let alone myself. Get back to your tent, crow woman.'

The sergeant frowned at her. He may not approve of beggars and vagrants, but these people had broken no law and served a purpose, no matter how small.

'Here,' he said, dropping a few copper coins into her hand as he reached out to grasp Asima's wrist and arrest her forward motion. As she jerked to a halt, her eyes flashing angrily, the sergeant turned to her.

'I'll pay to hear your future, just to be sure that in no way am I in it, Lady Asima.'

His charge glared at him as he turned and smiled at the old woman with the dishevelled hair.

'Tell her and I'll double your money when we leave.'

The old woman smiled a cracked smile and reached out gently for Asima's hand. The young lady recoiled in disgust, but the sergeant, his hand still on her wrist, pushed her hand out so that the fortune teller could reach. This she did and, with narrow, leathery fingers, she caressed the top of Asima's hand.

'You are a woman with a destiny,' the old woman said quietly.

Asima nodded.

'I hardly need a stinking old crow to tell me that!'

The sergeant treated her to an angry glare as the old woman went on, rubbing small circles on the back of Asima's hand before turning it over to examine the palm.

'Your life has been transition, constantly. Each time you feel you are nearing your goal, it is snatched away from you, yes?'

Asima stopped struggling to pull away, her brow furrowing. Her astonishment at the fact that the woman had so accurately summed up her life since the day the Satrap Ma'ahd came was compounded by the surprise at the old woman's soft tone and educated use of language. Despite everything in her that told her to push this woman away, Asima couldn't fight it... she was interested.

'The world has repeatedly promised you great things but never quite delivered them. You lash out when this happens and the result is often that you fall further away from your goal. You are beginning to believe that you are owed a great deal and are determined to squeeze the world until it pays.'

That was a bolt from the blue for Asima. It was horribly, cuttingly accurate and yet news to her; she had never realised this was the case.

'Stop.'

The old woman smiled.

'Everything happens for a reason, lady. You will achieve your destiny, but you must not fight it. Each time you fight it, your destiny pulls away from you. You need to follow the path you are now on and stop trying to change it.'

Asima frowned.

'I do not believe in Gods, or fate, or fortunes, old woman. A clever mind sees past the trickery. You are merely insightful and a good judge of character... but not a great one. If you were, you'd have steered well clear of me.'

The old woman laughed merrily.

'You do not believe? You who have murdered lords and ladies? You who have bought and sold souls and lives to climb the ladder of success? You who have sat with Kings and worn jewels that were worth more than M'Dahz has to offer? You who cannot stop yourself?'

'Stop!'

There was something in Asima's voice that made the sergeant frown; a great deal of irritation and anger, of course, but also a note verging on panic.

'Never, lady. You have taken a wrong turning at some point on the path of your life. You would have been poor but loved as a nobody. Sometimes you realise that and it makes you sad, but not sad enough to turn you away from the path you have chosen…'

'Stop!' Asima barked.

'Instead, you seek power at the expense of love. You care not what people think of you except when it is necessary to achieve something. You will not stop until you can look down on the Gods you deny and it matters not that the world will hate you for it.'

Asima made a lunge for the woman, but the sergeant still had a tight grip on her wrist and held her back, turning to the fortune teller.

'I think you'd best take the rest of the money and leave, woman.'

'Momentarily,' the old crone said quietly.

'Lady, I said I would tell you your fortune. I have only told you your past and the contents of your heart. I would be remiss, having been paid, not to perform my duty.'

Asima glared at her coldly, an angry rumble somewhere deep in her throat.

'I said that you are a woman of destiny. You may believe in what you wish, lady, but I have the sight and the knowledge, and I know beyond doubt and past certainty. You are destined, for better or for worse, to reach the dizzy heights that you seek. Before the next year cycles around, you will be acclaimed an Empress. You will rule with absolute power, uncontested, yet unloved. No one will sing your praise or welcome your accession, though I fear you care little about that.'

She smiled a humourless smile.

'You will be an Empress, lady, and as dark an Empress as ever walked beneath the heavens. I shudder to look further, so I must take my leave. May the sand devils grant you safe passage on your journey.'

With a smile, she wrapped her fingers tightly around the copper coins in her hand and shuffled off back toward her fire and tent.

The sergeant relaxed his grip.

'I'm not sure whether I'm glad I heard that, or not.'

He examined the young lady by his side. Asima had an unreadable expression.

'Come on. Get into the coach, so we can get underway. If your highness is going to be an Empress, I'd as soon it wasn't in my country.'

Shaking her head, Asima picked up her feet and walked off toward the coach, frowning as she went.

Behind her, the crooked old scarecrow woman in the tattered black pocketed her treasure and shuffled out of the open back to her tent. As the cavalry and their vehicles prepared to get underway, the old woman passed between two tents into the shelter of a couple of palm trees and scrub plants. Taking a quick glance between the shelters to make sure she was out of sight of the lady and her escort, she straightened, rubbing her back while sucking in air between her teeth. Grinning, she stretched and laughed quietly.

Samir was right. This girl was a real piece of work, and clever too. She was almost clever enough to have seen through it all, but Samir's insight had apparently been uncanny enough to throw her off kilter.

She laughed once more as she set off back toward the town walls and the secret way in that even few of the criminal underclass of M'Dahz knew existed.

In which Tain leads the way

Ghassan peered over the top of the crates a final time and then turned back to the men crouched behind him, each armed with a cudgel and a fierce and determined expression.

'Remember the rules: take them down as necessary, but I want to avoid killing wherever possible, and Samir would back me up on this. Any man I see killing someone when there is an alternative, I will leave for the authorities to deal with. Is that clear?'

There was a chorus of subdued agreement. Ghassan nodded with satisfaction. It did appear that despite their chosen path in life, these men of Samir's suffered the effects of a conscience and that made them the sort of people that Ghassan could use. Must have taken some work identifying men like this and manoeuvring them over the years until they formed the crew of the Empress.

Taking a deep breath, he beckoned to the man he'd selected earlier. It had been a simple choice. Most of the crew were long-time pirates with tattoos, long unruly hair, jewellery and piercings. There were few among them who matched the presentable manner expected of a military recruit. Young Tain was perhaps the only man among those around him that could do this. Fortunate they were that Tain was also fearless, well-spoken, clever, and as devious as a boy could be.

The young man, only a member of the crew for two years, left the crowd of his shipmates and approached Ghassan, picking and scratching irritably at the stolen guard uniform he wore.

'Ready?'

The young man laughed quietly.

'Ready as I'll ever be. I'd as soon go now an' get it over with, so's I can get this itchy crap off me!'

'Any moment now,' Ghassan smiled.

He glanced back across the port from where they lurked in the shadow of a dock-side warehouse, hidden from the jetty by piles of crates and barrels. He'd listened tensely and heaved a sigh of relief when he heard the midnight bell ring out. Since then he'd rarely taken his eyes off the dark roofs of the warehouse district and the guard compound that lay hidden among them.

The young sailor turned and cast his own gaze back there.

A few heartbeats passed and Ghassan grinned.

'Did you see that?'

'See what?'

The commander pointed into the dark distance and his young companion squinted.

'Can't see a thing, sir.'

'There's flames. Just small and just starting, but Ursa's in. It's begun.'

'You's got bloody good eyesight! I can't…'

His voice fell away as what had been a miniscule flicker of yellow, barely visible from this distance, suddenly exploded into a column of flame that reached up above the roofs.

'Do I go now?'

Ghassan shook his head.

'Count to a hundred slowly and steadily and then go. You need to leave enough time to have legitimately got here. They won't believe you flew.'

The boy shrugged.

'Never counted t'a hunderd. Is it long?'

Ghassan blinked at him and had to readjust his thinking. Just because the boy was clever didn't mean he was educated. Probably couldn't read either.

'Do you know the song 'Sharri the Mermaid?''

The young boy grinned and nodded.

'Rude version, though!'

'Hum four verses to yourself, then go,' Ghassan replied with a grin 'It'll be about right.'

He laughed quietly as he watched the lad concentrating on the song and noted a few of the more socially unacceptable of the lyrics in the rhyme as they formed silently on his lips.

'Get ready.'

A minute more and the young sailor grinned at him and nodded, standing and straightening his uniform. With a deep breath, he turned and ran back among the warehouses.

Ghassan returned his gaze to the jetty beyond the crates. The governor was taking no chances with this prize. The Dark Empress wallowed in the dock, tied fore and aft to the end jetty, the boarding plank pulled up on board. He would be willing to lay money on the oars having been taken away and impounded just in case, which is why they'd raided a storehouse earlier in the evening and brought a number of replacement oars with them to this spot. There were three of the port guard on duty at a brazier at the near end of the jetty, denying access to any possible visitors. Four men stood in position along the jetty itself with many more on deck. Ghassan had counted at least ten and estimated three times as many were aboard.

The sound of pounding feet from off to the left made him smile. Here came Tain.

Ghassan made several hand gestures to the men with him and watched as they split into three distinct groups.

'Fire!' came the warning.

Tain suddenly burst into the open in front of the jetty, having run like the wind around the back of three warehouses and arrived, panting, from the correct direction for a runner from the compound. The three men at the brazier readied their weapons. These soldiers were truly alert and prepared.

'Halt!' the leader barked.

Tain came to a stop, dropping his hands to his knees and breathing in deep gasps. After playing up the weariness a little, he straightened.

'Sir... Sarge at' barracks said he needs ya... Bin attacked at ammo store and... place's on fire... All pris'ners got out 'n' all!'

'Shit.'

The officer at the brazier turned to one of his companions.

'Take a dozen men and go help.'

Tain straightened and saluted before doubling over with a very impressive hacking cough.

'And you'd better stay here 'til you can breathe, lad.'

The young man nodded and shuffled over to a cleat to sit down. As he continued to breathe in deep lungfuls of air, he watched the second in command as he shouted to his men on board. A dozen guards came to the rail, dropped their spears over onto the jetty and then leapt the six feet down and across onto the wooden floor, some of them barely making it. Tain smiled to himself as he noted the random rope snaking away from the cleat upon which he sat and across the jetty. With a deep breath, he leaned back and began, surreptitiously, to move the rope an inch at a time with his foot.

Moments later, the guard detachment was away and marching through the port toward the now-obvious column of flame that marked the location of the ammunition store.

Ghassan made a single gesture with his hand and watched the groups with him burst into silent life. The first ran quietly along behind the piles of crates and barrels until they reached the end wall of the port.

Here the wall rose up behind warehouses, to nowhere near the height of the town walls, but high enough, and with a walkway. The guard that patrolled the top would be looking outward if he were paying attention at all. Likely he was now somewhere further inland, gazing toward the rising flames. Inside the perimeter, the first harbour was framed by the port wall and the jetty, the high sides of the Empress reaching up from the dark, glassy surface within.

The first group, silent and swift, crossed the space between the crates and the shore and disappeared into the black water with hardly a splash. Ghassan bit his lip, his heart pounding as he turned to the other two groups. The men at the near end had taken position in the cover of the barrels, close to the end of the jetty and just outside the circle of orange light cast by the brazier.

The third group, only eight men, but hand-picked by their companions for their abilities, remained with Ghassan at the centre.

He'd have liked, given the opportunity, to have gone with one of the main assault groups, but, no… He was in command and it was the job of a captain to direct and guide and from here he could continue to monitor what was going on until they were certain enough of the success of the plan that he could rush in and join them.

He turned his gaze back to the group in the water and watched, anxiously, as they slid through the black until they reached the ship. They disappeared from view at this angle as they moved along the far side of the hull and Ghassan took a deep breath, counting almost silently.

'One… two… three… four… five… six…'

Turning, he gestured with his thumb at the group near the jetty.

'Go!'

With a roar, the main party of pirates rushed out from their cover toward the two men by the brazier who reacted more professionally than Ghassan had expected, bellowing warnings and commands to the men behind and on board. Perhaps the officer had been prepared for something like this? If that was the case then Ghassan had to hope he'd out-thought the man.

As the raiders bore down on the jetty and Ghassan prepared for the next step, he almost laughed as he saw Tain, seated on a cleat, pull a rope by his feet until it tightened. The coils he'd been carefully manoeuvring with his foot straightened at the ankles of the two men by the brazier and, with a squawk, the officer and his companion were swept from their feet, the former landing on his back on the jetty, while the latter disappeared into the water with a splash.

With a wave to the small group beside him, Ghassan climbed to the top of the pile of crates. From their slightly elevated position, they had a better view of what was happening on deck.

The soaking pirates who had swum across and climbed the ship's side using the well-designed hand holds Samir had had carved for situations just like this finally reached the rail at their side and began to clamber over, just as most of the soldiers on board had rushed over to the jetty side to aid their comrades below.

'Now!'

Beside Ghassan, the men of his third party began to swing their slingshots and bolas and let the missiles fly at any target aboard that presented itself. Several men standing at the jetty side rail were caught unawares as the small stones pounded them. One man, unfortunate indeed, was the recipient of a thrown bolas that caught him at the knees, tying up his legs just as a small, smooth stone caught him a glancing blow on the forehead. Unconscious even as he fell, the guard toppled over the rail, alongside several of his companions. The men variously fell to the jetty with a thud or disappeared with a splash.

The distraction of the main charge was enough. The men who'd swum across and climbed the far side were now spreading out on the deck and disappearing into the doorways. It would all be over in a few minutes. Then would begin the difficult part: getting away from the dock intact.

With a nod of satisfaction, he noted that the assault group on the jetty had reached the far end, downing or pushing into the water anyone who resisted. Two men on board began to lower the boarding ramp as the others dealt with the remaining defenders.

Turning to his missile troops, Ghassan grinned.

'Alright lads. Let's fetch the oars and get on board.'

As they dropped down from the higher crates and rushed to collect the piles of long oars from the side of the building where they'd been stacked, Ghassan looked up when someone shouted his name. With a smile, he recognised Ursa and a number of men rushing down the main thoroughfare of the port and making for the Empress.

'Glad you could join us, mister Ursa.'

'Well, sir. You know how hard it is to leave a comfy fireside and come out in the cold.'

Ghassan laughed as the escaped pirates began to swarm across the jetty and up to the ship, preparing to get her underway. Ursa stopped amid the commotion and addressed his commander.

'Hope you've got something up your sleeve still? There are four navy vessels in port and they're all as fast as us. We're not away free yet…'

Ghassan smiled.

'We'll see, mister Ursa.'

In which paths diverge

The carriage rattled slowly and uncomfortably along the track toward Pelasia. Despite the fact that this was the closest she had managed to regaining what she had lost, Asima sat brooding and seething in the rickety vehicle. The encounter with that uncanny bitch at the staging post a couple of hours ago had sent her into a deep sense of disgruntlement and every time she tried to calm her mind or sleep, visions of that unholy ragged desert witch and her keen insights insisted themselves once more upon her thoughts.

'To hell with her.'

Many years ago, as an 'innocent' girl, she had travelled this very road in just such a coach with vapid, pointless companions on the way to Akkad. Strangely, that time she had been a virtual slave with an uncertain future and yet she had been relatively at peace. Now, while she was an adult with a sense of purpose, her destiny in her own capable hands and travelling on her own, something gnawed at the edges of her consciousness and made her unsettled. With a sigh she sat back heavily.

Ridiculously, this carriage was so old and dreadful that it was entirely possible it was the same damn coach she'd been sent in that first time.

Everything would be better when she got to Pelasia.

Another deep sigh and she realised that she was staring angrily at the empty seat opposite her. Reaching to her side, she pulled back the black curtain to see one of the cavalrymen riding alongside on escort duty.

The man, armoured lightly for a desert ride, wore his scarf wrapped around the lower part of his face, preventing the cloying sand and dust kicked up by horse and carriage from choking him. He paid no attention to the carriage and for some reason that annoyed Asima more than anything.

'How long until we reach the border, soldier?'

The man turned and raised his eyebrows.

'Should be just before dawn, ma'am' he replied, his voice muffled a little by the scarf.

Asima frowned and grumbled.

'Mind if I ask a personal question, miss?'

Asima shrugged and said nothing.

'Well,' he went on, 'we spent the last couple of decades pretty much at war with Pelasia. They're weird and have strange Gods and their noblemen are all... well, that way inclined, if you know what I mean.'

Asima furrowed her brow.

'And?'

'Well I was wondering why an Imperial lady such as you would want to go there. 'Specially since the sarge tells me that you're exiled from the place and you could get done over if you get found.'

Asima narrowed her eyes and wrinkled her lip.

'Outspoken, aren't you, soldier?'

The cavalryman shrugged.

'Just interested ma'am.'

Asima took a breath of tepid night air.

'A combination of ambition and revenge,' she answered darkly.

The soldier's brow furrowed.

'Ma'am?'

Glowering at the outspoken guard, Asima retreated into the darkness of the carriage and let the curtain fall back into place.

Prince Ashar would hang from the city walls for rejecting and banishing her and putting her through all of this. Her first stop would be the coastal town of Jeresh, where the satrap was a man of at least sixty years and of delicate enough health that he rarely ever visited Akkad and had remained absent throughout the troubles. Only two years ago the man's wife had died and it was said that he would take no other.

That would change.

What ageing lord wouldn't want such a stunning young woman on his arm?

And once she was with him, that satrap and his son would be the only two people that stood between her and a veritable kingdom of her own. A sizeable army and navy were centred on Jeresh, and the satrap was extremely wealthy.

Her timing would have to be careful, though. The son would have to die first… perhaps some sort of hunting accident? Hunting accidents happened all the time. Or possibly he would be attacked by brigands on one of his visits throughout their demesne. It would have to be something she could organise that would happen away from the city, in order to keep herself high above suspicion. Also, it couldn't happen for at least a year after she managed to wed the satrap. Arranging the incident and then disposing of those who could link back to her would be fun; just like the old days of the harem. She was good at that sort of planning.

And then, of course, the old man, already shaken by the loss of his wife and failing to find succour in the arms of his new bride, would be heartbroken at the death of his only son and heir. He would pine away and die in his sleep. Probably in his sleep. Perhaps it would be better if it happened in public?

She realised in the dark carriage that she was smiling for the first time since leaving M'Dahz. She was starting to get her life back in order. Half a year would be enough for her to insist herself upon the aging satrap. Married within the year and sole heir to his demesne, its wealth, title and military within two. That was the way to do things.

Then, of course, she would have to expand. A failed coup just did not bear thinking about. When she went for Ashar's head, it would have to be with certainty that she would succeed. The second step would require another powerful satrap. Perhaps a young and naïve one next; one with either money and influence or with military power. Didn't matter too much, so long as she was assured of being the one in control. Then, with the resources of two large and powerful demesnes, she would be able to buy or frighten a number of others into her cause.

It would take a while… could even take a decade, but her own rather tight timeline was based on a five year plan and she would try to stick to that.

She sat back, the tiredness finally beginning to settle over her, now that the thoughts of that old crow woman had been washed away by the plans of her future. As she closed her eyes and began to drift, she floated on through her future, picturing the day her army escorted her into Ashar's chamber and he stood before her, contrite and helpless. Would she bother with the immense satisfaction of executing the man herself or would that be beneath her?

Yes, she'd have to have him dealt with by her men. It would be unseemly to dirty her hands when she was about to grip the crown with them.

Of course she would be the power behind the throne, with her naïve, as-yet-unnamed consort the true King of Pelasia; but only for a year. Long enough to change the laws and become lawfully an equal ruling partner. Then she'd have to find a way to get rid of him, but that would be easy.

'Nice and easy,' she said quietly, smiling in her half-doze.

And then? Then she would have to turn the power of Pelasia to her own goals. That horrible island of pirates would already have been dealt with by the governor at M'Dahz or his superior at Calphoris. But Samir and Ghassan would be free. She was in no doubt that Samir would already be out somewhere and probably with Ghassan.

Was there no regret even deep down that she would have to deal with them?

She raised an eyebrow.

No… no regret. They had become an itch that she would have to scratch sooner or later. Not only would they both be harbouring a grudge against her after the events in M'Dahz, but also they knew enough about her that they'd inevitably find a way some day to try and take her on.

No. When she had the unlimited power of the 'God-Queen', she would demand both their heads of the Imperial governors. For certain, the authorities would not be happy with such a demand from a foreign power, but then one was a pirate and the other a traitor, and they would be hard put to find a reason to help them for fear of angering such a powerful neighbour as Pelasia.

Ghassan and Samir swinging out over the parapet above the sea at Akkad, creaking as they dangled in the wind. Perhaps…

Sleep swept over Asima like a comforting blanket, her smile one of sheer contentment as she ruled her dream-kingdom, drafting dream-laws and wreaking revenge on her dream-enemies.

The curtain lifted gently and two dark eyes sparkled as they gazed in on the sleeping occupant. The drape fell once more, masking the gentle snore that melded so perfectly with the rumble of carriage wheels on stony ground.

Samir pulled the scarf down a little to wipe his itchy nose. Why, in the name of Ha'Rish's fourth face, would people ever join the cavalry? Were these people numb from the waist down? Riding a horse was like spending hour after hour seated upon a bag of broken furniture. Still, that was about to end. It had been difficult and complicated waylaying and incapacitating one of the soldiers and taking his place in the escort; more difficult even than replacing the hired teamsters from the staging post with trusted men from the underbelly of M'Dahz.

He'd been hovering, even after everything she had done, on just leaving Asima to the fates to deal with. But he just had to know. He'd asked of her motives for returning to Pelasia and, though she had clearly spoken of ambition and revenge, he'd expected that anyway. What had clinched it for him, and Asima probably hadn't even been aware of it, was the slight sneer that crept into her expression when she said it and the deeply wicked and, frankly, evil look that welled up in her eyes as she spoke the words.

Whatever schemes she had laid out, and Samir was sure she'd planned for this, they would be at the expense of innocent people, including King Ashar, the legitimate ruler of Pelasia, and the man who had stabilised the realm and brought peace and reparations with the Empire. No. Whatever she was planning, she had to be stopped.

He smiled as he remembered the conversation he'd overheard between Asima and his friend the 'soothsayer'. It had been elaborate as a ruse; possibly overly-so, but as events unfolded in the coming days and Samir put his plan into action, it would be so much more helpful to have Asima going along with things, believing it to be in her own interest, rather than struggling against him every inch of the way.

'You will achieve your destiny, but you must not fight it.'

Samir smiled as he remembered the look on Tiana's face as she'd said that. So much furrowed concentration it looked like she was about to implode. What an actress! She was so wasted in the gambling pits when she could be on the stage.

With a smile, he let his horse drop back slightly, allowing the carriage to roll on into the night slightly ahead. Watching the baggage cart rumble past with its additional cargo of eight sleeping men, he grinned and nodded to the driver who touched his forelock in response.

Three more to deal with, then, or possibly just two, and the rearguard was the easiest. Allowing the cart to trundle on ahead, he watched the horseman at the rear catching up with him. As the two closed, the moonlight illuminating them, Samir was amused at the look of quiet incomprehension on the other man's face.

'What's up?' the soldier asked quietly.

'Lady in the coach asked if I'd give you this.'

The man frowned as the two converged and Samir reached into his tunic. The soldier watched with interest as the hand came out and reached toward him. Samir smiled as he turned the slow movement into a powerful punch that hit the man square in the face. The rider, stunned by the force of the blow as well as the shock, lurched back in his saddle, only the hand gripping the reins preventing him from toppling over backwards.

Samir smiled as he reached across and prised the fingers from the leather strap. The man, still stunned in the moment, opened his eyes wide as he was suddenly completely detached from the horse and slid gracelessly backwards and disappeared with a thump and a squawk in the night.

'That did not go as well as planned', Samir grumbled to himself as he grasped the reins of the riderless horse and trotted forward again. The blow was supposed to knock the man out and Samir had been damn lucky he'd been stunned enough not to bellow out a warning to the others. There was silence now, so the fall had either winded him or rendered him unconscious. Now he could have used Ghassan and those amazing little talents he seemed to have picked up.

Taking a deep breath, he trotted quietly up to the supply wagon and tied the reins of the riderless horse to the leash that connected all the spare horses to the cart. Nodding again at the teamster, he made a 'V' sign with his hand and rode on to the carriage. On the far side, opposite where he'd been riding, another of the soldiers sat ahorse, his gaze locked on the moonlit horizon.

Smiling, Samir rode alongside, nodding professionally at his peer. The horseman raised an eyebrow.

'Bored?'

'Hardly,' Samir smiled quietly. 'Terribly sorry…'

As the man frowned Samir's free hand came down behind him, knife gripped tightly, pommel downward. The heavy, carved ivory knob connected with the back of the soldier's head and he slid from the horse with a sigh, his eyes rolling up into his head. That was more how it was supposed to go.

Narrowing his eyes, he gazed out forward. The rider out front playing vanguard was perhaps a quarter of a mile ahead, paying attention to his surroundings in these sands that sometimes hid bandits. He wouldn't be looking back often, though. His job was to keep the way ahead clear while the two men with the carriage played close guard. Samir turned and nodded to the man leading the supply cart.

With a grin, the man reached around and unhooked the strap that kept the spare horses tethered to the cart. Stepping as quietly as possible onto the edge of the seat, the driver leapt, landing squarely on one of the unused steeds. With a smile, he began to usher the horses forward toward the carriage. Samir nodded again and then came alongside the carriage and nodded to that driver.

Moments later the carriage and almost a dozen horses veered off to the right, carving a new path toward the coast through the open rocky lands. Samir glanced back over his shoulder. The scout leading the way was little more than a dot in the distant grey, while the unmanned supply cart trundled on with its sleeping cargo, beginning to change direction as the oxen plodded along on their own route.

Samir grinned.

They would probably be early. So long as Ghassan was on time, anyway.

In which old tricks are useful

The Dark Empress slipped away from the jetty amid cries of distress and bellows of rage from the reserve port guard who were even now making their way down to the waterfront to find their compatriots largely unconscious or incapacitated. From where Ghassan stood on the command deck, he could make out more and more figures appearing from between buildings and rushing around the port. The town guard were now fully alerted and ever more reinforcements were being drafted into the harbour area. Ghassan smiled. They weren't the worry, unless they were superhuman swimmers.

He glanced away to his right as the Empress began to turn under the power of her determined oarsmen. They were the worry: the four Imperial daram docked further along the waterfront. Even now he could see their crews scrambling around on deck like a colony of ants, rushing to get the vessels underway and in pursuit of their escaping prize. He knew two of those ships well; knew their captains and some of the crew. They were good men and very capable sailors. Any pirate worth his salt would be soiling his trousers at the sight of those four beginning to burst into life.

Ghassan nodded with satisfaction.

Of course, he wasn't a pirate… not as such. But then he could hardly claim to be a naval officer these days. What he was, was an interested third party with a good, objective viewpoint. A smile slid into a grin. And, of course, because he was neither soldier not pirate, he was bound by no rules.

He staggered slightly as he tried to keep his gaze locked on those ships while the Empress completed her swing around and the reverse rowing stopped. Like one of those wind-up Pelasian toy birds, everything fell mechanically into place; this crew was every bit as good as the Wind of God's had been. The oars were repositioned once again and the ship drifted to a stop before beginning, very slowly, to pick up forward momentum. Staggering again, he looked down. The wound in his thigh, though it had been expertly dealt with, still weakened him and if he turned sharply or unexpectedly on that leg, he momentarily lost the strength in it.

Righting himself, he turned toward the stern to keep his eyes on the port as the Empress began finally to come straight and head out toward open sea. The commotion on the dock was immense. He watched tensely as artillery was cranked and loaded on the towers marking the seaward end of the port walls, where they gave way to the lower and non-defensive harbour wall. These catapults were a new defensive measure against invasion since Imperial control had once more been asserted, and it was they that were the first hurdle to overcome. Nothing for it but to pray and row. There was nothing they could have done with the artillery given their time and resources, but the pirates had two things on their side. Firstly, surprise: the Empress would hopefully be out of range before they were ready to fire; and secondly, even if that wasn't the case, the artillerists would have drilled for this moment, but would never yet have had the opportunity to fire a live shot in a combat situation. Their crews were trained, but green and inexperienced, and Ghassan knew just how hard it was to operate artillery effectively for the first time.

He nodded as he judged the distance. One tower might…

He held his breath as there was a distant 'twang' and a dull thud. A rock the size of a wine cask hurtled through the air from the nearest tower, followed almost instantaneously by a second from the other side of the port.

The near shot was clearly very badly aimed and not only fell some six hundred yards short of the target, but also around three ship-widths off to starboard. The other tower was far out of range and clearly no threat as the missile from there disappeared with a distant splash.

Grimacing, Ghassan turned back to the Imperial ships. They were already getting underway and, having been docked with their stern to land, as was the traditional way of the navy, they had no intricate manoeuvring to perform before they made for sea. There were times that any good captain had to rely on the abilities of others, when he himself had no bearing on the outcome of events… Ghassan hated those times.

Two of the four ships were already slipping from the jetty, with the others already moving. They would be very close on the

Empress' tail, or possibly even ahead of her. Even now, though he couldn't see it, he knew damn well that the artillery crews on all four ships would be loading and priming their own fire throwers and catapults, though they wouldn't begin to use them until they were clear of the harbour.

There was the sound of pounding feet and Ghassan turned to see one of the men, someone he vaguely recognised, running toward him.

'Yes?'

'Sir, Ursa wants permission to unfurl the sails.'

Ghassan shook his head.

'Tell mister Ursa the sails stay furled for now. Oar power only until I give the order.'

'Sir?'

'Just tell him.'

The man shrugged and ran off. Ghassan turned back to the four daram sliding through the water straight out to sea on an intercept course. He couldn't tell just yet…

He was still concentrating on the four ships and frowning into the night when he heard more boot steps. Without turning, he cleared his throat.

'No sails, mister Ursa.'

'We've got to catch the little wind there is to get out ahead! Look at that… the enemy ships have unfurled their sails. We're going to lose the lead we have in minutes!'

Ghassan smiled enigmatically.

'I may not be Samir, Ursa, but I have commanded a daram for years and I do know what I'm doing. I'm rather hoping that they match our speed or even outpace us, but I want to be ready to slow to a halt any minute.'

Turning, he unleashed what Ursa considered to be a mad grin.

'Here's your next job: we're angling toward the centre of the harbour to head out to sea. Before we turn, keep a sharp eye out. If everything is going according to plan and the Gods are smiling on us tonight, you'll spot a rowing boat. When you do, we need to stop and take its crew aboard. If it's not there, then we're in trouble and we might have a hell of a fight on our hands.'

Ursa narrowed his eyes.

'You're almost as irritating as your brother, sir!'

Ghassan laughed.

'Why, thank you. Now keep an eye out.'

Ursa nodded and peered off into the darkness, the sea sparkling and reflecting flashes of moonlight here in the harbour where the waves were low and the water remarkably still. The two men stood watching in a strange silence, while all about them was chaos; the roaring and grunting of the oarsmen as they heaved to bring the ship toward the centre of the harbour, the distant shouts and cries on board the enemy vessels, the commotion on the docks and the towers. It was almost unreal, standing calmly in the middle of this, particularly for Ursa, apparently, who appeared so taut he could snap at any moment.

Moments slid past with the dark water as the five vessels converged on the entrance to the harbour. Ursa ground his teeth.

'They're going to get there first and be able to block us in!'

'Faith, Ursa... faith,' Ghassan replied. 'Without faith, even Gods fail.'

The big, bald pirate glowered at him and mumbled something that sounded unflattering under his breath.

'There!' Ghassan called.

The first officer blinked. Damn it, this man's eyesight was good. It took a moment peering into the dark waters for the burly man to pick out the shape of the boat bobbing around in the darkness.

'Full stop!' he bellowed at the crew. The oarsmen, taken by surprise, took a moment to sort themselves out, but very quickly the Empress slowed to a halt, just beyond the small boat. Its four occupants rowed as fast as they could to catch up with the pirate vessel.

'This had better be important,' the big man grumbled to his commander. 'Those four ships are way out ahead of us now.'

Ghassan smiled.

'I think you'll be pleasantly surprised shortly, Ursa.'

The big man looked down at the four new arrivals who were beginning to climb the rope ladder at the side. Three men and a woman, all dressed in low-class utilitarian clothes and all dark grey and black.

'Who the hell are these people?'

Again Ghassan turned his smile to his second in command.

'My brother has the honour of knowing a great number of people in low places in the port of M'Dahz. I persuaded a few of them to rise above the waterline for an hour or two, in return for the promise of considerable recompense.'

'They're port dogs? Some of them have morals that would make an executioner blush!'

Ghassan nodded.

'But they have their uses, Ursa. We will be giving them passage out of the port for now and putting them ashore once again when we meet up with my brother.'

'*If* we meet up with your brother!'

That grin was starting to get on Ursa's nerves. Something about the tall officer's face actually managed to make his enigmatic smile even more irritating than Captain Samir's. As he grumbled under his breath, the last of the four dishevelled villains from M'Dahz climbed aboard.

'Get underway as fast as we can, mister Ursa. Still just the oars, though. Make for the harbour entrance…'

Ursa shook his head.

'Look sir. The navy are already there. They only have to manoeuvre into position and they can pull us to pieces.'

'Yes,' Ghassan grinned 'that could well have been the case. However, you will find in a moment that it actually isn't. As soon as we're at the harbour entrance I want hard a-port. Swing round and follow the coast west. As soon as we're out of harbour and in open sea and making for Pelasian waters you can unfurl as many sails as you like, but until then I want the tight manoeuvrability of oars alone. Your port turn might have to be the sharpest you'll ever make.'

Ursa narrowed his eyes.

'It would help us poor mortals if you and your brother occasionally shared your plans with the rest of us.'

'And spoil the surprise? Watch and learn, Ursa.'

The Dark Empress cut through the waves, bearing down on the entrance to the harbour where the four Imperial ships in tight formation had just arrived. From his position, following them, Ursa was surprised to hear sudden cries of alarm from the vessels ahead.

'What's happening?' he asked, of no one in particular.

Frowning and squinting into the distance, he watched the ships which, having begun to bank for positioning to blockade the Empress in, suddenly started jerking wildly around, two even colliding lightly as they continued on a roughly straight course, heading directly out to sea. There was a desperate commotion and the four ships were suddenly trying to sort themselves out and reverse their oars.

'What did you do?' he asked, turning to his temporary captain.

Ghassan smiled.

'Our four friends here have spent the last hour or two emulating what Asima did to my ship before you attacked us. These captains had no reason to bank until they reached the open sea, since they were facing the entrance while in dock. As soon as they got there ahead of us, they hauled on the rudders to turn and discovered that some villainous scoundrel has sawn most of the way through them. If you listened you could hear the cracks as they gave way and left them with no way to manoeuvre.'

His smile widened.

'They'll get back on track with steering oars, just like we did, but you'll remember the disadvantage that put us at. And, of course, because they're facing directly away from us, they can't fire their artillery without taking out their own masts.'

Ursa shook his head as he grinned.

'You're a clever bastard, sir... a mad one, but a clever one!'

'I hope your oarsmen are as good as they think. You've only got a small space there to take us to port without colliding with those ships.'

Ursa squared his shoulders.

'I don't think that'll be a problem, sir.'

Ghassan nodded as the heavy man ran off to issue the orders. Brushing that stray lock of black curly hair out of his eyes, he watched the havoc aboard the four daram as they desperately tried to manoeuvre. The Empress would be a dot on the horizon before they even made it back to the dock for an emergency refit.

'Alright, Samir. I've done my bit. Now let's see what you've been up to.'

In which a full reunion occurs

Samir nudged the teamster, who woke with a start.

'Smnff?'

'There's a sail. I think it's the Empress, but I want to be sure before I give the signal. What do you think?'

The man squinted off across the dark waves from their small and cold camp by the water's edge. They had arrived at the village of Khediv around an hour ago and rode on along the beach until they were safely a quarter of a mile from civilisation. Even then, Samir had refused to allow them a fire for warmth or food, in case they were spotted by the wrong people. The carriage driver sat awake in his seat, guarding the vehicle and its slumbering occupant.

'It's too big for a merchant ship and not flying military pennants, so if it's not your ship, it's another pirate.'

Samir nodded, satisfied, and finally retrieved his flint and steel, striking sparks on the dry straw, leaves and sticks until they caught and roared into life with an orange light that cast eerie shadows around the small camp.

Samir watched the ship out to sea as it gradually closed with the coast and nodded to himself once more as the Empress came to a stop just within safe depth and a lifeboat was lowered.

'Almost time to part ways, my friend.'

The teamster gave him a grin and raised an eyebrow. Samir looked down to see the man's hand out open.

'Yes, I remember the arrangement. You'll have to hang on until the others get here, though.'

As they waited, Samir strode over to the carriage and peered in through a crack in the curtains. He'd been doing so every ten minutes or so since they arrived, never entirely convinced that Asima would still be there the next time. He could have tied her, but would rather not have to. There she was, still slumped in the seat, fast asleep and believing herself on the way to Pelasia once again.

Samir smiled as he returned to the waterfront. The lifeboat was almost here now and Samir frowned as he realised there were six people in the vessel. Surely Ghassan hadn't brought an honour guard from the ship or some such rubbish.

He heaved a sigh of relief as the six occupants came into clearer view: Ghassan and Ursa were accompanied by four of the more resourceful but less reputable people he employed from time to time in port. The boat arrived at the gravel beach with a crunch and Ghassan stepped out. Samir smiled at him with a raised eyebrow.

'You've been using my contacts?'

'I used your name in the "Mermaid", yes brother. I had a little job I needed doing before we could saunter off to meet you.'

One of the four, a short, dark and badly-shaven man flashed a dangerous look at Samir.

'Your friend here offered us forty corona apiece and I'd hate to find out I've been stiffed, Samir…'

Samir laughed lightly.

'Hardly, Grim.' He turned to Ursa.

'You brought my bag?'

With a nod, the big pirate retrieved a waterproof sack from the boat and handed it over. Samir dropped it to the floor with a crunch and delved within, removing a bag of coins. Opening it, he began to count out large, gold discs and proffered them to the man.

'I'm afraid I'm rather low on corona at the moment, but I do have these sols, minted in Germalla. I believe the general exchange rate is around eight corona to a sol, so if I give you, say six sol apiece, the extra should make up for the inconvenience of having to change the currency, yes?'

The man glared at Samir and the captain shrugged.

'Bearing in mind that I'm in M'Dahz semi-regularly and you'll have plenty of opportunities to tell me if you have problems…'

'Seven apiece,' the man said flatly.

'You drive a hard bargain, Grim. Still, you have me currently at a disadvantage. Seven it is, but I shall expect preferential rates the next time we do business.'

As the others reached out to collect their payment, Samir doled out the coins with a smile.

'I presume I can leave you all here to work out the details of the return journey to the town? You have carriage, cart and plenty of horses.'

As they nodded and examined their coins, biting the gold to test its authenticity, Samir grasped Ghassan by the shoulder and walked him away from the crowd toward the carriage. The driver nodded respectfully down at him and reached out to take the coins the pirate captain proffered. As the exchange took place quietly, Samir leaned closer to his brother conspiratorially and whispered.

'Have a quick look inside.'

Ghassan frowned and, leaning across to the wagon, pulled aside the drape a little to peer into the darkness within. He blinked and then checked again to be sure his eyes did not deceive him.

'What are you doing, Samir?'

There was a groan from within.

'Now you've gone and woken her, Ghassan. Still, it's time she was up.'

Ghassan grasped Samir by the collar and pulled him close as the sounds of stirring came from within the coach.

'She cannot be trusted. She tried to kill me, Samir. She's sold us out more than once. She values nothing but her own comfort and power, and we were about to be rid of her, probably for good.'

Samir nodded.

'That's all certainly true, Ghassan, but you're the one who's always going on about duty and what's right. Do you think for a minute that we'd be doing the right thing sending her back to Pelasia so she can plot the downfall of King Ashar?'

Ghassan frowned as his brother went on.

'Pelasia's been nothing but trouble for the last two decades and now, at last, there's a good, reasonable, educated man on their throne; a man who wants to tighten ties with the Empire. He's the man who exiled Asima and, I gather, dislikes her intensely. Given that Asima knifed one of her oldest friends just because you were in her way, what do you think she has planned for the King of Pelasia?'

'But she couldn't...'

'She could, Ghassan. And she will if someone doesn't stop her. I asked her why she was going back and she told me flat that it was ambition and revenge.'

Ghassan continued to shake his head.

'She's a wild animal, Ghassan,' Samir said, shaking his head sadly 'and while I won't put her down, she needs to be tamed.'

'I'm a what?'

They both looked round to see Asima's face at the carriage window.

Samir beamed at her.

'Ah, the wildcat is awake. Good morning, Asima.'

The door burst open and their captive dropped heavily from of the vehicle, striding across the ground angrily to the brothers.

'What is the meaning of this, Samir?'

The pirate captain treated her to a warm smile.

'You've been selfish, Asima... very selfish. Now it's time to think of others for a change... people other than you. Time to give the world a breather and remove you from the game for a while.'

Ghassan shook his head.

'So that's the plan? We take her on board and flee? I presume there's more to your scheme than this?'

Samir nodded.

'Oh, far more, Ghassan. And, Asima? Bear in mind that despite everything you see, what I am doing is as much for your own good as everyone else's; possibly more so.'

Asima folded her arms defiantly.

'Is that so? Kidnapping me for my own good?'

Samir nodded.

'At some time since we were children, you came to a fork in the road and went down the wrong one and it's turned you into this. But the nice thing about roads is that you can walk down them both ways, even back to that fork so that you can go the right way this time.'

Asima blinked. Twice in a day she'd been told much the same thing, by both her oldest friend and that witch in the rags. Why was everyone so damn perceptive these days? Casting the blackest look she could muster at the brothers, she turned to the small, wiry man in black.

'On the assumption you are for hire, little man, I will pay you handsomely to protect me from these two and to escort me on the rest of my journey.'

Grim, a long-time resident of M'Dahz's most dangerous streets and a regular employee of Samir, grinned a largely toothless grin at Asima.

'You see, if it weren't for our "arrangement" with Samir, here, I'd be tempted to take you up on that offer, but be grateful I'm not about to cross him. Woman like you? You'd never get there. We'd have taken your money and then sold you to the desert traders for a lot more. Or maybe, we'd just have stopped for a while and had some fun on our own and left you in the desert. It can be a lonely life.'

Asima sneered at him and spat at his feet.

'Pig!'

He laughed.

'As I said, woman: be grateful.'

Samir stepped forward.

'You're coming with us, Asima. I would rather you came aboard quietly and willingly, but I will settle for any other way if necessary.'

He sighed as he saw the colour rise in Asima's face, her jaw clenching ready to launch into yet another tirade.

'Oh, for Gods' sake!'

Stepping past Samir, Ghassan swung a powerful punch, fast and unexpected, connecting with Asima's jaw and cheek so hard that it spun her on her feet and threw her to the ground. Samir blinked.

'You never cease to amaze me, brother.'

Ghassan shrugged and then bent to collect the unconscious woman from the floor and throw her gracelessly over his shoulder, staggering momentarily as his leg wobbled beneath him.

'Well, she was starting to get on my nerves.'

As Samir laughed, the pair of them nodded their goodbyes to the 'port dogs' as they gathered their gear and prepared for the long journey back to M'Dahz. Ghassan passed the silent form of Asima, a welt already beginning to show on her cheek, to Ursa, who took her, grinning, as the three turned toward the boat that would take them back to the Empress.

'Two mad bastard captains, now. This is going to be an interesting voyage.'

Part Five:

The kindness of strangers, the cruelty of friends

In which captains collude

Ghassan shook his head once again and tapped the table with his index finger.

'Nothing good can come of this, Samir.'

'I think that's blatantly untrue, Ghassan.'

Again, the shaking of the head. The taller brother sat in a heavy wooden chair opposite his sibling in the captain's cabin of the Dark Empress, swaying slightly with the motion of the ship through every dip and swell.

'I don't mean your plan in general. It's a good plan. I have nothing against your plan. In fact, it's the sort of thing I'd have liked to have come up with myself and I can't argue that I'm pleased you finally decided to take me into your confidence...'

'So what's the problem?' Samir grinned.

Ghassan ran his fingers through his wild, curly hair, getting them caught in the salty locks. Irritably, he raked his hand free and sighed.

'Actually, I can see a few gaping holes in your logic, though I can assume you've already spotted them and have some clever-arsed way around them. No. The big problem is Asima.'

'I think that just being near her befuddles your mind, brother,' Samir answered with a shrug. 'You're all over the place when it comes to Asima.'

Ghassan gave his brother a hard look.

'It's true,' Samir laughed. 'You don't trust her, but you still feel sorry for her. You agree that we can't just leave her to go merrily cutting a swathe through the innocent population of Pelasia, but you also don't want to confine or inconvenience her. You don't want her free, but you don't want her anywhere near us. You see what I mean?'

Ghassan shook his head again.

'You make it sound worse than it is.'

'Enlighten me, then.'

'What Asima has become is the product of what has been done to her. We remember her as a girl and she was one of us back then.'

It was Samir's turn to shake his head.

'I think you look back with rosy vision. When I think back on her youth I can see her playing the pair of us time and again. I think all that's happened has merely accentuated her selfish ambition.'

'I hope you're wrong. Even the most noble of people can be changed by events. Look at you. You've sunk ships, taken lives and robbed people, and we both know you were never that sort of boy.'

Samir laughed.

'Rosy vision again, I think, brother. I'm under no misconceptions that I was born anything other than a rogue.'

Ghassan was starting to get irritated now.

'Listen! We cannot just arbitrarily condemn Asima to anything without being sure that there is no other possibility. I live in constant hope that she will change, and while that doesn't appear to be happening, we've done nothing to help either. Perhaps if we try to push her in the right direction, we can get the Asima of old back?'

'You make it sound like I'm planning to have her executed. Alright, Ghassan. We've a little time yet. What do you want?'

'I want to give her the chance; I want to try to help her. I agree with your plan, with reservations, but I want to be sure that it's necessary first.'

Samir nodded slowly.

'Then for the sake of your conscience, I'll give her the chance to prove to us that she can change; that she can be reasonable. Healing is the province of Belapraxis and, as you know, everything with the 'desert lady' comes in threes. We'll give her three chances, but only three. Agreed?'

'Agreed.'

'So,' Samir sat back heavily 'what are your other reservations?'

'Lassos, basically.'

'And?'

Ghassan sighed.

'Samir, Lassos is the most infamous den of pirate iniquity in the world. Most criminals would be afraid to go there. As for us... well, I'm an ex-naval captain that's probably still on the top of their list of enemies to disembowel. The only person that might have knocked me off the top position is *you*, for what they likely see as betrayal and endangerment of the island. Neither of us is likely able to set a foot on that dock there without it being nailed to the timber by angry pirates.'

He grinned.

'There is a certain level of risk there, I'll grant you. I'm just trusting that my dice roll is high enough to make them fold without rolling themselves.'

'There's still only one of you and eleven of them. If you're wrong, the odds are going to be very heavily stacked against us.'

The smaller brother leaned forward over the table.

'I have other friends. Even if things go the worst they can, the odds aren't as bad as you suggest.'

'And what of the council? These are vicious old, hard-bitten pirates; they've only made it onto the council by being some of the most evil and remorseless bastards the world has ever known. They're not likely to fold easily and even if they do, they'll stay put at their table and leave it to us.'

Samir's grin intensified.

'I've already got that worked out. Just trust me, Ghassan.'

Ghassan sighed and then smiled a helpless smile.

'I love the idea, Samir... I really do. I just hope you're right and it all comes together.'

The captain stretched and stood.

'This has been years in the making, Ghassan. Things have been unfolding and I've been manoeuvring them for months now. Alright, there's a way ahead of us yet, but you have no idea how much work I've already put in and what's gone right so far. Everything now hinges on two things: our success or failure at Lassos and what the governor decides to do. The latter is out of our control, but at least we can take charge of the former and that'll be at least as much down to you as to me.'

The taller brother also stood, rolling his shoulders.

'I hope you're right and I hope we're up to it. Well, what now?'

Samir shrugged.

'We're still a way from Lassos and even then we'll have to loiter around for a while until we're sure of the path ahead. In the meantime, perhaps it's time we checked on our passenger?'

Ghassan nodded and the pair strode across to the cabin door, opening it and blinking as the fresh, salty air wafted across them.

Two cabins down, the doctor's cabin door remained firmly closed and locked, a specially selected man with no sense of humour standing beside it.

'Duro. We're here to see the lady.'

The big man nodded and withdrew a heavy key on a large iron ring from his belt. Reaching to the lock with it, he inserted the key and then paused to knock heavily on the door.

'People to see you. Step back from the door to the opposite wall of the cabin and there'll be no trouble.'

There was no sound from within.

'She never replies,' the big man shrugged 'but she's probably done it, cap'n. She's missed two meals from being difficult and disobedient, but she let us deliver the last one, so I think she's learning.'

Samir shook his head.

'I wouldn't be too sure about that, Duro, but we can handle her. Open up.'

The pirate nodded and turned the key in the lock. Stepping to one side, he turned the handle and pushed and the door swung inwards.

Samir ducked and Ghassan stepped lightly to one side as a fork, still covered in stew, hurtled through the doorway at eye height and bounced off the wall opposite, scattering away down the corridor with a metallic clatter.

'Asima, your aim is improving.'

Samir turned to his brother as he spoke.

'Does that count as one? Belapraxis is listening.'

Ghassan gave Samir a hard look, causing the smaller man to grin impishly as he turned back to the room and approached the doorway, the cabin's occupant out of sight around the door.

'If you're going to throw anything else, don't forget to adjust for height. I'm coming in first.'

Still sporting his cheeky grin, Samir stepped through the door, his hands wide and open in a conciliatory gesture.

'Good afternoon, my dear. The stew not to your liking?'

Asima sat on the bunk, fingering the handle of the knife on her plate thoughtfully.

'Have you come to gloat over your prisoner? Or perhaps to take advantage of me? I'll warn you Samir: men have tried that before. Some of them stopped being men that very day.'

Samir's grin widened.

'We're just here for a little chat, Asima.'

The woman on the cot opposite sat back and gestured to her surroundings. The doctor's room had been converted into what was, in effect, a prison cell. The many drugs and herbs and pieces of sharp or dangerous equipment had been removed, along with all the furniture barring the bed, a rickety chair and a small desk. The room was somewhat oppressive with just so much bare and dark wood. Moreover, the plank that had been nailed thoroughly across the exterior of the window, preventing its being opened, cut out around half of the light, making the interior dim and depressing.

'You can dispense with the pleasantries, I think,' she grumbled.

Samir and Ghassan entered and stood opposite her as the door was closed and locked by Duro outside.

'We're trying to decide how best to proceed with you, Asima.'

A sneer greeted that comment.

'You've made it abundantly clear how you will do that: you kidnapped me and prevented me from going home. Now you have three choices: kill me, free me, or imprison me for the rest of my life. Neither of you has the strength of character to kill me, and neither of you has the guts to free me. I just wonder how you will go about imprisoning me, and where you think could possibly be secure enough to contain me. Neither of you is very popular on either side of the law.'

Ghassan shook his head and opened his mouth, but Samir spoke first.

'Nothing has been decided yet. I have made certain potential arrangements, but I have yet to decide what to do about them. However, what you said does deserve a response.'

His smile turned cold and feral.

'I like to consider myself a good man, despite everything, but don't mistake good for weak. If I decide that the world would be a safer place with you at the bottom of the sea, believe me that I will cut your throat and drop you overboard myself. Ghassan is a better person than I, but I doubt that even he would stop me.'

He raised an eyebrow at his brother, but Ghassan said nothing, his expression unreadable.

'Also, do not think for a minute that I do not have the nerve to free you. No matter what you have done to us in the past, Ghassan and I know who and what you are, and I have no fear of you, Asima. The reason I took you away from your Pelasian dream is far from personal… let's say it's my little contribution to the peaceful relations between Pelasia and the Empire. To allow you to return to your games would be akin to setting a wild cat free in the famous royal aviary.'

Asima sneered and sat back, still fingering the knife.

'So you have no real decision to make.'

Ghassan stepped a pace forward, frowning.

'You say Samir prevented you from going home, Asima. You may be half Pelasian by blood, but you were born and raised in M'Dahz. You are one of us, whatever you've come to believe. Do you truly feel no kinship to your hometown?'

The sneer turned on Ghassan, but its owner said nothing.

'Your father was a good man,' the tall brother continued quietly, 'a man of the Empire; and he lies at rest in M'Dahz. I've visited his grave. Have you?'

There was no change in Asima's expression as she raised her head slightly.

'Are you finished boring me?'

Ghassan sighed.

'I believe so. Perhaps Samir was right about you. Belapraxis has closed one of her eyes.'

A trace of uncertainty passed suddenly across Asima's face, but disappeared in an instant, to be replaced by yet more disdain and disgust.

'Get out and leave me to eat this filth in peace.'

Samir and Ghassan exchanged a look and then turned to the door.

'Duro! Open up.'

As the key was jangled in the lock, a low and determined voice from behind them said 'Bear in mind, both of you, that I have been enslaved, imprisoned, exiled and sentenced to death and I have walked away free and unharmed every time. There is no power in the world that can contain me. It is my destiny to reign. Even the Gods have acknowledged that; and when I do, I will shake the world until it spits the pair of you out at my feet.'

Samir turned as the door opened and sketched a mock bow.

'Then, since I have no wish to anger the Gods, I shall do everything in my power to make sure that you achieve your goals, your magnificence.'

The gravy-spattered knife hit the door and dug deep with a wooden 'thunk' just as the lock clicked shut.

In which Asima rails against fate

Harus had joined the crew of the Dark Empress six years ago. Caught stealing food, he'd fled the guard in Calphoris, found himself at the docks and hid aboard the first vessel he could find, after which he'd never looked back. Even those first months after he'd been discovered stowing away, when the crew had been extremely harsh on him and he'd had the worst jobs they could throw his way, he'd been grateful beyond belief. It may have seemed to the rest of them that they were putting him through hell but the plain truth was that the worst they could dream up was heaven compared to life as a homeless beggar in the city. His muscles might ache, but his belly was full.

Six years of slowly clawing his way up from that inauspicious beginning, of forging a career as a sailor, learning the ropes in quite a literal manner, and of gaining the respect of his crewmates. Six long years of struggle, and it had to end like this, staggering against a doorframe, staring down at the blood gushing from his chest.

Harus felt like crying at the unfairness of it all, but the pain and the horror paralysed him. Was he dead? Was that it? He stared down at the tin bowl, its meaty, juicy contents spattered across the wooden floor. He was only delivering food! Could he do anything to prevent what seemed inevitable now? At least he could scream... that would bring help, and perhaps warn the others...

The cry died in his throat as Asima's dining knife came in for a second attack, slicing neatly across his windpipe and artery. With a wheeze and a sigh, pumping blood like the grand fountains of Calphoris, Harus slid down the doorframe and slumped to the floor.

Asima tutted irritably and brushed at the droplets that spattered the hem of her dress. Reaching down, she wiped the knife on the boy's tunic, cleaning the viscera from it so that it gleamed silver once again. Edging close to the door, she peered left and right. The corridor was empty and dark, the faint moonlight tempered by scudding clouds and not penetrating this far into the cabin section's interior.

Clearly Samir's cabin would be the one at the end. On the assumption this daram was organised the same as Ghassan's military one had been, the room opposite would be a social room for the more senior crewmen, while the four between here and the captain's cabin would be those of the first officer and the three other most senior crewmen. The nearest two to her would be less important, which meant that Ursa and Ghassan would be behind the two doors that flanked the captain's cabin.

Briefly she paused, wondering for the hundredth time since she had settled on this course of action whether it might have been better to steal a lifeboat and try to make for land; but she was no sailor and had no idea how far they were from shore now, so such an act would be reckless.

The old crone had told her not to fight against her fate, but that was assuming that there was such a thing as fate. Asima still struggled with the concept but, logically, if something were fated, then anything she did was already written and therefore she was following the path and not fighting it, whatever she did. That logic, when it had come to her this afternoon, had eased her tensions and helped her justify whatever needed doing.

This was a gamble, of course. The crew had no reason to support her, even though Ursa had been on good terms with her during their last brief stay at Lassos.

But this was the only real path left open now. In the navy it would be dealt with harshly, but among pirates it was said that strength ruled, and strength was something that Asima had in abundance. Realistically it should be Samir first. The way you killed a serpent was to cut off its head. Ursa could be last; he was clearly the least important.

But the more she thought of Ghassan and his self-righteous attitude, the more the thought of him pinned to the bulkhead with his eyes rolled up into his skull appealed to her. Samir could wait. Ghassan might just have to go first... call it a practice run.

Still pausing, Asima held her breath as she listened. The sounds from outside were muted in the night as the ship relied on sails, the oars shipped for the duration. The creak of timber was faint and, if she listened extremely hard, she could hear the distant murmur of low conversation between duty crewmen. There was no sound from the room opposite; presumably any eating, drinking and carousing they had planned, they'd done earlier in the evening.

Taking a quiet gulp of air, she stepped out into the corridor and silently padded deeper into the darkness. The wooden beams creaked gently under her feet, but the sound was lost amid the normal squeaks and groans of the ship's timbers.

She paused again as she reached the next set of doors. There was heavy snoring from the room on her left, but no sound from the right. Keeping a watchful eye on the silent door, she crept further, passing those rooms and approaching the end of the corridor, where the ornate door of Samir's cabin taunted her.

Perhaps she should go after the snake's head first, after all?

No. She'd made her decision. Second-guessing and indecision suggested failure in either the planning or the execution of any scheme. Now… which door?

Leaning to the left, she listened at the wood. The very faint sounds of someone sleeping within. Could be Ghassan… could be Ursa. Who knew? Crossing the corridor, she leaned toward that door. Again, the faint sounds of deep, relaxed breathing. It was a guess, then. One door held Ghassan and one Ursa. They would both have to die anyway if she were going to stand a chance of usurping command of the ship. She was sure enough of her own talents and persuasiveness that she didn't doubt for a moment she would sway the crew to her side, but not while any of these three lived to defy her.

Shrugging, she silently ran through a childhood rhyme to make her decision, the gleaming point of her sharp knife wavering back and forth with each line, pointing at one door and then the other.

The closing stanza of the rhyme escaped her lips and Asima looked down at the knife, then up to the door on her left and shrugged nonchalantly. Now for the first real test of her abilities. Leaning in close, she carefully grasped the handle and began, very slowly, to turn. There was the faintest squeak and she lowered the speed of turn more, moving the handle through a fraction of a degree at a time, all the while listening for any change in the sleep pattern within. It came as something of a relief when the door finally gave, just an inch. She'd half expected them to be locked and, while she was more than capable of overcoming that kind of difficulty after so many years' practice in the harem of Akkad, it represented an added degree of danger.

Slowly, the door cracked open. Once more there was a faint creak to it. Had she opened it at normal speed, the noise would have been loud enough to startle most sleepers awake, but Asima was nothing if not careful.

The door finally wide enough to allow access, she slipped inside. Briefly she considered closing it, but then, if she were caught out and there was a noise, a closed door would hardly protect her. Better to leave the exit clear for her to move on speedily.

Silently, she padded into the dark room, a drape hanging over the window and obscuring all but the faintest glow. As her eyes adjusted to the stygian gloom, she picked out various furnishings and, finally, the bed. For a moment she was a little disappointed to realise from the bulk of the figure in the bed that this was Ursa's room and not Ghassan's. Still, she told herself once more, they all had to go and this could be considered just an extra training run.

Slowly, she inched across to the bed. The great, bald man lay there, barely covered by a single sheet and naked barring a set of under-britches. He slept on his back, eyes tight and mouth purring gently in a manner so quiet and calm and even ladylike that it brought a smile to Asima's face; that great tattooed head uttering such a tiny, peaceful noise. Very easy positioning, of course. He would be a lot more peaceful in a minute.

Taking a deep breath, she raised herself up over the slumbering figure. Silent: that was the thing. Silence first. With a smile, she placed her hand ready over his mouth, not touching, but ready, should he get the chance to struggle.

The knife went in easily and slid across the neck to the ear opposite. She shook her head in disbelief at how easy it really was. Surely, they should have had more foresight than to give her a sharp knife to eat with. If she'd been their captor, they'd have been lucky to get a spoon.

Ursa awoke in understandable distress, his eyes wide as the life sprayed from his neck. He tried to shout something but it merely came out from his throat as bloody bubbles as he thrashed. Damn it. He was going to make too much noise with all this waving around.

Sighing, Asima drew the knife back, her hand going to his chest to try and hold him down. As he panicked, dying, she carefully drove her knife into his temple, delivering a paralysing, killing blow. The big body, a pile of sweating blubber, slick with sweat and crimson gore, shuddered and shook for a moment and then fell still, the man's glassy eyes staring lifelessly at the ceiling.

Asima nodded to herself. One down and two to go. And she'd learned a valuable lesson: silence from the mouth was only part of the job. She had to make sure the thrashing around was kept to a minimum. Ghassan would be a better job. Once more, she carefully cleaned the blade on the drape over the window. It wasn't a fussy thing, for the sake of cleanliness, so much as the need to make sure she kept a solid grip on the weapon with no slippery blood beneath her fingers.

Straightening and squaring her shoulders, she crossed the room once more and peered through the door. Still no sign of movement or noise outside. Quietly, she pulled the door to behind her, closing it with the faintest of clicks. A step or two and she was across to the other door.

Once again she repeated her procedure, turning the handle so slowly that the inevitable creaks and squeaks were almost dulled to inaudible levels; the door refused to budge. Shaking her head irritably, Asima retrieved a pin from her luscious, dark hair and set it into the lock. Her tongue protruding as she worked, she eased the pin left and right, finding the teeth of the mechanism and manoeuvring them into position. The harem had been a great teacher, for sure.

There was a slight click, and Asima stood back, holding her breath. The sound of breathing within continued without a change in pitch. Good.

The handle began to twist under her grasp and slowly, ever so slowly, she turned it and pushed. The wooden portal gave way quietly, inching open and revealing the dark cabin beyond. Drapes covered this window too, casting a deep darkness over most of the room. As her vision adjusted, she realised that the contents of this cabin almost exactly mirrored those of Ursa's opposite. The faintest gleam of silvery starlight shone from the window, where the drapes had caught on the frame and left a narrow triangle of clear glass. The beam fell across the bed and its occupant and Asima heaved a sigh of relief. Despite everything, she had half expected Ghassan to be standing behind the door, prepared for her, or Samir sitting in the chair, waiting. But no… that beam of light illuminated the tall figure beneath the sheet and those curly, ebony locks were unmistakably Ghassan's.

Silently, she crept across the room, approaching the bed. A different method was needed here. Ghassan was asleep on his side, his back to her. Given how dangerous he could be, she would have to make sure he was out of commission as soon as possible. A killing blow first, and then, as he woke, his life already ebbing, she would then have to make sure he stayed silent. She couldn't get to his throat without turning him over anyway, and that mass of curly hair made any blow to the temple uncertain. She might miss and merely crack his skull. Then he'd have the best of her.

Taking a deep breath, she looked up and down the sleeping figure of her childhood love before shrugging, bending and thrusting the knife to the hilt in his back. The blade rasped as it slid between ribs, making her shudder as the reverberation ran up her arm. As she dealt the blow, her other hand went straight around to the mouth, clamping over it to keep her victim quiet.

Ghassan's eyes opened wide, the shock of the sudden, incredibly forceful wound filling him. Asima yanked the knife back out, blood spattering both her and the floor as she did so, and raised her blood-soaked finger to her lips in a silencing motion.

'Shhhh.'

As her childhood friend's eyes blinked and his face went white, she turned him gently onto his back, her hand still over his mouth, and leaned forward, placing the tip of the blade on his throat beneath his ear, ready to finish the job.

And that's when it all went wrong. He should have been too panicked and weak; paralysed. He certainly shouldn't have the strength or presence of mind for this. She clenched her teeth and squeezed her eyes shut against the intense pain as Ghassan bit down hard on the hand over his mouth, his incisors meeting in the heel of her hand. She reeled, a chunk of flesh an inch across missing from her palm as Ghassan spat it out, his eyes filling with fury.

This wasn't possible. He should be dying. He was dying, but refusing to lie down and take it. He still hadn't cried out, though, and, despite the agony in her hand, neither had she, so there was still a chance. Gritting her teeth and ignoring the throbbing hand by her side, she reached in with the knife once again to go for the throat.

But Ghassan was already struggling to rise and, as she leaned forward, his arm came up like lightning, shaped into something resembling a claw, and delivered a sharp, precise blow to her neck, just below the jaw.

Asima was already unconscious when she hit the floor, the knife skittering away from her grasp. Ghassan stared and tried to rise from the bed. The agony in his chest and back was unbelievable and threatened to drain the consciousness from him. He tried to pull himself upright again and, instead, slid sideways and fell to the floor of the cabin, face down, his body shuddering and his legs flopping around.

Could this be it? Had Asima actually done for him? Had she already got to Samir?

His eyesight was already dimming.

'Samir!' he bellowed once before unconsciousness took him and he lay, motionless, next to the prone form of Asima.

In which the aftermath occurs

Samir noted with dismay the slick crimson coating of the doctor's hands and forearms as he entered the captain's cabin, one of the crewmen opening and closing the door for him. The man's face was unreadable, but that meant nothing. Samir had known him long enough now to know that Cale had long since seen enough horror for his face to give up expressing his emotions.

'Yes?'

The doctor reached down for the damp cloth at his belt and began to wipe the excess gore from his hands. Without looking up, he talked as he worked at his cleaning.

'The important thing is: he'll almost certainly live.'

'I don't like the "almost"…'

The doctor shrugged.

'I'm not about to give you any guarantee, captain. The next twenty four hours will be very telling, though. We were very lucky that you found him when you did; he'd have bled out in minutes longer. As it is, there's barely enough blood left in him to keep him going.'

'But blood heals, though, yes?'

The doctor's mouth curled up at the corner.

'It replenishes, yes. The big problem your brother had was not the loss of blood, but where the knife went in. Had he not been so weak and short of blood, I would have opened him up to check his organs.'

'His organs? Forgive me doctor... my medical knowledge is scant at best.'

The doctor sighed.

'His heart and his lungs. I'm fairly sure they're unharmed. His breathing is surprising strong, given the state he's in and his heartbeat is slow and measured, so I don't believe they've been harmed by the wound. This in itself is miraculous, as the blow was as precise as any assassin could achieve. The blade should have gone into his heart and he should, by all rights, be dead.'

Samir frowned.

'So why...'

'I'm not sure,' the doctor interrupted, 'but a Pelasian surgeon called Passides wrote a text on organs in which he noted discovering in his long career several people whose organs were not quite in the regular position. Without opening your brother up, I can't confirm it, but that's simply the only explanation I can think of. The knife went in between the fifth and sixth rib and was angled just right. Your brother is either very, very lucky or one of the Gods has a vested interest in him.'

Samir nodded, images of the cult statue of Belapraxis flashing across his vision.

'So he should be alright?'

'I'm pretty certain that's the case. There is the faintest possibility that the edge of the knife caught the cable down his back that the Pelasians call a "spinal nerve". If that's the case then he may lose the use of his legs, but that's a small possibility, so I wouldn't worry unduly about that until he's awake.'

Samir slumped back in his seat and let out an explosive breath.

'And when will that be?'

Again the doctor shrugged.

'I wouldn't expect him even to wake today. Tomorrow he might, but only for brief periods. He'll be very weak and very tired and his blood is so low that he's almost white. He may not be up and about for weeks.'

'I think Ghassan might surprise you on that. Can I see him?'

The doctor shook his head.

'Absolutely not. He is staying alone and undisturbed at least until the first time he wakes. I have my assistant sitting with him constantly. He's fine, but I don't want any disturbance for him.'

Samir nodded.

'Take good care of him, doctor, and thank you for all your efforts.'

'Now I may catch up on missed sleep and I suggest that you do the same, captain.'

'I'm beyond sleep now, Cale. Beside, the sun's made an appearance now and things will require my attention. We're nearing Lassos and things are afoot.'

The doctor shrugged and turned, approaching the door and banging on it with a clean elbow. A moment later it swung open and the man paused in the entrance for a moment.

'I'll let you know as soon as he wakes, captain.'

As Samir nodded, the man disappeared down the passageway outside. The man by the door began to shut it, but Samir waved a hand at him.

'Patus… where is the lady Asima now?'

'She's being held in the firepot locker, captain.'

'I trust you had the forethought to remove anything dangerous or useful from the room first?'

'It's as empty as a Germallan's head, sir,' the man grinned.

Samir nodded 'I've not known many Germallans but, for the sake of argument I will assume that means "yes".'

'Do you want to see her, captain?'

'No, I don't think so, Patus. If I meet her at the moment, I might just have to kill her out of hand and I made a vow to Belapraxis concerning her. The Goddess may have closed another eye, but until the third shuts, I've my hands tied in Asima's case. Has Ursa been taken care of?'

The smile slid from the man's face. The first officer had been a popular man and the crew were taking his death hard. Samir had the suspicion that Asima's ribs had probably met with a few boots during her apprehension and incarceration.

'His body's been cleaned up and wrapped. We thought we'd let him go at the eighth bell, if that's alright with you, sir? He never liked being up early, anyway.'

Samir gave a sad little smile.

'Agreed.'

'Anything else, sir?'

'No thank you. That'll be all.'

The man saluted and closed the door to the cabin, leaving the Empress' captain sitting silent and thoughtful in his chair. After a long pause spent staring at the desk, he turned and peered out of the window, past the great beam of the rudder and out to sea in the wake of the ship.

'Belapraxis? I'm not much one for praying, as I expect you've noticed. You've put me in an uncomfortable position. I said in your name that I'd give her three chances to redeem herself. Right now, I'm tempted beyond reason just to go and do away with her, but would that anger you? After all, Ghassan's life is also in your hands. Would it really piss you off that much if I got rid of her?'

He sighed.

'A deal's a deal, I suppose. When I'm sure I can spend long enough in a room with her without strangling her, then I'll give her another chance. But look after Ghassan.'

He sat quietly once more, pondering until a commotion on deck above caught his attention. Listening carefully, he heard someone calling about a sail. A sail on the horizon? And the footsteps were all above him, so they must be at the rear rail.

Frowning, he turned once more and peered out into the distance, squinting into the dark waters. The sun may be up, but only just and it wasn't making much of a difference in the west yet.

Was there a sail? He wished fervently that Ghassan was here with his sharp eyes.

'Dammit.'

Grumbling, he pushed back his chair and strode across the room, pulling open the door and marching down the corridor to the open air. Turning, he climbed the stairs to the command deck and approached the knot of sailors standing at the rail.

'Nice to know that something important enough to drag you all from your positions is not important enough to send someone down to find me?'

The comment was only half-joking and the faces of the men fell.

'Sir, we thought you had enough on your plate until we were sure what it was.'

Samir brushed the matter aside and frowned.

'So? Talk to me.'

'The lookout reckons he saw a sail behind us, but we're not sure. Can't see anything now.'

Samir shrugged.

'Well? We're not on that tight a schedule. Slow us up a little and we'll see what we can see.'

The men nodded and ran off, furling one of the sails.

Samir leaned on the rear rail and watched the horizon intently as he felt the momentum of the vessel lessen very slightly. More and more the pace slowed, and gradually the men drifted back to join him at the stern.

'See anything yet, sir?'

'Not yet. Perhaps our lookout's been dreaming.'

'What's that?' someone said.

Samir peered into the dim distance, where the purple sky met the black sea in the strange dawn moment. Squinting, he concentrated.

'That, my friend, is a sail.'

There was light laughter around him.

'Erm… captain?'
'Yes?'
'That's not a sail. That's three sails.'
Samir peered into the distance and smiled.
'More than that,' someone else added. 'I can see at least two more.'
'Bloody hell, it's a fleet!'
Samir grinned.
'Captain, why're you laughing? They're white sails and that means they're navy ships!'
'Yes,' he nodded. 'And now that I can see them a little better, I note there are a couple of black sails in there too. On the assumption they're not travelling with other pirates, I think our navy fleet out there has a few Pelasians in it too.'
He noted the uncertain faces of those around him.
'Do you trust me?'
'Of course, captain, but…'
'No buts, Mannius. Trust me. Everything is going according to plan. The governor is coming to see us and he's brought a few friends. I wonder what decision he's come to?'
'We can't face that many alone, captain?'
Samir nodded and smiled.
'You're absolutely right, my friend. All haste to Lassos, then. Get that sail back up and full of wind and let's get to port.'
The deck around him burst into life as sailors went about their business, leaving the captain alone at the rear rail where he peered off into the distance at the pursing fleet.
'What have you decided, governor? What are you going to do?'

In which the Empress goes home

'Back away from the door. If you're within reach when I open it, I'll break whatever I can touch!'

Asima was standing at the far side of the small, bare storeroom, an expression of glowering hatred on her face when the pirate finished with the lock and pushed the door inwards with a groan.

'What now?'

'Captain wants you on deck.'

'Does he indeed? Well, we'd best not keep him waiting, then.'

Asima was gratified to note as she stepped forward how the man moved carefully back and out of her way. If nothing else, her little exercise in butchery had earned her a reputation to be feared, and in many ways fear was more useful than respect or love.

'You don't have to be quite so jumpy, sailor. I'm unarmed and I'm hardly going to gut you in broad daylight in front of your friends, am I?'

She looked down at the wrappings around her throbbing hand.

'Besides, I'm hardly in a position to wield a weapon, am I?'

The big man gave her an unpleasant look and pointed at the stairs that led up on deck, the square hatch above letting in bright sunlight that stung her eyes after hours in the dark ammunition store. Nodding, Asima strode past him, her head held defiantly high and keeping her pace deliberately calm and controlled.

The deck was alive with activity, though curiously quiet. Asima frowned for a moment until she caught sight, between the working sailors, of the approaching jagged, black rocks. The pirates always seemed to fall into an awed silence around the reefs of the dead. Still, that explained Samir's sudden desire to see her: they'd arrived at Lassos. What he intended to do now was, however, still a mystery.

Goaded on by the angry-looking pirate, she strode along the deck, combing out the irritating knot in her hair with her fingers; this sea air really was no good for her. The sooner she could get all of this behind her, spike a few disobedient and irritating heads and set herself up in the palace of Akkad, the better.

'Ah, Asima.' Samir nodded at her as they reached the command deck. 'You have a curious look on your face? Contemplating murder again?'

'I was picturing your head on a spear tip, Samir,' she replied with a tight smile, 'and wondering where it would look best. Certainly somewhere I could admire it regularly; and somewhere near jasmine to hide the stench.'

Samir's grin was as unpleasant as her own and, despite the superficial smiles on the command deck, the undercurrent of malice was so thick and powerful that several of the sailors on deck moved further away from the pair.

'Sweet and charming as ever, my dear. Be grateful for Belapraxis.'

Asima frowned in incomprehension, and Samir squared his shoulders.

'We are about to arrive at Lassos. It will take a while to get through the rocks, as you'll remember, but then we'll dock and when we do I plan to move you to a secure temporary location to keep you safe from harm while I go to the council hall.'

Samir glared at his prisoner.

'I would have liked Ghassan or Ursa to join me when I went to address the council, but you appear to have gone through my crew like a plague. I dislike it when my plans are changed for me, but we will prevail.'

Asima shrugged carelessly.

'So,' Samir went on 'you will be coming ashore with me, along with a number of the more fearsome and trustworthy of my crew. We will be heading through the town and up the side of the hill. When we reach the council hall, I will leave you and my men will take you somewhere safe. I'm warning you about all this now, because I need to advise you against trying any of your madness. You may hate me, but remember that on Lassos I may be the only person not planning to drown you on sight. Stick with my men for your own safety.'

Asima frowned.

'What are you planning?'

'That is none of your concern, Asima. Just go with the men when they take you to the safe house and try not to kill anyone on the way. We'll speak again when I've finished with the council.'

Asima's frown deepened but she held her tongue. The two stood in silence for several minutes, watching the rocks as the Dark Empress reached the outer edge of the reef. The mist closed in on the bow of the ship and, despite the bright afternoon sunshine, within moments the Empress was cold, damp and gloomy.

As she peered ahead into the mist, she could make out the figures of the so-called ghosts or wraiths that occupied the glistening rocks. It was easy in this mist to lose track of the time, and turning to the stern, she wondered whether the mist had closed in behind yet. Suddenly she realised the Empress was not alone.

'Samir?'

'Mmm?'

'Who are they?'

Samir turned to look over the rear rail at the array of small white sails, interrupted by the occasional black triangle, dotting the horizon behind them.

'Oh, friends of yours, I think. Probably not friends of mine.'

Asima rolled her eyes. Samir never gave a question a straight answer and the longer she knew him the more it annoyed her. She really would have to put him out of her misery soon.

'You do realise that they're going to blockade the island now that they know where it is? Trap you all? And me along with you...'

Samir smirked.

'Is the governor's arrival not part of your plan, Asima? You told him about me, the Empress and the dead man's compass, so I can only assume you told him everything you know about Lassos, the reefs, the council and the ships.'

His smile was grating on her. Asima sighed.

'So they must have been following us since we left M'Dahz, then? You've very little choice now. You and your worthless friends are about to meet an unpleasant end as criminals and pirates. Want me to help? I can make it fast and relatively painless? Just a short sharp blow and it's over. Much nicer than swinging from a public gibbet.'

Samir's jaw hardened.

'Enough now, Asima. In around fifteen minutes we will reach the inner perimeter of the reef and approach the island itself. At that point things will become rather busy and I will be occupied. Remember that you need to behave, or I cannot guarantee your safety.'

His companion glared at him and then returned her gaze to the misty figures around the ship's hull, reaching pleadingly to the passing vessel. One day she would see to it that Samir and his crew joined them. The image of him on his knees on a rock, pleading for his life as she drifted past was a satisfying picture.

'Captain?'

A sailor's head popped up over the top of the steps from the main deck. Samir turned to look.

'Captain? The doc sent me. Your brother's awake and you can see him if you want.'

Samir grinned.

'My day just improved a great deal. Thank you, and lead on.'

As he stepped toward the ladder, he addressed the large pirate that had brought Asima from her cell.

'Make sure she's got at least four guards around her at all times and don't let her near anything important or dangerous. I'll be back before we dock.'

Reaching the stairs, he clambered down them after the medical orderly and entered the corridor, making for the open doorway of the doctor's cabin.

The scene that greeted him within made him start for a moment. His brother lay on the bed, on his side and facing away from the door with the doctor probing around his back. Ghassan's shirt was up around his neck and there was a nasty wound halfway up his ribs, laced with black thread and puckered with red, yellow and white flesh. The sight was momentarily horrifying until he realised that the shape and discolouration was largely due to the pressure the wound was under as Ghassan moved his arms and torso. Indeed, he appeared to be making windmill-like motions with his arms, causing the wound to ooze and change. Samir gulped down air.

'Is everything alright?'

The doctor looked up, surprised at the interruption.

'What? Oh yes. I'm just running a few tests. The wound may look unpleasant, but it doesn't seem to have done any lasting damage and this man seems to have a remarkable constitution. My orderly, may he be cursed with wakefulness for a thousand years, fell asleep on watch and when he awoke your brother was standing at the window, looking out!'

The body shook and Samir jumped before he realised that Ghassan was laughing.

'Ghassan? You need to be a little more careful. You nearly died last night.'

The doctor stopped prodding things and stood back as Ghassan rolled slightly and came up with a groan to sit on the edge of the bed. He was deathly pale, but the smile on his face was warm and full of life. The captain sighed with relief.

'Samir? Your doctor here tells me that I'm a freak?'

'I never used that word... Gah! Patients!'

Samir grinned.

'Well, you know what they say: the doc's a miserable old goat, but his heart's in the right place.'

'Well, he is a little impatient!'

Samir and Ghassan laughed as the doctor stood and scowled at them.

'Don't over-exert yourself,' he barked at his patient. 'I will be back in less than ten minutes and then you will be resting again, even if I have to knock you out myself to achieve it. Captain? Ten minutes, yes?'

Samir nodded gratefully as the man left the room.

'Ghassan, I am so glad to see this. I was worried that she'd have done some permanent damage to you. This may sound a little heartless, but it's a damn good job she came after you before me. You managed somehow to floor her before she could finish you off. I rather think if I'd been first that she'd have managed to dispatch me before I woke.'

Ghassan shrugged and then winced at the pain.

'Actually, though this is painful, it's not stopping me from doing anything. The doc says there's no reason I couldn't walk around and carry things, apart from the fact that I'm still weak from loss of blood, and even that'll heal in time. I've been waiting until he goes away for a bit so that I can get dressed and come above.'

'Stupid, but very useful, since I could really do with your help. We're almost at Lassos, the governor's fleet is hot on our tail, and I need to address the council, with you beside me if you can manage it?'

Ghassan nodded.

'Of course. Now, what have you done with Asima?'

'She's been held in a temporary brig,' Samir replied with a shrug 'but I've had her taken on deck under guard in preparation for our arrival.'

Ghassan nodded.

'Perhaps it's a good thing that I didn't kill her last night, given your plan, but I'm still vaguely sorry that I didn't. It's going to take a supreme effort of will not to push her overboard onto the reef.'

'I made a promise to you and Belapraxis, remember? Three chances. I figure she's had two. For us to kill her out of anger or vengeance before the Goddess has her judgment would be to defy the "healing mother", and defying a Goddess is never a good thing, especially when one is about to attempt such a thing as we are.'

Ghassan nodded again.

'Very well. Looks like the stage is set, since we're at Lassos. With Asima, you, me and the governor, all the players are here too. Now we have to get your little production underway.'

He grinned.

'We've still got a couple of minutes before the doctor gets back. Pass me my shirt and help me upstairs.'

Impulsively, Samir enfolded his brother in a hug, eliciting a groan of discomfort.

'I couldn't do this without you, Ghassan.'

In which the council sits

By the time the Empress touched the jetty, the hull bouncing away several times before settling, and men jumping off to tie ropes, a crowd had already gathered at the far end. A twitch crept into Asima's eyelid as she watched from the relative safety of the command deck. Down on the main deck, Samir stood with a sailor she didn't know, supporting the sagging figure of Ghassan. Her erstwhile victim had glanced at her only once in the few minutes since they had emerged from below decks and his expression might have been unsettling had she cared more.

The port was chaotic, with people flocking to the jetty, despite being involved in a thousand petty tasks of their own. Cargo was stacked everywhere and, Asima had noted, eleven other jetties were occupied, which meant that every ship based at Lassos was currently berthed here. It seemed unlikely that Samir had managed to engineer a situation where everyone was in port, so it could be pure luck, but then Samir, like her, made his own luck.

Asima heard the man behind her clearing his throat meaningfully and, as she glanced at him, he gestured that she should descend the steps and join the captain. Her bulky escorts gathered around as she moved forward and kept close pace with her as she climbed down and strode, head high, to the place amidships where Samir and Ghassan were watching the boarding ramp being run out to dock.

From here she had a better view of the crowd on the jetty. As she'd fully expected, their faces were not the smiling visages of those come to welcome their compatriots home. The word 'mob' better fitted the situation. In the old tales, she could have imagined this lot brandishing farm implements and shouting. Before she was roughly manhandled into position next to the brothers, she did note the striking and attractive features of Captain Faerus, Samir's friend, among those waiting. Faerus looked nervous.

The plank slid home onto the jetty and Samir and the other man helped Ghassan down. As soon as they reached the slippery timbers of the dock, though, Ghassan waved the man away and continued, wobbling slightly, on his own, his fingers locked round

Samir's arm for support, and tensing every time a badly-placed step sent a shock up his back. The large sailor behind Asima nudged her toward the plank and she tottered carefully down it to join the brothers.

'Stay with us all the way up the hill. This is not a good time for you to play games. A wrong step or word now could get us all killed before I can do anything.'

Asima nodded at Samir. Her time would come later, when he was less on guard.

Slowly, allowing for Ghassan's careful gait, the three of them walked toward the mass of angry-looking people at the end of the jetty, half a dozen burly sailors from the Empress following up and surrounding Asima, cutting off any path of escape. Samir came to a halt a few yards from the crowd and raised his voice.

'I need to call a meeting of the council, immediately.'

Faerus, shaking his handsome head, his jet black, long and straight hair whipping back and forth, filled the uncomfortable silence that followed.

'Too late, Samir. The council went into session the moment your sail appeared among the reefs. I expect they're busy right now deciding how many pieces to cut you into.'

A humourless smile crept across Samir's face.

'Good. Their timing is auspicious.'

He raised his voice to address the whole group.

'Let us through! I have to address the council, Faerus, but you had best get to it as well. The time we spoke of is upon us. I will meet you as planned in the safe house.'

Faerus frowned.

'So soon?' He paused a moment and then thrust out his arms, heaving people aside.

'Get out of the way and let Captain Samir through to address the council!'

The force with which he pushed caused a few spectators to stumble and fall, and the crowd quickly parted to allow them passage. Asima gave the tall pirate captain an appraising look. She recognised him in a vague way from the night she had spent in his lodgings on her last visit here, but the alcohol had dimmed her senses a little that night and she hadn't realised at the time just how enigmatic and attractive the man really was. Strikingly handsome, clean shaven and with immaculate hair, Faerus wore grey silks from the eastern lands beyond the Empire. He was in excess of six feet tall and had a powerful, smooth voice, like liquid honey. She had the feeling that if Faerus ordered them to, even the rocks would move out of the way.

'Shall I join you first?' the man asked of Samir.

'Best not. You and the others will have to be ready, on the assumption that I return shortly. Just meet me later and make sure Orin's aware too.'

Faerus nodded and sketched a bow as the three passed him and began the interminable climb to the council chamber on the hill. The walk up the sloping street was familiar to her and, if anything, even less pleasant than last time. On her previous visit she had been unknown and had elicited mixed reactions of interest, lust and suspicion. Now, however, every face hardened as it turned to them. Matters were made all the worse by the painfully slow pace of the journey, hampered as they were by the wounded Ghassan.

After minutes that seemed like hours, they reached the point where the street made a hairpin bend and marched off back across the hillside, through the upper tiers of the town. Here stood the council hall with its great marble columned portico, speaking volumes of the faded glory of the island.

'Alright... this is it. I shall speak first, then it's your turn, Ghassan. Are you alright? Definitely up to this? Your testimony is solid support, but I expect I can work them around myself if you can't manage.'

Ghassan shook his head. 'Leave it to me. I'll be fine.'

With a deep breath, Samir turned to Asima and her guards.

'Take her to Surafana's house on the hill. If Faerun and Orin have been efficient, it should be empty, but provisioned, and there should be a good secure room for Asima. Don't rely on the room though... I want at least two of you in full sight of her at all times.'

Asima glowered at him as the large pirate next to her nodded and grasped her upper arm tightly.

'We'll keep her nice and safe, cap'n. You be there soon?'

Samir nodded.

'Unless the council have other plans, Ghassan and I will follow you up very shortly.'

Asima continued to glare at Samir as she was turned away and marched in a no-nonsense manner up the slope in the opposite direction, doubling back behind the town.

Samir turned to Ghassan and smiled.

'Follow my lead, then.'

Ghassan, concentrating on the task at hand and keeping close attention on his brother, whose shoulder he still grasped for support, entered the fortress of his enemies for the first time, as a willing visitor. In other days he may have taken a more keen interest in this place that had been so sought after by his superiors for decades. Instead, he merely glanced briefly at the interior as they passed through the grand entrance and the outer room.

Making sure Ghassan's grip was secure on his shoulder, Samir threw open the door to the council chamber and stood in the doorway, gazing at the 'U' shaped table arrangement.

The seats were occupied by the motliest bunch that Ghassan had ever laid eyes on: mostly older, 'retired' pirates, they were sun-tanned and weathered like the faces of a sandstone cliff, displaying networks of scars, punctuated with jewellery and tattoos. Clearly the hawk-like, dry and emaciated figure occupying the central chair like an animated and mummified corpse was the most venerable member. Equally clearly, he had no love for Samir.

Glancing around, it surprised Ghassan that there was no one on guard either outside the doors or within the chamber, but then who, on an island of pirates, would dare to interrupt a meeting of their elders. Apart from his brother, naturally...

There had been a heated argument going on within as they entered, Samir striding out the front, while Ghassan dropped behind, closing the door after them. The last threads of the argument tailed off as the council regarded their visitors.

The last voice fell silent as the twelve most powerful men on Lassos stared in astonishment at the nerve of the wayward captain before them.

'Captain Samir? You have not been summoned... yet.'

Samir nodded and smiled.

'You have my apologies for the interruption, gentlemen, and I realise that I am currently not the Lassos' favourite son, but I am afraid that this simply cannot wait.'

An ebony-skinned man, pierced and covered in gold jewellery, narrowed his eyes.

'Captain Samir, you are insolent. The council is deciding your fate and you should not be here until ordered.'

Samir shrugged.

'This council can pronounce any judgment they wish... enforcing it is another matter entirely, but please allow me to speak. I am not here to argue with you, but to present you with the opportunity you need.'

Ghassan noted an almost instant polarisation among the faces of the councillors. The elder two thirds frowned and glared at the insolent young captain before them, while the remaining younger council members took on a thoughtful look, almost as if they had been expecting something of the sort. But then, Ghassan realised with a smile, Samir's reputation for innovative action and careful planning would already have made an impression on these younger councillors.

Ghassan muttered under his breath, just loud enough for his brother to hear.

'Samir? Concentrate on the younger ones. They're almost with you.'

Samir gave an almost imperceptible nod as the aquiline elder growled at him.

'This council has no wish to hear from you or your whore-son brother.'

'I'm not sure that's entirely true, elder Halcar,' Samir smiled.

'Let him speak, Halcar,' barked one of the younger men, dressed in crimson velvet and with a neat scar across the bridge of his nose. 'Samir is one of the best we have. If he says he has something of use for us, only the short sighted would do away with him before asking more.'

'Thank you, Master Culin. You are insightful as always. I'm afraid this will not sound good at first, but I must ask you to let us finish before you pronounce any judgments.'

The hoarse, older man at the centre with the parchment-thin skin and the aquiline face glared at Samir.

'You presume to order your elders around, Samir? Be very careful.'

Samir bowed slightly.

'No insult intended, Master Halcar, but this is very urgent and very important.'

'Go on,' the one called Culin urged.

'The time has come, Masters of Lassos, to conclude our business with the Imperial navy of Calphoris. As we reached the reefs on our way here, a fleet of Imperial daram with Pelasian support was close enough to breath down our necks. Even now they will be encircling Lassos, blockading us and effectively ending our time as a free port of non-aligned … raiders, if you will.'

The effect of the news was fascinating. The men of the council exhibited half a dozen different expressions on a theme of shock, anger and panic… all but Culin, who nodded sagely. Ghassan was interested to note no sign of surprise in the man's features. There was a strange pause for a second or so in which the room filled with an oppressive silence and then suddenly the council exploded in argument.

'Please, gentlemen…' Samir's voice cut across the noise. The arguments tailed off as the councillors turned back to the speaker.

'I am going to leave you to decide on the course of action when I have finished. I believe the only sensible choice is for the fleet of Lassos to arm up, crew up, and sail out en masse to meet the forces of the Empire. However, I realise that this sounds insane, so let me lay a few things on the line first.'

He spread his arms dramatically.

'For the last few years, Imperial control of the sea has been tightening notably. With Pelasia as an ally now, all the military have really had to occupy their time is making life difficult for the captains of Lassos. Our activity and takings have fallen dramatically in this time, and rarely do our captains manage an engagement without having to run for safety at the end. Things are becoming untenable unless we take back control of our sea. We are facing the extinction of Lassos lest we fight back. That is a painful conclusion to have arrived at, but I have been trying to find a solution for years now.'

A feeling passed among the audience. The council may not like hearing this, but there was no denying the truth of Samir's words.

'In addition, I see no other course of action as feasible. Lassos is not an abundant island. The vegetation here will support life, but only just. While people could live here indefinitely, their diet would be extremely dull and the food quantity would support only a handful at most. Our survival here has always relied on our takings, which are now too meagre to support the population. Our supplies may last a few months, but in the end we will be forced to take action against any blockade. We would be better dealing with it now, before they are set in and comfortable rather than later when they are fully prepared and fortified against us.'

'And why are they here, Captain Samir?' the elder growled. 'Why have you brought our enemies to us?'

Samir sighed.

'Quite simply we were betrayed, and I allowed it to happen in order to bring us to this point.'

There was another explosion of blustering and arguing. Samir stood back and crossed his arms, waiting for the noise to die down. As it did, Culin being the first to calm, the young councillor waved his arms.

'Samir asked us not to judge until he was finished. Let's hear him out.'

Samir nodded and looked over his shoulder.

'Ghassan?'

The taller brother stepped forward, still leaning heavily on Samir.

'You are all, no doubt, aware who I am. You may not, however, be aware of my current situation.'

There was a tense silence and the ebony-skinned pirate lord nodded quietly.

'Culin has informed us that you are no longer employed by the military of the Empire.'

Culin laughed.

'More than that, Saja. He's actively a wanted man. My people have been seeing wanted posters going up all over the coastal cities. There's a bigger price on his head at the moment than Samir's, though they're both sought after. I gather the pair of them blew part of the city wall to pieces in M'Dahz.'

Samir nodded, impressed.

'Your information is remarkably up-to-date, master Culin. That happened only just before we left to come here.'

The council members nodded, each involved in their own thoughts on the brothers before them.

Ghassan cleared his throat.

'A young woman named Asima who was here recently with my brother later took the opportunity to visit with the governor in M'Dahz. She sold out not only Samir and myself, but the location and details of Lassos... even the existence of the compasses you use. It is Asima who has brought the fleet here; I was in M'Dahz at the time and spoke to Asima myself and I can confirm the truth of this. Samir's only part in that is to allow her to do so.'

'That alone is enough to hang him, captain.'

Ghassan nodded.

'I imagine so, but Samir believes that you can fight the fleet and win. I am, I must say, considerably more sceptical over the matter, but when my brother is sure, he is usually correct, as I'm sure you're all aware. I myself am here for two reasons: firstly to give my evidence, as I just have, and secondly to seek sanctuary and safety with my brother, since I have nowhere else to go.'

Culin stood as Ghassan stepped back and frowned.

'I have no doubt that Samir and his brother are telling the truth, gentlemen. As you know, I have men in every port and some even hidden in places of authority in M'Dahz and Calphoris. Everything I have heard supports this story. The fact remains, however, that whether his intentions were good or not, Samir has brought our enemies to us. For that he should by all rights be put to death.'

Ghassan winced at the comment, but Culin was already going on.

'However, if he is right, we have an opportunity here and in that case, we really need any man we can get, and certainly one as wily and lucky as Samir.'

He turned to the brothers.

'I am tempted toward leniency, Samir. Convince us we can win.'

'Very well, Master Culin. Let me give you the full tale. I have been looking for a way to break the growing naval control of the Sea of Storms ever since I first took command of the Empress. Asima, while believing she has been playing me has, in her betrayal, been the very linchpin of my plan.'

He stepped forward once more under the suspicious gaze of the councillors.

'I had to find a way,' Samir continued, 'to bring the governor's fleet to battle with our own on favourable terms and this was far from easy, given the number of ships available to them, compared with our twelve. I could never have persuaded you to launch an assault on Calphoris, so I had to bring them here to provide you with no alternative. Once we clear the sea of the governor and his fleet, we can retake what is ours, and perhaps even more.'

The hoarse, wicked-looking old chief councillor snorted and pointed at Samir.

'We still have only twelve ships, Samir, while they have scores! What you have done is exterminated us, not saved us!'

Samir smiled.

'Not quite. What the governor does not currently know is just how many people I have placed in prime positions on board his ships in the last few years. Some of my less savoury friends from M'Dahz have been serving on board the Imperial darams for years, awaiting this very opportunity. As you know, I always plan things well in advance.'

In the silence that followed, a light voice chuckled and then began to laugh out loud. Master Culin leaned forward, steepling his fingers.

'Captain Samir, I would really hate to play you at dice. You have just answered for me one of the greatest mysteries of the past year.'

The other councillors looked at him in surprise. Culin laughed.

'On no less than four occasions in recent months documents have come into my possession that made no sense; documents referring to the hiring and transfer among the Imperial coastal forces of people that I wouldn't trust to open a door for me without stabbing me in the back and stealing my purse. I could never figure out why the governor was putting such dubious and dangerous people in such important positions.'

Samir smiled.

'I am a little disappointed in my associates leaving a paper trail, but you are correct, master Culin. If my moves have all paid off, the odds will be considerably improved. Several of the enemy ships should be in a position to switch sides and join us, and a number of others will find themselves the victim of sabotage. I do not like leaving things to chance.'

He noted the thoughtful looks on the faces of a number of the councillors.

'We have a chance. We have needed this chance for months, and now it is before you. It is up to the masters of Lassos as to whether they take it. We have a few hours; possibly even days, before we have to move against them, so we will go to Surafana's house, which lies empty, and settle in there until you reach a decision. You know where to find us.'

Samir turned and sauntered casually through the door and out into the entrance hall, Ghassan following close on his heels and closing the door behind them just as a loud debate began to kick in around the table.

Ghassan frowned as they stepped out into the fresh air and looked up the road toward their destination.

'That Culin seems to be supporting you, but I think you'll need to watch him. He's clever.'

Samir nodded.

'He is clever... very clever, and very well informed too, but that, Ghassan, is exactly what I'm counting on. Now come with me and I shall introduce you to the supporting cast in my little production.'

In which Belapraxis is honoured

The house of the former head of the council, the recently deceased Surafana, was more an eyrie than a mere home. A grand residence constructed on a narrow ledge, much of the building was held up by great supports formed from the boles of trees, driven at an angle into the cliff. The approach had taken Asima's breath away, partially from the sheer impressiveness of the structure and its positioning, but also with the thought that this house that looked to be held up against impossible conditions was about to be her home at least for a few hours.

It was not that she feared heights, or at least she'd never realised that she did, but this was something else; like being dangled over an immense drop with nothing to cling on to. Samir had chosen well. The only remotely safe exit from the building was the route by which they entered and there was no way she would be leaving without permission. Equally, of course, if things went badly at the meeting, this was clearly the most easily defensible position on the island.

And so she had been bundled into the house with no ceremony, waited while the pirates chose a room for her, and was then escorted to a very secure chamber with only one door and a window that looked out onto a precipitous drop to the roofs of the town more than a hundred feet below.

The escort had left the door open and one of their number sat on a chair opposite, his eyes locked on the makeshift prison cell. For the first five minutes of her incarceration, Asima had sat in one of the three chairs at the single table in the room and stewed over the situation. Once again, as so often in the last few years, she felt largely helpless and that aggravated her. Not being in control set her teeth on edge. Of course, her plans had now changed once more, so things were still quite uncertain.

Whether the old crone in the desert was right with her uncanny sight and her prediction of Asima's rise to power or not, Asima was sure of her future. Even if Gods and fate had nothing to do with it, she would make damn sure it happened. And now Samir was about to put her in a position to make it happen without realising it. She wasn't sure exactly what she would need to do yet, since that depended on how events unfolded. However, when they went back out to sea, she was sure she could find a way to sell him out to the Imperial fleet and deliver him to the governor.

And there were Pelasians among the fleet too. It was all coming together; she couldn't quite see how, yet, but conditions were falling into place. And when she finally achieved her goals and left Prince Ashar's corpse to the jackals while she sat on the veranda of the palace in Akkad, she would make the world pay for what it had put her through in recent years.

She smiled.

Oh yes. Streets would run with the blood of those who had got in her way.

Five minutes of musing relaxed her a little and she began to become impatient for news. Samir and Ghassan surely would be brief with the council. And then they'd come here and she'd see how the next small step in her plan fell into place.

Irritably, she stood, glancing at the pirate guard, wondering whether he would come and restrain her if she moved out of sight. He merely watched with scant interest. Of course, she could hardly escape from here.

Stretching her legs, she began to explore her cell. This was some sort of storeroom. From what she understood, the master of this house had been one of the council who had passed on recently. After his death, it appeared that the house had remained empty. A quick look at the dusty surfaces told her that no one had bothered tending to the interior, though the lack of valuables, decoration and useful items suggested that other island occupants had been through here like locusts, taking anything of value.

Arching her eyebrow in interest, she began to open and close cupboards and drawers.

Junk. The room was full, but full of junk; trinkets, knickknacks and miscellaneous rubbish. Every door she opened or drawer she pulled on revealed more of the pointless accumulations of a lifetime hoarding. She sighed. Not even anything that could keep her entertained while she waited. At least there could have been…

Her thoughts fell into silence as she opened a deep drawer at waist height in a tall cabinet and the next piece of her scheme fell into place. Asima smiled as she carefully and delicately picked up the hand-held torsion bow that lay abandoned amid the junk. It was loaded with a narrow, needle-like iron bolt, just under four inches long, which was exceedingly lucky, given that there was no supply of ammunition with it. She frowned at it and shrugged; she'd not a lot of experience with missile weapons, but she'd handled one of these before and it was nice and simple.

Taking a quick glance around the doorframe, she saw the pirate guard, still watching the room with a bored gaze. He couldn't see the cupboard around the corner and she smiled as she picked up the weapon, being careful to keep it angled so that the ammunition stayed in place. Just to be sure, she put her finger on the bolt and slid it back and forth a little. It was free and unjammed. A flick removed the catch that prevented misfires. Nodding to herself, she held it carefully in position behind her back and then returned to her seat, making sure she kept her front to the guard. He paid hardly any attention to her, merely looking up briefly as she reappeared from around the corner.

Slowly, ever so carefully, she manoeuvred the bow from behind her back so that it rested on her knees under the table. Every movement was kept tightly controlled and masked by innocent actions such as a scratch, a glance around or a yawn.

By the time she heard the activity at the front door, the weapon was securely held in both hands beneath the table. This next move required subtlety. She dropped her head dejectedly, apparently resigned to her fate and broken by captivity. Of course Samir wouldn't fall for that for a second, but it might distract him from what was really going on. With someone as sharp as Samir, it was a matter of throwing enough signals and suspicious activity at him that he didn't know which way to turn. Samir was sharp enough, but the iron bolt on her knee was sharper still and so was Asima's aim.

'Faerus and Orin will be here any time now with the most trusted senior members of their crews. The next few days will be a time that both the council and the governor will remember for many years.'

Samir's voice was light and betrayed a little excitement as he entered the front room of the house, helping Ghassan as he went. The taller brother was staggering wearily. Not surprising, after what she'd done to him, but it still surprised and irked her that what was undoubtedly a killing blow seemed to have done such little to him. Next time the opportunity came her way, she would make it slower and considerably more certain. He may survive a single blow, but see how long he lasted with no skin.

'I'll wait here, Samir,' her attempted victim said in a tired voice. 'I'll have a drink while we wait, but I just don't have the patience or energy to deal with Asima right now.

Samir nodded.

'I'll only be a few minutes, then we can get down to planning.' He turned to one of the other crewmen in the room. 'Jabir? Can you break out the drinks? I'll have one in a minute when I return.'

Asima's fingers tensed on the trigger as Samir strode toward the doorway. His face was a strangely unreadable expression. There seemed to be mixed hope, anger, irritation, desire and humour in roughly equal amounts. Despite some heavy competition, it won out as his most irritating look of all time.

'Asima...' he began as he turned and closed the door, leaving the two of them alone in the room.

She raised her eyes very slowly until her gaze met his. Her steely dark eyes held his as he squared his shoulders.

'As I've said, and I'm considered a man of my word, I will not harm you, despite everything you have done. When our business here is concluded, we will go our separate ways and, Gods willing, our paths will never cross again. I am bound by the promise I made when I took you back from Pelasia to try and help you achieve your goal.'

Asima shrugged.

'You are a liar, Samir. You veer wildly between vowing to help me on my path back to power and stealing me away whenever I get close, in order to save your precious "innocents". Innocents are merely criminals that haven't been caught yet, Samir. A man in your position should know that. Everyone is disposable... no exceptions.'

Samir shrugged.

'There are innocents, in relative grades, I'll admit, but I know they exist. You, however, Asima, are unable to recognise them, since I now realise that you were never one yourself, even when we were carefree children. Ghassan believes that you have become this person because the world turned its back on you. I personally believe that you were always this person, but it took certain events to trigger your release from the prison of youth.'

'Enough talk, Samir. I recognise that I have a struggle ahead of me, but it will be considerably easier without you standing in the way.'

Purposefully and smoothly, like the most professional Pelasian assassin, she stood, the chair sliding back and toppling behind her as she brought the hand bow up in a graceful arc and pulled the trigger to release the bolt at neck level. It was a speedy, smooth, bold, and deadly accurate move, the weapon aimed precisely for the centre of the throat.

Unfortunately for Asima, the result was a metallic click, a sad little 'twang' and the bolt rolling off the groove and falling to the floor. She stared in anger at the bow and then up at Samir's grinning face.

No... that was his most irritating look of all time.

'I see you found the bow. Good. I would have hated to have gone to such lengths with no appreciable result.'

'Why?' she demanded angrily.

'To appease Belapraxis, and to settle the matter in Ghassan's mind. Your tongue is more twisted than any serpent's, and no word that slips from it can be trusted, but your choices – your actions, even – tell us what your heart contains, and yours, Asima my dear, contains only black emptiness.'

She cast the useless, sabotaged weapon aside and crossed her arms defiantly as Samir strode toward her.

'And now that you've eased your conscience, you can drop the charade of your vow to help me and have me killed instead. At least have the balls to do it yourself and don't leave the job to one of your underlings.'

Samir smiled that vulture smile again as he came close, face to face with her and a yard away.

'Hardly, Asima. I keep my promises.'

With a snort, she turned her back on him.

'Good,' Samir said with relief. 'That makes it easier'.

His blow to the back of Asima's head was surprisingly gentle, but accurate and strong enough to knock the consciousness from her. Samir's only concession to his feelings was to let her fall heavily and painfully to the floor without catching her.

'Sleep well. All our worlds are about to change.'

In which the order is given

Samir opened the door just as the runner tried to knock on it, causing him to lose his balance and stagger a little. The young sailor was out of breath and quite red faced, and Samir waited patiently for him to regain his feet and take a deep breath. The lad looked up to see Samir waiting with his arms crossed, the tall, pale and gaunt figure of his brother at his shoulder and a collection of powerful men gathered in the background.

'Captain Samir…'

'The very same. Take your time… I'm sure there's nothing pressing?'

He smiled at the young man who flushed.

'Sorry sir. The council wants to see you. They've called an emergency meeting for all captains.'

'Now, I presume?'

'Yes, sir. Just the captains and their first officers.'

'Very well. We'll be along presently.'

'Yessir. I think…'

His voice trailed off as Samir shut the door on him and turned to the other occupants of the room. Quite a crowd had built up over the afternoon and into the early evening, with the eight men from the Empress having been joined by Faerus, Orin and their senior sailors.

'Are we all prepared? We all know what to do?'

Faerus nodded, scratching his chin.

'Still not all that sure I like it Samir, but you're absolutely right that it has to be done.'

Orin, a stocky, barrel-chested northerner with a forked beard and a surprisingly quiet and gentle voice, shook his head.

'I still wonder whether we could have done more.' He sighed. 'But yes… we know what to do and we're ready.'

'Then for the sake of Lassos and our continued survival let's go and do battle. You'd best head down to the council. I'll meet you there in a minute; just a few quick things to attend to here.'

The two captains nodded and made for the door, both stopping in the entrance to grasp Samir by the forearm in the age-old gesture of comradeship. As they left, taking their men with them, Samir glanced around the room at the remaining occupants and then closed the door.

'This is a dangerous course we've embarked on, gentlemen, and into unknown waters. We all know we can trust Faerus and Orin implicitly. I have other allies unrevealed as yet that will change the way today unfolds. Then there's the governor; we have no idea yet what he has decided to do, so he is a random element in the game. And finally, the council are almost entirely untrustworthy and have only their own safety and glory in mind. I have no doubt that they would sell out or drown any resident of Lassos without a moment's thought if they deemed it necessary. Today is an important day.'

He turned to Ghassan.

'Are you up to this?'

Ghassan laughed quietly.

'Unless you're expecting me to leap from ship to ship and head boarding parties, I can cope with standing on the command deck and watching what happens.'

'I had just a little more than that in mind. See, I have no first officer and it would be unthinkable to go to battle in that position. It might be a bit strange for you, being used to commanding a ship yourself, but if you could cope with it, I would really appreciate having you at my side?'

Ghassan answered with a grin.

'Samir, I'm not sure I could ever keep up with you, but I'd be honoured to take the post, yes.'

He sighed and shook his head, still laughing.

'It seems ridiculous in a way, since it's only weeks since I was a commissioned naval officer and now here I am, taking on the role of first officer with the most notorious pirate vessel on the sea, and fighting alongside Faerus and Orin, both of whom I've engaged in battle in the past. Strange how things turn out, isn't it?'

Samir smiled.

'I told you long ago, by the south gate stairs in M'Dahz, the day ma died... remember?'

Ghassan, suddenly taken aback by the memory of that horrible day, gave a sad little laugh.

'You told me things would be better. It's been long decades and finally things seem to be getting better, as you said. I just hope that's not just for today. I want things to stay better now. Do you think that's too much to hope for?'

Samir laughed.

'You've survived an invasion, repeated massacres and two decades of sea battles with pirates. You made it out of prison in an exploding tower; you've been knifed twice, once supposedly fatally, and yet here you are standing tall and about to lead a ship to war with me. I think that, despite everything we've been through, we've both got a lot to be thankful for, don't you?'

Ghassan continued to smile sadly and Samir turned to the other sailors.

'Mannius? Can you sort out Asima for me? Make sure she's carefully bound when you move her. She shouldn't wake up for a while yet, but you know how dangerous she is, and I don't want any harm to come to her. Once you've got her ready, take three of these lads and move her out of here. Ghassan and I need to go attend the meeting, but we'll meet you at the ship shortly.'

The thin, wiry man nodded as he holstered the knife he'd been idly playing with.

'We'll be there and ready, cap'n.'

Samir nodded and turned to the tall, heavy-set man next to the door with a scowl moulded permanently to his features.

'Duro? You and Rashad need to take care of the other thing. You'll find the tools and the paint in the room back there. Make sure that Faerus and Orin have taken theirs. If not, you'll have to deliver theirs before you start work.'

'What are you up to now, Samir?' Ghassan frowned.

'Oh, just a little surprise. Nothing important. Shall we go?'

Ghassan continued to peer at him through narrowed eyes and finally sighed, shrugged, and opened the door.

'After you, my captain.'

'Thank you.'

As the room became a hive of activity behind them, Samir and Ghassan stood straight and began to stride down the sloping road in the warm, purple dusk toward the council chamber at the first bend. The noble scene was only slightly marred by the fact that Ghassan winced and gasped with every other step and quickly began to lean on Samir for support once again.

'Don't worry. When we get on board, all you have to do is lean on the command deck rail and shout commands.'

Ghassan nodded.

'I shall be grateful to stay still for a while. I think all this movement may have torn a stitch or two. Your doctor's going to be furious with me.'

The two walked on in silence, each contemplating the coming day with a mixture of excitement and nervousness. Slowly they approached the council hall, the great, peeling colonnade towering above them as they closed on the doorway.

'You're sure they'll go for it? You've sent everyone off ready as though they'd already announced their intention to go to war.'

Samir shrugged.

'I can't see as they really have any other choice. Besides, whether they say yes or no, we'll still have to get underway, so best to be prepared. Are you ready for this? We might not be over popular tonight.'

Ghassan answered with a nod.

'In we go.'

The entrance hall was empty as usual, though the door to the main chamber was already open and the commotion within could be heard as far out as the colonnade. Dozens of raised voices argued a dozen different points, each trying to be heard over the others. Samir smiled as he and Ghassan entered and took up position leaning against the door and closing it with a loud click.

The room fell silent at the noise and a number of faces turned to them.

'Good evening, gentlemen,' Samir said with a tight smile.

There were a number of growls and low-voiced threats from the assembled group, but the banging of a knife pommel on the central table brought the silence to bear once more.

'Captain Samir... present yourself and your brother before the council.'

The crowd parted, allowing the pair room to face the hawk-like figure of master Halcar, who frowned at them.

'The council has concluded its deliberations, Captain Samir, and come to a decision as to the best course of action for Lassos and its occupants.'

Samir nodded but remained silent.

Someone nearby said in low tones 'I's gonna slit yer throat, real slow, Samir...'

Ghassan's head whipped around, but in the press of people, the source of the voice remained unknown. The comment was ignored by the mass and the council.

'Whatever your motive, Captain Samir,' Halcar went on 'you have betrayed the people of Lassos and we do not tolerate betrayal in any circumstances. You have put us in an awkward position, even though some of our number believe that this time was inevitable. The judgment of this council is that war must be prosecuted. The twelve ships of Lassos will sally forth at dawn when the mist is thickest and will engage the fleet of the governor. Your unique position, with traitors on board the enemy ships, makes you irreplaceable. Therefore, you will lead the way out of the reefs and into position.'

He smiled humourlessly.

'The possibility that this is some sort of trap has occurred to us and, if this is the case, you will have the option of falling into it yourself or revealing its existence.'

Samir nodded.

'That is fair, of course, Master Halcar.'

'Be quiet! We are not finished. In addition, the council will sail out aboard the ships. It is important both that we add our long experience and expertise to the command, and that we take part in what is, after all, a battle for our survival. Masters Culin, Saja and myself will come out aboard the Dark Empress with you in order to avoid any... unfortunate decisions being made, and we will be bringing a guard with us, of course.'

He squared his shoulders.

'More than half the council and many more among the captains have called for your death for what you have done, Samir, and some demand that you be tortured to death. It is only the irreplaceable position you currently hold that is keeping you alive. Therefore, once battle is concluded, if we have taken the day, you will be deemed a traitor to Lassos. You will then hand over your compass to us and you will be taken back to Lassos. There, you will be skinned, salted and then boiled for your crimes.'

Ghassan straightened.

'No!'

Samir shook his head, but Halcar nodded.

'You will prosecute the war to the best of your ability and then submit willingly to your fate, because we will allow your brother to live, banished from Lassos back to the mainland. If you refuse to submit or attempt to trick us, we will do the same to both of you and to every man who serves on your ship. You may believe that mercy is a prime trait in a pirate captain, but you are alone in that belief. Is that all clear?'

Samir frowned, his head down.

'Very clear, Master Halcar.'

'Go, then, and prepare the Empress for battle.'

Samir bowed, making sure to keep steady for Ghassan's support and the pair turned and opened the door, passing through before closing it quietly. In the hall outside, as the room behind them burst into noisy life once more, Ghassan shook his head.

'This had better work, Samir. I'm not going to see you skinned.'

Samir smiled.

'I have no intention of ending my days bobbing pink and white in a barrel, Ghassan. We've laid our cards on the table and so has the council. Now we just need to know what hand the governor holds.'

Ghassan nodded.

'We'll find out first thing tomorrow, I suspect.'

In which the fleet sails

Ghassan leaned on the rail, wincing. His back had begun to ooze a little this morning and Samir had worried enough to consult the doctor, who'd merely become irritated and incensed that the taller brother was being too active and not resting enough to allow the wound to heal properly.

Samir gave him an admonishing glare as he squeezed his eyes tight and fought down the sharp pain.

'It's alright, Samir. He says I'm in no immediate danger and, given the situation, I think that's a better than average estimate.'

He gestured at the command deck in front.

The Dark Empress had set off at first light, leading the other eleven vessels from the docks of Lassos and heading into the nightmare reefs in thick fog; the most dangerous time to attempt a passage of the sharp teeth that protected the island. The three members of the council had come aboard just in time to sail, with an escort of more than a dozen hand-picked men chosen from the crew of the other, more dependable, ships.

Halcar was taking no chances with Samir's potential treachery and had organised the ship and the fleet so that those vessels who were likely to be more sympathetic to him, under Captains Faerus and Orin, had been manipulated into 'safe' positions, far back in the line from the Empress and between more traditional captains who owed their success to the council. Ghassan could see no way that Samir could pull anything out of this mess.

'What will we do about that?' he asked very quietly, gesturing subtly in the direction of the three masters of Lassos who stood side by side, leaning over the rail at the front of the command deck, keeping a close watch on the activity on deck, while their guard kept a close watch on their safety.

Samir shrugged.

'They're not a problem. If they don't deal with it themselves, we'll handle them when the time is right.'

'Samir, we are rather seriously running out of time.'

'On the contrary, my dear brother. We have all the time in the world. Quite possibly,' he added, grinning, 'we have the whole rest of our lives.'

Ghassan glared at him.

'I just wish you'd tell me everything. I've got the main plan straight in my head. It's a good plan... or at least it would be if the council weren't hog-tying us. But there are so many things you haven't explained. How are we going to rally your friends? What are you going to do about the three councillors and their thugs? How are you going to stop the others from fleeing back to the island? I'm just too nervous about the uncertainty of everything.'

Samir nodded.

'I understand, but there really is nothing to worry about. In fact, I think something is about to fall into place that I'd only tentatively hoped for. The only thing that still makes me tense is the governor. What will he do?'

Ghassan shrugged.

'He'll do as you asked. It's to his advantage.'

Samir nodded with a distinct lack of enthusiasm.

'That may be so, but there are other ways he could look at it. He'd be taking a fairly serious risk and putting his own career in jeopardy. And that's even if he trusts or believes me, which is a fairly tall order on its own.'

Ghassan nodded.

'I don't worry about the governor. It's the problems that are a little closer that worry me.'

'Regardless, Ghassan, right now we need to prepare and steel ourselves. All hell is about to break loose and we need to be ready. Can you see how far back the other ships are?'

Ghassan narrowed his eyes as he turned and peered over the rear rail.

'Not really. The fog's too thick. I can see two behind us, and they're keeping very close, paying attention to the signals.'

He raised an eyebrow.

'I suppose you've given thought to the possibility of having your man give a false signal? You could scupper the whole fleet within the rocks. Not a ship would make it out.'

Samir shook his head.

'There are good people back there that I wouldn't leave behind. Besides, I've only got one of the compasses. I don't know yet which captain was given the other, but it'll be somewhere near the back and someone that Halcar trusts. Even with the chaos I'd cause, it's more than possible that a ship or two would escape back to Lassos and with the compass to boot.'

Ghassan nodded.

'You're right, of course. I just don't like uncertainty.'

'Cheer up,' Samir smiled. 'We're about to leave the reefs.'

'A great relief, I'm sure,' Ghassan replied sourly.

The last few glistening rocks with their sad and pleading occupants slid toward the bow of the ship and washed past in the oppressive, velvety silence, the figures pawing at the timbers as though they could help. Ghassan shuddered. No matter how many times he passed these reefs, that sight would still make him shudder.

Tensely, he watched the slick rocks drift past and into their wake, where his attention was drawn, as the mist thinned and finally evaporated, to the Hart's Heart behind them, captained by a particularly notorious man named Gharic, and currently also host to two more of the council's elders.

'Ha'Rish shine a good face on us today.'

Samir's mouth turned up at the corner cheekily.

'Are you intimating that our favourite Goddess has ugly faces?'

Ghassan flashed a glare at Samir, who merely laughed.

Suddenly, with the veil of mist lifted, the Sea of Winter Storms reflected the dancing sunlight back to them in all its glory, revealing a wide swathe of open horizon and drawing the viewer's attention squarely to the array of sails positioned in a rough arc around the sea into which they sailed. In other circumstances it might look pretty; it was certainly impressive. Perhaps forty or fifty daram of varying sizes and construction face the Empress as she emerged from the fleecy blanket. Three quarters of the sails were white, bearing aloft the colours of the Imperial navy, punctuated by the less common black sail of the fleet of the King of Pelasia. And in the centre of the arc, a particularly outsized daram, bearing the blue insignia of the governor of M'Dahz.

Ghassan frowned.

'It worries me that the governor's flying that pennant. If he'd agreed, I would expect to see a different insignia there.' He ground his teeth. 'But then they're all here… they haven't blockaded the entire circuit. Isn't that a good sign?'

Samir shrugged.

'Either very good, or very bad. Hush for a moment. One of my more interesting coin tosses is about to come down. Let's see whether we win or lose this one…'

Ghassan frowned again as he looked past Samir. Master Culin of the Lassos council was strolling toward them, hands clasped behind his back, while the other two councillors remained at the rail watching the events ahead unfold. As he approached, Culin stopped by the group of menacing looking guards that the councillors had brought aboard and selected half a dozen of them, gesturing for them to join him. Ghassan winced inwardly and realised that his breathing had become shallow and fast. He forced himself to calm down. Culin was the sort of man who could read emotions and appeared to have an intuitive mind, almost a match for Samir.

'Captain...' the man addressed Samir, and then nodded at Ghassan.

'Master Culin. What could I possibly do for you?'

Culin smiled quietly.

'Samir, please... you are not the only one here able to see beyond the end of his nose. I'm not entirely sure how you're going to do it, but I have a pretty shrewd idea of what's about to happen. Somehow, despite being outnumbered more than three to one by an enemy fleet and having most of your own fleet out for your blood, I have this disturbing feeling that next to you may be the safest place to stand today.'

Samir sketched a light bow.

'Master Culin, you flatter me. I am a mere gambler with an eye for good odds.'

Culin's answering grin was equally self-assured.

'As am I, Samir. I have been watching you and my peers with interest and trying to decide what to do about my suspicions. As a matter of duty and sense, I fear that what we should most do right now is to dispatch you both and tip you overboard before you can do any more damage.'

He sighed.

'My somewhat acute sense of self-preservation, however, presses me to other courses of action. When your little game plays out here, Samir, I would appreciate it if you remember the choice I made.'

Samir nodded, his smile fading to a grave expression.

'You are, as you have been for a while, foremost in my thoughts, Master Culin.'

The councillor nodded and then turned to the men with him.

'Stay with the captain and first officer. You know what to do.'

The burly pirate he addressed nodded respectfully as the master turned and strode back to the rail to join his peers. Once he was out of easy earshot, Ghassan leaned close to Samir and spoke under his breath.

'I don't know what you're up to with him, but that sounded good?'

Samir grinned as he nodded.

'Master Culin has revealed his hand and, I think, that the balance in our own fleet has just tipped in our favour.'

He smiled curiously.

'How prophetic I was…'

Ghassan frowned and Samir laughed.

'Later, my brother.' He squared his shoulders. 'Can you see the ships behind us now? Your eyes are so much better than mine.'

Ghassan squinted off behind them.

'Most of them. They're coming out of the fog and they're all as close as the ones just behind us. Shall I give the signal?'

Samir waved his hand noncommittally.

'Best ask the council for permission first.'

As Ghassan stood tensely, Samir stepped forward and cleared his throat, addressing the pirate leaders in a loud and clear voice.

'Masters? May I ask your indulgence and allow my brother to give the order to call the fleet to battle lines?'

Halcar turned his sour, hawk-like face back to them.

'You do not have to send any messages to your people yet?'

Samir grinned.

'That's taken care of, Master Halcar. We should see a reply any time. Permission?'

Halcar looked at Culin and Saja, standing to his left at the rail. Saja shrugged his bare ebony shoulders and Culin raised his brow.

'Why not?'

Halcar turned back to Samir.

'You have the council's permission to prepare for the attack.'

Samir nodded and turned to his brother.

'Alright Ghassan, let's get this fleet into position while we wait for my other coin to fall.'

In which other coins come down

With the practiced ease of veteran sailors, the eleven assorted vessels accompanying the Dark Empress from the reefs fanned out into a battle line. Given their hushed conversations the previous night, during which Samir had given his brother a complete rundown of the ships, their captains and any crew or tactics that he knew of, Ghassan rubbed his chin and glanced to the left and right trying to size up the fleet. Careful attention as the ships spread gracefully out into the line had given him the time and leisure to put together a mental map of the battlefield, as it were.

The Empress held the centre of the fleet. Stretching away to starboard lay six ships. The first, the Hart's Heart, clearly held little love for the Empress and her captain. The artillery master on the vessel had two of his weapons charged and angled to fire on the enemy fleet, below the rigging and past the mast, but the third weapon stood on a pivot and continually straying back and forth along the hull of Samir's vessel. Ghassan sighed. The Hart's Heart would be the most dangerous foe here. Beyond her lay three more ships captained by the more barbarous of Lassos' occupants, each of whom would have no compunction about sinking the brothers without a moment's pause. Beyond them, and almost out of useful reach of the Empress, lay one of their few allies: Orin's vessel, the Southern Fang, itself being shepherded carefully by another council-loyal vessel at the far flank.

Ghassan gritted his teeth. There was nothing they could do to help Orin that far out, and equally nothing that Orin could do to help them, but that was not their problem. Their own great problem would be Captain Gharic of the Hart's Heart, a northern barbarian come south decades ago in search of warmer blood in which to wade. Samir had painted a frightening picture last night not only of the captain's exploits, but also of his personal pastimes. Gharic would not leave the day without murdering the pair of them, and so he was clearly the most dangerous.

Except…

He turned to look across the port rail. To their immediate left wallowed the great dark bulk of the Sea Witch, now under the command of a strange easterner called Sho-han, but until recently the vessel of the very councillor Saja, who now leaned across their own command rail, scratching his ebony scalp and playing idly with one of his ear-rings as he scrutinised the Imperial fleet opposite.

Yes... the Sea Witch could well be as much trouble as the Hart's Heart. Whatever good Master Culin thought could come of this and however sure Samir was of their situation, the hawk-like Halcar had trapped the Empress between the two ships that held the firmest connection to the council. Ghassan would be unable to manoeuvre without presenting a soft side to one or the other.

Therefore it hardly mattered what Ghassan thought of the two other enemy ships beyond the Sea Witch, or Captain Faerus' Golden Dawn that lay trapped between other more vicious pirates on that flank.

In short, they could rely on only three of the twelve vessels and each of those was thoroughly constrained by the other pirate ships. He shook his head once again.

'Captain?'

Ghassan blinked and reined in his wandering and somewhat gloomy thoughts at the parchment-thin voice that had called from the rail.

Samir smiled at Ghassan and raised his brow, flicking his eyes toward the three council members in the most commanding position on the bridge. Ghassan pulled himself away from the rail with a groan of discomfort and joined his brother as they strode across to join the masters of Lassos. The tall first officer wiped the eternally bothersome curls from his forehead where they kept becoming plastered down with a mix of salty mist and sweat. This strange calm while the two fleets sat facing one another was almost too much to bear. Every ounce of command experience in him told him they had to make a move soon.

'Master Halcar?' Samir asked lightly.

The elderly pirate turned a sour face on the brothers.

'Your lookout says there is a signal showing from below the bowsprit on the enemy flagship. I would be interested to know how you got your men on the governor's own ship?'

Samir ignored the question and squinted through the rigging.

'We should get a clear view from over there,' he said, pointing at the side rail.

Without waiting for a reply, Samir strode to the port side and leaned over the edge where he could just see the winking lantern against the dark timbers of the massive daram's hull across the open water that separated the fleets. He grinned.

'That's our signal at last, Master Halcar.'

The older councillor, along with the ebony-skinned and somewhat grumpy looking Saja leaned across the rail next to Samir and peered off into the distance. There was a long, silent moment as Halcar and Saja translated the flashing signal. Halcar turned to Samir, his face an uncomfortable mix of suspicion and confusion.

'What does that mean: "yes"?'

Samir smiled.

'It means that all my coins have come down right-side up, Master Halcar… my apologies.'

Halcar's brow furrowed for only a moment before shock and terror swept across his mean and twisted features when the glistening dark bulk of councillor Saja heaved him over the rail with an easy push. The eldest and most senior pirate lord of Lassos disappeared beneath the waves that splashed against the timbers of the Empress, but not before his head had struck the hull with a heavy 'clonk'.

Ghassan stared as the ebony pirate master turned and flashed a brilliant white grin at Samir, squaring his shoulders.

'He was really beginning to get on my nerves, Samir. I couldn't have waited much longer!'

Ghassan's mouth flapped open and closed a few times as the two pirates before him clasped hands. Behind them, Master Culin strode across the deck, the dozen burly men at his back now.

'I daresay you could use another dozen good men right now, Samir?'

The captain of the Empress laughed.

'You have no idea, Culin. I think my brother will find places for them.'

Finally, Ghassan managed a hoarse exclamation of astonishment. Samir turned his irritating grin on his brother.

'I don't like leaving things to chance, Ghassan… you know that!'

Ghassan laughed.

'Then the Sea Witch…?'

Councillor Saja beamed at him.

'Is awaiting my signal, master Ghassan.'

Samir turned again. A noise attracted their attention from the starboard rail. Someone aboard the Hart's Heart had apparently noticed that something was wrong. Perhaps they had seen Master Halcar taking his final dive into the brine. Whatever the cause, there was no time left to ponder. Samir straightened.

'Ghassan? Pass the word to the boarding parties and the artillerists and have the lookout give the signal.'

Ghassan nodded as he turned, wincing once more at the pain in his back. Whatever the future held, it would all be decided within the hour, now. After a youth spent bouncing from one horror to another that had hardened them for their adulthood, and then decades spent in bloody opposition as they both lost sight of their original goal, the sons of Nadia, the sweetest flower of M'Dahz, stood side by side, doing what they both knew to be right, and with an opportunity at last to change the world.

Despite himself, he found himself grinning like the little boy who had won the fiercest rooftop race that Samir had ever devised and sat in the cool shade of the temple tower as he basked in his own achievement. He laughed a carefree laugh, drawing curious looks from the men around him.

'Artillery section? Make your target the Hart's Heart.'

The artillerist saluted as he ran off among the small detachment that manned the cruel machines at the central fortified section. Ghassan turned his gaze upward and cupped his hands to his mouth to bellow aloft, but removed them again with a smile as he saw that the lookout was already doing the job. Samir's crew were almost instinctively fast.

Ghassan beamed up at the Imperial naval pennant that unfurled, blue and green and bursting with pride, fluttering in the wind and changing the entire nature of the vessel.

The act must not have gone unnoticed, as the commotion that broke out on board the other vessels clearly indicated. Ghassan laughed as he watched an identical pennant unfurl aboard the Sea Witch. From captain in the Imperial navy, to vagabond, then second in command of a pirate vessel and now full circle back to a naval first officer! Strange, the turns that life can take a person down. He jogged back to the command deck just as he heard the first crashes of artillery, beginning the action proper.

'Samir? Everything's set. I've got firepower concentrating on the Hart...'

The last comment may have been unnecessary as he was forced to duck to avoid the horrifying flying splinters that exploded from both ships as their artillerists sought to do as much damage as possible, despite the close range hampering their ability to aim scuttling shots. As the shower of deadly shards dissipated, claiming three men on the deck to their horrifying points, Ghassan gestured at the enemy vessel next to them.

'I'm still not sure whether four against eight is a good number, Samir!'

Samir laughed.

'Aren't you forgetting about the governor's fleet?'

'Don't be ridiculous, Samir. By the time they get underway and reach us, it'll all be over!'

Master Culin leaned across between them, grasped Ghassan's arm and turned him deliberately to port, where he pointed at the Imperial fleet, sitting silent across the calm sea. Ghassan frowned for a moment and then his eyes widened as he saw a great ball of fiery hell catapult from one of the governor's ships. His eyes followed the flaming arc as his mouth dropped open. With an almost unbelievable accuracy, the great mass came down on the deck of the pirate three ships to port. The effect was instant and frenzied. The pirates panicked at the sudden realisation that, not only were they within artillery range of the Imperial fleet, but they had been sitting in place long enough to give the artillerists plenty of time to get their aim just right.

Ghassan turned to stare at his companions on board the command deck as, behind him, four more flaming missiles came hurtling across the open water to strike into the heart of Lassos' most vicious predators.

Culin was laughing so hard his eyes were streaming. Samir turned that ever-infuriating grin on his brother.

'Care to tell me how you arranged this?'

Samir cast a semi-apologetic look at the pirate councillors beside him.

'A few well-placed coins among some of Culin's contacts. You see, we all know that Culin has a man in just about every office of the southern provinces. Feeding information around is ridiculously easy when you know the right people.'

Ghassan shook his head.

'But how do they know which ships to attack? They can't see the pennants from that distance.'

That grin was beginning to irritate him beyond reason.

'Master Saja here was the one who persuaded the council to put the ships in this order. He fed me the plan long before he told the council.'

Ghassan laughed helplessly.

'Is there anything you don't think of ahead?'

Samir shrugged.

'There are a few things left to work out yet. The edge is with us now, but the Imperial fleet won't fire on the centre for fear of hitting us. They're concentrating on groups of enemy ships, not individuals.'

He paused his conversation as a massive crash indicated that the Empress had been hit with a pot of heavy canister shot. Whole sections of deck were ripped violently away.

'So we're going to have to deal with the Hart's Heart ourselves, and quickly. The Sea Witch can try and help Faerus out.'

Ghassan frowned.

'The Hart is beginning to move. They've reversed oars. Can they get back to the island?'

Samir frowned and flashed a questioning glance at Saja and Culin. The pirate leaders shrugged.

'Halcar entrusted the other compass to Captain Gharic. If he reaches the reef, he can get to safety.'

Samir shook his head.

'Can't have that... my deal with the governor was to empty Lassos and deliver everyone there to him as either ally or prisoner. We'll have to turn and take him out before he gets to the reef.'

He smiled as something occurred to him.

'Ghassan! In all the commotion, I forgot to show you the new paint job. While we get underway, can you find Duro or Rashad and tell them to do their duty?'

Ghassan strode off to find the dour giant or his peculiar assistant, his brow furrowed and ignoring the strain he felt in the wound on his back. He shook his head as he walked. Try as he might, and he considered himself a bright and intuitive man, he just could never keep up with Samir. That man had probably already planned out his afterlife.

The crew of the ship ran madly about their business and, as the oars shot out and began to dip in desperate time to try and catch the Hart's Heart, already speeding back toward the reef, two men dropped into the water a rough blanket that had been pegged in place over the ship's nameplate. The rough, timeworn planks with their black and green insignia in southern script had been replaced with new, clean and carefully-cut planks.

The Imperial ship of the line Redemption cut away the last of its ties to piracy as it chased down the one vessel that could still mar the day.

In which the fleet engages

Captain Faerus held his breath, his black locks whipping behind him in the gentle breeze as his gaze passed for the hundredth time from the ship to his left, her watchful captain and crew keeping their eye more on Faerus than the enemy, to the Imperial fleet across the open water, silent and brooding, and then to the other pirate ship to starboard hemming in the Golden Dawn. Samir has assured him that the odds were good, but that some risks had to be taken and the Golden Dawn would be at great risk for the first few minutes.

He realised that he'd bitten his lip hard enough to draw blood. This was ridiculous! Faerus had served with the Imperial navy in great engagements along the eastern shores of the Sea of Storms until the collapse of the military. Even after that, when he tried to form a militia for some time, he'd remained active, keeping his home city safe from their local lords that tried to take advantage of the failing of Imperial power. Only with his capture and escape had he turned to the last remaining avenue open to him: piracy; and since then, while he'd tried to retain an honourable attitude, he'd fought hard and dirty against every form of vessel: military, pirate, trader and mercenary. He'd only lost three engagements in ten years of commanding the Dawn and had had the sense and control to get out in time in each of those.

And now here he was, part of a ridiculously fragile conspiracy of pirates against other pirates, relying on the planning and brains of a man over a decade younger than himself, outnumbered, and waiting for some unknown sign to move. Of course, Samir was a man after his own heart and certainly the best man for this job and, if he managed to pull this off, he would be responsible not only for ending the threat of piracy in the Sea of Storms, but also for returning those who deserved it to position in the military. It was a master stroke. Faerus just hoped he lived long enough to enjoy it. The plan had sounded so good, but now, trapped between hostile captains and barely able to even see his ally through the rigging, he was beginning to doubt the strategy.

'Sir!'

Faerus blinked as he turned to locate the shouting sailor. One of the juniors was pointing to starboard. Shaking his head irritably, Faerus tried to see through the rigging of the pirate vessel that sat alongside them and to the ships beyond. Through the mass of ropes, sails, masts and men he could see the next pirate ship and then just make out the colours of Sho-Han's Sea Witch beyond that. The Dark Empress was entirely lost behind them all. What the hell had the lad seen?

A sudden and tremendous 'boom' answered his question as artillery went off in the centre of the fleet. He shook his head again. Samir said he'd know the signal when he heard it, but that was just ridiculous! Turning to the first officer, he took a deep breath.

'Alright, Alif... These two ships won't know what's going on, but it won't take them long to realise and, as soon as they do, they'll be down on us like a sand devil on a wounded camel. Everything we planned, and all at once. Alright?'

The desert-dweller who had served faithfully as Faerus' right hand man for the best part of a decade grinned.

'Everything at once, sir, aye! Let's hope we can make enough room eh, sir?'

Faerus ground his teeth and spoke under his breath into the breeze.

'This is it, Samir. I hope you know what you're doing.'

He smiled as there was a muted and distant thud, way out across the waves. As he watched, a ball of flaming mass arced up and over the water, trailing a line of oily black smoke behind it as it flew with relentless speed and surprising precision straight into the bow of the ship to starboard of Faerus. He turned to watch his orders being carried out as several more horrifying missiles began their journey from the Imperial fleet.

The ships to either side of the Golden Dawn were in chaos, just as Faerus had expected. The sudden launching of hostilities within their own fleet, followed by the beginning of a surprise bombardment from the governor's ships had left them panicking and trying to pull themselves into enough order to either engage or flee, though neither captain would have had the leisure to make even that decision yet.

Faerus' crew had been with him and worked together for so many years that the orders were carried out with the minimum of wasteful activity and fuss, and events unfolded before him in perfect order and precision.

Aloft, the pirate pennant was cut loose as the great Imperial replacement fluttered free in the breeze. He'd questioned Samir as to whether it would have been more sensible to wait to reveal their intentions until after they'd attacked, giving them more surprise, but Samir had been adamant. As soon as this action began, he'd said, it began with them serving the Empire and to do that they had to be honourable and open. In a way Faerus agreed, but with a nod to the need for surprise, he'd waited until the very last minute, pushing all his actions into one frantic moment.

As the green and blue flag whipped in the breeze, a cloth was discarded into the sea and the Golden Dawn was no more. The pirate ship that had been Faerus' home for decades had gone, to be replaced instantaneously by the Imperial ship of the line Retribution, which was already bursting into life with impressive speed and efficiency. Even as the oarsmen began to heave on the oars and the ship started to turn sharply to port, the artillerists had their weapons loaded and trained to the rear.

Shouts of alarm went up from the ship they were turning toward as the crew saw the sudden movement of Faerus' vessel, turning sharply sideways while remaining in the line, and they noted with horror the great iron ram and spike listing ponderously toward their hull. Their captain leapt to action trying to get his vessel mobile as fast as possible and move out of the way of this sudden menace.

Behind and to starboard as they turned, the captain and crew of the other vessel were already in a panic, trying to deal with the massive damage caused by the Imperial fire catapults. The forward section of the main deck was ablaze, and flames were leaping up the foresail and racing along the rigging as men tried desperately to cut the ropes and contain the fire. It would be out soon, Faerus noted, as men were already hurling water and sand across the flames, but the damage had crippled them long enough to give Faerus the edge.

As the Retribution turned, the artillerists finished lining up and levelling their weapons and released in unison. With a deafening crash, the already beleaguered and flaming vessel found itself the sudden target of a second ball of oily fire that burst at the base of the stairs to the command deck, filling the corridor inside with flames and cutting off the officers from their men, while two canister shots ripped through timber, sails, rigging and crew. In among the carnage, an officer trying to rally the crew in desperation was picked up bodily by one of the long iron bolts and pinned to the burning timbers where he burst into flame before the life could pass from his eyes.

Faerus turned his face from the doomed ship. Horrible and dangerous as that was, that had never been the gamble. This was the gamble: there simply was not enough room for Faerus' ship to fit lengthwise between the two enemy vessels and they had to keep moving away from the burning ship before the flames engulfed the whole vessel and she became a hazard to the Retribution.

That all meant that the only way Faerus could get safely to a position where he could manoeuvre and involve himself further in the action was to go through the outermost vessel. As he watched, the prow of the Retribution closed on the side of the enemy ship's hull. Their captain had been quick to get his oars out and into the water, and even now the enemy ship was starting to move ponderously forward. He'd never get out of the way in time, of course, but that wasn't what was worrying Faerus. Ramming someone at slow speed and at a three quarter angle was not a recipe for success.

'Artillery? Phase two!' shouted the second in command and Faerus nodded tensely. Without speed and a direct frontal blow, the ram and spike would probably just jam and lodge there, locking the two ships in a deadly embrace while the fire behind them drifted ever closer. The only hope was to break up enough of the ships' structure before the ram hit so that half its job was already done.

Behind him, the artillerists, their weapons already reloaded, were swivelling their machines of war on the small castle amidships, and taking aim at their next target: the hull of the ship directly ahead of the Retribution's prow.

Faerus held his breath as the two ships closed with an unstoppable force. The Retribution continued to pick up speed as the oarsmen strained and heaved like they had never done before.

The first two shots of heavy iron ammunition punched into the enemy ship in tightly-aimed locations, one just below the waterline, ahead of their ram, the other smashing into the rail and shearing the main deck as it smashed through the timbers, ripping up boards. Squinting at the need to be perfectly accurate, the artillerists released the third and fourth shot only a moment later. Both of these hit in the areas previously devastated by the initial shots, entering the main structure of the ship and ripping apart beams and bulkheads.

New cries of dismay went up among the crew of the enemy ship and the captain rushed to the rail of his command deck to survey the damage, waving his arms and shouting to his juniors, but there was no hope. His orders went unheard as the faster-thinking members of his crew ran to either stern or prow, whichever was closer, and threw themselves into the water, far from the site of the impending breach.

Faerus shut his eyes as the shadow cast by his ram slowly made its way up the side of the enemy ship, marking every inch as they closed. This was it... they were either going through, or down...

At the far end of the fleet, another tale was unfolding, though this was far from a happy one. The barrel-chested and fork-bearded Orin, captain of the newly named Revenge, surveyed the damage and sighed, scratching his chin. He would have liked at least once to have stood on the deck as it entered port a legitimate naval vessel. He was no longer a young man and had long ago begun to tire of the attitudes of his peers. When Faerus and Samir had tentatively approached him with the plan, it had been a dream come true.

But then all dreams faded.

As soon as the first shot was fired, the ships on either side of Orin had leapt into action. The Imperial fleet had taken its toll on a number of vessels between here and the centre of the line, but the ones flanking Orin had been sharp enough to launch an immediate assault on him, even before he'd had a chance to strike the new colours.

By the time his artillerists had launched their first shot, the prow had already been hit by a ball of oily fire and leapt into a flickering blaze. He'd had the oars run out to try and begin pulling back from the line, but the solid and canister shot from both sides had been aimed at the banks of oars and he'd lost half the rowing capability only moments after the oars touched water. As he'd watched in horror, trying to decide how best to deal with the growing nightmare, the second and third fireballs had hit, one amidships at the mast, effectively ending the use of his artillery, while the other burst through the side of the ship, below the command deck, ravaging the cabins within.

Orin ground his teeth in anger as he felt the boards beneath his feet beginning to warm with the fierce heat of the flaming cabins below.

He'd had plans, for certain, but they'd relied on him having at least a second to breathe before the fight began. But the shrewd bastards to either side of him had clearly been planning on taking him out regardless of the day's actions. Their artillery must have all been loaded and trained on him from the start for things to have happened so damn quick.

He sighed again. There was no other option.

'Leave that!'

The crew amidships looked up in surprise at their captain where they worked tirelessly with buckets of water, trying to douse the ever expanding flower of billowing flames.

'The Revenge is done for, but we'll not go down alone, eh lads?'

There was a somewhat half-hearted cheer. He couldn't really blame them, of course. Many of them would now be wondering why they ever decided to turn against their colleagues. Still, Revenge was both the name of the ship and the order of the day… he'd see those bastards to either side whipped through three hells for what they'd done to him this morning.

'Grapple lines… every available hand on both rails!'

The men stood for a moment in confusion, but then realisation dawned on them and they ran to get the ropes and grapples. The Revenge would burn for a while yet before she began to sink. The other ships were so busy concentrating on taking him down that they hadn't given thought to pulling out of the range of danger themselves.

With enough strength on the grapples, the Revenge would pull its assailants relentlessly in until they all three became one great flaming mass. But he would have to make sure that did for them too...

Scouring the deck, he spotted the dejected face of the second in command of artillery and beckoned to him.

'We'll make use of your stuff yet, Khaim. Drop that grapple and get three men with you down to the armoury. Remove the protective coverings on all your firepots and get them charged and up on deck. As soon as we're within reach of these bastards, we're going to turn this ship into the biggest explosive you've ever seen!'

In which the line breaks

As the Redemption, formerly the Dark Empress, backed out of the chaotic line of vessels, making for somewhere with enough room to turn, Ghassan and Samir stood at the rail with Saja and Culin, trying to make sense of what was happening. Almost every ship in the line was now moving, though there was an unplanned, chaotic and desperate edge to the action.

The left flank of the line was one of the main areas of trouble, though Samir had felt sure that Faerus could handle whatever the morning threw at him. The ships to either side of him were in trouble, one thoroughly ablaze and already starting to lean badly, the other...

Samir laughed as he watched his friend's ship in the distance hit the enemy vessel amidships, tearing through the hull as though it were parchment and passing through, cutting the pirate ship in half in the process. How he'd managed that without more damage to his own ship, Samir couldn't fathom, but he'd certainly be asking him if they got out of this well.

So at least one of their allies was safe, he thought as he watched Faerus tear through the last of the ship and out to open sea where he could turn and manoeuvre. And in the process he seemed to have crippled or destroyed two of the remaining eight enemy vessels.

The two remaining ships on that side of the rail were now heavily locked in close combat, Captain Sho-Han of the Sea Witch having, not surprisingly, declared for his old commander who now stood side by side with Samir on the command deck. Those two vessels were an even match and far too close for effective use of anything other than small shot artillery. It would come down to man to man fighting on deck, which would be nasty for both sides but, whatever the outcome, that meant the entire line to the left of Samir was involved or dealt with.

The Imperial fleet had finished its bombardment, but that was expected. The agreement had called for only one volley since, by the time a reload had been effected, the pirate fleet would be moving and likely mixing among one another, making targeting almost impossible for a crew at such distance. Still, from the roiling smoke that filled the bright morning air and the steady roar of flaming timber, their single volley had been devastating enough to turn the fight immediately Samir's way.

To the other side...

Samir rocked back on his heels as he turned and the far end of the fleet suddenly exploded in a fireball the like of which Samir had never even imagined. The expanding mushroom of red and orange boiling flame engulfed several vessels at the far end and Samir blinked in shock. Second and third subsidiary explosions marked the detonation of spare ammunition among the vessels involved in the conflagration.

It took a moment for Samir's reeling mind to pull itself together in the wake of the mind-numbing blast. With a deep sadness of the soul, he realised, from the direction of the blast, that Orin's ship was somewhere in that fireball. Precious little hope of anyone surviving that... if there were any survivors at that flank it would be those who had the foresight to jump from the rails and were underwater when the blast occurred. Samir shook his head and turned to his friends to realise that they were all standing, staring, as shocked as he.

'Orin knew the risks. We need to concentrate on what's still to do.'

As if shaken from sleep, the three other commanders on the deck blinked and nodded. As Ghassan ran to the rail to yell orders at the men and Culin put a rare and expensive spyglass to his eye, Saja fumed at the Hart's Heart, already completing its turn and heading for the reef ahead.

'We'll have go some to catch them,' he barked.

Samir turned away to examine the line once more. The fireball had contracted once more and left three ships in a state of almost complete destruction, hardly anything standing above deck. Fragments of wood and other, more unthinkable, things rained down from the sky, trailing little flames like falling stars, while chunks of timber and bodies floated in the water around them. Oh, it was too far away for Samir to actually see what it was that darkened the waves around the ships, but he'd been in enough brutal engagements these past two decades to know what caused that stain.

Trying not to think how many of those tiny dots that speckled the water had shared a drink with him in the bar on Lassos, Samir forced his gaze away from them and to the remaining two enemy vessels on that side. Along with the Hart's Heart they were the only remaining enemy ships that were not engaged. The question was: what would they do? Faerus' ship, the Retribution, was at the very other end of the line and too far away to engage, Orin's vessel was a burning shell and the Sea Witch, their surprise ally, was already engaged with another ship in vicious hand-to-hand.

Samir shifted round the rail to keep watch on them as the Redemption turned as fast as Ghassan could manage, trying to catch the Hart's Heart in open water.

There was clearly chaos on board both enemy vessels, though that was hardly a surprise, given the sudden turns of events in the past few minutes.

As he watched, sliding his hands along the rail while the deck turned, he frowned. The nearest of the two vessels was beginning to wheel around. Given that they now had plenty of room to manoeuvre and no close enemies and could simply pull forward out of the line, turning meant only one thing: they were planning to head the same way as Samir and his prey, though whether in order to engage the Redemption or merely to try and hook up with the Hart's Heart and try to return to Lassos remained to be seen. Either way, in a few minutes Samir and his crew would be trapped between the ship they were pursuing and this new one following them in. The situation could turn unpleasant then.

His lip curled into a slight smile as he realised that the remaining unengaged ship had struck out at full speed for open sea, past the three burning wrecks. More fool him... the governor could spare up to half a dozen ships to chase him down and apprehend him, but the likelihood was that, now they had all had a chance to reload their artillery, the running fool would be used as target practice. He wouldn't get a half mile away from here before he touched the sea bed. Still, that was one ship that he didn't have to worry about.

He turned back to the two pirate councillors standing at the rail.

'How far are they from the reefs?'

Saja, his bright eyes flashing anxiously in that dark face, turned to Samir.

'Not far enough. They'll be among the rocks before we can touch them. They've got away.'

Culin, next to him, nodded unenthusiastically.

'He's right, Samir. With the best will in the world, I know your crew are good, but unless you happen to have a God in your pocket, there's no way we can catch them. Lassos is theirs and it'll be hell trying to lever them out then.'

Samir shook his head.

'That would be no use anyway. My deal with the governor stipulated all the folk of Lassos and their ships. We let Gharic get back to the island and we've broken our side of the deal. While I can't guarantee that the governor would renege on his side, I'm not about to take that chance.'

He smiled wickedly.

'I have a plan. We don't have to catch them.'

As Saja and Culin narrowed their eyes suspiciously, Samir turned to his brother.

'Ghassan? Give us every bit of speed you have, but count to fifty and then bring us to starboard at a narrow angle, as though we're trying to come alongside from behind.'

Ghassan frowned for a moment and then shrugged, turning to the crew and muttering something unheard under his breath before bellowing out the orders once more.

Samir smiled and brushed his fingers along the edge of the object in his pocket.

So, Gharic wanted to run back to the island, did he?

Captain Faerus heaved a sigh of relief as the Retribution pulled free of the mass of the stricken pirate ship. It had been, he had to admit, a dangerously lunatic idea. The whole idea of the ram was to puncture the enemy and then pull out and flee while they sank. Nobody, to his knowledge, had ever attempted this and, despite the awesome weight and strength of the Retribution's ram, it was still idiotic. But then, the fiery mass that was the other ship behind them was listing in their direction, and any attempt to reverse after impact would be to present themselves to a whole new burning danger.

After the initial collision, his main worry had been that they would stick fast, or even that the rudder would jam on the wreckage before they could get clear. It had been a fascinating and heart-stopping minute and a half as his ship had sliced somewhat messily through the midsection of the enemy vessel.

The initial heavy shots had been well placed enough that they had shattered the main beams and bulkheads in the hull, and Faerus' ship had long been renowned and feared for its outsized ram; just under a ton of iron, fifteen feet long and reinforced all the way from the keel up along the breakwater and to the bowsprit. As they had struck, the ram had punched through with ease, the iron breakwater shattering the remaining boards as they met. The main problem had been that the Retribution had not had enough room to build up ramming speed and the initial impact had slowed their ship further. In danger of grinding to a halt, jammed across their enemy, Faerus' artillerists had begun to fire shot, both solid and canister, into the structure of the ship ahead, beside and below them.

Even then, they had almost become wedged. The oarsmen, given their objective, hauled their oars in at the last minute, a couple of them in the front half of the ship waiting too long and watching helplessly as the long wooden implements shattered on the enemy hull while they came up. Most, however, had managed to get the oars up in time and spent the next minute using them to push the disintegrating hull of the enemy ship away from them, heaving as hard as they could as though they were punting a barge, every ounce of strength adding to the ease of passage.

Had the crew of the pirate vessel had their wits about them, they could have taken the opportunity to pick off many of Faerus' crew as they sawed their way through, but the imminent demise of their own ship had them panicked and those that hadn't already run fore or aft and dived into the water before impact were desperately running up the tilting deck away from the scene of the destruction.

By the time the Retribution was far enough through the enemy hull for the foremost oars to be dipped into the water once again, the pirate ship had separated into two neat halves and was beginning to disappear below the waves.

'Are we clear?'

Alif, the weathered second in command, standing on the main deck above the hatch, shivered and rubbed his head.

'I can't believe you even tried that, cap'n, let alone that it worked!'

'But are we clear?'

Alif nodded.

'We're able to manoeuvre a little, but we've taken a hell of a lot of damage, sir. The prow's a mess and people are shouting up from below that we're taking on water in a dozen places.'

'Critically?'

Alif shrugged.

'Water coming in is never good, captain. In a perfect world, the water stays on the outside of a ship.'

Faerus smiled. That his grouchy subordinate felt the subject worthy of humour spoke volumes.

'Then let's get those holes plugged as best we can and set the crew to emergency repairs only. We've not got time to effect a full repair; I want to get us back into the fight as soon as possible.'

'With respect, captain… you're barking mad! Has anyone ever told you that?'

'You have, Alif, and on more than one occasion.'

The swarthy man grinned.

'At least five minutes for a desperate patch up before I'll feel safe even trying to make a turn, alright sir?'

'Whatever you say, Alif.'

He sighed as he stood back and leaned on the railing. His ship may have taken a pounding from this, but they came off better than the other two vessels. He watched with a slight undercurrent of sadness as the last timbers of the shattered ship around them disappeared beneath the waves. A glance behind revealed the burning mass of the other vessel, now leaning at a dangerous angle as it began its descent to the underworld. Unfortunate for the crew, caught between the choice of a fiery death or a watery one. In the most perfect of worlds they would help the stricken sailors bobbing in the water and shouting for help, hauling them aboard to save them.

But that was for military engagements with men of honour, such as Faerus had faced in the old days. He knew those men in the water from the last decade or more, though. Most of them would gut him the moment his back was turned and, realistically, what chance did they stand? If Faerus relented and rescued them, he would have to deliver them to the governor, who would hang them in Calphoris of M'Dahz, watching as they jerked and soiled themselves in front of a jeering crowd. Better that they disappeared here, forgotten.

Better for him and better for them.

He smiled sadly at the ship of the line Retribution. Five minutes and no more. Then he would go and help Samir and Orin.

In which threads come to a close

S amir shook his head.
'Not yet.'
'But we're in range. A heavy firepot might stop them.'
Samir turned from the rail to look at Ghassan.
'Not yet!'
'But Samir...'
'Listen! Gharic is far from stupid. He's seen what's happened up and down the line. Hell, he knew he was beaten that first moment. While the other captains started fighting back, Gharic knew they were done for and fled. Not brave, but clever. He's seen what shots have been fired and he knows what we'll do. He'll be expecting the fire shot by now. Every man who's not on the oars will be standing by with poles and water to sort it out. At best we'll create a minor distraction and singe the deck. No. I need that catapult ready.'

Ghassan ground his teeth.

'Then tell us what you're planning. Damn it, Samir! I know you have this whole personal superiority complex where you need to know things that other people don't and be ahead of the game, but now is not the time!'

'I am who I am, Ghassan,' Samir grinned.

Ahead, Saja, leaning on the rail amidships, turned and shouted back to them.

'He's reached the rocks and slowed. Any minute now we'll lose him in the mist.'

Ghassan growled at his brother.

'Alright, Samir. This is it. Whatever you're going to do, do it now.'

Samir shook his head.

'One more minute. We need one more minute; let him get safely in the rocks.'

The exasperated Ghassan turned to look out to stern. The remaining active pirate ship was bearing down on them, matching speed. They would catch up the moment Samir turned... on the assumption he was going to turn and hadn't planned merely to fly over the reefs.

Moments passed in tense silence and finally the deep voice of Saja called out.

'That's it... she's gone into the mist. Two minutes and we'll hit rocks and fog ourselves. Hope you've got the compass ready, Samir?'

The captain of the Redemption grinned.

'You have no idea, Saja.'

Reaching into his tunic, he withdrew the disc with its mummified finger. With a laugh, he beckoned to Culin and Ghassan and made for the steps down to the main deck.

Frowning, the two officers followed him down the stairs and out onto the deck where the crew worked tirelessly, the oarsmen on their benches hauling and grunting, trying to bring the ship within reach of the now-invisible target. As the three approached the midsection, Samir striding out ahead, Saja hurried over from the rail to join them.

'Alright, Samir... what's going on?'

The diminutive captain smiled his most irritating smile and passed the compass to the ebony-skinned councillor.

'What have you given me this for?'

'Watch and learn,' laughed Samir.

Still grinning, he reached into his pocket and withdrew a key. Flourishing it like a showman, he held it aloft.

'Behold the end of Captain Gharic.'

He became aware of the tense irritation around him and stepped forward to the set of five steps leading up to the fortified artillery castle by the main mast. There he crouched down and inserted the key into an almost invisible hole in the timbers at the base of the tower.

'You see, the compasses have been Lassos' closest guarded secret for centuries, but my old captain, Khmun, had an even closer-guarded secret than that. To this day, the only person he ever told was me, and he had this little compartment fitted to hide away that secret. He never used it, to my knowledge, and I only used it once myself, when I last fled Lassos with a pirate fleet hot on my heels.'

With a click, he swung open the wooden plank, perfectly hinged and expertly hidden, and slid out a dark, metal container.

'I think you'll like this.'

Reaching into his pocket, he produced a second key, which he inserted into a lock in the container.

'The box is made of lead. Don't ask me why is has to be lead. I don't even know how Khmun knew that, but there it is: only lead works. Now...' He grinned up at them. 'Keep an eye on the compass.'

With a flourish, he opened the box and, as the other three stared down at the bronze disk in Saja's hand, the finger within suddenly jerked as though alive and then swung wildly round to point at Samir where it hung for just a moment before beginning to spin at a dizzying speed in circles.

The three commanders stared at the precious item in their hands, rendered entirely useless by... by what?

Samir grinned as he stood and unwrapped the bag he'd retrieved from the lead casket. A lump of metal fell out into his hand, rusty and red like the rawest iron. Laughing, he thrust the lump close to the compass and the pointing finger within picked up speed, spinning so fast it almost fractured and fell apart.

'How the hell are you doing that?' Ghassan blinked.

'It's the metal. Don't ask me why. A gift from the Gods maybe? All I know is that it totally messes up the compass' ability to give a reading. At a distance it makes the needle waver a little. Closer and it'll point toward the metal. But anywhere within a couple of ship lengths and it makes the finger do this.'

Culin laughed.

'We spent a week arguing about how you did that the last time you left here. You almost sank half the ships of Lassos on those rocks!'

Samir's smile faltered slightly.

'I never intended that. There were friends in that fleet. I just revealed the red metal from a distance and gave them enough to worry about that they had to work hard and forget about me.'

He smiled grimly.

'Now, however, it's not only time to stop Gharic and his crew, but to seal off Lassos forever.'

Turning, he climbed the five steps to the platform.

'Who's the best shot in your crew?' he asked of the artillery master.

The bearded man scratched his chin.

'I'd like to say it was me, but that would be young Kayri here.'

Samir turned to the young marksman.

'There's enough gold corona in it to buy your own ship if you can fire this thing and land it close to the Hart's Heart. Think you can do it?'

The young lad frowned, casting a professional eye over the red lump in Samir's hand.

'May I, captain?'

Samir nodded and passed the lump to the young man, rubbing his hands together and wiping away the red dust.

'Not very heavy. It'll be a tricky shot, sir. I've never fired anything this light. Can't guarantee it.'

'So we have to make it heavier?'

The lad nodded as he regarded the lump.

'That would be good, sir.'

Samir grinned, retrieved the item, and reached across to one of the foot-high barrels of canister shot. With a flourish, he produced his belt knife, levered off the lid and scooped out a couple of the rocks within. Concentrating, he dropped the iron lump in, replaced the lid, and hammered the pins back down with the hilt of his knife. Lifting the barrel, he stood and turned to the lad.

'More the right sort of weight?'

The artillerist nodded and reached out, taking the canister.

'That'll be easy, sir, but bear in mind that if it doesn't hit a rock, it'll just sink with your metal lump inside it.'

Samir shrugged noncommittally.

'Nothing short of a lead casket would make a difference anyway. A few yards of water and a wooden box won't matter.'

He nodded to the lad and stepped back down to the main deck as the artillerists began to adjust the catapult's aim.

Ghassan flashed a nervous smile.

'Let's hope he's up to it.'

Samir laughed.

'He was good enough to cripple your ship, brother. I think he'll be alright. To be honest, anywhere remotely near them will do the trick, anyway.'

Saja sighed as he gazed out toward the rocks.

'Of course, that means we can never go home, Samir. You realise that?'

Samir shrugged.

'My home is M'Dahz… always has been. Lassos was only ever a temporary haven.'

The four officers fell silent as they heard the creak of the winch. Staring out ahead, they couldn't help but flinch as the catapult fired, not six feet from where they stood, with a loud crack and a bang that shook the deck nearby. The canister that Samir had produced disappeared, arcing out silently into the mist.

'Shouldn't we hear it land?'

Culin shook his head.

'Too small. It'll only be a little splash, muted by the fog.'

The four watched tensely as the reefs grew ever closer. Now, if Samir concentrated, he could see the shapes of the desperate wraiths as they called out helplessly from their slippery platforms. Everything was eerily silent and the mist closed on the bow.

'Best take us to starboard sharp and bring us about. I've no intention of foundering on those rocks,' Samir said.

Ghassan nodded and turned to call to the man at the rudder but as he opened his mouth there was a muted crash. As they all fell silent and listened from deep within the mist there were desperate cries and the sound of splintering timbers, crashes and splashes. The smile dropped from every face. Gharic may have been a cold hearted and vicious bastard, but to crash among those rocks… well, everyone knew what that meant.

Ghassan heaved in a deep breath and bellowed to the helmsman.

'Come about to starboard; sharp as you can manage!'

Saja sighed.

'No more Lassos. It'll be strange being legitimate. It's been so long since I could hold my head up in an Imperial city that I can't even remember what it's like.'

Samir gave a light laugh.

'I daresay you'll adjust, my friend. You'll...'

Culin grasped his wrist sharply and Samir looked down and then across at the councillor in surprise, his words immediately forgotten.

'What?'

'Our pursuers! They're almost on us. It's not over yet.'

In which the brothers are beleaguered

Samir rushed to the port rail, cursing himself. He'd been concentrating so hard on catching and dealing with the Hart's Heart that he'd paid scant attention to the vessel that had broken the line to pursue them. It had been unclear initially whether the captain of this last operational pirate vessel had been planning to launch an attack on them or try to flee past them to Lassos.

The latter course of action was no longer open to them anyway, given the fact that, of the two compasses that existed and could navigate the reefs, one was now at the bottom of the sea among the rocks and the other was on board Samir's ship. Regardless, the objective of the pirates appeared to have been Samir and his men from the start. Rather than making course for the narrow channel that led into the reef or pulling about after the Hart had disappeared, the pursuers were bearing down on Samir at a surprising speed, both billowing sails and splashing oars bringing them to a ramming speed.

Samir eyed the iron spike on the ship's prow; not the work of destructive art that adorned Faerus' ship, but enough to punch a hole in the side of the Redemption and cripple her. Samir's mind raced. They had a minute at most. Given their own ponderous speed since they'd come to a stop to fire the strange package among the rocks, presenting their portside to the enemy in the process, there simply was not enough time to get the ship out of the way. Their only hope, then, was to stop the enemy before they managed to ram.

He shook his head angrily. How the hell could they do that?

Turning, he saw Saja and Culin deep in panicked discussion, while Ghassan desperately shouted orders to the crew, trying to get the Redemption moving and out of the way of the ship bearing down on her.

'We've got to stop her! Ideas… come on!'

Saja and Culin glanced around at him as they argued, but neither looked hopeful.

'Ghassan?'

Samir looked across the command deck at where his brother had been only a moment earlier, shouting out commands. Now, however, there was no sign of him. Squinting, Samir cast his eyes around the ship and finally spotted Ghassan racing up the steps to the artillery platform amidships.

Running after him, Samir shook his head. There would only be time to get one shot off, and there wasn't time to prime a fire shot. They might do a little damage, but not enough to stop them. As he reached the foot of the steps climbing up to the artillery castle, the lead casket still lying open nearby, he clambered up to see Ghassan in deep conversation with the young artillerist, waving his arms to illustrate some point he was making.

Samir stopped, panting, at the top of the steps and Ghassan turned to him, a look of quiet determination on his face. Behind him, two artillerists loaded heavy solid shot into the catapult.

'Ghassan? What are you up to? There's no time for this.'

Ghassan nodded absently.

'There is. There's time for one shot. Just pray that it's enough and that your men are that good.'

Samir frowned at his brother and, as the artillerists began to line up the catapult, tightening the ropes a last few turns and checking their trajectory, he and Ghassan leaned over the wooden battlements and watched the scene unfold, their breath held.

The enemy ship was perhaps half a minute from them and still on a ramming course, having to adjust only a few degrees occasionally as the Redemption slowly slid forward.

'Gods, I hope you're right, Ghassan.'

They stared bleakly at the ever closing bow of the enemy ship with that horrific iron spike, the oarsmen heaving like they'd never rowed before to achieve a crippling ramming speed. Samir closed his eyes tight and held his breath.

Crack.

Behind them, the artillerists let loose the only shot they would have time for.

Samir opened one eye as the great, heavy shot sailed over their heads on a remarkably low trajectory. For an artillerist to manage such a low and straight shot from a catapult was a remarkable enough feat, let alone with the perfect precision targeting that the shot displayed.

Through his squinted eye, Samir saw the shot hit the banks of oars on the port side of the enemy vessel, smashing and shattering them and bouncing along the shafts, cracking and breaking more as it disappeared with dreadful momentum down the side of the ship and disappeared into the water with a loud splash.

Samir blinked. Just as he'd once done to Ghassan's ship! One carefully aimed shot had removed almost half the rowing power on the enemy's port side, the remaining oars on that side now disjointed and out of time, in chaos.

The effect was immediate and astounding.

With little forward motion on the port oars, while the starboard banks ploughed on as fast as they could and the sails billowed with the wind, no amount of rudder control at the rear could stop the ship turning. The men of the Imperial ship Redemption watched with fascination as the enemy vessel slewed wildly to port, momentum still carrying it forward at a strange quarter angle.

Samir barely had time to take it all in before he realised what was coming next. The ramming spike had skewed left and out of line with its target, but nothing was going to stop the two ships colliding under the circumstances.

'Brace!' he bellowed and, grabbing tight hold of the artillery fortification, ducked to floor level.

The enemy vessel hit them at that quarter angle, the timbers of both ships crashing and breaking, amidships for Redemption and to starboard of the forward deck on the pirate vessel. The damage was far from fatal for either, but the crews of both ships were shaken, those who were not fully braced being swept from their feet. A number of screams and splashes from various directions announced men overboard among both crews.

The Redemption listed frighteningly following the impact, slowly righting itself as men were hurled from the rail. Similar events appeared to be occurring among the pirates.

Ghassan grasped Samir and the two hauled themselves back up to the crenellated top of the fortification.

'We're not out of the shit yet, Samir,' Ghassan breathed heavily. 'You've got a skeleton crew at best now, while they're fully manned.'

Samir nodded, biting back an undeserved retort. Ghassan was right. The men on his ship were brave and among the best he'd ever seen, but the odds would be three or four to one, and no amount of heart was going to even that out.

'I'm not letting them have the Empress, Ghassan.'

'The Redemption, Samir.'

The smaller brother shot an irritated look at his sibling.

'If things get too bleak, make sure you throw that compass over the side. That has to be the end of it.'

Ghassan nodded soberly and Samir turned and cupped his hands around his mouth.

'To arms. Prepare to board!'

Ghassan stared at his brother.

'Board? Are you mad? We should be trying to repel them. You don't try and board a ship that outnumbers you by four men to one!'

'Indeed,' replied Samir, 'which is why it'll throw them completely off track!'

Behind them, the men of the Redemption drew their weapons as they picked themselves up from the deck and clambered across the wreckage toward the rail.

'Samir, they'll die.'

'Better to go out trying than cowering, Ghassan. I'm leaving you in charge of the Redemption and the compass. You know what to do when things get too bad.'

'Oh no you don…'

'Yes I do. Good luck, brother.'

As Ghassan launched off on a tirade at the smaller man, Samir, grimacing, leapt down to the main deck and ran to join the men who were even now clambering at the rail.

Ghassan watched from the command deck, helplessly. Samir, however irritating, was right. Someone needed to stay back in charge of the compass. It must not fall into enemy hands. And since his back was still weeping when he moved wrong, Ghassan was the obvious choice. He thumped his hand on the rail as he surveyed the scene.

It was a mess. Many of the oars on both ships had been smashed when the collision occurred, and the pirate vessel had slid to a stop side by side with her prey, both ships rocking and shaking. The gap between the two hulls was almost narrow enough to leap, but if a man missed, given the fact that the two hulls kept washing against one another, drowning would be a blessed option. Ghassan had seen men crushed between two ships' hulls before and it was never pretty.

The sailors of both sides were clamouring at the rails, awaiting the chance to cross and cause havoc, but neither was ready yet. The collision had left both ships in a state of chaos. No one was willing to take the leap between ships and neither side had expected a boarding action, so the boarding ramps were being brought up hurriedly on both sides.

The crews, who looked largely identical, roared their anger and defiance at one another and the sight was almost comical, given both crews' inability to actually reach their enemies until the ramps were in place.

Ghassan, however, a veteran of so many years of combat, could see a subtle difference in the two crews.

Not the numbers. There was nothing subtle about the fact that the enemy ship's rail was crowded by a throng of bloodthirsty cutthroats at least four men deep, while there were few enough men on board the Redemption that small gaps remained at the rail.

No. The difference was in the tone of the shouts. The enemy ship had that roar of true violence. They knew they had the upper hand and that they would be safe if they overran the Redemption, stole the compass and retreated into the reefs. They had every reason to believe that the fight would go their way.

Samir's crew, however, knew they were doomed. Though their cries were as angry as those of the enemy, the undercurrent was that of resignation. The crew of the Redemption knew that they were likely to lose here and that the enemy would leave no survivors.

The roaring intensified as the boarding planks were run out on both sides, falling to the opposing deck and jamming there as the iron teeth fitted to the end dug into the boards; yet another potentially humorous moment unfolding as both sides tried to charge one another before the other could prepare.

The result was, of course, chaos. Men from both ships ran out onto the same boarding planks, meeting at the centre between the two vessels. The forces clashed in a sea of bellowing colour, men screaming and hollering as sword blows landed and helpless, desperate men fell from the planks into the churning waters, only to stare terrified and boggle-eyed at the hulls of the two ships as they trod water. The waves brought the hulls inexorably closer and closer together once more until they met with a crunch.

Ghassan winced at the sound of a dozen desperate cries being cut off instantly with that wooden bang.

The initial attack was beginning to slow. The numbers were thinning out and more people now fell foul of the drop between the hulls than made it either forward or back to either deck. The gore and viscera of the vicious fighting had, within the first minute, coated every ramp, making the crimson timber slippery and treacherous.

Anger was quickly giving way to frustration and desperation, as men from both sides fought as carefully as they could. Then, as Ghassan watched in horror, the figures of Samir and Saja appeared out of the rear of the Redemption's massed crew, nodded at one another, turned, and ran, using the banks of rowing seats as a launch pad.

From his vantage point on the command deck Ghassan watched, his heart in his throat, as the two men leapt across the gap with its bloody boards, crushing depths and battling men and came down in a heap on the enemy deck, amid a pushing crowd of surprised pirates, knocking a number of men to the deck as they hit.

The pair vanished from sight in a pile of men and the area suddenly became a focus of intense fighting. Ghassan closed his eyes.

'Samir, you bloody idiot!'

A call escaped his attention for a moment as it was almost lost in the noise of the battle raging around him and it took precious seconds for Ghassan to realise that the voice was addressing him from somewhere above. Raising his eyes and sheltering them from the brightness of the blue sky above, he spotted a young sailor at the top of the smaller rear sail, hanging onto the cross bar.

'What is it?'

The young man shouted something garbled that Ghassan couldn't quite make out and pointed toward the enemy ship's rigging. Ghassan frowned as he looked across at the sails, ropes and masts of the pirate vessel, with the shouting men dotted here and there among them. There was nothing unusual there. He frowned again and was just about to turn and try to frame a mouthed question at the lad when he saw it…not among the enemy ship's rigging, but behind them.

Two vessels! Not just one, but two! Saja's former ship: The Sea Witch. She'd not been officially part of the rebellion, so she had no new name and no Imperial pennant to fly, but she'd dropped her own colours and was sporting a plain green flag the captain had found somewhere.

And she was bearing down on their aggressor at a frightening pace, with Faerus' Retribution at her side, like a charge of heroes from the tales of old.

Ghassan took a deep breath.

'Stay safe, Samir. Help is on the way…'

In which a last assault begins

There was a moment when the madness of the act flashed across Samir's mind and almost shocked him to a standstill. He was a man who never did anything without a plan and at least one card up his sleeve. He had rarely in his adult life entered into any situation that he was not already absolutely sure of. There always had to be a way out.

Not this time.

For years he had bent every effort and guided every possible thread he could find to one end: to this very end. But once the governor had accepted the deal, the pirate fleet had been coerced or dealt with and the passage through the reefs had been sealed for all time, there had been no more plans. And now he had found himself fighting a sea action for which he was unprepared and which seemed to be heavily weighted in favour of the enemy. And the upshot of everything was that he had to do what he could without that all-too-important card up his sleeve.

In the press of men pushing up against the rail of the Redemption, trying to get to the rabid pirates on board the enemy vessel, Samir's mind had finally gone blank, leaving him floundering with no plan; directionless. He and his men had to gain the advantage over the much larger enemy, but he just kept coming up blank; there was no clear way.

Around him the men of his crew pushed and shouted, itching to prove their worth over the one remaining enemy vessel, and Samir could do nothing but watch helplessly.

He had jumped and almost lashed out when a hand clamped down on his shoulder. Swinging round, he found himself staring helplessly into the eyes of Saja, ex councillor of Lassos, renowned pirate lord and tactician and equally famed warrior. Saja's face wore a deep frown of concern, causing some of his tattoos to meet around the corner of his eye and his various gold adornments to move hypnotically around his face. Samir, his mind reeling with the unfamiliar feeling of uncertainty, found himself lost in the movements of the various rings and studs.

He suddenly realised that Saja was saying something to him, just as the man stopped and raised his brow, waiting for an answer.

Can't show my growing panic, Samir thought... not amid the crew.

Taking a deep breath, he held his hand to his ear, miming that he couldn't hear Saja over the rabble. The large, ebony-skinned captain nodded and, grasping Samir's shoulder harder, turned and propelled him back through the press and toward the open deck behind them.

As they left the heavy crowd, the councillor leaned close to Samir.

'We have to do something to break them.'

'Yes,' Samir nodded emphatically, 'but what?'

'It's up to us. Men fight twice as hard when they are led by men they believe in; you know that, Samir. It's up to us to turn the tables on the enemy.'

Samir nodded again, uncertainty still freezing his mind.

'But how?'

Saja shrugged as they neared the open space.

'We have to lead the attack. Give them something to aim for.'

Samir nodded, the uncertainty still filling his mind with emptiness. He had to do something. He was never this useless; always had the next five steps worked out.

So... they had to get ahead of the press and onto the enemy ship. They had to give them 'something to aim for' as Saja said. There was plainly only one thing they could do.

'We'll have to dive in feet first and come up fighting. We need to be the incentive.'

Saja nodded.

'Swing down from the rigging?'

'Too slow. Things could go badly by the time we've climbed up there and swung across. We need to get our men over there now, before they break us and we all end up fighting on the Redemption!'

'Then we need the clearest area and a good run up.'

Samir nodded and scanned the deck as the pair finally came out of the rear of the massed sailors.

'There... past the main mast. The place with the least men. That'll be where they break through first!'

Saja followed Samir's gaze and then turned to him and nodded. The two men jogged back across the deck, angling themselves so that when they turned back to the press, they were facing one of the remaining gaps where the mass of shouting sailors was thinnest.

'See you on the other side,' Samir laughed, the sudden direction giving him purpose and clearing his mind of the fluff that seemed to have settled there.

'Ha'Rish smile on us with a good face.'

The pair grinned and then ran. There was surprisingly little run up across the deck, and the charge was hampered a little by the many obstacles on the wooden boards, but the two men reached the raised benches of the oarsmen just behind the press of men and took an agile step, jump and then leap from the highest point, drawing their weapons as they rose.

Ghassan would not approve, Samir thought briefly as he watched the surprised upturned faces of the men of his ship while he passed over the top of them, and then the equally astonished raised faces of the enemy just before reality reasserted itself and the two men crashed back to the floor in a tangle of body parts. Fortunate they were that the enemy had been so taken by surprise that they'd not had time to react. Just one man having the forethought to raise a sword to the descending men could have put an end to the foolhardy attack all too soon.

As Samir and Saja felt the squashed bodies of fallen men and the hard surface of the deck boards beneath them, a roar went up from behind. Their attack had enthused the Redemption's crew and, hopefully, spurred them into a stronger push. The two had precious little time to think, though, and could pay no further heed to what was happening behind them. Already the effects of their shock arrival were wearing off and men nearby were picking themselves up and collecting weapons.

Samir struggled to his hands and knees, his fist wrapped around the hilt of his short sword and supporting his weight as he tried to take stock of the immediate situation. As he turned, he found himself face to face with one of the pirates, picking himself up in the same fashion. As their eyes met, the man tried to free the blade in his hand enough to manage a stab at this mad captain. Samir, instinct taking over as always, had already considered and then abandoned the sword as an option. Still leaning on that hand, he lashed out with his free fist, punching the crouched pirate full in the face, shattering his nose and knocking the man flat.

As the stunned man toppled to the side, his hand came up and Samir reached out and calmly plucked the longer, curved blade from it. Standing slowly, hefting his shorter Imperial sword in his right hand and the long, curved desert blade in the other, Samir remembered a day, so long ago, when he had stood on a ruined tower at the edge of M'Dahz with their uncle Faraj teaching them the difference between the two and why they had to learn the use of different weapons.

He smiled grimly as he twisted his wrist and spun the straight blade in his hand. The nearest pirate took a look at his face, the man's gaze passing down first to one hand and then the other, and he carefully backed away into the press of men.

Behind him, Saja had acted with much less flourish, style and honour, but with considerably more effect. As the big man had come to his senses on the floor, on top of two fallen pirates, but surrounded by many more still standing, he had brandished his weapon, elbowed a little room and then taken as strong a swing as he could.

Despite the lack of space, Saja was a powerful man, huge muscles rippling under his dark and decorated skin, and the golden bangles jangled as he scythed out with his own curved blade, cutting easily through calves, shins, knees and hamstrings. The effect was horrifying. Blood pumped from a dozen wounds and begun to flood the area as men collapsed in a screaming mass at this sudden and debilitating attack. And, as the pirates above him fell like a field of wheat before the scythe, Saja rose from the mass, slowly, covered in fresh blood and brandishing his evil blade while grinning like some monster from legend.

Samir stood slowly, a sword in each hand, and nodded to his companion. The attack had certainly started something. Back among the press, he could see occasional faces he recognised from the crew of the Redemption, snarling and shouting among the enemy. Samir's crew had begun to push once more.

The pirates were being pressed by a considerably smaller force, against all odds, and Samir and Saja grinned as they faced a motley collection of nervous-looking men, waiting for the tense standoff to break, after their initial onslaught.

The first strike came suddenly, after three heartbeats had passed, which had felt like months. The man closest to Samir lunged with the speed of a viper and Samir had to step back to parry the blow with his short Imperial blade, stumbling slightly into Saja, who consequently almost fell foul of a simultaneous attack from the other side.

In the brief moment that followed before all hell broke loose, Samir took the opportunity to swap hands with the two blades, the heavy, curved sword in his right, striking hand, the smaller straight Imperial blade in the left for parrying. He barely had time to get a full grip before the force hit them.

The men around Samir and Saja came in like a tide, the ripples of a cast stone in reverse, swinging curved blades and lunging with short swords and long knives, the attack only faltering a little through lack of organisation and room to manoeuvre.

Samir found he had no time to make an attack of his own, being forced instead to raise and shift both swords in a constant whirr of steel in order to block the various blades that thrust, swiped and cut at him. Even so, in the massive press of men, he felt three blows land in the initial flurry: one glancing blow cutting a thin sliver of flesh from his upper arm just below the shoulder, another taking a small piece from his earlobe and the third cutting deep into his outer thigh.

Another set of blows like that and he'd be down! He was damned lucky none of those three had been debilitating, as they easily could have. Behind him, Saja yelped as a blow bit home somewhere on his powerful physique.

And then there was chaos. After the initial surprise and the standoff, then the tentative lunges, the full-blown assault by the enemy had given the defending men all the incentive they needed, and Samir and Saja found themselves beleaguered and fighting desperately for their lives, parrying blow after blow and managing only rarely to get in a thrust or swing of their own as opportunity allowed.

Again and again Samir felt the shock of swords hitting his desperately-raised blade and sliding with a jarring, grating feel down the blade. More blows connected, drawing blood and leaving fine lines or small wounds on his flesh. Samir was a good swordsman; maybe as good as Saja, even, but no man could hope to hold his own for long in a pressing circle of dozens of bloodthirsty, screaming enemies.

This was it. No regrets, of course. What they did, leaping in among the enemy, had been the spur the men of the Redemption had needed and had changed the whole direction of the battle. Ghassan and Culin had better take advantage of the change and use it, or their sacrifice would have been in vain.

Another blow, well placed while Samir's own swords were raised to block other attacks, swung in beneath his guard and cut deeply just above his left knee.

Some muscle or cord had been severed, Samir realised as he desperately swung with his curved blade. The strength left his leg instantly and he collapsed like a sack of grain, the blade spinning out of his hand and bouncing along the boards between the legs of the attackers. He watched with dismay as the curved weapon came to a halt perhaps a foot out of reach among the stamping feet.

He stared at it as he crumpled, his head hitting the deck, hard. A foot, perhaps, but it might as well be a league. Out of reach.

He tried pushing himself up, but his vision exploded in shards of white light and he realised through the heavy pulsing of his blood as it pounded round his brain, that the deck beneath his head was slick with dark blood that was pouring from his own skull.

He flailed and tried to raise the short sword in his left hand, but there was so little strength there and no coordination in his head. The blade wobbled for a moment before it toppled from his grasp and fell to the floor.

He realised he'd fallen back again only as the board hit the cracked area at the back of his skull and his vision blurred.

He'd always wondered how it happened. When Ha'Rish turned her masked face to you and your soul went with her, did you see the Goddess? He squinted through the shattered fragments of white light and the growing fug deep in his brain, trying to see whether Ha'Rish had come for him personally.

Perhaps not, he sighed, as his vision briefly swam into focus long enough to identify a heavy-set man with a blue whorled pattern tattooed on his face as the pirate raised a straight and wide sword in both hands, point down, to drive it through Samir's chest and finish him at last.

Given the rather insistent pain, it might be a blessing. Samir let his limbs loosen and fall to the deck as he watched the glinting point of the sword descend.

Somehow, superimposed over the falling blade, he finally saw the masked face of Ha'Rish.

She wasn't as beautiful, even in her death-masked image, as he'd expected. In fact, she might very well be said to be quite ugly.

Samir sighed as the blackness descended. At least she could have been pretty…

Saja grasped Samir by the shoulders, a sudden panic descending on him as the men of the Redemption swept around him and began to push the desperate pirate crew back. The Sea Witch and the Retribution were moments away, their own boarding ramps already raised and ready to help. In mere moments, the whole attack had been turned. The two commanders' attack had begun something that simply could not be stopped, even by sheer weight of numbers, and the sight of their sister ship and Saja's old vessel bearing down to help them had lent renewed vigour to the attack.

The news had, however, had a somewhat different effect on the pirates. Their earlier resolution lost, panic had set in. There would be no hope for them. If they surrendered, only a gibbet and a very public death awaited but, if they stayed here they would only be carved to pieces by the three victorious crews.

And so they had broken, some diving overboard, others trying to find somewhere to hide from the now overwhelming enemy force.

Saja frowned at Samir's still form. Only a moment ago, as he'd swept aside the last pirate who'd been intent on finishing the job, he'd seen Samir, eyes open and smiling. And then suddenly he'd gone limp and slumped.

With breath held, heart thumping in his throat, he leaned down to Samir's chest and put his ear to the man's tunic.

A voice from above spoke in a leaden, hollow tone.

'Well?'

Saja looked up and his ebony face burst into a wide, toothy grin.

'He'll be alright, Captain Ghassan. So long as that head's bound quickly. He's a survivor, your brother.'

The tall first officer brushed the ever-present curl of black hair from his eyes and sighed with relief.

'Close, Saja. Too close for you two mad bastards!'

In which Retribution is the watchword

The governor's flagship was a magnificent vessel. Ghassan could hardly take his eyes from the thing as he was greeted at the top of the rope ladder and gestured toward the main deck by a deferential sailor. Waving aside the man, he turned and helped Saja bring his wounded and bandaged brother up the last section, Master Culin below adding support as he pushed Samir toward the top.

The governor stood on the command platform with a number of important looking personages and Samir shook his head gently as he reached the deck and planted his wobbly legs as firmly as he could on the timber, accepting Ghassan's offered arm for support.

Saja and Culin took up positions in surreptitiously supportive places around the young captain who had, against all odds and despite the innumerable immense obstacles, brought a fleet of vicious pirates to battle against one another until the only ones that remained afloat flew the flag of the Empire. The four men waited a moment until the windswept head of Captain Faerus appeared over the edge of the deck.

'I see no one feels the need to help me aboard, just because I didn't have the idiotic bad sense to try and personally tackle an entire crew of howling lunatics.'

He grinned as Culin reached down and grasped his hand, hauling him aboard.

The five men, the leaders of the pirate rebellion, stood for a moment, recovering, before following the beckoning form of the second officer aboard the Pride of Calphoris.

The climb up the stairs to the command deck was easier, though still a little delicate, given the condition of three of the five men. Ghassan still winced occasionally as movements pulled the stitches in his back, Saja was criss-crossed with minor cuts and abrasions and Samir... The doctor on board the Redemption had been typically sarcastic, but had begun work on stitching and binding the various wounds before the captain had even been given a sedative; a testament to how bad he considered Samir's condition.

That had been almost five hours ago and the doctor had been quite vocal in his refusal to let Samir out of his sight, even at the governor's request until, Ghassan had given him a direct order to his quarters.

While the doctor had worked, the crews of the three ships had swept the site of the battle, noting the locations of the various sunken wrecks mostly from the flotsam and jetsam and the bobbing, bloated bodies that had not yet been pulled down as they lay draped over random spars of wood or shattered pieces of broken deck.

The saddest had been the site of Orin's ship, the Revenge. No sign had been found of any survivors in the area, but the pieces of charred timber and the various unpleasant things the searchers did locate had told a horrible story.

Still, Orin had fought, like all of them, for what he believed to be right and it was partially through his sacrifice that the five remaining leaders reached the top of the stairs and crossed the command deck of the massive, outsized daram to the waiting officers opposite.

Marshal Tythias and Commodore Jaral, standing to one side of the governor, bore unreadable expressions. Ghassan realised he was having a little difficulty meeting the gaze of his old captain, even in Jaral's new exalted role as commander of the navy. The presence of a clearly very important Pelasian Satrap, dressed in his elegant black robes, and sporting numerous marks of rank and decorations, was more of a surprise. Ghassan recognised some of the markings that identified the officer as the commander of the Pelasian royal fleet.

'All five of you?' the governor asked in surprise. 'I thought I saw one of your ships disappear in a fireball. I was expecting only four.'

Samir nodded wearily, wincing at the pain in his head.

'I beg a slight change in the contract, governor.'

The man frowned suspiciously.

'One does not usually change the conditions of a deal after it is done, Captain Samir.'

'I'm aware of that, Excellency, but there are… circumstances.'

He glanced along the line.

'Captain Orin, as you astutely noted, is no longer with us, having given his life for the cause. However, we were very fortunate to have, as a last minute ally, Master Culin of the Lassos council.'

'Culin?' the governor snapped. 'The man is wanted on a hundred different charges! Piracy is merely somewhere on the list. This is hardly what I agreed to!'

The target of his bile stepped out from the line and bowed slightly to the governor.

'With respect, your Excellency, you will find upon investigation, that more than half of those charges are erroneous or at least inflated.'

As the governor glared at him, he cast a mischievous smile back.

'Indeed, if you give me a couple of days, I think you'll find that my charge sheet is almost clear!'

'What?'

Culin grinned.

'Come now, governor. You must be aware of just how many people I have among your people. If I'd wished, I could have cleared my name years ago. But I would rather it were done in a legitimate manner.'

The governor glared at him and then turned the look on Samir.

'You could do far worse, governor. Master Culin truly is a master, of many things. I think you would find him a serious asset in the admiralty. Certainly I'd rather have him working for me than against me…'

The governor's glare refused to shift and Samir sighed and withdrew a folded and worn sheet of parchment from his tunic.

'And this particular item was not part of our agreement, but I will proffer it as an extra incentive to accept the change in terms.'

The governor reached out and accepted the parchment, his scowl remaining deep as he unfolded it and read the neat script on the inner surface.

'What is this? A list of names? Who are these people?'

Samir's grin became darkly mischievous.

'Those are all the people I slipped aboard your ships over the last few years. You may want to honourably discharge them all, since they've done you no harm and served as well as any other sailor.'

Next to him, Ghassan blinked.

'You really did have men on board their ships? I assumed that was a lie to goad the council into action?' he asked, his voice hovering somewhere between astonishment and anger. 'Not sure I'd have gone along with this if I'd known that.'

Samir laughed quietly.

'I like to have a cushion to fall back on, Ghassan. You know that. There was always the possibility that the governor would not accept my offer, and I had to be prepared.'

Ghassan stared at his brother helplessly as Samir turned back to the governor.

'Straight deal time, governor. You accept the five of us with amnesty into your service and I give you a guaranteed end to the pirate island.'

The governor turned and whispered something into the ear of Marshal Tythias. The two men, along with Commodore Jaral retreated a few paces and then fell into a brief whispered discussion while the Pelasian admiral watched them, an unreadable expression on his face. After a long minute, the three officers turned and strode back across to them.

'Very well. The deal is this: Samir, Ghassan, Saja and Faerus will be pardoned entirely and accepted into the Imperial navy at the rank of captain, with their own commands, as per your original request. Our offer with respect to master Culin is on different terms, however. We offer an amnesty for all his crimes to date, but without Imperial naval enlistment and on the understanding that he "disappears" as far as we are concerned.'

Samir shook his head.

'That's…'

He was cut off mid-sentence as the Pelasian admiral gestured at Culin.

'In that case, I would like to offer a position to this man. The Pelasian navy is more than aware of Culin's accomplishments. I think we can use you?'

Culin shrugged.

'How's the weather in Pelasia.'

'Hot,' the man replied with a tight smile. 'Always hot.'

Samir looked back and forth between the two until Culin gave a small nod.

'Looks like you have a deal, governor, though I think you've let a major asset slip your fingers there. Be very wary of the Pelasian navy now.'

The governor nodded.

'Then only one thing remains.'

His eyes rose to the mist on the horizon and the black rock of Lassos' peak rising from the centre. Samir nodded and turned to his brother.

'Ghassan?'

Fishing in his tunic, the taller brother retrieved the bronze disk with its grizzly needle and displayed it openly to the men before them.

'And I have your word this is what you said it was?'

Samir nodded.

'The dead man's compass. Since the Hart's Heart took the other one to the bottom of the sea a few hours ago, this is the last. Moreover, I have taken extra steps to cutting off any future hope of navigating the reefs. You need have no more fear of the pirate island, governor. This is an end of it.'

He turned and nodded at Ghassan and the tall captain strode across to the rail nearby. With a curious smile, he changed his grip on the bronze compass and, nestling it in an underarm position, cast it with all his might out into the sea, where it hit the surface, skimmed three times and then disappeared with a plop, sinking to a watery grave.

The governor nodded as Ghassan returned to the group.

'Then our business is complete, Captain Samir. Welcome to the Imperial navy. I believe Commodore Jaral has had rather a large cask of some corrosive liquid stored below deck in order to celebrate... I have it on authority that there are rites of passage you must endure that defy official terms. I presume you are in no rush to return to your ships?'

Samir glanced back and forth between his friends and noted their grins.

'I think we can spare some time to carouse with our fellow officers, Excellency.'

Epilogue

The sun was beginning to sink below the horizon as Ghassan and Samir rested on the side rail of the Imperial flagship and stared out across the glittering sea. Ghassan had been careful with the drink below, aware at all times of the gaze of Commodore Jaral, and not entirely sure of where he now stood with his former captain, Still, he was back in a position of command and, even if Jaral still held misgivings, Ghassan would soon put them to one side and make his name a noble one again.

Life was suddenly a sea of possibilities. He smiled at the smaller captain by his side. Samir also had partaken only of a couple of drinks, the thumping of the blood in his wounded skull making him light-headed and fuzzy after only a few mouthfuls.

'You did it, Samir. You redeemed both of us.'

Samir nodded, wincing.

'More than that, Ghassan, I think, but it wasn't just me. I may have been the central peg that held things together, but this was the work of several of us, including the governor and Culin and Saja… but most of all, I agree, it was the sons of Nadia.'

Smiling, he raised his cup to the darkening sky.

'To mother and uncle Faraj, wherever you may be. Your boys have made you proud at last.'

Ghassan raised his own cup and took a quick sip.

'It seems like a thousand years since mother died and I lost all hope. And it was you. It was always you, with your "things will be better", that kept me going. Through everything. Everything we lost and so many times we met as enemies, but you never lost sight of that, did you? Everything "being better" was always your goal.'

Samir smiled.

'After what we went through, I think we deserve a little of everything being better, don't you?'

Ghassan laughed quietly.

'It's to be hoped we never go to war against Pelasia again. I'd hate to come up against a navy with Culin behind it!'

Samir laughed a genuine laugh and the two fell silent, watching the light fade in the west, taking with it the old world and bringing the possibility of the new.

The desert nomads have a saying.

'When something is broken it should never be discarded. So long as the pieces remain, the whole can be remade.'

Karo was, and he'd be the first to admit it, not a nice man. He'd never been one and piracy had been a natural course for him. After years of fighting in the pits in Calphoris to harden himself, he'd turned to mugging folk as a way to make ends meet. He'd discovered how much he liked to kill that very way, when a mugging went wrong and he'd been forced to dispatch the target. It had been messy and gratuitous. And he'd enjoyed it so much that he'd repeated it the next time; and the next.

Only when the heat from the authorities had become just too much had he had to flee the streets and make for the port where he began the long journey that would lead to him, more than a decade later, being the commander of a boarding party aboard the pirate vessel Diamond Devil. He'd had an illustrious career serving under Captain Corun and everything had been rosy until the last couple of days. Then that damned Samir and his treacherous friends had come back and brought disaster with them.

Corun had dithered when the fleet suddenly started attacking itself and it had taken the first officer's presence of mind to persuade him to turn and chase down the Hart's Heart and the Dark Princess, in the hope of killing Samir and getting back to Lassos. And then everything had gone wrong. Somehow, despite being in the favourable position, things had gone so damn badly wrong that he'd had to stop in the middle of scalping some bastard from the Empress and jump into the sea to avoid capture and death following the sudden arrival of the Sea Witch and Faerus' damn ship.

He'd seen a few dozen others hit the water around him. Some had been crushed between the hulls. Others had probably drowned, but he paid them no mind. Now they were no longer on the ship, it was every man for himself. A question of survival. And so he'd struck out for the rocks.

Of course, people said things about the reefs, and he'd seen the ghosts himself, but they were there to stop ships getting through, not individuals. It would take a long time for a man to get from rock to rock all the way to the island, but he knew he could do it.

The first rock felt cold and slimy. He slid his hands up the clammy surface until he could peer over the top. There they were in the mist: figures in grey, robed and threatening. But, just as he'd thought, none directly around him. They were a deterrent. They always appeared nearby, not on the rock where you actually were. A deterrent, pure and simple. They must be some sort of magic, as they couldn't really exist.

He grasped the top with his fingers and hauled himself up.

The next rock was clear too. He'd make it there and then decide where to head next. Hauling against the wet, cold stone, he pulled himself over the crest to a dip beyond and found himself staring up at a grey figure.

His eyes widened as the phantom smiled and the effect, as that wet and rubbery grey face stretched and contorted to show a hundred needle teeth, was truly terrifying.

'Gharic?'

His heart stopped in shock, but not before the cold, dead, grey hands of the former captain of the pirate ship Hart's Heart closed on his cheeks and the wraith fed.

Asima awoke to silence. She was clearly in some sort of hold. The bulkhead timbers and barrels reminded her of the room that Samir had last kept her held in. Well, this time there would be no sweetness and complicity... Samir would just have to die. She'd like to do it slowly; to peel the flesh from his limbs while lightly salting him, but she might just have to go for a knife in the back. That hadn't done for Ghassan, though. Maybe the neck. A blade straight through the side and then ripped out of the front; that would do it. Everything vital in one go... messy, but quick and sure. Ghassan may be deformed, but nobody could claim their throat was in a different place.

She moved and groaned.

How long had she been unconscious here? She could hear the lapping of waves but no voices. She moved again and realised that some of her discomfort came from the piece of wreckage under her head.

She squinted, her eyes gradually becoming accustomed to the dimness in here, a boarded up window letting in only minimal light. There was a shattered lump of wood she'd been using as a pillow; several broken boards torn from the wall of a building or some such. Her head tilted to one side as she examined the boards and sudden anger flashed deep in her eyes as she realised where they had come from, their origin betrayed by the elegantly painted slogan: Dark Empress.

She raged silently for a moment in the privacy of her head.

He was going to have to suffer, after all. No quick kill. Trouble or no trouble, Samir deserved slow and painstaking. She pulled herself up to her knees and realised that a note had been pinned to the bottom of the section of hull that had been torn from the side of Samir's ship.

Angrily, she ripped the square of parchment from the shattered timbers and straightened, stretching. Who the hell did that little monster think he was? When Asima got hold of him, she'd stretch his death to take days, or even weeks. She looked around the small cabin and noted the faint glimmer of light around the cracks of a door. A proper cabin on a daram, then, and not down below in the hold somewhere.

Unfolding the parchment and concentrating in the low light, she read the short note as she approached the door, her expression moving slowly as she read down the page from puzzlement to anger and finally to plain horror.

She read the last line and allowed the paper to fall from her shaking hands as she threw open the door to see not the corridor and deck of a daram, but a jetty marching back through the water to the harbour of Lassos, the black mountain hovering high above.

Her cry was heard by no living soul. Nor would any other she ever made.

My dearest Asima

I feel that the situation is painfully obvious, but I do believe that your arrogance blinds you to certain truths and so I feel the need to explain this to you.

My ship, the Dark Empress, is no more. Like the phoenix of legend, she has risen from the flames of battle and been reborn as the Retribution and, if you think just a little, I believe you'll understand why.

The ship has a long history, and 'Dark Empress' is not the first name by which it was known. Back in the early days of the Emperor Quintus, the ship was commissioned under an Imperial order and, with its sister ships of that order, was named for members of the Imperial family. This ship took the name of Sabinia, the Emperor's mother. She was, as you may be aware from your histories, one of the family line that fell foul of the hereditary insanity of the dynasty. When she began to manifest her vicious madness in acts of random, senseless violence and megalomania, and was finally 'disappeared' for the good of the Empire, the Imperial ship of the line Sabinia became the 'Dark Empress', for that is what Quintus' mother will ever be remembered as.

But the ship, like her captain and crew, has been redeemed.

We are reborn into Imperial service and the title of Dark Empress, passed from Sabinia to my ship, needs to be passed on, to divorce us from this wickedness.

But, and I imagine you can see where I am going with this, there is an obvious successor. Like Sabinia, a promising, beautiful and clever young woman who descended into vicious madness and megalomania, this new 'Dark Empress' has reached the point where she needs to be 'disappeared' for the good of the world as a whole.

And Lassos will be no more. No living foot other than yours will step on the cursed island ever again. You can no longer visit your evil upon the innocent people of the world but, like a soothsayer friend of mine once told you, you were destined to rule as an Empress.

I hope your Empire trembles at the sound of your commands.

I wish you luck in your rule. May it be long and peaceful.

Your friend,

Samir.

Read on with the future of the empire with all the books in the series, including the latest instalment Insurgency (2016):

INSURGENCY

BY S.J.A. TURNEY

PROLOGUE

There is a strange saying among the northern folk:

'A tripod may stand solid, but a ladder can be climbed.'

The Emperor Kiva moved about his court like a gilded moth, flittering from flame to flame, moving on briskly before his wings were singed. A tall, willowy figure with slim build and slender fingers, a wise contemplative face and his father's eyes, Kiva played the role of ruler of the civilized world with aplomb. He was a master of tact and tactics, playing down the argumentative, suppressing the sycophantic, embracing the distant and fending off the o'er-close. Even now, as he was cornered by some brash western lord with rosy cheeks and an even rosier nose, Kiva laughed off some accidental slight, deftly swiping a crystal goblet of wine from a passing tray, slipping it smoothly into the drunken lord's hand and removing the empty with barely a glance. As the lord realized he had a full glass once more, he reached down and took a deep swig. When he looked up, the emperor was gone, swirling in the dance of sociability, quick-stepping with an ambassador from Pelasia.

Quintillian watched from the sidelines.

Not for him the pageantry of the imperial celebrations. He danced with the best of men, but only when his hand held a blade and the end of the dance meant the end of a life. Instead, the younger brother of the emperor, senior marshal of the armies and lord of Vengen, stood on a narrow, balustraded balcony overlooking the grand events of the evening, half hidden in the shadows above the hall. Here, in the old days, musicians would sit by lamplight playing their hearts out. In these times it was more common for such entertainment to be placed among the guests for better captivation of their melody.

The balcony was dark and Quintillian smiled as he took a sip of his wine and watched his brother at work. They had always been close, he and Kiva, closer than most brothers. But their father had brought them up like that – to believe that family was all and that nothing in the world had the right, nor the power, to stand between two brothers who loved each other. Their father, of course, had suffered in his life, losing the friend who had been as close as a brother – Quintillian's namesake, in fact – during the great interregnum. And he had lost a father – a *great* father – before he had even found out who he was. And so the Emperor Darius had instilled in his sons the need for that bond and for a closeness with no secrets.

No secrets…

Some secrets were kept out of love, though. Hadn't their father ever considered that?

It had been a hard time, five years ago, when their father had died. Darius had been an active emperor and a good one, long-reigning. After the 20 years of civil war and anarchy, he had put the empire back together, healed the wounds of the land and its people, and initiated a golden age that had lasted longer than anyone could have hoped. When he had finally passed on, in his chambers on the island of Isera, it had been after a full life and with a reign fulfilled. And he had followed all his friends to the grave, knowing that they were all waiting for him in the afterlife, for he was not a man to believe in the divinity of rulers, just like his sons.

Kiva had taken the purple cloak and the obsidian sceptre, the orb of the heavens in his other hand, the very next day. There had, of course, been no dissent over the natural succession of the eldest son, though there *had* been a few voices that had expressed the quiet, careful opinion that the younger brother might have been stronger in the role. Not that they would have pushed for a change, and most certainly Quintillian would have refused. Not that he couldn't have done the job, not that he would be unwilling to, but his brother was natural heir and that was all there was to it.

And Kiva was good at it. There was no denying that.

Five years to the day since the accession and the blessings, that purple cloak almost gleaming in the sun, so well brushed was the velvet. Five years of growth for the empire and of peace within its borders. Five years of strong economies and excellent external relations. It had seemed wholly appropriate to celebrate such a milestone in this manner, with everyone of any rank both within and without the empire all gathered at the palace in Velutio. And among the tanned visages of the imperial lords, governors, officers and administrators, there were different faces – *interesting* faces. The King of the Gotii beyond the Pula mountains with his retinue, for instance. It was the first time those violent raiders had visited the capital – the first time in the empire's history when relations between the two peoples had been good enough. The Gota king sat with his three wives and his close companions not far from the emperor's seat. He was a tall and broad man with a flat face, strong jaw, flaxen hair and ice blue eyes. His wives were... well, Quintillian had oft heard it said that the Gota prized strength and ability to bear children above simple looks. It had taken Quintillian some time to distinguish the wives from the bodyguards, of whom there were five, including relations of the king himself. They had been denied the right to carry weapons this close to the emperor, but there was no doubt in Quintillian's mind that each of them could kill in the blink of an eye with just their bare hands. And there was the king's seer: an old man with hair down to his backside, who wore dirty rags and the pelts of a number of unfortunate small animals, their bones clattering in his hair as he moved. He gave Quintillian the shivers, not least since he seemed to be the only person aware that the younger brother was here, having looked up into the shadows directly at him.

There were other northern chieftains who were in the process of buying into the imperial model in Kiva's new world, too, though they all looked a little like the Gota king would have, had he tried to assimilate into imperial culture.

There were two kings from the dark-skinned lands south of Pelasia. *They* were interesting, but required a translator to pass even the slightest time of day, and Quintillian's brief introduction to them at the start of the celebration had been hard work. Their world was so alien, and most of Quintillian's hungry questions had been lost on them with no mutual frame of reference. Invitations had even been sent to the lords of that peculiar eastern world beyond the steppes from whence silk came, though they had not come. Very likely the messengers never reached those lands. Few did, for the route to the silk lands crossed the most dangerous territories in the world. That had been a shame, though.

Quintillian liked the feel of silk and it was said that the sharper a blade was, the more likely the miraculous material was to turn it aside. The idea of a light fabric that could stop a blade was simply too fascinating to him. One day, if they did not come here, he would have to go to them.

And, of course, there were the Pelasians. Three of their highest nobles were present, including a prince of the realm. Young Ashar Parishid, though – son of Ashar the great, and God-King of Pelasia – sadly could not be here. A riding accident had left him with a badly broken leg a week earlier, and he had been advised by the best physicians in the world that he would recover fully, but there was simply no way he could leave his chambers for several weeks. It must have been a terrible blow for Ashar, for while he and the emperor – and Quintillian too, for that matter – were as close friends as it was possible for neighbouring rulers to be, Ashar would be particularly missing the opportunity to visit his beloved sister.

Jala.

The empress.

Jala, unlike her husband, sat upon her comfortable divan at the heart of proceedings, smiling and doling out compliments. Each of her honeyed words was as sought after as a lordship or a chest of gold, and each was prized and tightly-held once received. Her soft skin, the light brown of the deep desert, was more on show than was traditional among imperial ladies. But then Jala was no ordinary imperial lady. She was a Princess of Pelasia, sister to the god-king, and now, for five years, wife of the Emperor Kiva. And she was exquisite.

Yes, some secrets had to be kept for the good of all concerned.

For two years now, Kiva had been pushing him to marry – to take a wife from among the many beauties of the imperial court. His brother simply could not understand why Quintillian remained alone. But how could he marry a woman knowing that his heart was already in the care of another. It beat silently, deep in his chest, only for Jala. And it would beat silently for her until the end of his days, for even the hint of such a thing carried the scent of tragedy, and neither Kiva nor Jala deserved such a thing. So Quintillian would remain alone. What need had he of a wife, anyway? True soldiers should not take wives, for a warrior took a promising girl and turned her into a hollow widow. It was the way of things. And while there was no true need for an officer of such high command to involve himself directly in combat, there was something in the song of steel and the dance of blades that called to Quintillian. He could no more refuse to fight than he could refuse to breathe… than he could open his heart…

Something was happening now, down in the hall. Quintillian squinted into the thick, cloying atmosphere of oil lamps, braziers and incense.

An argument had broken out between two guests. Ordinarily such things would be unthinkable in the imperial presence, but the variety of uncivilized figures present had made such things almost an inevitability. That was why his favourite marshal, Titus, son of Tythias, had positioned burly, competent imperial guards in strategic positions around the hall, subtly armed.

Quintillian contemplated descending from the balcony to deal with the problem, but Titus's men were already moving to contain the trouble, so the younger brother relaxed a little and leaned on the balustrade, watching.

'Trouble,' muttered a familiar voice behind him. Quintillian didn't rise or turn, simply smiling as he continued to lean on the balcony.

'Titus. How did you know where I was?'

'I am your brother's best officer and commander of his guard. I know where *everyone* is. It's part of my job.' Titus Tythianus slipped in next to Quintillian, leaning his scarred forearms on the stone rail, waggling his nine remaining fingers.

'Yes, it seems there's a spot of trouble,' Quintillian noted. 'Shall we intervene?'

Titus snorted. 'Not unless they threaten *imperial* guests. In some of these cultures they murder each other for entertainment. If it gets out of hand my men will deal with it. It's unseemly anyway for a member of the imperial family to involve himself in a brawl.'

Quintillian chuckled and watched as the two arguing groups moved closer.

'I recognize the Gota one, but I can't place the white-haired one,' Quintillian said conversationally.

Below, the crowd was beginning to pull apart, leaving a circle at the centre where one of the Gotii – a strapping young man... not a woman? No, not one of the wives. A big strong warrior with a face like an abused turnip was stamping his feet like a petulant child, roaring imprecations in a tongue that sounded like someone gargling with broken glass. The crowd was fascinated, though not enough to involve themselves any closer than at the level of interested spectator.

At the far side of the expanding circle, one of the northern lords was sneering and waving a deprecating finger at the Gota warrior. But it was not that lord who was stepping forward. It was a strange pale figure. Both northerners – lord and servant – looked in build and physical make-up to have far more in common with the king of the Gotii than their imperial hosts, yet they wore breeches and tunic in the imperial style, if of an outdated northern cut and in semi-barbaric colours.

Borderlanders.

It was a recent process, begun by the Emperor Darius, but continued by Kiva in the same vein. You took the barbarian tribes who lived around the borders and you brought them to the empire. You introduced them to the benefits of imperial culture, engineering and science, and you dazzled them with what they could have. Then you offered to send them men to help build aqueducts and temples, bridges and mills. You often built their chiefs palaces to house their egos. And all you asked in return was that they pay lip service to the emperor and protect the borders from the less civilized barbarians beyond. As a system it made sense. And it had proven to work, too, for already, a decade on, some of those barbarian nobles had brought their lands into the empire entire, becoming lords in their own right and expanding the borders through gentle, subtle assimilation, as the same process then began on the tribes beyond.

But they were decades away from being true imperial subjects, even if that were *ever* to happen.

Certainly, looking at the behaviour unfolding in the hall below, this particular northern border lord seemed to be far from cultured.

'The noble is Aldegund, Lord of Adrennas,' Titus said quietly. 'He's one of the ones your father first settled. He's been a lord now for over five years, and two more semi-barbarian border tribes owe him fealty already. He's all right, I suppose. A bit brash and still far from courtier material, but he's loyal and he knows he's onto a good thing. His ghost I don't know, but he's a reedy fellow. Don't much fancy his chances against the Gota.'

'Will you have your men stop it?'

Titus shook his head. 'Aldegund should know better, and his man is about to learn a horrible lesson. But once he's seen this, he won't do the same again. The Gotii take insults very personally, and they cleanse their spirit of insult with the blood of the offender. That pale, ghostly fellow is about to die. Unless he's very lucky. Maybe the Gota warrior's feeling generous and he'll just rip off an arm. They are celebrating and having a drink after all.'

The Gota warrior had removed his leather vest and was stretching his arms, moving like a dancer. Quintillian appreciated his form. He was a warrior bred to the art. The white-haired, pale northerner opposite him just sneered and took another drink from his cup.

'He really doesn't know what he's in for,' Titus snorted.

Quintillian frowned. 'A gold corona on the pale one.'

Titus' eyebrow ratcheted upward. 'Are you mad?'

'He's not afraid.'

'Maybe that's because he's stupid? Aldegund certainly seems to be. And that half-naked warrior is the third bastard son of the Gota king. He'll have been trained with the best of the Gotii.'

'There's something about the white one. I think you're underestimating him. Is it a wager?'

'Damn right it's a wager,' Titus retorted. 'And make it five.'

'Five it is.'

Down below, the crowd was now in a wide circle around the two combatants, Titus's guardsmen in plain evidence, making sure the duel was contained. The Gota was snarling again in his horrible language. The icy white opponent was examining his nails.

'Make it ten,' Quintillian said quietly.

'Done.'

At a command from the king, the two men moved towards one another. On the balcony, Quintillian glanced to the side. Titus looked hungry, like a spectator at the pit fights, and the sight of him leering down at the two men made the prince smile.

The Gota warrior struck the first blow, which had seemed inevitable. Stepping the last pace into the fight, the hairy north-easterner with the naked torso and the leather kirtle delivered a powerful punch to the ghost's upper left arm at a point that would surely deaden the muscle for some time. Barely had the white-haired northerner had a breath to recover before the second blow took him in the gut, followed by a head-butt that sent him staggering back a pace. The Gota threw his arms out and roared as his father and the other Gotii cheered him on. The crowd thrummed with inappropriate interest.

'Easiest money I'll ever make,' snorted Titus.

'I'm still not so sure.'

The white man was stepping slowly back, regaining his senses as he went, while the Gota played to the crowd, roaring and beating his chest.

'He's not really got going yet,' Titus hissed. 'I've fought Gotii. This is just warming up. I kid you not – he'll rip off the man's arm. I've seen it done and by smaller Gotii than him!'

'He's predictable. The ghost isn't.'

'*I* predict he's going to die,' said Titus. 'He never even raised a fist to block that flurry!'

'Precisely. He never even tried. He was seeing what the man could do. Testing him.'

'If he's very lucky he'll test him to death.'

The pale figure had stopped now and was pacing forward again. He still didn't appear prepared for the fight. He was sauntering as though he wandered quiet gardens. The Gota warrior snarled and came on once more, smacking his fists against his hips and then bringing up his hands into a fighting stance. As they closed to three or four paces the Gota leapt, swinging his punch, aiming for the pale man's other arm to deaden a second muscle and leave him largely helpless.

It all happened in such a blur that the pair on the balcony almost missed it. A moment later, the ghost was standing behind his opponent and the Gota was dead.

Titus blinked.

As the burly warrior had swung and stepped into the strike, the white-haired man had simply bent like a stalk of grass in the wind, slipped beneath the lunging arm, and delivered his own blows – three in such quick succession that they were almost invisible to the naked eye. But Quintillian had seen the angle of the moves and could see the results clearly enough to identify the strikes. The numb arm he'd been unable to raise but he had instead used it to grab hold of the pronounced hamstring behind his opponent's knee, wrenching it agonizingly. And even in the blink of an eye that his opponent had begun to collapse, white-hair's other hand had jabbed twice. The first blow had struck at the point where shoulder meets neck, paralysing the muscle there and thus – along with the hamstring – rendering the Gota's entire left side useless. But as quick as the thumb had left the flesh, it struck again, a jagged thumbnail tearing a small nick in the neck. It was a minute hole. But it was well placed. The vein beneath was an important one, and the dark blood was jetting from it with impressive strength.

The white man straightened, examined his nails again, and now chewed off the jagged point he'd deliberately left as he strolled around the stricken man and back to his lord.

'Shit on a fat stick!' breathed Titus, slapping the balustrade. 'How the hell did he do that?'

'Planning,' Quintillian smiled. 'He was willing to take a couple of blows to size up his chances.'

'I'm glad he's on our side. At least I won't worry so much about the northern borders any more!'

Quintillian chuckled as Titus slipped the coins grudgingly into his palm. Down below, Lord Aldegund was congratulating his man in a quiet, steady tone – the white man's name, it transpired, was Halfdan. No one seemed to be paying any attention to the dying Gota at the centre of the circle, who had collapsed to the floor, entirely useless and paralysed on one side, desperately trying to hold his vein shut with his other arm as he slipped and slid in the growing pool of his own blood. But the pressure was too much and he was already becoming weak. The warrior looked up imploringly at his father, the Gota king, but all he found there was contempt as the king turned his face from the bastard son who had so clearly disappointed him.

The Gota champion died unsung and alone on the floor, and such was the speed and efficiency of the palace staff and the guard that within a matter of minutes all that remained to mark the passing of these events was a clean, damp section of marble.

Quintillian gave an odd half smile as Titus disappeared back to the stairs, muttering to himself. The younger brother could see the emperor moving among them now, absolving Aldegund and his man of any blame in what had happened and giving reassurance, then passing on to the Gota king – not commiserating, since clearly the king cared little – but *empathizing* and discussing the qualities of warriors. Kiva may not have the makings of a fighter himself, but he knew what made one, and he was a consummate politician.

Perhaps Titus was right and men like this Halfdan were the future of border defences. It certainly freed up the military from dull garrison life on the edge of empire and made them useful for such things as construction of roads and aqueducts, keeping banditry down and clearing the seas of pirates. The north, then, was protected, and with Pelasia tied to them by marriage, the south was settled. To the west: the open ocean. Only the lands to the east were still troublesome, but they would ever be so.

For a moment, Quintillian wondered whether the nomad horse clans of the steppe would be amenable to a similar arrangement as the barbarians in the north. No... they had no concept of home or ownership. They were nomadic. How could a people who never stopped moving guard a border? Besides, trying to get the thousand disparate horse clans to agree on anything together would be like trying to nail fog to a tree. The east would always be a fluid border with the risk of banditry and raids, and the imperial military would need to keep men around that edge of the world for safety.

Lost in thought about the strange eastern land of silk-makers, the ephemeral nature of the horse clans and the solidity of imperial frontiers, Quintillian had no idea he had company until there was a faint rustle behind him. He turned, startled.

Jala stood silhouetted in the faint light of the stairwell, the back-glow making her robe surprisingly gauzy and throwing her shape into sharp relief most inappropriately. Quintillian swallowed down his panic and his desire somewhat noisily and threw a fraternal smile across his face.

'Dearest sister.'

'Quintillian, why will you not join the festivities? Must you lurk here in the shadows like some monster in a poor play?'

She reached out and grasped his upper arms in her warm, sensuous fingers, and Quintillian gave an involuntary shudder.

'I... I don't like parties. I don't socialize well.'

'Nonsense.' Jala smiled. 'I have seen you do just that many times.'

'I'm not in the mood, Jala.'

Her lip stuck out slightly in a barely discernible pout, and Quintillian almost laughed despite himself.

'Come on, dear Quintillian.'

'I really cannot. I should be doing many other things. And you should be with your husband down there.'

Without warning, Jala leaned close and planted a kiss upon his lips before leaning back with a strange smile. 'Your brother is too busy with affairs of state to keep me company, and I tire of all these rough northerners. I need company, Quintillian. *Good* company.'

Quintillian stared in abject panic.

'You look like a hare caught in the hunter's gaze.' She chuckled. 'Will you come join me, then?'

Quintillian's voice seemed to have vanished. It was there somewhere, though, deep inside, and it took a great deal of coaxing to draw it up into his throat where it still wavered and croaked.

'I'll be down shortly.'

'Don't keep me waiting.' Jala smiled, and swayed off back into the stairwell.

Quintillian stared at her retreating form and continued to gaze at the empty archway long after she had gone. His mind was churning like a winter sea, his heart hammering out like a cavalry horse at the charge. Had that been innocent? Was he reading something into what just happened that wasn't truly there?

But Quintillian prided himself on his ability to read people. Had not his instincts just won him ten gold corona? And he had seen Jala's eyes as she'd lunged forth and kissed him. It had been as deliberate a blow as any he'd ever struck with a sword. It had been no kiss of brother and sister, for all its seeming innocent from the outside. He had seen *through* her eyes. He had seen into her soul. And there it had been: the reflection of himself. The longing. The desire. Suppressed beneath a veneer of civilization and correctness. She had wanted him as he wanted her!

The realization almost floored him.

He turned back to the room, suddenly aware he was trembling and sweating coldly. Down below, he saw Jala emerge once more into the hall, barely noticed amid the rich and the powerful. Kiva spotted her through the crowd and gave her a warm smile, which she returned easily, but he was trapped in conversation by a pair of stocky, swarthy lords and as soon as smiles had been exchanged he was back again, drawn into their talk. Jala took her seat at the room's centre once more, where she became an island amid a sea of busy socializing.

Quintillian stared at her.

What should he do? What *could* he do?

A line had been crossed, a barrier broken. And no hand in the world could repair that barrier. No digit could redraw the line. Why were human hearts such fragile things? As fragile as an empire, perhaps? An empire could not ruin a heart, but for certain a heart could shatter an empire if misused.

The panic was gone, but it had left a desolate, hollow uncertainty in its place.

He had to do something, but what?

He made the mistake – *or was it a mistake?* – of looking down at Jala just as she looked up at him from her divan, and his gaze swept in through her eyes and deep into her heart once more, leaving him in absolutely no doubt now that Jala shared his feelings. Oh, he did not doubt that she loved Kiva. And so did he. And therein lay the worst of the problem, for he could no more hurt his brother than he could strike off his own head.

Fragile. Hearts and empires.

Whatever he did, it would have to take him away from Jala, he realized, for if they remained in the same place, no matter how hard they might fight it, trouble would be inevitable. One man could live with impossible, unrequited love, no matter how painful. But to have that love shared could bring down the whole empire.

No, he had to find a way out somehow.

And soon.

If you enjoyed Dark Empress why not also try:

The Thief's Tale

(First book of the Ottoman Cycle)

by S.J.A. Turney

Istanbul, 1481. The once great city of Constantine that now forms the heart of the Ottoman empire is a strange mix of Christian, Turk and Jew. Despite the benevolent reign of the Sultan Bayezid II, the conquest is still a recent memory, and emotions run high among the inhabitants, with danger never far beneath the surface.

Skiouros and Lykaion, the sons of a Greek country farmer, are conscripted into the ranks of the famous Janissary guards and taken to Istanbul where they will play a pivotal, if unsung, role in the history of the new regime. As Skiouros escapes into the Greek quarter and vanishes among its streets to survive on his wits alone, Lykaion remains with the slave chain to fulfill his destiny and become an Islamic convert and a guard of the Imperial palace. Brothers they remain, though standing to either side of an unimaginable divide.

On a fateful day in late autumn 1490, Skiouros picks the wrong pocket and begins to unravel a plot that reaches to the very highest peaks of Imperial power. He and his brother are about to be left with the most difficult decision faced by a conquered Greek: whether the rule of the Ottoman Sultan is worth saving.

Marius' Mules: The Invasion of Gaul

(First book of the Marius' Mules Series)

by S.J.A. Turney

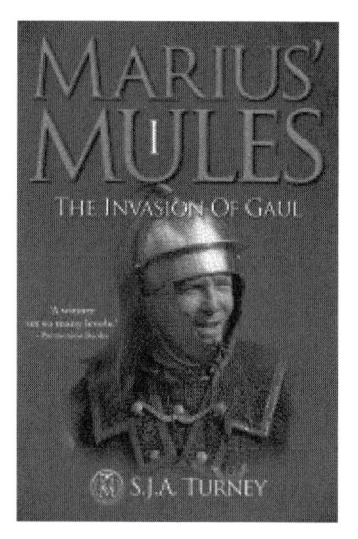

It is 58 BC and the mighty Tenth Legion, camped in Northern Italy, prepare for the arrival of the most notorious general in Roman history: Julius Caesar.

Marcus Falerius Fronto, commander of the Tenth is a career soldier and long-time companion of Caesar's. Despite his desire for the simplicity of the military life, he cannot help but be drawn into intrigue and politics as Caesar engineers a motive to invade the lands of Gaul.

Fronto is about to discover that politics can be as dangerous as battle, that old enemies can be trusted more than new friends, and that standing close to such a shining figure as Caesar, even the most ethical of men risk being burned.

Praetorian: The Great Game

(First book of the Praetorian Series)

by S.J.A. Turney

Promoted to the elite Praetorian Guard in the thick of battle, a young legionary is thrust into a seedy world of imperial politics and corruption. Tasked with uncovering a plot against the newly-crowned emperor Commodus, his mission takes him from the cold Danubian border all the way to the heart of Rome, the villa of the emperor's scheming sister, and the great Colosseum.

What seems a straightforward, if terrifying, assignment soon descends into Machiavellian treachery and peril as everything in which young Rufinus trusts and believes is called into question and he faces warring commanders, Sarmatian cannibals, vicious dogs, mercenary killers and even a clandestine Imperial agent. In a race against time to save the Emperor, Rufinus will be introduced, willing or not, to the great game.

"Entertaining, exciting and beautifully researched" - Douglas Jackson

"From the Legion to the Guard, from battles to the deep intrigue of court, Praetorian: The Great Game is packed with great characters, wonderfully researched locations and a powerful plot." - Robin Carter